"Do you think we should seal our bond in blood?"

he asked lightly.

Julie met his gaze and shook her head. "No, Dev. Remember? I'm the 'dancing girl.' We seal our oaths with a kiss."

The laughter died in his eyes. "I don't think that's very wise," he said softly.

She smiled at his refusal. "Only a kiss, Dev," she mocked. "Nothing else. I assure you, I know my place," she said with a carefully controlled bitterness.

"For days that place has been at my side," he said quietly, acknowledging her courage and endurance. But that was not, of course, what she wanted.

"Are you afraid?" she asked, goading him. She was tired of his nobility. She wanted the touch of his mouth.

"One kiss," she offered again, and her eyes were soft and dark with the dangerous invitation....

Dear Reader,

In Gayle Wilson's first book, *The Heart's Desire*, Dominic Maitland, the Duke of Avon, found unexpected love with Lady Emily Harland. In the sequel, *The Heart's Wager*, the duke needs rescuing and it is Emily's brother, Devon, who follows his brother-in-law's trail to revolutionary France. March Madness author Gayle Wilson has once again created a compelling hero and heroine who must overcome great danger just to survive in this suspenseful tale set in the Regency era.

Also this month, we have Claire Delacroix's *Pearl Beyond Price*. Thierry de Pereille loses his heart to a beautiful Persian captive on his journey to France to discover the truth about his heritage in this, the second book of the author's Unicorn Series.

And be sure and keep a lookout for our other two titles: *Land of Dreams*, a heartwarming Western from March Madness author Cheryl St.John, and *The Bride's Portion*, a captivating medieval tale from author Susan Paul. We hope you enjoy them all.

Sincerely,

Tracy Farrell
Senior Editor

Please address questions and book requests to:
Harlequin Reader Service
U.S.: 3010 Walden Ave., P.O. Box 1325, Buffalo, NY 14269
Canadian: P.O. Box 609, Fort Erie, Ont. L2A 5X3

Gayle Wilson

The Heart's Wager

Harlequin Books

TORONTO • NEW YORK • LONDON
AMSTERDAM • PARIS • SYDNEY • HAMBURG
STOCKHOLM • ATHENS • TOKYO • MILAN
MADRID • WARSAW • BUDAPEST • AUCKLAND

ISBN 0-373-28863-8

THE HEART'S WAGER

Printed in U.S.A.

Books by Gayle Wilson

Harlequin Historicals

The Heart's Desire #211
The Heart's Wager #263

GAYLE WILSON

teaches English and history to gifted high school students. Her love of both subjects naturally resulted in a desire to write historical fiction. After several years as the wife of a military pilot, she returned with her husband to live in Alabama, where they had both grown up. She has one son, who is at school in England.

To my own soldier knight

Prologue

Paris—January 1815

"Gentlemen, you may now place your wagers."

The pleasantly pitched and very feminine voice carried clearly above the din to the gamesters who clustered eagerly around the table. Juliette de Valmé's slim fingers, with their shockingly tinted nails, hovered over the faro bank, allowing them time to lay down their stakes.

"My dear, can you offer an explanation for this phenomenon? Why do we come each night to lose our money to a dealer with such prodigious good luck?" one of her patrons teased.

"Perhaps if you were wiser in placing your bets," another answered, laughing, "you'd not bother Juliette with ridiculous questions. I, personally, can think of no one to whom I'd rather lose a wager. Julie, my beloved, my heart and my money are yours," he finished, sketching the lovely banker a courtly bow.

"I believe you're right," she said smiling, indicating with a graceful movement of her hand the winning pair she had just drawn from the bank. Laughter

circled the table at her comment and at the evidence of
her continuing good fortune.

"Apparently we are all in that same predicament—
so enamored that we endure our losses in the hopes of
winning a smile, a kind word, and less importantly, of
course, the occasional wager," said the Baron du
Deffand.

"But how ungallant, Deffand," argued another of
the young aristocrats who languidly jockeyed each
evening for the positions at this particular table. "I,
my dear, have no interest in winning any money from
your father's establishment. I don't care how many
Louis you wrest from my quite willing fingers. It is
sufficient that I am allowed to bask nightly in the ra-
diance of your presence. With that I am content."

Julie's dark eyes smiled up at him from under a
sweep of impossibly long lashes, and she asked lightly,
"Ah, but the question is, when you have tallied your
losses, will you still love me tomorrow?"

"My heart is yours through eternity," he answered, putting his hand over his breast to signify the
sincerity of that pledge.

"Then I can only hope, my dear comte, that your
bankers are as faithful and that your accounts with
them are as deep as your devotion," she answered, her
delicate fingers expertly gathering his stake from the
table. Laughter at the nobleman's expense echoed
again through the vast room, and more than one jealous gambler, unlucky enough to be relegated to play
at another table, wondered what sally the "Divine
Juliette" had made to cause such merriment.

The blaze from the Austrian chandeliers and the
noise that swelled and ebbed from the densely packed
throng who crowded the rooms of this elegant house

in the Marais district of Paris were as familiar to Juliette de Valmé as was the beating of her own heart. She had spent most of her life in one gambling den or another, and she understood very well why the English called them hells. Souls were bartered on the turn of a card, the spin of the wheel. She had seen more than one loser leave the table where his fellow sportsmen had avidly watched the death of his hopes, to go out to end his life in some Parisian alleyway when he realized the enormity of what he had done.

At least her father's house was honest. The odds, of course, were still heavily in favor of the establishment, but there were no Johnny Sharps or shaved decks here, and the roulette tables had not been tampered with. Her father had insisted on fair play, and in these last years, as she had taken from his increasingly frail hands the reins of this business, she had respected his rules. Satisfyingly, the profit margin had remained healthy, especially now, after the defeat of Napoleon. Since then an influx of English gamblers had swelled the select group that sought admittance each night to what had become the most popular club in the city.

She knew that its popularity, to a large extent, was due to her presence here each evening. She considered it part of her professional duties to display both wit and unfailing good humor; to charm recalcitrant drunks out of whatever retaliation they threatened for their losses; and to deal baccarat, vingt-et-un and faro with a skilled line of patter that she could, and indeed believed she often did, deliver in her sleep.

She was well aware that the gentlemen who gathered around her table seldom watched her skillful fingers, uncaring if this particular dealer employed some sleight-of-hand in arranging the cards. Their fascinated eyes were more apt to dwell on the gloss of the blue-black, upswept curls, or on the artfully enhanced lashes that alternately hid and then revealed the laughing, expressive sparkle of her dark eyes, or on the revealing décolletage of whichever expensive dress had been delivered that week from LeRoy, the most fashionable dressmaker in the most fashionable city in the world.

Tonight the gown was bloodred, and she had highlighted her cheeks and lips to complement the glow that vivid color gave her ivory skin. She knew that every man here realized that the beauty nature had generously bestowed by virtue of her Anglo-Gallic heritage had been supplemented with her carefully applied cosmetics, but she knew also that none of them cared. They enjoyed in Julie what they would vehemently decry in the women who graced their drawing rooms.

She casually watched the action at the dozen tables without seeming to neglect in the slightest the entertainment of those crowded around her own. She had become aware some minutes ago of the heightened excitement that whispered around the rooms and centered on the heavy betting of a handsome and extremely drunk young English aristocrat who was being urged on by a group of his fellow Corinthians.

She had also caught Jean's warning, so she unhurriedly finished the game and, to the accompaniment of disappointed groans and lighthearted rebukes, she gracefully moved to the table she had been watching.

The Englishman was rather cheerfully disclaiming his bad luck, which he didn't seem to blame on the house. But drunk he certainly was, and her father's policies forbade taking the last ecu from those who did not, even if they should, know what they were doing.

She moved closely enough that by the costly scent she wore, if by nothing else, he was made aware of her presence. She smiled at his surprise in finding such a charming *mademoiselle* under his elbow, and she saw clearly the flush the unaccustomed alcohol had given to the downiness of his cheeks. A lamb ripe for the taking, but if he stupidly desired to lose his entire fortune at the tables, he would have to do it somewhere else.

She placed her small, carefully manicured hand lightly on his arm and watched in the unfocused eyes his interest in the table die a quick death, to be replaced by interest in a far more entertaining activity his body was trying to suggest to his brain.

"I know a quiet place where we can be alone," she whispered in unaccented English, softly enough that only he could hear through the swirling noise.

His sweating palm came up to cover her fingers, and with a minimum of fumbling, he managed to convey them to his lips with a rather charming ineptitude.

Certainly not a rake, she thought with amusement, turning to thread her way through the tables.

She knew from experience, knew without looking, that he would follow her. She was aware also of the dark figure that moved parallel to her own path, separated from the ongoing drama by the width of the room. The man, through whose efforts she had succeeded at taking control of this business in what had been exclusively a man's world, was again supporting her decision.

They were already out the rear door and into the bite of the evening air before the boy had realized their destination.

"Do you remember the address of your lodging?" she asked quickly, hearing Jean move behind her in the darkness.

"Of course," the Englishman answered in surprise, wondering if she intended to go home with him. Even in his befuddled state, he could imagine how his hostess, a friend of his mother and father, would feel about his bringing a demimondaine, no matter how beautiful, into her house.

"Then tell him," she said, and, taking his right hand, she pressed into it a small, heavy purse that clinked full of coins. "And tell your friends that neither they nor you will be admitted to this house again during your stay. If you intend to lose every centime you have, it won't be here. *Bonsoir, monsieur,* and welcome to Paris, where one seldom gets a second chance to make a fool of himself."

She turned quickly, leaving him in Jean's very capable hands. She could hear his soothing, persuasive voice quieting the boy's questioning protests, and then she forgot the incident in her professional assessment of every corner of her kingdom. She had hardly known any other way of life, except during the years after her mother's death, unhappily spent in one of the convent schools.

When her father had realized how little, other than etiquette, she really knew, he had brought her to live with him and had engaged the first of a series of tutors. And so it was in his Paris casino that she had been educated by her teachers in the classic texts and, perhaps regretfully, by her life in the various depravities and dishonesties of which the human soul is capable. She had, in her twenty-three years, literally seen it all.

"I put him in a hired coach and sent him home." Jean's deep voice spoke softly against her ear.

She turned and smiled up into the scarred face of the man who had been like an older brother for the last three years. Her father had found Jean, and she would never know what argument had been used to convince him to take over the physical aspects of the running of the casino. But only Jean's intimidating presence, his quick eye and even quicker intelligence kept the kind of tight control necessary to manage a successful gambling operation in these uncertain times. He received a generous salary, of course, but not nearly what she knew he was worth, and she often wondered why he stayed.

Her father had always maintained that there was some mystery about the gambler's past. He was far too well-traveled, too knowledgeable and sophisticated, too sure of his abilities, to fit the personal history he'd offered when he'd applied for the job. But through the years, Jean had given no other explanation. And they both knew that his past, like the scars he bore, were forbidden territory.

She supposed that Jean, like so many of those who inhabited her world, was running from something, although she had yet to see anything or anyone frighten the Frenchman. He was as tall and as dark as Satan, and as handsome, too, she thought, in spite of the marred right profile and the black patch securely held in place by the ribbon that lost itself in the matching midnight of his hair. She became aware suddenly that his hazel eye was lazily watching her, and that he knew she was thinking about him in a way that was unusual for their relationship.

To her, he had always been simply Jean, a part of her family almost as much now as her father. And so the smile he bestowed in response to her scrutiny did nothing to quicken her heartbeat, as it would have that of almost any other female in the city. She no longer even thought about the rather endearing crookedness of his smile, the damaged corner of his lips scarcely moving in response to any emotion revealed in those dark features.

"I thought he was a little old for rescuing," he said softly.

"He was a child," she said, knowing she was being chided about her determination to follow her father's strictures.

"He was older than you," Jean said in amusement. His smile faded, however, at the flash of pain his unthinking comment had caused in the depths of her dark eyes.

"I'm older than he by a thousand years, and you know it."

He heard the surety in her voice, but he said gently, his thumb touching under her chin, "Not so old, little one, as all that. Young enough, I promise."

His smile this time coaxed an answering one from her lightly rouged lips.

"And what do you promise I'm young enough for, my friend?" she questioned lightly.

"For all the things you want," he responded immediately.

"Better wines at cheaper prices, a house run to rival that we had in October, for the coal merchant to forget to present his bill," she listed, laughing.

"No," he said softly. "For a time when you don't have to worry about all those responsibilities. For someone who will take care of you, for a change."

"I'm a little old for fairy tales," she mocked. "Go tell the boy you just deposited in that coach those fantasies. That's not what lies ahead for me. And to be truthful, I'm not sure anymore that I would be happy doing anything other than what I have done for so long. Somehow, I can no longer envision myself married to the coal merchant and dutifully producing a child a year. I think I'll be satisfied with the evils I know."

"And are you so sure that marriage is an evil? I have it on the best authority that some people even manage to enjoy the state of wedded bliss. And I didn't have the coal merchant in mind," he denied.

"Then who?" she said, laughing again as he had intended. "The only men I know are the merchants who come to this house to collect their bills. And our noble customers. Are you suggesting . . ."

"I'm suggesting that there are other men than those. And that you'll eventually discover that interesting fact."

"And, of course, those men would be interested in me?" she questioned sarcastically. "The proposals I've had have not been marriage proposals, I assure you. Nor are they ever likely to be."

She had never thought of Jean himself in the light of a lover. She needed him in a different way, and so she read nothing into his remarks beyond the gentle camaraderie they always shared.

More aware of her dependence on his friendship than she realized, Jean smiled and reached to tweak a dark curl between his long fingers. "Then if you're determined not to trade your expertise at running a hell for the running of a household, I suggest you return to your courtiers, who eagerly await your majesty's return."

He bowed deeply, every movement of his body smoothly controlled. His slimness belied a strength that had been tested only occasionally when he was new to the house. By now his reputation had eliminated any need to prove there was steel underlying the velvet.

Julie kissed her fingertips and blew a swift kiss in his direction, but he was already forgotten as she turned and began to make her way back to the endless watch over the busy tables, unaware that he tracked her graceful movement through the crowd. Then there was a slight disturbance at one of the roulette wheels, and Jean, too, returned to the demands of the small world they shared.

It was after three when Jean deftly slipped into Julie's place at the faro table, conveying her father's message, and in almost the same breath, piquing the interest of those who might protest the change in dealers by offering new odds that seemed to put the house at a disadvantage. Her father's summons in the midst of a successful evening was unusual enough that she found herself hurrying toward the office in which he presided now only over the accounts of the business he had begun many years ago.

He was seated at his desk, his frail shoulders draped with a heavy woolen shawl against the night air that he felt so painfully. His thin, long-fingered hands, the hands of the English aristocrat he had been born, rested on the surface of his desk. He and Julie both knew, and had known for several months, how ill he was, but the careful facade of normality had been strictly maintained between them. Tonight, however, she could sense his unaccustomed agitation as soon as she entered the room.

"Lock the door," he ordered quickly and waited until she had completed that task. "You know that I would never ask you to do anything that was not for your own good."

"Of course," she began, but he quieted her with a gesture and continued to speak rapidly, holding her eyes.

"I'm afraid, my dear, that I've endangered you by my activities on behalf of my country. I know that you must be aware that this establishment has provided a cover for those activities through the years, and now it seems that the French authorities are also aware of my role in the downfall of the Emperor. They see it as a betrayal, as spying on my adopted country, but England—"

His voice broke suddenly. They both knew that he would never see his beloved homeland again. She put her hand comfortingly over the fragile bones of his shoulder, but he cleared those memories and began again, speaking with a sense of urgency that was so foreign to his usual tranquillity.

"But now... because of me, because of my espionage for England, you must disappear. Take the money from the safe and run. Bury yourself as deeply as you can in the countryside, as far from Paris as it will take you. There are those who will want you in their power because they will believe, since you're my daughter..." He hesitated again, shaking his head. "They're capable of anything to secure information about my contacts in England. Torture, Julie, or even worse. You cannot imagine the depths of depravity to which you would be subjected if you fall into their hands.''

"But I have no information. I know nothing," she began and stopped as her father's eyes shifted suddenly toward the front rooms where there seemed to be a slight difference in the normal flow of talk and laughter, and then they came back to focus on her face.

His trembling finger pointed to the safe behind him, and she quickly removed the small, heavy pouch that was resting alone on the shelf, as if prepared for this moment, for these bizarre instructions. But she noticed that the papers her father had always kept locked in that strongbox were no longer there.

"We have even less time than I thought. Remember, my dear, how much I love you, how much I have always loved you.''

She was bewildered by what was happening, but she, too, heard clearly now the disturbance that was moving through the casino as a tear, once begun, runs through fabric.

"Jean," she whispered, turning unthinkingly toward the door to the main salon. The gambler had taken her place at the table, perhaps putting himself in danger. She knew that she had to warn him.

"No," her father said, frantically catching her arm. "My God, don't you understand? Jean is delaying them, giving me time to get you away. And you're wasting those precious minutes.''

"Do you think I'll let Jean be the sacrifice here?" she argued, pulling against that frail white hand that held her prisoner with its death grip. "Do you believe that I'll accept my freedom at the cost of his?"

"They're not interested in Jean. As far as they're concerned, he's a loyal Frenchman. And besides..." Her father hesitated, and then hurriedly continued his reassurance. "There is nothing to taint Jean with what I've done. But they won't believe *you're* innocent. They'll think, because you're my flesh and blood, that you'll know something they can use," he said urgently. "Don't throw away the opportunity Jean's providing. You know he's far more capable of taking care of himself in this situation than you would be. If you fall into their hands... There is nothing, or no one, that can protect you in a French prison, Julie. Nothing..."

Again the sounds of raised voices from beyond the closed door clearly gave evidence of an altercation of some kind, and her father opened the drawer of his desk. She saw the gambler's sleeve gun and wondered how he intended to stop anyone with that toy.

"Don't be a fool," she said, putting her hand over the small pistol and trying to push it back into the drawer. "You can't fight them with that."

"I don't intend to fight them," he said quietly, but he raised his eyes and held hers unwaveringly. Finally the pressure of her fingers against his eased as she understood what he intended.

"I've always hated the thought of this lingering death. What more could you wish for me, my love, than to die for England? What better end? But not in their hands. Not tortured to death to reveal the names of those I've served so long. As *I* choose, Julie. *My* choice."

There was no fear and no regret in his dark eyes as they held hers.

Slowly she released the skeletal hand that gripped the weapon and put her arms around her father, pulling him close against her trembling body. She buried her face in the sparse white hair and fought the burn of tears behind her lids. Finally she bent to place her lips against the crepelike skin of his cheek, speaking, without words, her last goodbye.

"Be brave, my dear heart," he said.

"As brave as my father," she whispered. His hand lifted to push her away, and she stepped back in obedience to his command.

"Go," he said as before, and she nodded, against all her own instincts, giving in to his wishes, because, as he had reminded her, he would ask her to do nothing that was not right.

Pulling a cloak from the peg, she cautiously opened the door to the alley that backed the house. There was no one there, and she had already begun to cross the threshold when she heard her father's urgent whisper behind her. "The Limping Man, Julie. Look for the Limping Man. When I realized they knew, I shut down his network, but I sent him word, and he'll come..."

Then the crash of a heavy body resounded against the locked door of his office, and at his frantic gesture she pulled the street door closed and ran out into the pitch blackness. None of this made any sense. What had he said about a limping man?

She heard behind her the single crack of the tiny pistol, and after it, the inevitable splintering of the wooden door, and with those sounds, whose sequence she agonizingly understood, she acknowledged that whatever was now happening in that small room was no longer of any concern to her.

And so she ran from sheltering darkness into deeper shadow, but always into streets that led away from the only home she had known for over half her life.

Chapter One

London—March 1815

No one in the Horse Guards would be surprised to find the lamps burning late in this particular office. Considering the news that was slowly filtering like wisps of smoke from the Continent, the light in the office where Colonel Devon Burke pored over the stack of encoded dispatches was certainly not the only one still lit in Whitehall this particular spring midnight.

But the man who sat at this cluttered desk had, in the course of these last months, too often watched dawn touch the sky through the tall mullioned windows that now stretched blackly behind him. For him, work had become a refuge, and an escape, from the emptiness.

Finally the tightness in his neck and the numbness that in the last hour had begun to radiate unpleasantly from between his shoulders signaled that tonight he had gone beyond his body's limits. Placing both hands on his desk, Colonel Burke pushed himself up, feeling the price he would pay for this night's vigil in the cramping tightness of his back and in the unresponsiveness of his right leg. He walked to the windows, limping slightly, flexing his shoulders and trying to stretch out the aching muscles along his spine.

He paused before the divided glass that mockingly threw back his reflection. The gleam of the short chestnut hair, the intensity of the dark blue eyes, all the subtle marks etched on the ruggedly handsome face by his experiences were, of course, hidden in the blackness that stretched beyond the panes. The breadth of his shoulders and the muscled chest covered by the elegant coat, the narrow waist and the strong length of leg revealed by skintight pantaloons and gleaming Hessians were, however, clearly mirrored and appeared, remarkably, exactly the same as when he had been commissioned.

The changes that had been wrought in Devon Burke by the last two years were no longer outwardly visible. Invalided out of the army after Salamanca, he had been brought home from the Peninsula to die. Instead, he had surprised everyone by surviving, despite the massive damage inflicted by the explosion of a French shell directly behind him.

He had lived, but for months his confined existence had been governed by the threat of some movement of one deadly sliver of metal that had rested precariously against his spine. Those were months that he no longer allowed himself to remember.

One of many things he tried not to remember.

And that was why, of course, he was here, surrounded by an environment that was totally masculine. He was always surprised by the minor stimuli capable of setting off the memories that he sought to block—a breath of lavender or even the gracefully erect posture of some woman on the street. And with that admission, they were there again, running fleetingly through his mind.

Elizabeth, he thought, and against his will felt the cold, clenching sickness of her rejection in his gut. For he knew that these images of the woman who had haunted his dreams, both waking and sleeping, for the last five years would inevitably be followed by the darker ones he also fought.

Only the knowledge that Elizabeth was waiting for him had kept him sane in the hell of countless battles, and—with the possibility of recovery provided by the French surgeon his brother-in-law had miraculously found—even through the agonizing months he had spent attempting to become the man he had been before the injury. Only for her had the grinding pain of rebuilding his shattered body been worth it, only for her was the endless effort justified.

And then ...

God, he'd been such a fool. He had never realized that Elizabeth's life would not, of course, have remained as static as his during those long months. And so, as soon as he had deemed himself fit to ask, he had gone to beg again for her hand.

He found her already married to the Earl of March, a man old enough to be her father, and heavily pregnant with his heir. Devon suddenly closed his eyes, to force out of his brain the picture of Elizabeth with March, an unspeakable vision engendered by the whispered reputation of the aging roué she had chosen over him.

In these intervening months, he had moved beyond anger, even beyond the sense of betrayal, but the bitterness of disillusionment still had the power to threaten his hard-won acceptance. Fighting against emotions he had long ago rejected as self-pitying, he leaned forward, his forehead resting against the cold glass and the knuckles of both hands pressed too hard into the unyielding sill of the window. And unbelievably, he heard behind him, sharp and unmistakable, the opening of the door to his office.

Bloody hell, he thought, steeling himself to face whoever was invading this refuge, an intrusion that demanded a control he was far from feeling.

Devon removed his hands from the sill and allowed his fingers to tighten over the pen he'd unthinkingly carried with him from the desk, deliberately bending it until he felt it snap. He turned and threw the ruined instrument against the papers scattered over the desk.

"Damned nuisance," he began, but the words died in his throat as he raised his eyes to the figure by the door.

"You need to get out of this office more, and then the paperwork wouldn't become such a chore. Even his grace knew that," the quiet, familiar voice offered.

"Moss?" Devon said incredulously, recognizing the small gray-haired man who stood before him. At first he could imagine no reason his brother-in-law's very unusual and highly trusted valet might be calling on him in the predawn hours. But then his mind began to formulate the kind of message that would send this particular agent of the Duke of Avon to seek him out.

"What are you doing here?" Devon whispered, dreading the answer. He knew very well that Moss was always under the direction of Avon, that his every action was dedicated to the service of that brilliant and enigmatic man who was married to Devon's only sister. "What's wrong with Emily? Or is it Will?"

"There's nothing wrong with your sister or with your nephew. Not that you'd know, of course. Your not having been to your sister's home in some weeks now. But it's not her grace I've come about. I need your help, Colonel."

"Of course. You know you have only to—" Devon began, and Avon's valet cut him short.

"I want you to understand that the decision to seek you out was not lightly made. But considering how you feel about Dominic..." Moss hesitated for the first time, and Devon recognized that he was weighing his words carefully. "And also considering what you owe him," the valet suggested softly. They both knew that suggestion would never have been allowed by the man they were discussing. The Duke of Avon called due no debts from those he loved.

Two years ago it had been his grace, the Duke of Avon, who had offered Devon a job in intelligence, an opportunity to perform valuable work for the war effort despite the uselessness of his body. And it had also been Avon who had persisted until he had found a surgeon willing to risk the removal of that fragment of metal that had held Devon captive in an imprisonment that was, for him, far worse than death.

"And I remembered what you told him the day he left. So I thought you might be willing..."

"I owe Dominic more than my life, Moss. And he is my friend. Whatever you think—"

"I think," Moss interrupted again, "that you're the brother he never had. And I'm probably the only man alive who knows what that relationship means to him."

"And to me," Devon affirmed softly. "So why don't you tell me what Avon wants me to do."

"It's not exactly— You see, the duke didn't send me." Again Moss paused, and Devon waited, knowing that what the valet had come to ask must be something he knew his master would disapprove of. And obeying Avon had been Moss's habit for twenty-five years. But Devon could never have anticipated the valet's next words. "I need you to find the duke."

"Find the duke?" Devon repeated, his voice unconsciously rising as he grasped the import of what had been said. "What the hell do you mean, find the duke?"

"Dominic's disappeared. And I can't contact anyone in France. None of his agents responds. It's as if they've all vanished from the face of the earth. And the duke with them. But I can't go. I gave him my word I wouldn't leave the babe and the duchess. He told me he was no longer my concern. That they were. I've never broken my word to him, and so that leaves you."

"Disappeared. My God, Moss, do you know..." Devon began the unthinking question, and then realized that the valet couldn't possibly know what was happening in France. Only yesterday had the dispatch marked "Most Secret" crossed his desk. Napoleon had escaped from Elba and was even now marching toward Paris.

"How long since you've heard from him?" Devon asked, his mind already considering the intelligence aspects of the disappearance of the man who had been so vital to the Emperor's defeat. Not only was Avon his friend, the husband of his sister, but he was also

England's master spy. And his disappearance in these circumstances could not be coincidental.

"Almost three months," Moss answered, and Devon felt shock wash through his body.

"Three months," he repeated. "But that's impossible. Emily's had letters—"

"That he wrote before he left. He knew he'd have no way to write her from France, and he didn't want her to worry. So he left them for me to give her. But I've run out, and she's sure to suspect something's wrong. He never intended to be gone this long. I'm certain of that. I would have come to you earlier, but he's more than capable of looking after himself. I know that. He'd call me an old woman," Moss said, and they both remembered the mocking tone with which Avon greeted any expression of concern over his very dangerous activities. "But *three* months, Colonel. Something's very wrong, and I knew it before he left. I tried to tell him—" The valet deliberately cut off the almost frantic desperation.

"Three months," Devon repeated, remembering his own forebodings as he had stood in the shadowed hall of the duke's town house that December morning, listening to Dominic's quiet explanation of this mission. Avon's chief agent in Paris had sent a brief warning through the espionage network, which had once stretched across France, but the duke had been unable to reestablish contact with him after that communication. And so he had gone himself, disguised, to investigate the breakdown in the system that had provided invaluable information during the war.

Someone's taken a hand in the game the diplomats think is being played out in the Congress at Vienna, the duke had said, *and the stakes are too high to chance how a new player might affect the outcome.*

And remembering that cold dawn, Devon remembered, too, his own whispered vow to the man to whom he owed so much.

If you need me, Dominic, he had promised, responding to the dark presentiment that had brushed icelike along the brutal scars that marred his back, *you have only to send word. You know I'll come,* he had pledged grimly, meeting the calm silver eyes of his brother-in-law, *if I have to climb out of the very pits of hell.*

Devon Burke's comrades-at-arms would have said that he had never known what it was to be afraid, even in the most desperate charge, the most furiously fought battle; but standing in the quiet foyer of Avon's elegant town house, he had known that they were wrong. He had been very much afraid, inexplicably terrified, for the man to whom he was saying goodbye.

Then, in his own selfish concerns, he had lost the troubled conviction, which Moss apparently had shared, that Dominic's mission to France was more dangerous than anything he had undertaken before.

Three months, he thought again, wondering if the trail were too cold to follow. And with the news from the Continent, he also wondered if it would now be possible to even make the attempt.

France—A week later

To the amusement of the watching crowd, the boy who twisted futilely in the hold of the burly farmer was protesting his innocence with a blustering combination of excuses and profanities. Since the evidence of his crime bulged in the pockets of his stained, tattered smock, it seemed a ridiculous performance. Although the child was clearly outnumbered and outmatched, none of the good French villagers had felt the urge to go to his aid. The man who held the writhing figure was dragging him relentlessly to the wagon he had driven into these quiet, sun-dappled streets only a short time before. He had been bringing the winter apples to market and had naturally resented the urchin's theft of even so small a part of his crop.

The boy's fists beat ineffectually against the massive forearm wrapped tightly about his thin body as the farmer prepared to toss him up into the bed of the wagon where a helpful villager waited. The apples had been shifted to the front of the wooden conveyance, their sale apparently forgotten, at least temporarily, in the much more satisfying endeavor of bringing such a dangerous criminal to justice.

"You won't go stealing no one else's apples," the peasant promised, as he added his other arm around the struggling body and locked his hamlike hands together over the front of the heaving chest. The child kicked back with the wooden sabots he wore on bare and very dirty feet, but the farmer stepped nimbly out of the way. As the only reward for his valiant attempt, the boy lost one of his shoes. The crowd laughed appreciatively, and he cursed again and tried to bring his shod foot down on the toes of the man who was still holding him quite securely, in spite of his efforts.

The child was undoubtedly helpless against the forces determined to control him. Perhaps it was that very helplessness and his rather gallant resistance that stirred the pity of the blue-eyed stranger who quietly surveyed the unfolding scene. He had stopped to ask about accommodations at whatever inn might be nearby, and his attention had been attracted by the crowd's laughter and the boy's shrill, angry protests.

For several minutes now he had been sitting on the roan gelding, unnoticed by the mob. Had this lively entertainment not been provided, they would certainly have been aware of the outsider in their midst. The gleaming Hessians and the doeskin breeches, both covered now with the dust of the road, would have clearly marked for the crowd his class, in spite of the simple lawn shirt and the leather waistcoat that covered his upper body. In response to the bright winter sun of the March afternoon, he had put away in his saddlebag the woolen cloak he had worn against the morning's chill.

Helpless, he thought again as he watched the uneven battle, and compelled by his memories, he urged the well-trained mount into the middle of the melee.

The crowd parted reluctantly before the horse, and the rider stopped in front of the farmer who held the struggling urchin.

"Let him go," the stranger said softly, and at the quiet tone of command in that slightly accented voice, all activity stopped, even the frenetic struggles of the child, whose dark eyes gazed with sudden hope out of a small and remarkably dirty face.

His savior sat militarily straight on the back of the huge horse. As he watched, the man reached into the pocket of his waistcoat and flipped a coin worth more than the entire cargo of apples to the feet of the man who held him.

The peasant stood frozen, not responding to the generous offer. The villagers started to mumble their disbelief, wondering at his hesitation in accepting such a gift from Providence.

"Let him go," he said again, as quietly as before. "Your apples are more than paid for."

The brute who held the child studied the calm face of the man above him. The straight nose was slightly sunburned, the chin square and resolute, but it was whatever he read in the depths of the dark blue eyes that finally caused his sausage-shaped fingers to reluctantly free their prisoner and pick up the gold that gleamed temptingly from the dust of the street.

At the release, the child shot like a shaft from a crossbow to stand against the dusty boots that rested in the stirrups of the worn but obviously expensive saddle. Looking up into her hero's face, Julie watched the quickly concealed amusement push at the corners of the well-shaped lips.

Then the stranger turned the horse in the direction of the inn. Julie jumped when she realized she was alone again in the middle of the uncaring crowd and hurried to resume her place at the side of the ambling thoroughbred. It seemed the rider was in no hurry to reach his destination, and she had no trouble keeping pace.

She was aware that the blue eyes had flicked over to her stumbling figure. She hopped on one foot until she could pull off the remaining clog, in spite of the cold ground, and offered helpfully, "*Monsieur* desires a guide?"

The man looked down to study the eager, upturned face.

"Do you know the White Horse?" he asked consideringly.

"But of course," she assured him and moved to the front of the slowly moving animal.

The rider didn't approach the entrance of the inn, which was nestled snugly under the trees that shaded its doorway from the afternoon light. He turned the gelding instead into the dimness of its stables.

Julie stopped on the threshold and raised her nose like a scenting puppy. The smells of hay and oiled leather and the sharp, friendly odors of horses and manure colored the air. She breathed deeply and looked up to find the stranger's blue eyes focused on her face with the same intensity with which they had stared down the bully. She again watched the man's hand find and toss a coin, which her quick fingers caught spinning in midair.

It was not as large as the bribe the stranger had offered her tormentor, but it was a more than generous reward for the small service rendered.

The stranger's lips slanted into a smile at the skillful, one-handed catch.

"Thank you," the man said simply and turned the gelding into the interior of the long dim aisle that stretched between the stalls.

Julie looked at the coin and then again at the stranger who had begun to dismount. She watched the quick grimace distort that handsome face and heard the softly spoken English expletive. English, she thought in sudden understanding. That explained so much. The stranger rolled his shoulders and then stretched the long muscles of his back, the sighing breath Devon released as he moved clearly indicating the unpleasantness of the entire operation.

Julie's mouth twitched upward, her smile hidden, she hoped, in the gloom of the entryway.

"*Monsieur* does not ride?" she asked ingenuously, recognizing, she thought, the muscle fatigue of an inept or inexperienced rider who has just spent too many hours in the saddle.

She watched as the blue eyes, wide with shock at the unexpected question, swung to her face.

And then the Englishman, a man who had literally ridden before he had walked, laughed with genuine and ironic amusement.

"Apparently not," he agreed softly, almost to himself, "at least not anymore." Still smiling, he spoke again. "What are you waiting for? The adventure's over. Go home and ask your mother to say a prayer for all fools," he laughingly commanded.

Julie nodded reluctantly, and although her eyes remained locked on the stranger's face, she bit professionally into the metal of the coin to test its value. Then, apparently satisfied with the genuineness of the gift, she turned and began to move out of the dark shadows of the barn and into the pleasant afternoon shade.

English, she thought again, smiling. No wonder the stranger had come to her aid. The English—forever slaying dragons and rescuing fair damsels. *Especially* fair damsels. Her lips quirked again in amusement.

Julie moved into the coolness of the approaching twilight and, her mind still occupied by her savior, she was totally unaware of the man who waited beyond the inn yard. She pushed her cold hands into the deep pockets of the smock and found with surprise one of the apples that the farmer had stuffed there to justify his attempt. She bit into it and made a face and spat the offending morsel onto the ground.

She had raised a slim arm to toss the rest of the rotten apple away when her hand was instead pulled behind her, and she was again locked in her pursuer's grip.

"You're clever," the man whispered into the disordered cap of short black curls that covered the girl's well-shaped head, "but not so clever as to outsmart me."

His laugh turned into a pained yelp as Julie's even white teeth bit down hard on the palm that blocked her mouth.

As soon as the offending fingers were removed, Julie filled her lungs and released a remarkable scream for so small a body, and kept on screaming until she was slapped hard across the face and then backhanded with equal force. The tears started unbidden in the furious brown eyes, but determinedly the mouth opened again, only to be filled with a gag, hastily contrived from a sweat-stained kerchief.

Julie's hands were twisted behind her, and she was thrown onto the back of the farm wagon to roll hard against the wooden side. She lay stunned by the force of her landing a few precious moments, and then realized her predicament was more serious than this afternoon's as the horses pulling the wagon began to gather speed.

The horses were, however, merely hired hacks and certainly no match for the well-bred muscles and boundless stamina of the stranger's gelding that had already carried his master so many miles today.

The roan raced behind the flying wagon, its long legs eating the distance between. The rider was stretched out along the reaching neck, and it was only as he raised himself and shouted to Julie that it became obvious he was riding bareback.

Monsieur does not ride, indeed, she thought in quick amazement as she removed the gag, and then, realizing the intent of the rapidly approaching rescuer, she scrambled to the rear of the wagon.

The command was given, a command seen more clearly in the shape of the firm lips than heard, one word shouted above the noise of the drumming hooves and the creak of the rocking wagon bed.

"Jump," he ordered, and the slim figure launched unhesitatingly into the rapidly closing space between the back of the wagon and the galloping steed. Jumped and was caught too low, so that all the weight of the small body, light though it was, rested for long, agonizing seconds in one corded arm and against the straining pull of the damaged muscles of the rider's back.

Dark eyes locked with blue, and both were aware of the scope of that struggle. Neither spoke, knowing that words could not change the outcome nor alter the terrifying consequences should his strength fail. The brutality of the effort that finally lifted the length of the slim body securely into the saddle in front of his own had blackened the air around the rider's head, and he had to fight to remain conscious, to stay upright, to hold on as two feminine arms twined trustingly around his neck.

Finally he was in control enough, despite whatever he had just done to the recently healed muscles of his back, to put his left arm around the slim waist.

"Not the apples, then?" Devon questioned softly, attempting to hide what the rescue had cost.

He watched the brown velvet of the girl's eyes come up to answer the ironic amusement in his own.

"No, not the apples," she agreed with matching mock-seriousness.

He gripped the reins, turning the horse in a direction that would take them away from the bouncing tail of the wagon. But the fight to pull her into the saddle had taken too many long, dangerous seconds.

Julie felt his body jerk as the shots she had expected from the beginning rang out clearly now from behind them. Devon dug his heels again into the sweating flanks of his horse, sheltering the fragile form that he now knew, with absolute certainty, did not belong to a child, as they outrode the determined pursuit.

The exhausted horse had slowed to a stumble. The body that held Julie had begun to tremble several long minutes before, and the shirt crushed against her ragged smock was drenched with cold sweat.

"I know a place," she said finally, recognizing their surroundings. "It's not far," she continued reassuringly.

"Wherever," he said, "it had better..."

The muscled arms that had held securely during the wild ride suddenly relaxed, and without warning, the tall figure that had been wavering slipped off the horse's back to lie sprawled in the dust of the road. She jumped down from the gelding and knelt beside the fallen man.

Her slender hand felt his forehead and then gently and unthinkingly caressed the stubbled cheek. His head turned restlessly, and a low moan escaped. Even in the darkness she could see the blood that covered the white shirt. So much blood, and there was no way, without light, to ascertain even the location of his injury, much less to treat it. She had realized, finally, that he'd been hit, but their pursuer had been too tenacious and at times too close for them to do anything about the wound. Even now...

Julie looked up from the fallen man to examine the road that stretched behind them in the moonlight. There was no sound. So perhaps it was safe. And she really had no choice. The Gypsy's camp was tantalizingly close, but she hated to leave him even the short time it would take to get help. She sighed, unaccustomed to uncertainty about any course of action. But then she had seldom been responsible for the welfare of someone else. And she wasn't sure she liked that responsibility.

Finally making the decision that was inevitable, given the situation, she pulled the weary animal to a nearby stump and struggled to mount. Both bare heels bounced against the heaving, foam-flecked flanks, and the courageous heart again answered the demand. The gelding turned to look once more, questioningly, at the figure lying in the moonlight, and then gave himself up to the guidance of the small fingers that now controlled his reins.

Much later those same cool fingers rested again against Devon's forehead, edging his mind into an unwanted consciousness. He listened to the muffled sounds around him, but since there were none he could identify, he gave up that attempt and opened his eyes.

The glint of silver danced in the light of an oil lantern, and he wondered idly what she was going to do with the knife. Then he focused clearly enough to realize that the tip of the blade was moving dangerously close to his body. His hard fingers latched onto a fragile wrist, and he looked up into the dirty face of his afternoon's companion. He twisted his hand slightly, and the knife dropped onto the wooden floor on which he was sitting, his aching back propped against something hard and unyielding.

"What are you doing?" he asked hoarsely, barely recognizing his own voice.

"Shh," her low voice soothed. "I'm just going to cut up your sleeve."

"Why?" he asked, trying to remember where he was. His eyes closed, exhausted by the loss of blood that had left him drifting in and out of consciousness as they had loaded him into the pony cart and brought him here. Wherever here was. He remembered other hands and voices. Masculine voices. And the girl's. But nothing clearly, and nothing that made much sense.

He finally forced his eyes open again and found dark velvet eyes studying his face, the same eyes that had this afternoon met his so bravely when he had almost let her fall beneath the deadly, flashing hooves of the gelding. And their beauty, framed by the dirty face and disheveled black curls, was as incongruous as he had found it then.

"Why are you dressed like a boy?" he asked, the question he had wanted to ask her during their escape.

"How did you know?" she asked softly and picked up the knife. He watched it disappear under the smock and into the waistband of the grimy, shapeless trousers. "No one else . . ."

"Maybe no one else has ridden for miles holding you against his chest. Your body may be boyish—"

"Boyish?" the undisputed toast of the Parisian underworld interrupted. Her eyes narrowed slightly, and then she smiled. She realized with some surprise that the man who had rescued her was totally unaffected by the practiced lowering of lashes and the provocative smile.

"A very believable boy," he said, but his eyes closed again with the effort of explaining.

Julie wondered at the spurt of anger she felt at his assessment. It was, of course, what she had intended. She had entered into the role with all the considerable acting talent she possessed and had been pleased with its success. So she couldn't understand why she was disconcerted by his compliment on the success of her disguise.

"Let me," Devon heard another voice say, remembering it as the authority that had directed the men who'd moved him.

The Gypsy leader, impatient with the conversation, pushed the girl aside and gripped Devon's sleeve in one gnarled brown hand. He inserted the point of his own knife, ripping up the fabric without hesitation.

He grasped the edges of the slit and pulled them apart until the hole the apple farmer's ball had made was exposed. He turned the arm slightly, so that the light of the dim lamp better illuminated the wound. An involuntary gasp was wrenched from Devon's suddenly colorless lips at that movement, but he locked his teeth into the bottom one, determined not to react any further to the examination.

"Move your fingers," the old man ordered, and Devon found that he was able to obey.

"And the wrist."

Again the order was carried out.

"Nothing broken," the old man said with satisfaction, turning to reach behind him for something on the table. The gold earring glinted though the silver strands of his hair, and Devon's fascinated eyes lowered to take in also the gaily embroidered shirt he wore. He glanced at the girl, who was now kneeling beside him holding the lantern for the Romany. She was certainly dark enough, Devon thought, but there was something about the heart-shaped face that...

"Here," the Gypsy said, holding out a stone bottle.

At Devon's hesitation, he gestured again with the container. "Whiskey. Drink it," he ordered. "You'll need it."

"Why," Devon asked, but given his experience, he was afraid he knew.

"Because I'm going to clean the wound. It's only a flesh wound, and the ball went through. Inflammation's the greatest danger, so if we can prevent that..."

"How?" Devon asked softly, his eyes resting on the old man's face.

The stone bottle lifted again, the glaze on its brown surface glinting softly. "Even the Romans used wine to speed healing," the Rom explained.

Devon took a deep breath and reached for the whiskey. He drank as long and as deeply as he could, the burn as unpleasant as that which was beginning to throb like flame through his arm. He head swam suddenly, the effects of the alcohol on top of the loss of blood.

He lowered the bottle and wiped his mouth on his left sleeve. And then he handed the whiskey back to the old man.

"Hold his arm," he ordered the girl. Her dark eyes, wide with shock, raised to the walnut brown, lined face of the Gypsy. He laughed suddenly.

"If you're going to faint," he said derisively, seeing the blanched features, "I'll get one of my men."

But having had an opportunity to assess the character of this girl during the weeks she had lived among his people, he wasn't surprised when the long lashes fell, hiding the glaze of her eyes. And when she raised them again to his face, they were as calm and as steady as the blue ones of the watching Englishman who lay propped against the wall of the caravan where they had laid him.

"I don't faint," she said deliberately and took Devon's right hand in her left. She put her right palm under his elbow and held the arm out for the old man's ministrations. And the small fingers that gripped Devon's didn't tremble.

The burn of the alcohol was as terrible as he had imagined it would be. He thought he could feel it tracing the path the ball had taken through his arm, cauterizing with its agony. He was unaware that his fingers had tightened unbearably over the small ones that held his, held still without trembling. He had made no sound beyond the first gasping inhalation as the whiskey bit into the damaged flesh.

And finally it was over. The old man's fingers were surprisingly gentle and reassuringly competent as he mopped up the liquid, pink-tinted with the freely flowing blood, and then almost professionally bound the wound tightly with strips of cotton.

At last, Devon found he was cradling the injured arm against his stomach. He opened his eyes, and the Gypsy handed him the whiskey bottle. He realized, as he drank, trying to hold the container steady in his left hand, which seemed determined to shake, that the girl was gone. Grateful for her absence, he lowered the bottle and tried to hand it back.

"Keep it," the old man said. "You'll need it."

Devon closed his eyes, allowing his head to fall back against the hard wall behind him. And he thought that the Rom was probably right.

Julie had stopped at the corner of the caravan she had just left. She stood, gulping long breaths of the cold night air, her head swimming, still smelling the fumes of the liquor the old man had used.

"I don't faint," she had said within the caravan. But now she lowered her head, comfortingly hidden by the darkness, and thought how close to being a lie that particular claim had just come.

Chapter Two

The next morning the curtain that barred entry to the caravan where Devon lay was pushed aside by the old man. Because he had no choice, Devon accepted the Gypsy's help in accomplishing the morning's necessities. The arm, too, was examined and rebandaged, and he was grateful beyond words when, in spite of a definite tender swelling around the wound and the slight fever, the Gypsy didn't suggest a repetition of last night's treatment.

After the old man left, Devon lay back down on the narrow cot and thought how worthless a rescuer for Avon he was turning out to be. All because of an ill-conceived feat of quixotic derring-do to save a Gypsy girl who, for whatever reasons, had been masquerading in boy's clothing. Possibly his mission to France had been the fool's errand he had feared from the beginning, but it had been one he was more than willing to undertake for the debt he owed the duke. And instead of success, he had only proven himself to be the fool he'd suspected from the start.

He didn't even open his eyes when the weight on the steps leading up to the caravan indicated his privacy was again about to be invaded. He hoped whoever it was would believe he was asleep and leave him alone.

It wasn't until she had moved so close to the low bed he could smell the aroma of the stew she carried in the chipped bowl that he gave up his pretense of sleep.

She was dressed as a girl today, the shining dark hair combed into a riot of loose curls all over her head and threaded through with a scarlet ribbon. The beautiful heart-shaped face was clean, and the smooth cream of her bare shoulders was only a shade or two darker than the low-necked peasant blouse that also left most of her slender arms exposed. The long, patterned skirt swirled around trim ankles and slender, slippered feet.

Julie waited for the expected impact of her careful toilette to appear on the features of the man who lay watching her. She had been frequently and lavishly assured of her beauty most of her life, but for some reason, his dismissal of her face and figure last night as "believably boyish" had rankled. And so she watched for the accustomed admiration and was again disappointed in the unwavering assessment of the dark blue eyes.

No wonder she'd made a believable child, Devon was thinking. She was tiny, probably less than five feet tall, and perfectly proportioned for her height. There was no denying her rather exotic beauty, but since that beauty was the opposite of everything he had ever admired in a woman, he wondered at the sudden lurch in his stomach at the sight of this startling transformation.

He allowed himself to briefly picture Elizabeth's blond perfection, which he knew, for him at least, was the epitome of womanly attractiveness. Her cool, poised elegance had always left him breathless, and he wondered how he could find in the slightest way appealing someone so different from that old ideal. The response he had felt was obviously for the enticing aroma of the food she had brought, and not, of course, for the dark, slim beauty of the girl herself.

"I thought you might be hungry," she offered, taking her own inventory. The fine lips she had admired as he'd struggled yesterday not to reveal his amusement at her supposed hero-worship were today tightly set. The lines around his mouth were too distinct for his age, but she found that she liked the multitude of laugh lines that fanned richly around his eyes. And his lashes, dark brown and shading to gold at the tips, were as long and as thick as her own.

"No," he said, but she knew by the pause, a pause that had stretched long enough to allow her to consider what she had found so appealing about his face yesterday, that he had at least thought about the food. Which meant he was probably as hungry as she suspected, in spite of what she was beginning to recognize as the same stiff-necked English pride her father had always displayed.

"I'm not suggesting that you let me feed you," she said and held out the slim hand that had supported his arm so firmly last night.

The debate between pride and hunger was brief, and Devon put his left hand in hers and let her help in the awkward struggle to sit up. She made no comment about the stiffness of his wrenched back. Instead, as soon as he was upright on the edge of the bed, she placed the bowl of stew on the small table that crowded the central aisle of the caravan. She swept a few scattered items that had rested there out of the way and then removed from the pocket of her skirt a small loaf of bread wrapped in a clean napkin and laid it down beside the bowl. She poured a cup of water from the pitcher that had been left for him on the table last night. He hadn't noticed the water, but then he'd gone to sleep almost as soon as his head had touched the narrow mattress, drugged by the old man's whiskey, blood loss and the exertions from the first days he'd spent in the saddle in over two years.

He realized suddenly that she had completed her preparations for his meal and was waiting for him.

With his left hand he grasped the post of the bed, using it to pull himself to his feet. It wasn't a particularly smooth ascent, but he was up and moving fairly normally toward the table before he realized that the girl's dark eyes had watched and evaluated the entire operation. And he knew sitting down would be just as awkward.

What the hell, he thought suddenly. Given his condition six months ago, he found himself grateful that yesterday's activities hadn't resulted in more serious impairment today. Just strained muscles, and he knew that the soreness would work out.

He put his left hand flat on the surface of the small table, hoping it was stronger than it looked, and then lowered his body by careful stages onto the chair.

This time he didn't even glance at her face. Whatever her reaction, he'd seen it before. He'd seen them all. And since this particular injury was a result of his efforts on her behalf, it certainly was not cause for embarrassment in front of her.

He picked up the spoon with his left hand and began to eat. In spite of his real hunger and the awkwardness of having to use the wrong hand, there was no lapse in his innate good manners.

Julie was well aware of what that revealed about this man. His speech, his dress, even the equipment and the valuable horse he rode, all had marked him as a member of the class Julie had learned long ago only tolerated people like her on its own terms. Only for the "services" they could render. And now his manners confirmed the suspicions she'd had yesterday about his place in the world. Intent on his meal, Devon wasn't aware of the cynical smile that touched her lips.

He reached for the small loaf of bread, realizing as soon as he touched it that there was no way, one-handed, he could break it apart. And he refused to add trying to manage the damaged arm to the show he'd already presented. Since he was as incapable of tearing chunks off the whole with his teeth as he would have been of beating his horse or of cheating at cards, he simply gave up the thought of the bread and turned his attention back to the stew. Considering the primitive nature of the meals he'd eaten on the Peninsula, the stew alone was a feast for kings.

Having seen that decision reached and, having now firmly fixed his position on the rigid social scale that governed society, Julie took the loaf and began to tear it into small pieces.

Devon noticed the slight swelling and discoloration of her left hand as she worked, and he wondered if that had happened yesterday in her battle with the apple farmer, whoever he really was.

"Thank you," he said automatically when she had reduced the bread to manageable portions.

"What happened to your back?" she asked softly. He had known the question was inevitable, but he'd hoped. He always hoped.

His head remained down, eyes locked on the flavorful meat for a few seconds. His close-cut chestnut hair caught the light from the open curtain. That and the hand holding the spoon were all that she could see of her rescuer.

His eyes, when they were raised to her face, revealed only amusement.

"Well," he began, in the time-honored fashion of storytellers, "there once was a boy who was caught stealing apples..."

"No," she interrupted. "I saw you before. In the stables. That's why I thought you couldn't ride. Before—"

At the sudden break in that sentence, Devon realized that her insult to his horsemanship had just been acknowledged. And he judged rightly that this was the only apology he was likely to get. But the question she had asked still lay between them.

"Shrapnel," he said concisely and turned back to the stew. It was, after all, the complete explanation.

"Shrapnel?" she repeated with surprise. "Then... you were a soldier."

He didn't interrupt his eating to agree to the obvious. And the loss of his profession was not a topic that he was able to discuss dispassionately. Not that he'd ever tried. Not with anyone other than his father.

"Somehow..." she began, and when she laughed instead of finishing that thought, he glanced up. "Somehow," she started again, studying those tired blue eyes, "I'd decided you were something quite different."

His question was asked with raised brows and a slight tilt of his head.

"An aristocrat," she suggested. "A very proper English *milord*," she said, her low voice rich with sarcasm.

"And you don't like milords?" he repeated, retaining her mocking inflection. "Then you'll be glad to learn that I'm not one."

"No fancy English title?" she asked.

"Not even a minor one," he said, and his lips moved into the upward slant she was learning to anticipate, the smile she had enjoyed yesterday.

"Perhaps growing up with the Revolution's lack of respect for titles is to blame for how I feel about the nobility," she said, knowing that the real reason was her treatment by the men of that class. The sexual innuendos, the offers, the speculative gleam in leering, amorous, oh-so-noble eyes. She had found nothing to admire in the blue bloods who had crowded her father's casino. "And Bonaparte's new aristocracy hasn't managed to change my opinion," she acknowledged truthfully. "Have you ever known an aristocrat who deserved the titles he bore?" she challenged.

"Spoken like a true revolutionary," Devon said, smiling gently at the understandable class rebellion of the Gypsy girl. "No wonder royal families all over Europe dreaded the spread of those doctrines. And yes, I *have* known noblemen who lived up to their titles and positions," Devon said, thinking of the man he had come to France to find. "Not only those born to wealth and power abuse them. I should have thought that Robespierre's bloodbath would have convinced everyone of that."

"I wasn't in Paris then," she said and quickly stopped that revelation. She could trust no one, not even someone who had risked his own life to save hers. Coming back here had been dangerous enough. If they had been able to track her to the village where she'd lived after she'd left the Gypsy's camp, then they might be aware of where she'd spent her time before she'd so successfully become the orphaned urchin. And if so...

"Do you think you might find me a razor somewhere?" Devon asked, and her mind came back to the present. He had finished the stew and the bread she'd broken. "I'd like to try to get rid of these," he said, running long, tanned fingers over the stubbled cheeks.

Following that movement with her eyes, she wondered irrationally if his beard would be blond if he let it grow. The morning sun was touching it now with the same gold that tipped his lashes. She realized suddenly that the direction of her thoughts was too personal, too intimate. She was intrigued with his beard. Thinking about its color and texture. As she had thought about his smile. And the thick lashes that surrounded the blue eyes. The laugh lines. God, she thought, her self-discovery catching her by surprise, I'm attracted to him.

The emotion was so foreign to her usual wary reaction to men that she was unsure at first of the validity of her surmise. But a quick assessment of the attractiveness of the strong, angular planes of his face, of those tiny lines around his eyes, of his mouth... My God, she thought again. She wondered why he was looking at her so strangely, and then she realized that she hadn't answered his question. What had he asked? she thought, trying desperately to remember. A razor. Something about a razor.

"And you're going to try to shave left-handed?" she managed.

"Unless... I had wondered if you might be willing..." His voice faded at her expression, trying to analyze what it meant.

"I've never shaved a man before," she said. Her usually decisive voice was almost a whisper. She cleared her throat nervously, and forced her eyes away from that beautifully masculine face.

"Well, you certainly can't do any worse than I'd do left-handed," he said, laughing.

The pleasantness of that sound drew her eyes back, and she found herself confronting the full, unleashed force of his smile. Her knees were suddenly water.

What's the matter with me, she thought angrily. But she knew. Even the thought of touching him, of holding his face, of standing close enough to him to accomplish what seemed to her now the much too intimate act of shaving him was disturbing.

"I'd ask the old man, but somehow the thought of a razor in his one hand and my throat in the other..." He let his voice trail off with that suggestion, and smiled at her again, inviting her to join his amusement.

But there was no answering smile. Her eyes were as wide and dark as they had been last night. He wondered what was wrong, and then he realized that he'd just insulted the Gypsy. His irreverent sense of humor had made him a popular member of Wellington's staff, but it had also gotten him into trouble on more than one occasion. And now, when the old man had been good enough to take him in, he'd offered only insults in return. Maybe they were even related, he thought suddenly. Maybe...

"Your father," he said, putting it all together. "He's your father. I'm sorry. I didn't mean to insult him. I just—"

"My father!" Julie repeated incredulously, thinking about the gentle, dignified English aristocrat who had pampered and spoiled his only daughter, such a contrast to the brutal, despotic old Rom. "He's *not* my father," she denied vehemently, as if the suggestion were too ridiculous for discussion. "But you were right. He'd cut your throat for a centime, and without a second thought. And he's *not* my father," she said again.

She turned and, angrily pushing the partially opened curtain out of her way, she left him alone.

Behind her in the silence of the caravan, Devon looked at the curtain that moved, swinging, for several moments in the violence of her departure.

Not my father, she had said. And he wondered at the strength of that denial. Why would she be so adamant about the impossibility of that?

The thought, when it came, was as repulsive as the images of Elizabeth and March. The old man and the beautiful, dark-eyed girl. He remembered the touch of her slender fingers on his arm, and somewhere in the back of his mind came the sudden, sure remembrance of their gentle tracing over the stubble he had just asked her to help him remove. And unbidden and unwanted, the image of those slender fingers moving, caressing and enticing, through the long silver locks of the Rom. In the sudden bile that filled his throat he knew that, in spite of its contrast to Elizabeth's cool perfection, the girl's beauty had *not* left him indifferent.

He fought the pull back to the comfort of the narrow cot and was still sitting at the table, methodically flexing and unflexing the swollen fingers of his right hand. He was just as methodically avoiding any thoughts of the girl when a dip in the steadiness of the caravan toward the curtained doorway announced his next visitor. He took a deep breath and looked up from his self-appointed task to find the Romany watching him with amusement.

"Sore?" he questioned rhetorically. "You think that will help the soreness?"

"It can't hurt," Devon said simply, having no desire now to talk to the Gypsy. He hadn't been as successful as he'd hoped in convincing himself that whatever was happening between the Romany leader and the girl was none of his affair. It had nothing to do with him or the reason he was in France. And that mission was all he intended to think about from now on.

"It won't matter," the old man said, his high good humor apparent. He was very satisfied about something. "The girl's fingers are nimble enough for you both," he finished, thinking of the very lucrative proposition she had just made.

The old man didn't understand the sudden sharp movement that locked those slowly flexing fingers into a fist. But the English were a strange breed. Besides, discussing the girl's newly revealed talents was not the purpose of this visit.

"I brought you a shirt," he said, dropping the indigo garment on the table in front of the Englishman.

The long fingers eventually unclenched and touched the smooth softness of the material.

"I can't pay you," Devon said, controlling the anger that had surged through his body at what he viewed as a confirmation of his earlier suspicions. "All the money I had was in my saddlebags. When I rode after the child...after the girl," he amended, and then knew there was no point in explaining his foolish, unthinking gallantry. "I left them in the stable at the inn. I can—"

"It's all right," the old man said dismissingly as he turned to leave. "The girl will more than compensate me for the shirt."

The crash of the chair in the confines of the small wagon drew his dark eyes to stare in amazement at the man standing across the table from him. Despite the strained muscles, there had been no hesitation in the surge of movement that had this time brought Devon to his feet.

"No," he said bitterly. "I don't know what your previous arrangement has involved, but she won't pay for *this* that way." He grabbed the shirt from the table and, balling it angrily in his fist, he threw it suddenly at the old man. It hit him squarely in the chest but, bewildered by the Englishman's actions, the Gypsy made no effort to catch it. The cotton slithered to the floor, its fall unwatched by either pair of eyes.

In the dark ones of the old man there was only astonishment. And briefly, complete puzzlement. But something in the rigid jaw and furiously blazing blue eyes must have given him a clue as to the source of Devon's anger.

"You think..." he began, and then the ludicrous suggestion was dismissed by a universal and contemptuous gesture of his liver-spotted hand. "You think I would sleep with children," he mocked.

And with that taunting ridicule, the tight disgust that had knotted in Devon's stomach since the inception of that thought loosened.

"I have grandchildren older than she," the Gypsy said derisively, his distaste apparent. "My wife would cut her throat. And probably mine," he finished, his good humor and his vanity making the Englishman's suggestion now a source of enjoyment. His accusation would make a good story.

"Then how—" Devon began, only to be cut off.

"You ask her. Like you, she's my guest. In her case, a paying guest. And her secrets are her own. I haven't asked what an English aristocrat's doing in France in these ... unusual times," he said, choosing his words cautiously.

But in the very carefulness of that phrasing Devon recognized that the Rom knew about Napoleon's slow yet inexorable march to the capital. And he wondered at the old man's sources of information.

"And I haven't asked the girl why she's here," the Gypsy continued.

"Then she's not a member of your..." Devon stopped, unsure of correct wording of the question he needed answered.

"Harem?" the old man suggested sardonically, one thick white brow raised. "Family," he supplied at Devon's embarrassed head shake. "I don't believe in asking questions of people who obviously don't want to answer them. It's a practice you might consider."

He turned again to leave, almost stepping on the crumpled shirt. He bent to pick it up and tossed it accurately to land in the center of Devon's chest. Although he hadn't been expecting it, Devon's reflexes were still well-honed enough to make a quick left-handed grab at the material, preventing its fall.

"And you may consider the shirt a gift," the Romany said, pushing aside the curtain and descending the three short steps from the caravan to the ground.

The man who stood in the slightly rocking wagon wasn't thinking about the Gypsy's displeasure, as dangerous as he knew it probably was. He was thinking again about the girl. A guest, the old man had said. If she didn't belong here, then who was she? He knew he wouldn't get the answer from the Gypsy. The Rom had made that clear.

Devon looked down at the dark shirt he held. A touch of red that gleamed brightly against the indigo caused him to take a closer look at the old man's gift. Forcing himself to awkwardly use the aching right arm, he held up the shirt until the embroidered flowers that decorated the collar and wide cuffs were plainly revealed.

An involuntary smile at the thought of the picture he'd present in this grew into a broad grin. Never in his life, he thought, shaking his head, had he ever worn anything so exotic. The array of picturesque uniforms he'd donned through the years never entered his mind, because, of course, he'd never seen anything even remotely unusual about those. They were simply the very honorable garb of his profession.

And then he turned his attention to the Herculean task of getting out of the bloody, mutilated shirt he'd worn for the last two days and into this. But the entire time he was undressing, the small self-derisory smile quirked the corners of his lips.

He managed a rough bath using his ruined shirt and the cold water remaining in the pitcher. He combed dampened fingers through his hair, leaving it curling over his forehead. And he was wearing the shirt. At least he felt clean and more in control. He had learned in Portugal the almost miraculous boost in spirits that a bath and a shave could provide. He ran his fingers over his face, feeling the two days' growth with disgust. But it seemed there was nothing he could do about that.

The shifting dip that announced visitors to his small room could be clearly felt again. As popular as the punch bowl at Almack's, he thought in amusement, mocking one of the more ridiculous rituals of that artificial society he'd long ago come to view with disdain. The Marriage Mart, the bachelors had nicknamed the popular club, and at the remembrance of the hopeful mamas and their dressed-up charges, he smiled again.

He hadn't stopped to analyze the upswing in mood he'd experienced since the confrontation with the Romany leader. If he'd thought about it at all, he'd have put the near-elation down to the effects of clean clothes and a relatively clean body.

He turned to the door, expecting to greet the old man again, and instead found the girl, carefully balancing a brimming basin of steaming water, a razor and piece of white flannel.

Julie met the shock in his eyes with a practiced smile, her emotions very much under control now that she'd had time to assimilate his effect on her senses and to rationalize those feelings as a very understandable gratitude. He had, after all, saved her freedom, if not her life. And at a not inconsiderable cost to himself.

My hero, she had mocked herself as she prepared the necessary equipment to provide the shave he'd asked for. She had accepted the task almost as a challenge. She was certainly sophisticated enough to shave a man without swooning over the length of his lashes or the shape of his nose. Or the blue of his eyes. The almost navy blue of his eyes, she found herself thinking now.

For the first time she became aware of the indigo shirt he wore. The embroidered collar and cuffs and wide, flowing sleeves looked so exotically out of place with the skintight English doeskins that molded the long length of muscular legs and disappeared into the tops of the now-shining boots. It was the deep blue of the shirt that enhanced the color of his eyes and warmed the pallor yesterday's ordeal had given his face. The short chestnut hair was still damp from his ablutions, which she suspected had been accomplished from that same pitcher from which she'd poured the water that had earlier accompanied his meal.

"That's a very attractive shirt," she said, trying to command her twitching lips into obedience.

"It's ridiculous, I know, but at least it's clean," he said, smiling easily at her amusement.

And in spite of the determined admonitions she'd given herself, in spite of her careful mental enumeration of all the despicable characteristics of the men of his class, she felt a fluttering warmth in the center of her heart. A heart that had always remained remarkably untouched until she'd met this Englishman who knew how to laugh at himself.

"Are you still interested in a shave?" she forced herself to ask calmly and registered the surprise in his eyes.

"Of course," he said. "I'd be very grateful. I had just thought that a shave would complete..."

"The transformation," she suggested when he hesitated.

"The recovery," he said, almost on top of her words.

"You *do* look better."

"I'm fine. I need only a shave to be a new man," he said.

"I didn't find much wrong with the old one," she admitted carefully. "I haven't told you how grateful I am for yesterday. I really—"

"A shave, and we're even," he broke into her expression of gratitude. He'd never wanted that. He was always uncomfortable with thanks, especially for those actions that anyone would have undertaken. The idea that a child could be abducted without anyone lifting a hand to prevent it had demanded his automatic response, unthinking and unquestioning. Although one heard stories of stolen children sold to sweeps or Gypsies... He smiled at the irony of his thoughts of the previous day as he had struggled to mount the gelding he'd just unsaddled.

"I think you'd better sit down," she suggested, wondering what had caused that smile. "You're too tall."

He lowered himself into the chair, and she was pleased to note that the movement this time was far less careful than it had been before.

She put the objects she'd carried into the caravan on the table and took the soap she'd begged from one of the women from the pocket of her skirt. She efficiently coaxed a slightly soapy foam from the harsh, lye-based lump. Eventually her hands were covered with the watery mixture. But when she realized it was time to transfer the soap to his face, she hesitated. He glanced up as water dripped onto his thigh and saw her standing, still as a statue, with soapy hands extended.

"What's wrong?" he asked.

She shook her head, breaking the spell she'd created by thinking about touching him. She resolutely put her palms against his cheeks and wondered if he could feel the almost physical jolt of reaction that moved through her body at the pleasantly rough warmth of his skin. She rubbed his face determinedly, and then, resorting again to the soap, transferred more onto his chin and the narrow area between the strong, nearly Roman nose and the molded lips. He had turned his head accommodatingly as she'd worked, and she struggled to keep her reaction to touching him from being communicated through her fingertips.

When she had finished soaping his face, she unconsciously released her building tension in a soft sigh. The sound caused the blue eyes to open, and Devon realized that he had shut them almost with the first stroke of her fingers against his cheeks.

There had been something strongly sensuous in the caress of those slender fingers against his face, and there had also been an immediate response to the soft, very womanly breasts, which had been exactly on the level of his eyes. As her body had shifted slightly, moving with the stroking movements of her hands, the clean, pleasant aroma of that small, perfect body had wafted under his nose. He had closed his eyes to fight the response he'd felt to both her touch and to that fragrance.

He forced himself to picture the icy mountain streams in the Pyrenees, imagined himself wading knee deep in their frigid waters. And then deeper. Allowing the ice to cover his thighs. But nothing was interfering with his awareness of those fingers playing over his cheeks, of her breasts moving just in front of his face. He shifted uncomfortably in the chair and carefully crossed his legs.

"Are you all right?" she asked suddenly, wondering about his back. There had been something in that sudden movement that had communicated his discomfort quite clearly.

"Of course," he said, his voice slightly unsteady. He unnecessarily eased the injured arm into his lap. That movement served more than one purpose, and apparently it was convincing, for she picked up the razor and tilted his face to allow her better access to his cheek.

The pressure of the moving blade was better than her hands, but wielding it had required that she move her body closer to his. She was leaning now, almost touching him, her knee resting against his thigh and her breasts again in too-close proximity to his face. He had only to move the fingers of his hand, or to lower his head to give his lips access to that dark, fragrant valley...

She stepped back suddenly, and he wondered if she could know what he'd been thinking. He opened his eyes and found her critically assessing the area she'd just finished. Her tongue was protruding slightly between small, even teeth, and when she became aware that he was watching her, she smiled at his expression.

"Not very professional, I'm afraid," she began to apologize.

"It's fine," he said. "It's bound to be better than before." Just get it over with, he thought, before I embarrass us both.

He wondered suddenly if, because she was not one of the elegantly poised women of his circle, he was more inclined to think about... The realization of exactly what he had been thinking surprised him. It was so against the rigid code that had always governed his actions where women were concerned. Because, he was forced to admit, he had been thinking about making love to her. A woman alone and apparently unprotected beyond the purchased sanctuary of the Romany camp.

"This way," she said softly, directing his chin with those slender fingers. He'd been unconsciously resisting her placement of his face, lost in his thoughts.

Too long without a woman, he mocked himself ruefully. And she was very beautiful. And perhaps... He deliberately blocked that idle fantasy.

He wasn't aware of the bitterness of his slight smile at even the thought of exposing himself to the kind of pain Elizabeth's rejection had inflicted.

And so until he knew the secrets this woman was hiding, he decided grimly, whatever emotions she was able to evoke would be very carefully controlled.

Chapter Three

It was almost dusk when Devon descended the three steps of the caravan for his first look around the camp. After the girl had left today, he had taken advantage of his solitude to rest. And in the peaceful lull of the spring afternoon, that rest had, due to the continuing low fever, turned into sleep.

One of the Gypsy women woke him when she brought his dinner—bread and a small cheese—and he'd forced himself to eat it all. The quicker he got his strength back, the quicker he could continue his search for his brother-in-law. It was that which had brought him to France and not whatever was going on with the girl.

As if in response to that thought, his eyes drifted across the circled camp to find her sitting under the shelter of a tall oak, a small table in front of her stool. She appeared to be manipulating something on its surface. He looked around at the scattered caravans and found that, in the growing twilight, no one was paying the least attention to the girl or to himself. Driven by an emotion that certainly wasn't logic, he walked across the dusty compound and stood watching her swiftly moving fingers.

Julie glanced up, smiling, and then her eyes returned to the flashing hands and the shells they were directing.

This morning she had been forced to consider the pitiful hoard of coins she carried. She knew that the old man's hospitality was based strictly on a guest's ability to pay. He had taken her in when her father's money had paid the way, but her remaining treasury would not have covered the cost of her own food, and this time she had brought another mouth to be fed.

So she had made the dangerous, but necessary, offer and had watched the shrewd Romany mind assess her value. She had not been surprised when he had demanded a demonstration, and although he had hidden his elation well, she knew he had been pleased.

But even if the Gypsy hadn't noticed, she had known that she was out of practice after three months away from the casino's tables. Not that this was, of course, a game her father had ever countenanced there. It depended on deception more than skill or strategy, and he would never have approved of what she was doing for the old man. But she had no other choice. Not if she wanted his protection, both for herself and for the man who now stood watching her.

Her left hand betrayed her suddenly, the ball dropping from between her fingers to roll across the table and into the grass at her feet.

"Damn," she said under her breath, knowing that if that happened at the fair tomorrow, she'd end up in the village gaol or with a knife in her back. Unthinkingly, she flexed the slightly swollen hand.

Suddenly long masculine fingers were resting under her small ones. Devon turned her hand in the fading light, seeing again the slight discoloration he'd noticed earlier.

"What happened to your fingers?" he asked.

She found that she had no answer, the sight or the sensation of his hand supporting hers robbing her of her usual ready wit. And so she sat, silent as the village idiot, while he held her hand. His thumb caressed her knuckles, and her mouth went dry.

"It looks like..." he began, and then he remembered crushing fragile bones last night when the old man had poured the whiskey into the rawness of his wound.

"My God," he said softly. "I did that."

He waited, hoping for her denial, but once again her eyes were simply locked on his face. He had never in his life hurt a woman. Except, apparently, this one. And the small bruised fingers rested still so trustingly in his.

"I'm sorry," he said softly. "I never meant..."

The soft palm was lifted from his, and she smiled, shaking her head.

"It's nothing. I probably hurt it when he threw me into the wagon." The lie easily made, she changed the subject by gesturing to the shells on the table. "But it makes this a little challenging."

"This?" he questioned, uncertainly.

"Le jeu des gobelets."

"Le jeu..." he began to repeat without comprehension and saw her quick smile at his obvious puzzlement.

"Thimblerig," she said in English, and he realized suddenly that she had spoken English all along, from the time she had answered his question about the apples until her unexpected reply just now in French.

Surprisingly, her English was as pure, as educated and cultured and as unaccented as his own. He could have carried her into any ballroom in London, and no one would have had the least suspicion that she was anything other than another attractive debutante come to the capital for her season.

"My father was English," she said simply, as if that alone would explain the enigma of her identity. She watched the thoughts chase across his face.

"Thimblerig," she said again, closing the door to the questions she could see forming by bending to pick up the ball she'd dropped. "Do you know it? It's all the rage. The Gypsy's willing to accept our addition to his band in exchange for my expertise at the game. The crowds we'll attract at the fair tomorrow and their wagers will more than cover whatever our food and lodging costs him. He'll be more than compensated for his kindnesses."

"Thank you for taking care of me last night, for bringing me here," he said, thinking back with somewhat ironic amusement on all the Gypsy's "kindnesses." She smiled away his gratitude.

"We're even. Remember?" she said, but the reminder of his words in the small caravan this morning brought back too strongly the memory of that pleasant intimacy. She wondered why, with him, she couldn't seem to keep the distance she usually had no trouble maintaining in her dealings with men.

"Would you like to watch me practice?" she asked, again deliberately moving away from the personal.

"Of course," he agreed, and her quick fingers began to manipulate the shells in ever-faster circles.

When she looked up at him and arched her brows in question, he said with a great deal of assurance, "The middle one."

And she lifted the shell to expose to his disbelieving eyes the nothing that rested beneath it.

"How . . ." he began, and she laughed.

"One doesn't ask a magician to explain his magic. And the shells can't lie. You must not be watching closely enough. Try again," she offered generously.

It hadn't seemed possible to him that her fingers could move any faster than they had before, but when she stopped and questioned his choice with her eyes, he wasn't as sure as before. And, of course, he was just as wrong.

"At least you aren't betting any money," she said, laughing. "Again?" she suggested and, without waiting for his reply, began the slow, preliminary movements that so convinced the unwary they were, this time, going to succeed in following the ball's course.

She looked up to find his eyes, not on her hands as she had expected, but watching her face. Her fingers hesitated in their practiced motion, and the air was thick with some element she couldn't identify.

"Who are you?" he asked softly, his eyes still intent on hers.

She placed her palms over the shells and sat too still for a moment.

"For now, a Gypsy girl," she said finally. "Only a girl who has a skill the old man can use." The dark eyes flashed, her smile carefully maintained. "Deception," she said, her tone almost challenging. She turned her hand palm up, and he could see the ball he thought she had placed under one of the shells held snugly hidden in the space between two of her fingers.

She watched the faint crease form between his brows, and she swept the shells and the ball into one small hand and rose smoothly.

But she was still smiling when she warned, "The only skill I have is the ability to make people believe they see one thing, when in reality..." She stopped because of what was in his eyes.

"You cheat," he said, surprised at how pained that accusation sounded. He was no innocent, given the years he had spent in the brutal conditions of Iberia, but the thought that she would deliberately set out to deceive those who would play tomorrow was abhorrent.

"And if you make the enemy believe that your forces are stronger than they are, or that you intend to attack from one direction and then charge from another..." she began to argue and saw him shake his head.

"That's not—"

"Deception?" she questioned softly, mockingly.

"That's not cheating," he finished doggedly.

"You're such a child," she jeered. "The English and their damned rules. And if you break one—" She stopped, knowing that in her bitterness at his judgment she had given away too much.

"And if you break one?" he repeated quietly.

"Then you're never forgiven. You become no one," she finished, her voice a whisper.

"What's wrong?" he asked, watching the struggle for control, the dark eyes glaze quickly with unshed tears. "Why are you crying?"

"Crying," she said, laughing suddenly, her tone derisive, and the long dark lashes quickly veiled whatever had been in her eyes. "I'm not crying. I don't cry. I never cry," she said more strongly. The eyes she raised to his were angry and mocking, but the moisture was gone, so he was forced to doubt what he'd seen. Maybe he *had* been mistaken.

"Who are you?" he asked again, but she turned away, unable to look at the condemnation in his eyes. Now she knew what her father had faced, some small part of what had driven him from his country and from the judgment of men like this.

She heard him say something else, but she didn't turn back.

"No one," she whispered bitterly to herself, repeating the only possible answer to his question. But she moved across the compound with the deliberately swaying walk that made the colorful skirt swing enticingly around her bare ankles, knowing that he was watching her.

The afternoon had been long and successful. The ancient crossroads bustled with people who had come to take advantage of the presence of the merchants and entertainers.

The ache that had begun to gnaw between Julie's shoulder blades attested to the hours she had enthralled the succession of yokels who begged to be taken in by her nimble fingers and distracting spiel. She had been watched over by the hawklike eyes of the old man, guarding his investment, as the members of his band exhorted the wagers of the crowd.

It was unusual enough to have a woman, especially one so beautiful, openly engaged in the games of chance that her patrons had far outnumbered those of her numerous competitors.

One of those patrons was a drunk who had crowded close to the table where she entertained. Since this particular customer had been betting with increasing frequency and with a total disregard for his losses, the old man had indicated with a small upward movement of his chin that he desired her to milk his inebriation for all the profit possible. So she had laughingly endured the drunk's occasional fondling touch on her arm. His fingers had even once trailed across the bare skin of her exposed shoulder. With the Romany daggers so readily at hand, she knew she was in no danger, other than to her sensibilities. She blocked her distaste and began again to invite the crowd's fascinated attention.

Halfway through the practiced performance, she felt the drunk's moist hands rest heavily on her shoulders and then begin the caressing descent downward. Her quick twist from his hold and the grimace of disgust were reflexive. She shivered convulsively at the thought of those hands against her breasts.

She heard the muttering complaint of the crowd at the interruption in the swift movement of her hands. She looked up to offer some laughing reassurance and met instead the coldly furious eyes of the Englishman who stood before her table like some medieval warrior.

"Don't touch her again," he said softly, his gaze locked on the drunk's flushed face, locked without any trace of fear. He was as calmly in control now as when he'd compelled her captor to release her in the village.

The man lurched belligerently around the table and toward the Englishman. Devon braced himself, knees bent and legs slightly apart, preparing to meet the wild charge everyone was aware was coming.

The drunk's fist swung with more control than his drunkenness should have allowed, but a small, carefully timed twist of Devon's upper body caused the blow to pass harmlessly by his left ear. Then his circling movements mirrored the aggressor's, whose staggering steps and upraised fists made it clear he intended to try again to land a fist on that calm and watchful face. Instead, Julie slipped her small body under the drunkard's elbow and stood between his raised arms. She leaned back, pushing strongly against the malodorous body, and at the same time she spoke to Devon, who stood, still in that almost relaxed fighter's stance, watching her.

"Stop it," she hissed, outraged by his intervention. "Go away. My God, what do you think you're doing?"

Something flared hotly in the narrowed blue of his eyes, and then they moved away from her face to his attacker's.

"You belong to him?" the drunk questioned, reading more in her defender's face, perhaps, than she had.

He moved from behind the barrier of her slender body and swept Devon a low and clumsily mocking bow. "My apologies. I didn't know she was your whore. I thought she was fair game. After all," he continued unwisely and looked up just as Devon's well-placed left exploded against his nose, and the rest of whatever insult he had intended remained unspoken.

The crowd had not particularly liked the interference of the drunk in their entertainment, but he was one of their own. Seeing him so suddenly defeated, they began a threatening surge against the lone figure who stood over his downed and forgotten foe, his eyes riveted now on the features of the furious girl.

"How dare you?" she said. "Do you have any idea, damn you, what you've done?"

Disbelief moved into his face, and his hand closed suddenly on her elbow, but she jerked from his grasp far more violently than she had from the drunk's. She watched his lips tighten, but she was too angry to care. She knew very well what the Gypsy's reaction to the loss of such a ripe pigeon for plucking would be. And now the watchers were hostile, wary. All her hard work to develop a rapport had been for naught.

Then the Rom was there, pulling her away in a grip far harder than that she had just broken. A grip she knew better than to fight against.

"Tomorrow," he said to the disgruntled crowd. "Come back tomorrow. The game's closed for the day."

"What about our money?" a voice questioned and, in the sudden remembrance of bets that had already been fixed and then forgotten in the ensuing excitement of the fight, the question was picked up to be repeated in a multitude of demanding tones. The Gypsy signaled his men, who began to repay the wagers as he pulled her from the middle of the mob and pushed her angrily before him down the road to the encampment. And his touch was not gentle.

"You control your man," he said harshly, as soon as they were out of earshot of the crowd, "or you leave. That," he said, with a quick twist of his head in the direction of the jeering comments that followed their retreat, "will not happen again. I swear I'll put a knife between his ribs myself."

"He's not my man," she answered hotly, "and I can't control him."

"Then get rid of him. Or I'll do it for you. You didn't tell me he was a fool. What did he think he was doing?" he asked in disbelief.

At the sudden realization of exactly what he had been doing, her anger evaporated.

"He thought he was protecting me," she said softly, knowing that was the sum of his reasons. And if they made no sense to her or to the old man, that didn't mean in his world they were invalid. Protecting me, she thought again. A small feeling of wonder began to grow.

"From what? You were never in danger. You knew that," the Gypsy said, still furious over the rich prize the Englishman had driven away, over the profitable afternoon's loss.

The girl looked up suddenly, her expression unreadable. "Not from that," she said. "From what he did. From touching me."

"He wasn't hurting you." The girl's explanation was ridiculous, quickly rejected by his practicality.

"He put his hands—" she said, and then stopped. She knew she'd never make the Gypsy understand how outrageous that touch was in the Englishman's world. Not in theirs perhaps, but in his. And to have been protected in that way, as he believed women should be, was surprisingly pleasant. Jean would have laughingly lured the drunk away, taking care never to anger the customer. But Devon had chosen instead to defend her.

"No more. You tell him. You make him understand or by God..." the old man threatened, his eyes
brooking no defiance. She knew her position was such
that she couldn't afford to question his authority here
where his word was literally the law.

Perhaps she was valuable to him, but the Englishman was not. He was nothing more than a burden that
the Rom, thus far, had put up with for the ample pay-
ment her skills were providing. But if the Englishman
persisted in interfering in that contribution, she knew
the old man would do exactly what he had indicated.
He would swiftly and without the least compunction
destroy what he saw as a hazard to the success of his
ventures.

She took a breath to control her emotions and
promised grimly, "It won't happen again. You have
my word."

The ancient eyes looked deeply into hers for a moment, and then he nodded and strode on, leaving her
standing alone on the dirt road.

Near twilight, directed by one of the men who had
helped placate the afternoon's angry mob, she found
Devon at the stream where the horses had been teth-
ered. She had ignored the admiring gleam in the young
man's dark eyes and had thanked him for the information without making any explanation.

The Englishman was standing quietly by the water's edge, the gelding contentedly nibbling grass
nearby. He held a stick in his long fingers, and she
watched as he idly broke pieces from it and threw them
to swirl aimlessly in the water that rushed through the
small stream at his feet.

Although Julie's slippers had made no noise on the mossy slope, he turned and watched her approach. She thought he might make some comment about what had happened today, but instead he simply waited for her to speak.

"If you ever interfere again, the old man will kill you," she warned. She would have expected disbelief or even anger from most men at the blunt message, but instead amusement replaced the patient wariness that had been in his eyes.

"My God," she exploded, her fear for him fueling her words, "do you think that's a joke? He means exactly what he said. And here—" her hand swept to encompass the grazing horses and the wagons circled in the gathering dusk "—he's king, judge and executioner. There's no law to prevent him if he wants to murder you in your bed. This isn't London."

"Believe me, people have been trying to kill me for a number of years," Devon said, smiling at her. "And the law has seemed remarkably unconcerned about those attempts. I don't suppose he'll succeed any better than the others have." The amusement lurked still in his eyes as well as in the calm voice. There was no arrogance in that statement, but rather a smiling resignation.

"Excuse me," she mocked bitterly. "I see I was wrong. I thought you were merely foolish. Now I can see that you're stupid, as well. At least you've been warned."

His continued calmness in the face of the warning infuriated her as much as her fear for him had earlier.

"Don't you understand," she began, but his quiet voice stopped her, and there was now no humor in its tone.

"I don't understand why you were angry today. I should have thought—"

"I was angry because you interfered in something that wasn't your affair. I had made a commitment to the old man. And your heroics lost him a very profitable customer. Over nothing. There was no reason..." she stopped as she suddenly remembered she knew his reason.

She had found, even in the hours she'd spent thinking about what she should say to convince him of the danger the old man represented, that his action, although ridiculous, was also, somehow, very pleasant. As soon as she'd convinced him that the old man would stand for no more meddling in his enterprises, she might allow herself to savor that pleasantness. But for now...

"It's no wonder he was furious, and he still is. You don't know how dangerous he is."

"And what his profitable 'customer' did? And said? It didn't bother you to be pawed? It didn't bother you to be called a whore?" he questioned softly.

"Your whore," she reminded him bitingly. "And your interference alone was responsible for what he said."

He said nothing in response to that accusation, and although she knew she was being unjust, she continued her attack. "Why should I take offense at what an amorous drunkard says? Believe me, I've been called much worse," she said, smiling defiantly, but he heard the bitterness that underlay her claim.

"Worse than my whore?" His voice was still quiet, but it probed too deeply the pain she was trying to hide.

"I'm nothing to you. Don't defend me. I don't want you to. I don't need or want a knight-errant. And I certainly don't need your *valorous* protection," she lashed out, hating Devon's soft repetition of the insult. It hadn't bothered her from the man at the fair, but, somehow, to hear herself characterized as a whore by this man...

"Then you're satisfied with the Gypsy's 'protection'?" he mocked softly. "Somehow, in what happened this afternoon, I wasn't aware that anyone was concerned with protecting you."

"Because I wasn't in any danger."

"Not physically, I suppose. But—" he paused, seeming for the first time to be uncertain. "But your reputation, your honor—"

Her laughter was derisive. "My reputation," she repeated and laughed again. "And my honor." She shook her head, but the smile with which she mocked him was almost twisted. "I don't have any honor. And my reputation? Perhaps you should have listened to the drunk today. He seemed to have a much better idea—"

Her words stopped with painful suddenness, cut off by the belief that whatever had been in his eyes when she had shown him the ball hidden under her palm was there again. And against her will, she hated it. So she set out to destroy any possibility that she might ever have to face its censure again.

"I lie. I deceive. I even *cheat,*" she said with mock horror, deliberately ridiculing his rigid code of behavior.

"And you whore?" he asked softly into her defiance and saw the question take her breath, stop the jeering words.

She swallowed hard, the sudden movement running the slender length of her throat. His eyes followed that reaction, coming to rest again on the shadowed warmth of the darkness between her breasts, café au lait against the ivory.

"How much?" he asked, forcing his eyes back to her face. She could read nothing in his voice beyond the calm seriousness of his question.

"What?" she whispered, not understanding.

"If you're a whore, then how much?" he said again. And he touched her as the drunk had today, bringing both hands to rest lightly on the bare skin of her shoulders, exposed by the low neck of the peasant blouse. His lips smiled at her, but whatever was in his eyes hadn't changed.

"No," she denied, wanting to erase what was happening between them. This was what she had wanted him to think, but the reality was far more painful than anything she could have imagined. He had treated her before with a gallantry her world mocked. And now that he was trying to move into the lie she had created, she hungered for what had been between them before.

His hands moved caressingly down her arms, and she could feel the broken, blistered skin of his palms, caused by their prolonged and unaccustomed contact with the gelding's reins. Their roughness moving over her skin was the most seductive sensation she'd ever felt in her life.

Devon had intended to use his mouth to punish her. For her anger, perhaps, or for being what he didn't want her to be. But the fragility of the collarbone that he had touched, the silk of her arms...something had changed that harsh intent.

Her eyes closed when he tightened his grip, pulling her to him by his hold on her upper arms. And so she didn't see the sudden tenderness of the smile that recognized the involuntary nature of that reaction to his touch.

And then his mouth was over hers, turning to caress, fitting against her lips that answered, instinctively welcoming. He kissed her twice, softly, his lips tracing over hers, gentle and undemanding. When he lifted his mouth away, hers followed, wanting more than the touch of his. Experienced far beyond what she might have guessed, he accurately read that desire and lowered his head again, using his tongue to command entrance. Teasing and probing, until her lips opened, the breath shivering out, warm and sweet, to meet his. And then inside, moving, hard and demanding. Coaxing a response from the small body that he was holding almost totally off the ground.

Julie swayed against him, unconscious of what she was communicating to him as surely as if she had put her feelings into words. Words that she would never say because she had no right. Because she knew the barriers that were between them. As her body apparently did not.

She had no idea how long the kiss went on, his mouth softly ravaging, robbing her of any ability to deny whatever he wanted. But finally his hands put her from him, holding her steady as the strength his touch had stolen slowly flowed back into her legs.

She opened her eyes to find him watching the wonder in them that she was not enough in control to even try to hide.

"Whatever else you are—" he began softly, savoring the unpracticed and spontaneous reactions he had just elicited from her. But when fear moved into the velvet brown of her eyes, he smiled at her before he finished. "You are *certainly* a liar."

"What's your name?" she asked without thinking, a question she hadn't intended, for it opened the possibility of his corresponding one. But she wanted a name. It and this memory might be all she'd have.

He briefly considered the wisdom of telling her the truth, then rejected arbitrarily all the arguments that could be made for not revealing this small part of who and what he was.

"Devon," he said simply. "Devon Burke."

"Devon," she repeated, thinking that its unusualness was right because he was, of course, unique. In her experience, at least.

"I'm not a whore," she said, unable now to maintain the pretense, unable to let him leave, believing that.

"I know," he said, as softly as the question he'd asked before.

"But," she began, unsure of what she could tell him, the old man's threat ever present in the back of her mind. She owed it to this man to protect him from the Gypsy's code that was as foreign to him as his chivalry had been to her. And from her other enemies. She had sought to create bitterness and enmity between them. But now that wouldn't answer. And so she settled for the truth. At least part of the truth.

"I really don't need your protection. I'm grateful for what you did in the village, no matter how this sounds, but I'm the last person to need someone to look after me. I've been looking after myself for a long time now. I'm well able to defend myself from the attentions of men like those today. I'm accustomed to doing it. I don't need—I don't *want*—your help."

"You seemed to need my help before, in the village."

"I would have thought of something," she said. "And besides—"

"Besides?"

"You'll only get hurt. Like you did then. I don't want that."

"Don't you think," he said, smiling, "that I'm capable of taking care of myself?" She could hear his amusement at the thought that *he* needed *her* protection.

"Why? You don't think I'm capable of taking care of myself."

His lips lifted suddenly into the smile she liked, the lines around his eyes creasing slightly.

"That's a little different, I think."

"Why?"

"I'm not the one with the enemies," he reminded her.

"Everyone has enemies," she said. "And I'm afraid that you made a very dangerous one today."

"I'm not even afraid of the Gypsy," he said, still smiling.

"Then you're the fool I called you before. He'll kill you. And I don't want your blood on my hands. I think you need to leave. In the morning. I think you'll be safe tonight."

"And you? Will you be safe tonight?" The husky tenderness in his voice matched that which she had not seen in his eyes. But she couldn't allow herself to react to that. He didn't belong to this dangerous world she understood so well. And so to protect him from its harsh realities, she rejected his concern.

"I told you," she said strongly. "I don't need you. I don't want you."

And despite what her body and eyes had just told him, Devon reacted to that repeated denial, unconsciously remembering the rejection of the last woman he'd allowed himself to care about.

He turned away, gazing over the swift stream into the woods that stretched on the other side. She waited a long time in the gathering dusk, but he didn't look at her again. Finally, recognizing that she had destroyed, as she'd intended, the strange bond she'd felt with this man from the first, she turned and left him. And she knew that this time he didn't watch as she walked away.

Chapter Four

Julie had been deeply asleep on her pallet when the old woman's words pulled her back into wakefulness.

"The Englishman," she'd whispered, and Julie's immediate and unquestioning response had been to rise and put on the skirt she'd discarded before she'd lain down. There was little moonlight as she hurriedly descended the narrow steps and found the Gypsy leader waiting for her.

"Follow me," he said simply. She drew the ends of the heavy shawl more tightly around her shoulders against the night's cold. She was trying to think what could have happened that would make Devon send for her and walked without suspicion behind her host. It was not until she was face to face with her nemesis of the apples that she realized what a fool she had been.

Although she knew it was useless, she couldn't resist asking the Gypsy, "Why? Wasn't I worth more to you here, alive? Working the crowd for you? No more golden eggs if you sell the goose."

"Perhaps." There was no guilt in the black eyes that met hers unwaveringly.

"You told him where to find me the first time," she accused, recognizing his treachery. The old man was the only one who could have sent her father's enemies to the village. "Why? I've done nothing to you."

"Because you have powerful enemies and dangerous friends. And I do what's best for my people."

"And my 'dangerous' friend?" she asked, thinking of Devon. Was the same fate in store for him, the same betrayal? "What are you going to do with him?"

"He's still asleep. I don't know who his enemies are, but they haven't yet made me an offer."

"How fortunate for him," she said mockingly and was aware that her helpless anger amused him.

"Fate," he said, smiling. "My daughter, you must learn to accept your fate."

"A fate arranged by your greed," she said bitterly.

"That's enough," the apple farmer ordered impatiently. He was no longer dressed for that role. His cheap clothing marked him clearly as a city dweller, as did his accent. Paris, she recognized at once, and knew that in spite of all she had done to carry out her father's instructions, she had failed. They will do anything, he had told her, because they will believe you have information. The irony, and also the danger, was, of course, that she had none.

With the old man's help, the Parisian subdued her quickly. She fought, but this time she didn't cry out. She knew that if she called, Devon would come, but after what she had said this afternoon, she had forfeited any right to seek his help, and so she said nothing, even as she struggled futilely against the restraints.

It was the old man who removed the knife she carried and who laid the shawl with a curious gentleness over her bruised shoulders after he had helped put her, hands bound, on the gelding. She wondered if he had sold the horse with as little emotion as he felt over selling her.

"I thought you said he wasn't your man," the Rom mocked softly, for her ears alone. He, too, apparently, had known that Devon would come if she screamed and that, because she cared about him, she had chosen to protect him. The old man stepped back, waiting for the buyer to mount, then handed him the roan's lead.

She thought about what the Gypsy meant as the man he'd sold her to led her horse out of the clearing and into the stream. She wished she could honestly deny what his words implied. She wished also that she had at least said goodbye. And then she forced herself to concentrate only on the difficult task of balancing as the gelding picked his way carefully over the slick rocks.

The old man sat hunched over the fire as dawn fingered faint pink-and-yellow streaks onto the horizon. The coffee he cupped between his palms had been dosed with brandy against the night's chill and perhaps even against something he was forced to acknowledge might be the stirrings of regret. That unaccustomed emotion was almost as disturbing to him as the visions of what might now, as he sat by the secure warmth of his campfire, be happening to the girl.

He found himself remembering the mute and futile struggle she had waged against the casual brutality of the man to whom he had sold her. But times were increasingly dangerous, and as he had truthfully told her, he knew the quality of her enemies.

He suddenly became aware of the figure standing before him against whose set face the flickering flames cast light and shadow. He didn't allow himself to react even when the fingers of the Englishman dropped to grasp talonlike into the colorful kerchief around his neck. They twisted into the cloth and then pulled it upward. The Gypsy controlled the fear that clutched instinctively at his gut as the band tightened painfully.

The sentry's knife was at his assailant's throat almost before the final twist was completed. Only the Romany leader's guttural command, occasioned by his guilt over what he had done to the girl, halted the plunge of the blade into the strong column of Devon's neck. As the tip bit into the skin, a drop of blood swelled and hovered, gleaming in the firelight like some obscene jewel, until it rolled smoothly down the blade, to be followed by the slow welling of another.

The old man's eyes looked up into the deadly gaze that had locked unflinchingly on his as the blade had pierced the skin. There was no fear reflected even now in the lucid midnight blue.

"Where is she?" Devon asked softly. Despite the ridiculousness of the emotion, given the vulnerable position of his questioner, the Gypsy felt a shiver of fear again ice down his spine. And he was a man who had spit in death's eye more times than he cared to remember.

"It's difficult to be afraid of a man when I've helped him..." he began, with a bravado he didn't feel.

"Don't." The threat in the whisper was as convincing as the drunk had found it. As convincing as the farmer had believed it to be in the peaceful, sun-dappled streets of the village.

"What have you done with the girl?" he repeated.

"I sold her to the highest bidder," the Gypsy admitted defiantly, but he felt again a brief remorse for that action move through his eastern-European pragmatism.

"But you didn't give any other bidder a chance," the Englishman's voice taunted. Devon's fingers tightened their grip imperceptibly, tightened so skillfully that the man holding the knife to his throat was unaware of the increased pressure against his commander's.

"And do you have a bid?" The old man struggled to produce the question, interested in spite of himself.

He knew now that he had underestimated this man who had lived so quietly among his people these few days. It seemed that there might be more to his resources than had been apparent at the beginning. And there had also been, of course, the sacrifice the girl had gallantly made for him with her silence. Perhaps there was more to this man altogether than he had imagined.

"I want the directions—correct directions—to wherever the bidder has taken her and enough money and provisions to get me there." The Englishman listed his demands concisely.

"And a horse," the Gypsy added with dangerous mockery and was rewarded with another reactive tightening of the impromptu noose.

The struggle became one to pull enough air into his lungs past the constriction on his throat. But for some reason, he didn't want to give the signal that would result in the quick death of this interesting new player in what was, to him, an old game. He watched the flow of blood increase sluggishly down the knife's edge, glad to see that his sentry had at least been aware enough to recognize the last movement.

"Where's my horse?" Devon asked. His voice had become even softer, but he loosened his hold enough to allow the old man to answer.

"I sold him with the girl. She needed a mount," he said, as if that were the only consideration. "What do you intend to offer in exchange for these very expensive commodities I'm to provide you?"

The Romany's pause was mockingly expectant, and then the body of the man holding him straightened. In one fluid motion, he released the kerchief and reached over the arm that had held it to fasten his hand on the wrist of the man pushing the knife against his throat. The sentry was suddenly on his knees, his arm twisted and held high behind his neck. The knife dropped from his nerveless fingers. Using his booted foot to push the kneeling figure aside, Devon bent to pick the dagger out of the dirt. Then the Englishman rose to face the two men who had just observed a sleight-of-hand as practiced as any the girl's slender fingers had performed before the fair-goers.

"Tell your boy to go to bed," Devon suggested. "This is between the two of us."

"My 'boy' is older than you," the old man said, trying to identify what he had seen in his guest's eyes as he'd handled the sentry. The look was gone now, faded into the same blue serenity as before.

"No," Devon said easily. He spoke with conviction. "He's much too young to associate with the likes of us, and you know it."

The Rom finally gave the required command, and the sentry rose from his knees to stumble out of the clearing, still clutching his injured wrist.

Devon's fingers fumbled against the blood-soaked neck of the shirt, lifting the gold chain and Avon's seal from its position against his heart. Moss had provided this talisman because he had insisted that if Devon were to succeed, he would need the help of the men most familiar with the dark world of espionage in France. The seal, used on all secret communications from the duke, was something whose authenticity would be easily recognized by Avon's primary agents in France. But it was, of course, its intrinsic value that Devon was counting on now.

He slipped the chain over his head and placed the glittering links and their precious burden into the horny hand of the Gypsy, the hand in which now rested the fate of the girl, as well.

A variety of emotions churned in his stomach as he watched the old man study the gold holder with the secret seal carved into the emerald it held. It was, perhaps, the key to finding Avon, and he had just offered to trade it for the dubious assistance of a greedy, treacherous old bastard who would put a knife into him as soon as he'd spit a hare for his dinner. Trade it for a girl whose name he had never learned. But the seal was all he had of value, and in spite of his success with the sentry, Devon knew he was far from holding the winning hand at this table. And so he waited.

The dark eyes, when they finally rose from their contemplation of the emerald to meet his, gleamed in the light of the dying fire with some emotion Devon could have sworn was humor.

"I told the girl she had powerful enemies, and that was true," the Gypsy said. "But it seems that you, my friend, have even more powerful friends. Why have you waited so long to show me this?"

Hope flared, and Devon said, lying to give himself time to think what the recognition of Avon's seal by this old bandit might mean, "Because I didn't need your help until now."

And the old man laughed with the first genuine amusement Devon had heard him express.

"Three days ago you needed my help to piss," the Romany king cackled. In the face of the man's continued delight in his own joke, a slow smile finally slanted Devon's lips, and then, incredibly, they were laughing together. Neither was aware of the questioning eyes that watched from the curtained doorways of the encamped caravans. And they watched wonderingly because it had been years since anyone could remember hearing the old man laugh that hard.

The chain and the emerald seal had been restored to their hiding place around Devon's neck. The saddlebag on the horse had been packed with provisions and a small pouch of gold coins. The bloodlines of the mare the Romany had provided were not as obviously aristocratic as the gelding's, but he believed the old man's promise that she would carry him without fatigue and without faltering to the end of whatever journey he set for her.

The Gypsy had talked the whole time the preparations were being carried out, and Devon believed the information he had provided was the sum of what he knew. The problem was that, by design, Avon's agents operated almost independently of one another. Their dealings with Avon were carried out by an intricate system of reporting procedures that left them unaware of the identity of those above them in the chain of command.

"Except for the Spider in Paris and, of course, the Limping Man," the old man had explained. The Spider everyone in the network knew by reputation. He was the hub of the web Avon had woven across France. It was from him that the order had come some months ago for Avon's agents in France to disappear. But the descriptive nickname was all the information the old man had. And Paris.

In the other sobriquet Devon recognized his brother-in-law. Whatever disguise Avon might undertake, he would always be the Limping Man, marked by nature with a twisted knee, a dangerously distinctive characteristic in the avocation he had chosen.

The sharing of information was not reciprocal, and the Romany didn't seem to expect a return for any of the things he had provided. Seeing Avon's seal was apparently sufficient in itself to obtain his cooperation.

When Devon was ready to leave, the Gypsy dismissed his followers who had, at his command, rushed to accommodate their departing guest. Now he alone stood by the mare as Devon unnecessarily checked the girth again.

Because he could still feel the results of the last day he'd spent in the saddle, Devon had unconsciously been delaying this moment. His unwillingness to mount finally communicated itself to the watcher, who asked bluntly, "Do you need a hand into the saddle?"

The amused blue eyes lifted from the cinch to rest briefly on the seamed face.

"Only if I come off the other side. Otherwise, whatever happens, just put it down to poor horsemanship," he answered, smiling as he had at the girl's question.

He put out his hand to the old man, and the black eyes moved down to it and then back up to his face.

"That's not our way," he said. A jeweled dagger lay suddenly on the Gypsy's palm. "We swear our loyalty in blood. A primitive custom to you perhaps, but I've never betrayed a man whose blood I've shared." He waited while the Englishman considered the offer.

"I should think you'd spilled enough of my blood tonight," Devon said with grim humor, but he took the proffered dagger and, without hesitation, sliced into the fleshy mound at the base of his thumb. He allowed the blood to flow around and under his own outstretched hand to drip slowly into the absorbing dirt as he held the knife out to the Romany.

The old man made the same cut and then moved his palm to rest above Devon's, his fingers locking the handclasp.

"What makes a man unafraid to die?" he asked softly as their blood mingled. "I've never before met anyone whose eyes betrayed no fear of a knife at his throat."

The pause was so long he thought the Englishman was not going to respond, but then he answered simply, "Maybe knowing there are many things worse than dying for something you believe in."

"And what do you still believe in, my son?" the Gypsy questioned, watching the darkness he had seen before stir in the blue depths. Again the silence stretched thinly between them.

"I believe in my country, in family and friendship," he said quietly, "and in honor."

"And in nothing else?" the old man persisted.

"There *is* nothing else," Devon said. He pulled his hand away and put it to his lips to suck at the edges of the cut. He was aware of the jet eyes still studying his face in the growing light of dawn.

"And into which of those does your quest for the girl fit?" the old man asked, smiling at the sudden blue flame of reaction in Devon's eyes.

Finally the Englishman shook his head and, setting his foot into the stirrup, lifted his long body into the saddle. His hands gathered the reins, his horseman's thighs communicating his surety to the animal who acknowledged his command. He never looked back, because they both knew he had no answer for the old man's question.

The girl's captor had stopped at twilight in a clearing beside a stream whose current ran with bloodred glints in the last rays of the dying sun. He had pulled her unceremoniously off the gelding and had shoved her to sit with her back against the rough bark of one of the slender trees that shaded the water. He had tied her bound hands to the tree, knotting the rope well above her head.

She had no choice but to watch as he cared for the horses and built a small fire from carefully selected deadfall. In spite of his city background, the resulting flame hardly smoked at all. He didn't intend to be interrupted by unwanted visitors.

As she watched him eat his cold supper of bread and cheese, she became aware that his small, porcine eyes slid frequently over her breasts, which, with her arms stretched above her head, were outlined too obviously against the thin cotton of her blouse. She thought she could not have been more sickened had his hands been caressing her. His gaze skimmed hotly over the smooth hollow and the delicate column of her throat and touched on the dark cleavage. Her nipples tightened with the cold fear that clenched her stomach, and she knew that he watched their tautness grow because she felt the oily touch of his eyes there, too.

But when he finally approached her, she decided that she wouldn't give him the satisfaction of knowing how terrified she was. And she was determined to fight, despite her bonds. She didn't intend to make it easy for him. Her pupils were dilated with fear, but her face was controlled, studying him as he moved closer, waiting for any opening that would allow even the slightest chance...

Then he used the tip of the knife to cut through the cord that gathered the low neckline of her blouse and to slit the material, exposing her body. Pushing aside one edge with the cold blade, he allowed its tip to score lightly down an ivory globe and circle the rose areola. She realized she was holding her breath, and if she released it, if she moved at all, the blade would cut the delicate skin.

"You bastard," she said softly and forced her eyes to meet his. "You damned coward. Is this the only way you can get a woman? To tie her up and take her by force?" Knowing there was nothing she could do to protect herself, she decided she had nothing to lose by defying him. And her brave words helped control her fear.

When he looked up from his contemplation of the knife point against her skin, she spat in his face, her eyes full of contempt.

But instead of angering him, her puny rebellion seemed to amuse him. He used his sleeve to wipe away the spittle, and then he smiled at her, revealing broken teeth. She could smell on his breath the fetid ripeness of the cheese.

"Why shouldn't I have a taste of what half of Paris has already enjoyed? I'm not as rich as the *aristos* that swarm around that fancy club, but that won't matter once I've had you."

In his eager anticipation of that thought, he allowed the tip of the knife to move slightly away from her breast, and knowing this might be the only opportunity she would have, she kicked upward suddenly. But he had read her intent, signaled too clearly by her eyes. He turned his body to avoid the kick and used his fist to stop any further attempt at resistance. The girl's head lolled back against the tree in unconsciousness. But in striking her, the Frenchman had shifted the knife away from her body.

The long form that launched itself from the gathering darkness had been silently and patiently awaiting any such opening. There was no hesitation in Devon's attack. He had lost none of the decisiveness that had served his troops so brilliantly on the Peninsula. As he had intended, the force of his body pushed the man with the knife well past the girl's unconscious body.

While they were still being carried by the momentum of his leap, Devon's fingers had fastened around the wrist that held the blade. He was aware suddenly of the slight weakness in the injured right arm, but he forced the pain from his mind, blocking it from consideration. After all, he had a lot of practice in exercising that control.

The man twisted under him, trying to bend his knees to get his legs up enough to throw him off. Devon pressed his body down over the larger one beneath him, fighting to hold him still while his left hand sought a grip on his opponent's throat.

The knife jabbed upward suddenly, seeking Devon's face, and he was forced to pull his head out of the way. The resulting shift of his body gave the Frenchman a chance to twist away from his reaching fingers. But Devon's reflexes were too good, and in the flurry of movement, he managed a quick, short punch into the man's Adam's apple. The resulting choked gag was reassurance that he hadn't lost his touch.

Dealing with that unexpected agony, the Frenchman's hold on his weapon loosened slightly, and with Devon's sudden jerk against his wrist, the knife fell, lost somewhere on the dark turf. Realizing that the blade no longer offered any danger, Devon grasped for the man's throat. Now that he had control, his fingers closed around the muscular neck, methodically squeezing, until he felt the windpipe collapse, crushed under the pressure of his thumbs. He kept his fingers tight a long time after the struggling body under him had stilled. There was no chivalry in the business of killing. And killing had been Devon's profession for a long time.

With the knife of the man he had just fought, he cut the cords that had bound the girl's wrists, then chafed them to restore circulation to the cold fingers. As they rested still unmoving in his hands, he began to be afraid that she had some wound, afraid that the Frenchman had already inflicted some injury with the knife he hadn't been aware of in the gathering darkness. He examined her carefully, pulling the ruined blouse gently back over the small, perfectly shaped breasts.

His throat tightened when his fingers brushed unintentionally against their ivory softness. And then, because he could find no marks other than the abrasion caused by the Frenchman's fist on her chin and the raw wrists, he sat down against the tree to which she had been tied and held her against his chest, cradling her in his lap. He folded the icy hands so that they rested caught between the warmth created by their bodies.

He found himself imagining what would have happened had he reached the clearing only minutes later, if he had stopped to rest or had missed the faint indications that the pair he followed had left the road to make camp. With the vision of what had been about to take place here in this peaceful spot, his arms tightened protectively. He wondered at the force of his reaction to her danger, a reaction he could allow only now, when that danger had passed.

The shivers that eventually began to shake her frame made him aware that she was returning to consciousness. He held her securely, but without restricting the first stirring movements. Her palm turned to lie flat against the hard muscles of his chest, and then he felt her head move. He smiled down into the open eyes that knew, now, his face.

Her fingers were warmer, and they lifted to trace lightly over his cheek, stubbled again with this day's growth of beard. Her thumb moved to caress the lines that fanned from the corner of his eye.

"Devon?" she whispered in disbelief.

"It's all right," he said, answering what her eyes had asked.

"How..." she began. He watched her tongue moisten dry lips and felt the shuddering breath vibrate through the body he still sheltered against his strength.

"He's dead," he said. He didn't explain how it had been accomplished. "You're safe. I promise," he finished softly.

She swallowed and nodded once, trusting him, as she had from the beginning. She laid her head back against the warmth of his chest, hearing the even rhythm of the slow, steady heartbeat. She eventually became aware of the stiffness of the cloth under her cheek, and her hand lifted again to touch the blood-stained shirt.

"You're hurt," she said. She pushed away from the comfort of his body to look for the source of the blood.

"No." He laughed suddenly, shaking his head. He read puzzlement in the anxious brown eyes. "A souvenir of your friend the Rom. We're blood brothers, in more ways than one," he explained, and felt her relax as she heard the amusement in his voice.

"I don't understand," she whispered, but her cheek nestled again into the curve of his shoulder. She took a deep breath, the masculine aromas of his body soothing. The evening noises in the woods around them had resumed, and the campfire was fading to a dim glow.

"How did you know where to find me?" she asked. In the peaceful security of his arms, her mind was beginning to function again.

"The old man," he said. Unthinking, he brushed the dark curls away from her temple, and his fingers remained, tangled in their softness.

"But he's the one... That doesn't make sense. Why would he sell me and then tell you where to find me? He must have known that you'd—" She stopped, wondering how she could explain her conviction that everyone had known he would come. She didn't understand how she herself had been so sure, sure enough that she hadn't dared cry out, hadn't wanted to put him into danger again, even when the Frenchman was taking her away.

"He sold you because he's afraid of the man who's hunting you."

"The man—"

"Fouché. Even the Gypsy respects Fouché's power," Devon said softly, wondering if she'd tell him why one of the most powerful men in France had, according to the Gypsy, literally put a price on her head.

"Fouché?" She echoed the name of Napoleon's former minister of police, who was much more than that simple title implied. Fouché had held a position in France under the Emperor that corresponded very closely to that which Avon occupied in the British government.

"You didn't know?" he asked.

"But why would Fouché—?" she began and then took a small, shivering breath as she realized the head of French espionage had obviously been the one who had discovered her father's activities, and that Fouché was now seeking her for whatever information she could provide about them.

"The old man said he told you that you have powerful enemies," Devon said, again inviting her confidence but trying not to probe into whatever secrets she guarded. He hadn't revealed all that had brought him to France, and so, he supposed, she still had a right to her privacy as well.

They didn't speak for a long time. The pleasant night sounds increased subtly around them as the last light faded from the western sky. He wasn't even aware that his hand was now moving in slow, caressing patterns across her shoulders. He felt her inhale, and her whisper was barely audible, even as close as she lay to his heart.

"Why would he tell you how to find me?"

"One of the women told me that you were gone, that he'd sold you. I think she felt sorry for you, for what he'd done." His voice was almost as quiet as hers. "And then I convinced the Rom to tell me where Fouché's agent was taking you."

"Did you kill him, too?" she asked, but there was no remorse for the Gypsy in the question.

Devon laughed at the contrast between the image created by her question and the reality of their encounter.

"We parted on the best of terms. I told you. We're blood brothers."

"I don't understand," she said again. "How could you convince him to help you?"

"I reminded him of someone he fears, or respects, more than Fouché. I wish I'd done it sooner. It would have saved us all a lot of trouble," he said. She could

see the corners of his mouth lift into the smile she had
thought she would never see again.

She put her thumb over his lips, brushing lightly
across, and was surprised to feel them part. They
touched her finger in what was almost, she decided, a
kiss. He turned his head slightly until his chin lifted,
unconsciously nuzzling the roughness of his beard
against the knuckle of her thumb.

"Devon," she whispered and watched his gaze come
back to her face.

"Hmm?" he said, smiling down into her eyes.

"I'm sorry."

He waited, and when she didn't explain, shook his
head.

"Sorry? For what?" he whispered. "What do you
have to be sorry for?"

"For saying that I didn't need you. That I didn't…"
She stopped, realizing what she had been about to admit. If she was sorry she'd said she didn't want him,
then that implied, of course, that she did. And although that was certainly true, she couldn't tell him.

He laughed and pulled her tighter against the
warmth of corded muscle and solid bone.

"Don't," he said, his chin resting against the fragrance of her dusky curls. "It doesn't matter. I know
you were only trying to protect me."

She could hear again his amusement that she would
think that necessary. But because she didn't know his
hard-earned fighting skills, she didn't understand.

"But *I* need you now," he said lightly, knowing she
would have to realize any danger from this henchman
of Fouché's, who had so relentlessly hunted her across
France, was over. "You're going to help me dispose of
that body. A winch couldn't get me back on a horse

again tonight, but that doesn't mean I intend to sleep next to that bastard's corpse.''

Together they rolled the stiffening body into the stream's flow. Even in the near-moonless night, Devon was aware that she clutched the remnants of her torn blouse over her breasts with one hand as they worked. And aware, also, that she was sometimes unsuccessful in her efforts at concealment.

Finally he pulled the bloodstained shirt over his head and held it out to her. He doubted he'd sleep anyway, and he'd be awake early enough to slit one of the blankets to wear as the peasants in Spain did. Until then, the darkness would cover his back, would hide what he knew was a shockingly unpleasant sight.

"I'm sorry, too," he said, smiling, when she hesitated over taking the shirt he offered.

"Sorry for what?" she asked, answering his smile, knowing from his voice that she was about to be teased, but unable to anticipate his target. "For again saving me from Fouché's clutches. For coming after me, in spite of what I said. Sorry for—"

"No," he said, interrupting her litany of thanks. "I'm not sorry for any of those. But I am very sorry that I called you boyish. That, my dear, was an unforgivable error in judgment."

In the darkness he couldn't see the slow blush, and he couldn't know that she was unable to remember the last time a man's words had provoked that reaction. But he saw the white hand reach finally and take the shirt from his.

"Thank you," she said softly and was rewarded once more with his smile.

While he saw to the horses, she replaced the ruined blouse with the shirt the Gypsy had given him. The fall of indigo reached almost to her knees. She removed her skirt and spread it over a low branch and wrapped one of the blankets the Gypsy had provided around her body. And waited.

She watched him walk back across the clearing, the pale doeskins lighter than the exposed skin of his chest.

"You're limping," she said, noticing a slight hesitation in his long stride, the result of too many long hours spent in the saddle.

"If only I'd known you were watching, I assure you I would have tried much harder not to," he said, smiling at her. "Forgive me, but sometimes I limp." He paused, feeling no obligation, after his success tonight, to explain his injuries. And so he finished, teasing her with what she'd suggested about his abilities as an equestrian. "Especially, incompetent horseman that I am, if I've ridden all day."

"The Limping Man," she interrupted. She saw shock wipe the smile from his face. "That's what my father said. I'd forgotten until just now. He said he'd sent for the Limping Man. He told me to look for him. Are you— Is that why...?"

"No," he said sharply. "No, you're wrong. I'm not the man you're looking for. But I have to know exactly what you know about him and the circumstances under which your father told you. I asked you once before, and you wouldn't answer me. But now I think you must, whether you trust me or not. Who are you?" he asked again, as he had in the Gypsy camp.

This time, she knew, that in spite of her father's warning, she would tell him.

Chapter Five

Dawn touched the sleepers in the clearing, its light rimming the muscles of a hard masculine arm stretched protectively over breasts that rose and fell with each breath sighing through the girl's parted lips.

Julie had told him her story last night. She omitted nothing, from her flight after her father's instructions in the office of his Paris casino until the time when Devon had found her in the arms of Fouché's agent. He realized her father had been the Spider, Avon's chief operative, driven to his death by the French authorities because of his valuable work for the British Crown. And his daughter had been left with a vague reference to the Limping Man and ordered to disappear.

Her odyssey had led her fortuitously to the Gypsy's camp, where she had bought obscurity with her father's gold. But eventually she had ventured, well disguised as one of the homeless orphans who roamed the countryside, to the village where Devon had found her. She had remembered its name on more than one of the documents her father kept locked in his office safe. She had hoped for some connection there to the people her father had worked for, and her conjecture had been shrewdly accurate.

The name of the agent who had lived in the village was one of the few Moss had been able to provide Devon. But, following the Spider's orders when the French had begun to unravel the network, he had already disappeared, long before Devon had arrived. And so he and Julie had met.

Devon spoke little, an occasional question to clarify some point in her narrative until it had become his turn to explain his reasons for coming to France, to tell her about the man he sought, whose code name her father had whispered that night.

She had listened to all that was revealed by his tone, if not by his words. She wondered at the quality of this friend whom he clearly admired above all others. What kind of person must the Limping Man, this mysterious Duke of Avon, be, she wondered, to attract the loyalty of men of Devon's caliber? And of her father's?

When they had finally exhausted most of their questions, they had lain down on opposite sides of the campfire he'd rebuilt against the late March chill. But in the unfamiliar noises of the rural night, she had heard too many echoes of what had almost happened today and had remembered the cold threat of the knife blade tracing with provocative slowness over her breast.

Finally she had come to stand over the long form covered by the blanket. Surely, by now, he must be asleep, but as she stood there, wondering if she dared to lie down nearer the safety of his body, he spoke to her.

"What is it?" he asked softly. "Are you cold?"

"I can't sleep," she answered and watched him sit up, the blanket falling away from his shoulders.

"What's wrong?" he asked, his hand reaching to take hers.

"Let me sleep..." she began. He felt her fingers tremble in his as she realized what she was asking.

"I'm sorry, Dev," she whispered, "but I can't forget— I can still feel that knife. And his eyes. Please, just let me sleep beside you. I know..."

The attempt to explain her need for human comfort faded in recognition of what he must be thinking.

"My sister calls me Dev," he said, pulling her down to cradle her against the long, hard warmth of his body. "Go to sleep, little one. No one's going to hurt you tonight."

"Julie," she reminded him softly, wanting to hear him say her name.

"Julie," he repeated obediently, his breath stirring the dark tendrils. "I promise, Julie, tonight you're safe."

Except from what I have begun to feel for you, she thought. Except from the dangers that those feelings represent to what my life has always been.

She lay awake a long time, held securely in his arms, and finally when she felt his breathing even into a slow rhythm and knew that he slept, she turned slightly to face him. Unable to resist, her fingers moved to touch the softness of his hair. Then they returned to curl under her chin, and she watched him in the dying light of the fire until she, too, slept at last.

She woke first and decided to slip from under the pleasantly confining weight of his arm to take care of her morning needs. She carefully inched upward, to sit finally with Devon's left arm lying loosely across her thighs. She looked down at the glaze of soft, light hair that glinted over his forearm. A smile touched her lips at the memory of the intimate position they had shared last night, and while he still slept, she decided to allow herself a brief, private moment to admire the long, muscled body stretched out beside her. He was lying almost on his stomach with his head resting on the shoulder of the right arm that bent above it.

The smile froze and then faded at the sight of the grotesque network of scars that marred the whole of his back. Some were wide, irregular circles, their colors ranging nearly to purple, pitting the skin like craters on a battlefield. Others were deeply furrowed and elongated. And over several were thin, precise lines of neatly stitched surgeries, some redder and more recent than the fading paleness of earlier ones.

The blue eyes of the waking man watched her face a moment, and then reacting to what he thought was revealed there, Devon sat up. He rejected his inclination to reach for the protective covering of the blanket that lay over his legs. Instead, he turned so that his back, and the damage he had never fully seen and could only imagine by the reactions of those who did, was hidden.

Her gaze lifted slowly to his face, and the emotions, evoked both by the thought of what he must have endured and by the realization of the extent of the injuries he had hidden, were still exposed, raw in the brown eyes.

Shrapnel, he'd said, the understated simplicity of that explanation made ridiculous by what she had just seen.

"God, Dev..." she began and knew by his closed features that any of the comments her brain was formulating would be construed as pity or horror or disgust.

And so she forced her frozen lips to say instead, "What a very expensive doctor's charge you must have had."

She rose, using his broad shoulder to help her stand. She could feel one of the thick, ridged marks under her fingers, and because of that, she let her hand rest there a moment longer than she required to find her balance.

Her shapely calves and ankles were now on the level of his lowered eyes, and he thought irrelevantly how small her feet were, pink toes gripping in the grass like a child's.

She left him sitting on the blanket they had shared and deliberately spent a long time several yards downstream. Hidden from the camp by the thick undergrowth, she removed the shirt and stepped into the frigid water. She scrubbed her skin and washed her dark hair, shivering but refreshed by the sense of having removed the filth of yesterday's captivity from her body.

She used the blue shirt as a towel, and when she had finished drying off, she rubbed at the stain at the neck, rinsing it with the cold water of the stream, until she had removed most of the blood. In spite of its dampness, she put the shirt on, and on her way back to the campsite took her skirt from the branch and stepped into it and into her slippers.

Devon was feeding the fire, dressed as he had been on the day she'd met him in the neatly mended and freshly laundered lawn shirt and the leather waist-

coat. He had found them carefully folded in the saddlebag the Romany had had his women pack.

He straightened, but he didn't speak as he watched
her from across the clearing. He was remembering his
physical response last night to the very feminine body
that had fitted so perfectly into his. And when he had
first awakened this morning, long before the sun had
moved above the horizon, he had been forced to ease
his growing arousal away from the soft buttocks that
were resting trustingly against his thighs. Because no
matter how much his body desired to carry their relationship into a different path, he knew he couldn't.
Her story last night had placed restrictions on the
emotional response that had been growing between
them. Avon was not here to provide the protection she
was entitled to. Therefore, because of her father's
service to the country both he and the duke loved, that
obligation now rested in Devon's hands. And it didn't
include making love to her, especially as vulnerable as
her father's death and his enemies' search had made
her.

When she had asked to share his blanket last night,
he had known there was nothing sexual in that request. She had wanted the thing she had so adamantly denied before—simply his protection. And
when he had taken her hand, he had undertaken to
provide *only* protection. Even if it meant protecting
her against himself. Especially if it meant that. As she
gracefully crossed the remaining distance that separated them, he could feel the pressure of his body's
response even now to her unconsciously sensual appeal. Despite the horror he had seen in her eyes when
she'd become aware of the scars. But her comment
had robbed that look of its ability to hurt. No pity. No

emotional expression of concern. Well done, Julie, he saluted silently. Far better than most.

She couldn't know that he was mentally commending her reaction. Especially from his face. His features were still as set as when she had left. She glanced down at the open bag at his feet and dropped easily to her knees beside it.

"What did the old man send for breakfast? 'Fillet of a fenny snake? Eye of newt and toe of frog'?" she quoted Shakespeare's witches lightly, her fingers busy among the carefully wrapped packages that included simple medical supplies and even fishing hooks and a line. "Or perhaps something less literate and more deadly—toadstools boiled in bats' blood? No, nothing so exciting, I'm afraid. A cheese and winter apples. Why do I find those so familiar, I wonder? And so unappetizing."

She finally looked up to meet his blue eyes, calmly resting on her face. She held out one of the apples to him, but he didn't move to take it.

"Actually," he said softly, "you handled that better than most people. Even Dominic looked away."

Her hand with the offered apple dropped to rest in her lap. She swallowed the lump that had grown in the back of her throat, but she held his eyes.

"It wasn't because..." she began to explain and then stopped. "It was just so unexpected. You acted as if whatever had happened to your back was nothing. An inconvenient soreness."

"That's all it is," he said. *Now,* his mind finished the thought, but he didn't intend to ever remember what it had been before.

"I'm going to Paris," he said, changing the subject. "I think your father's casino is where my search will have to continue. But I'll take you back to the Gypsy first. I promise you'll be safe with him now."

"No," she said, rising smoothly to stand before him. "I know you trust him, but I'm afraid my memories of his treachery are all too current. And I'm *not* his blood brother."

The corners of his mouth lifted slightly, and he said, "Then wherever you want me to take you. You have only to say."

She hesitated, wondering about her motives, and told him what she wanted to do.

"In spite of what my father said, I think I need to go to Paris, too. I can help you find whatever information might be in his office. I think he meant for me to try to find the Limping Man, your friend Avon, and since you have the same mission . . ."

She waited for his refusal, but the blue eyes rested steady for a heartbeat on her face; then he nodded, examining his motives without thinking to question hers, and she began to breathe again.

He had estimated the journey would take three days, but they didn't make the distance he had planned on the first. He called a halt at sundown, finding a location for their camp near another stream, enough like the first to cause a slight shiver when she saw it.

She dismounted quickly, fighting memories of the previous twilight. Her skirt caught on the saddlebow, and she struggled to release it, not thinking about the length of slender leg the mishap had revealed. When she had freed the material, she glanced at her companion and realized he was still in the saddle, watching her.

He lowered his eyes, ashamed of that natural reaction. He knew he was losing control where she was concerned, and he wondered how he was going to manage this journey he had foolishly agreed to. He hadn't realized what a test of his restraint living beside her for days was going to be. But he hadn't been reluctant to agree to her suggestion.

Unconsciously, he shook his head at the confusion of emotions she evoked. Protection, he reminded himself grimly as he dismounted. She's under my protection.

"If I ever get back to England," he said, stretching rather obviously the long muscles in his back, "I'll never sit on a horse as long as I live. Have I told you that? As long as I live. And I used to think of riding as a pleasure."

He rolled his shoulders, the material of his shirt smoothing tight against the flexing muscles of his upper arms. He began to strip the equipment from the two horses, accomplishing the task with an economy of motion that argued long practice. She watched his efficiency, the easy movement of his strong body, but she saw again in her mind's eye the scars. It was hard to imagine him wounded, incapacitated. He was too vital, too strong. Even in the Gypsy's camp, even after he'd been shot, there had been no doubting his strength. Or last night when he'd rescued her again.

She realized that he'd finished staking the horses and was studying her face. She'd been staring at him. Not seeing him today, but remembering scenes from the few days he'd been a part of her life. Daydreaming about him, she mocked herself. He'd think... She could imagine what he'd think, so she forced her eyes away from his face and made them focus on the stream that reminded her of last night's camp. She shivered suddenly.

"What is it?" he asked. There was something haunted about her face.

"I was just wondering," she answered, trying to think of any topic of conversation she could introduce to cover the awkwardness. Her fascination with him seemed to be robbing her of her ability to think.

"Do you think there might be fish in that stream?" she tried to ask matter-of-factly. "I have to admit the prospect of dining again off the provisions in that pack is not thrilling. Are you a fisherman? Or shall I try my hand?"

The blue eyes continued to examine her face a moment and then moved to the stream as if considering her suggestion. They came back to smile into hers, giving in to this deception. Fishing had been the last thing on her mind a moment ago. That much he was sure of.

"I am probably," he said lightly, "the best fisherman of your acquaintance. I've caught fish when everyone else had despaired. All we need," he said, looking around the clearing for a slender branch that would be supple enough to use, "is a suitable pole."

"If you're any fisherman at all, you're the best of my acquaintance. I doubt any one of them has ever even attempted to catch a fish, and certainly not one to eat. While you're providing our supper, I think I'll find a spot downstream and clean up."

She forced herself to move away from him. She knew she had to stop thinking about him, stop dreaming about what could never be.

Nothing can come of this, she thought. The distance between our worlds, our experiences, is too great to ever be bridged. It will be better to end it before it becomes something else.

But even as her intellect produced all the logical arguments against what she was feeling, her heart still wanted the something else.

"I can't remember ever before sleeping out under the stars," she said much later. She couldn't remember eating fish cooked over a fire, either, but she had found it delicious. His expertise had not failed him in the catching or the cooking of their dinner.

He sat leaning against a tree while she was cross-legged, poking at the small fire with a stick. She glanced at him as she spoke and saw that his head was back against the trunk, his eyes closed. The firelight gleamed down the exposed column of his throat until its tanned length disappeared into the shadowed neck of the white shirt. He had used her absence this afternoon to clean up also; his sleeves had been turned back to expose strong forearms, and his hair curled damply.

"For a city dweller, you've adapted to camp life very well. Most women..." He stopped, thinking of his sister's elegance now compared to the life she had lived on the Peninsula. Julie would be another woman who would be capable of surviving under those conditions, he realized, admiring her courage and her adaptability. Another woman whose strength would be equal to any challenge.

Most women? Julie was wondering, responding to whatever assessment he intended to make with a reaction she recognized as jealousy. She didn't want to hear about other women he knew. And given his physical attractiveness, his appealing ease of manner, his sense of humor, she was sure there would be many of them. She wondered what the women of his circle in London would have done in her situation. Perhaps he might have preferred that she swoon or have the vapors or throw a tantrum when confronted with everything that had happened.

"Most women?" she asked aloud, deciding perversely that she wanted very much to hear the completion of that thought.

"Sorry," he said, "I was thinking of something else. I don't remember what I intended to say."

"Something about most of the women you know. Or are there too many to make a general statement about their possible reactions?" she asked with a touch of tartness.

"Too many?" he repeated, laughing. "If you're imagining that I know a number of women... I'm not a rake, if that's what you're implying. As a matter of fact, there was always only one—"

The amused voice stopped suddenly. The silence beat painfully against her heart. *Always only one.*

"I think if we're to make an early start tomorrow," he said, his tone emotionless now, "then we better get some sleep. You have the other blanket, don't you?"

"Yes," she said, ignoring, as he had done, the chasm that had opened between them. "I have it."

She wrapped her body in the rough blanket and lay down beside the fire. She knew that no matter what nightmares or remembered images disturbed her rest tonight, she would not seek the comfort of his arms. He had put the barrier there, not deliberately, she thought, but with his unthinking response to the ridiculous notion that he might be attracted to anyone other than the woman whom, it had been obvious by his voice, he loved. And Julie was not, of course, that woman.

The only possible relationship she might have with this man was the one the drunk at the fair had surmised. And it was not the one that had evoked the deep tenderness she had just heard.

The next afternoon's rainstorm caught them unprepared. They had been lucky the unpredictable spring weather had been kind until then, but the pelting fury had thoroughly soaked them before Devon spotted the dilapidated barn. He motioned her to follow and then gave the gelding his head. The animal responded with a burst of speed that signaled his annoyance with the sedate pace his master had been carefully maintaining out of concern for the woman who rode beside him.

When Julie breathlessly clattered into the sheltering dimness of the barn, she knew the farm had been deserted a long time. In spite of her city background, she recognized that its smells were all ancient, the air musty from disuse and abandonment.

Like the gelding, she'd enjoyed the hard gallop. Her eyes were full of laughter as she allowed them time to adjust to the interior gloom. When her vision cleared, she saw that Devon had already dismounted and was standing at her stirrup, ready to help her down.

"Why did you do that?" she asked, still smiling. "We were already soaked. We couldn't have gotten any wetter."

"I don't know," he admitted. One of the filtered shafts of murky light that intruded like fingers through the missing boards of the roof caught in her hair, glittering in the damp jet of her curls. Her eyes were rich with humor, inviting him to confess to the little-boy exuberance for speed that had made him release his horse's head.

"I just thought of shelter and wanted..." He paused, finishing mentally, *To get you inside, safe and protected.*

"Come on," he ordered softly instead of telling her what he had been thinking. After all, she'd made it clear that she didn't want the protection his friendship for Avon obligated him to provide.

She considered that invitation and wondered if he were thinking about the privacy the shadowed building offered them.

He lifted her from the saddle, his lean hands almost spanning her slender waist. She rested her palms on his shoulders, and for one long moment as he supported her, their eyes locked. Finally he allowed her feet to touch the floor and released her. And instead of looking down into the fathomless depths of his blue eyes, she was looking up into a face that was again guarded and closed. But for an instant, she thought, for a moment, he had been unable to hide what was there. And then the control was back, and with it the distance.

"I don't think this will last long," she said. "They seldom do. Afternoon storms, intense but quickly over. One moment it's black and terrifying, and then the next, the sun's out, and it's hard to remember what went before."

She was talking too much, but she was too aware of his carefully imposed restraint. His self-discipline. Suddenly, dangerously, she didn't want him to be disciplined. She wanted whatever he would give her. Whatever of himself he would share with the Gypsy girl who, for the first time in her life, desired something she couldn't have.

Except, of course, she could. She had known that from the beginning. She knew from his physical responses that she could seduce him, could grasp with both hands the opportunity this journey had offered, and then... But that, of course, was what he had known from the beginning, Julie thought, and, in his inherent nobility, had resisted. There would be, for them, no "then." Whatever they shared could not be permanent. He was too far removed from what her life had made her.

He had moved away from her to rummage in the pack the Rom had provided. He walked across the hard-packed ground, his steps raising dust motes that danced briefly in the shafts of light he crossed until he was again standing before her.

He held out the peasant blouse, and for a moment she didn't understand what he wanted her to do. She wondered if he intended her to wear the damaged garment.

"Dry your hair," he said. "It's too cold to leave it wet. I'll get you a blanket, and you can at least wrap up."

She took the material, dry and warm, that he handed her and began to blot the water from her face. That accomplished, she raised her arms to rub at the dripping curls. Her nipples, tight from the damp coolness she was just beginning to be aware of, moved upward with the motion, outlined against the shirt.

She glanced up to find his eyes resting on her breasts, which were as clearly revealed under the clinging indigo as if she were standing before him nude. She could see the pulse beating under his jaw and the rigidity of the muscle beside his mobile mouth. Even the breath he eased, unaware that she was watching his every move, trembled slightly. The navy eyes moved upward suddenly, as if becoming conscious of her scrutiny. Then, as he had before, he turned away, retracing his steps to the patiently waiting horses and the promised blanket.

She finished drying her hair and didn't know how lovely the halo of dark curls, clustering loosely around the rain-touched clarity of her skin, was. She only knew that again he had retreated from the tension that was between them, that had flowed between them from the first betraying touch of her fingers over his cheek.

Then he returned with the rough blanket. He stood holding it out to her, and determined to break through the reserve that governed his responses, she dropped her eyes. The practiced sweep of long lashes dipped and then lifted, revealing the coquetry she had used to such effect in Paris.

"I don't think that's going to keep me warm," she began, hesitating as if she were thinking about the best thing to do in the situation, "unless..." She let her voice trail off. Her fingers moved to the open throat of the shirt, and she glanced up again at his face. His eyes were fastened on the hand that was touching the wet material.

She allowed nothing of what she was feeling to show in her face. Instead she pivoted slowly until her back was to him. She removed the shirt and waited.

He had known what she intended. What she was inviting. But something about the delicate curve of her shoulders and the narrow channel of her back, through which the slim, perfect column of vertebrae ran upward to disappear into the dusky curls on the nape of her neck, stopped his breath. She was so exquisite. And in that way lay madness, he thought, fighting for control.

He didn't know why he was resisting. She was obviously attempting to provoke the painfully surging desire that was moving through his body. She seemed to know exactly what she was doing, and that knowledge argued a great deal of experience in the game she was suggesting, so he wondered why he hesitated. He wanted her. God, how he wanted her. But somehow, even in the face of her deliberate provocation, he knew that making love to her here was an action he'd eventually regret, an action that went against everything he believed the mission he'd undertaken required.

She turned, the dark material of the Gypsy's gift held against her breasts, crushed tightly in both small fists, an effective shield. The creamy skin of her shoulders above it contrasted to the wet richness of the shirt's color.

"The blanket," she suggested softly, seeing again the harsh reality of what she was doing to him revealed in the taut mouth and slightly narrowed eyes, in the vein that jumped in his temple. And she reveled in her ability to affect him this way. She hadn't been mistaken about his feelings.

"Don't," he whispered. "Don't do this unless..."

"Unless?"

"I want you. You seem to be very aware of how much." He stopped because her eyes were suddenly uncertain.

She had never played with this fire, had never flirted in a situation where anything might come of it. She had used her skills only professionally, well-guarded by her father and then by Jean. Her provocations had all been aimed at intriguing the unwary gambler and never the prospective lover. And faced with the tightly leashed passion that was in Devon's face, she realized that she was unprepared for the flame she had ignited.

But seeing her uncertainty, he, at least, was again sure of the path he had chosen.

"I've never taken a woman in a barn before," he said. The pain that flashed through the dark eyes at that brutal choice of words reassured him. He *had* been right. Whatever her actions had indicated, she had not been prepared for that response.

"Don't," she whispered, denying the phrase he'd just used. But she realized that if she had been successful in destroying his control, that's all it would have been. All it could have been to him. He wanted her, but that's all it meant.

Taking a woman. He'd probably had many women through the years, she thought. He'd been a soldier. And she would be only one more. One more in a line of women who had offered him their bodies because that was all they had to give. And he had given only his body in return. Obviously, that was all he intended to give her. *I've never taken a woman...*

"But I suppose that's no reason not to." He lowered his head suddenly, and his lips found the silken skin stretched over the thin bones that spanned her shoulder to the hollow of her throat. His mouth moved, warmly inviting and slightly damp. Her eyes closed in response.

"And we'll probably need the blanket after all," he murmured against her neck, his tongue tracing upward until his breath stirred against the sensitive shell of her ear. His fingers caught the material she still clutched tightly against her body. Feeling the gentle pressure exerted to remove that barrier between her nudity and the hard wall of his chest, she stepped back, away from the very reaction she had set out to provoke.

"No," she whispered. In the blue eyes there was neither surprise or anger. But it was only much later that she would think to try to identify what she *had* seen in their dark depth.

"No?" he repeated.

"I didn't mean..." she said. "I don't..." There were no words to explain. "Please," she begged instead.

"Then you don't want..." He left the question unfinished, apparently as uncertain about what to call what was between them as she.

"No. I'm sorry. I know what I did, but no, I don't want that. I didn't mean..."

"You didn't mean..." he repeated softly, mocking her words. He took the blanket he had brought and draped it loosely over her shoulders. "Then, until you do mean it, I want your word that what's between us won't be allowed to interfere in what we have set out to do. Do you understand?"

"What's between us?" she repeated softly. "And what *is* between us?" She wanted his assessment of what was happening. She knew what she felt for him, but she needed to hear his explanation.

"This," he said instead and lowered his mouth again to hers. His hands locked as they had before over her upper arms, separated this time from the softness of her skin by the rough wool of the blanket. But his kiss was as sensuously moving, plundering her

emotions until she again clung, mindless and helpless
against the force of what he could make her feel.

And he released her to stand shivering before him.

"When you want to finish that," he said, certain
now that she had not really thought about the inevitable results of her actions, "then tell me. But until we
reach Paris, our relationship will remain strictly..."

He hesitated, not sure what kind of relationship
they might have, now that the barriers had been lowered and a grudging admission of the passion that
smoldered too near the surface had been made.

"I understand," she said, humiliated at what he
must be thinking. But it really didn't matter what he
thought. Because he was right. Until she decided that
she could be satisfied with the only thing he could offer her, it was better that she not invite his lovemaking. But she knew she had moved closer to that
decision. Until Paris, he'd said. He had left it up to
her. The only offer he'd ever make, she thought. The
only one he could make, given who she was—and she
had until Paris to decide whether or not to accept.

The nearer to the capital they came, the more fre-
quent their contact with people. They chose routes
that paralleled the main thoroughfares, but even on
those dusty rural byways, they attracted attention. The
quality of both the horses they rode and their equipment, along with the combination of garments Julie
wore, and perhaps even her exotic beauty, occasioned
too many speculative stares.

"I think we'll have to find more appropriate apparel for you before we enter the city," Devon said
after the interested eyes of the farm wife they had
asked for directions followed their departure.

"I have clothes in Paris. I don't think we need to spend our limited resources on something for me to wear. Besides, what could be more appropriate for our mode of travel than what I have on?" she asked humorously, touching the faintly stained, gaily embroidered collar of the Gypsy's shirt.

"And on the streets of Paris?" he questioned. "I think someone who knows that Fouché is searching France for her would be more concerned not to attract attention."

"Then why not plan to enter the city after dark? We can go to my father's and be inside, safely hidden before daybreak."

"Don't you think they'll be watching the casino, hoping you'll return?"

"After all these weeks? I should think they would have given up that idea. Besides, there's an entrance through the cellars. I discovered it by accident when I was a child. I don't know when, or why, or even if my father had it constructed, but I'm sure he found it invaluable in his endeavors for your friend. We can leave the horses in the shed that conceals the passageway and be inside the house with no one the wiser, not even Fouché's watchers, if they exist. What better place to hide than under his nose? There's something that appeals to me about that."

Devon turned slightly in the saddle to answer her mocking challenge to her enemy's omniscience. But, out of the corner of his eye, he caught a glimpse of a detachment of dragoons, their uniforms glittering smartly with gold braid. He grasped the bridle of the mare and, digging his heels into the gelding's side, directed both horses off the road and out of the path of the oncoming troop. They watched from the shadowed verge as the cavalrymen cantered briskly by.

"Devon?" Julie breathed the question as the last of the horsemen disappeared around the bend. She turned to find the blue eyes still on the direction the soldiers had taken, but there was no shock in their calm depths such as she knew was reflected in her own.

"I know," he said softly. "The fleur-de-lis of the Bourbons has disappeared once more from French arms to be replaced by the imperial eagles. The Emperor has returned."

"You knew," she said, the accusation clear in her voice.

"Before I left England. One of the advantages of working in Whitehall. My position provided me with enough knowledge to be aware of the dangers the Continent holds for the unwary. I wonder how my countrymen who have been enjoying the sights of Paris for the first time since the Peace of Amiens dealt with Napoleon's return."

"And Fouché?" she said, her eyes resting on the calm, sun-browned face of her companion. "I wonder how the Emperor's return will affect the plans of our friend Fouché."

Devon's blue eyes shifted to her face and he smiled grimly.

He thought of what the intelligence reports had suggested about Fouché's plans to stage a coup much like the one that had originally given Napoleon control of France. And in place of the unpopular Bourbon Louis XVIII, Fouché intended to put another royal claimant, the Duc d'Orleans. A puppet ruler, with Fouché pulling the strings. But with the popular Napoleon back in the game... Devon smiled at the thought of Fouché's frustration. He wouldn't be the power behind the throne as he had dreamed. Only Bonaparte's flunky once again.

"I don't think he's going to be at all pleased with the return of his master. Not at all pleased," he finished with satisfaction.

Chapter Six

It was well after midnight of a long third day of travel when they finally reached Paris. Julie led the way to the small lean-to that sheltered the entrance to the secret passage into the darkened casino.

She slipped off the mare and left Devon to handle the task of settling the tired horses for the night. By memory she traversed the dark tunnel, standing a long time in the kitchens when she reached them, breathing in the familiar scents of home. Then, shaking off those ghosts, she pulled the shutters over the windows and left candles lighted that would guide their way back into the house. When she returned to the shed, she found Devon waiting for her, patiently leaning against the rough planks of the wall. The animals were already unsaddled, watered and lipping the grain they'd purchased yesterday.

"What did you find?" he asked, reading in her expression how difficult this homecoming was. She had left this house the night her father died, and she had not been back in all those weeks.

Her exhaustion was also openly revealed in her face, the fine skin stretched tightly over the perfect bone structure. Although she had never complained, he knew how difficult the long hours spent in the saddle and camping in the most primitive of conditions each night must have been. And now she was forced to deal with the memories that the casino represented.

"Everything seems to be the same. It's so strange. It feels as if I've been away a lifetime, but nothing has changed. I almost expect to open the door to the salon and hear the noises." She paused, unsure of how to explain. "I've changed," she whispered, knowing in how many ways that was true, "but everything else seems to have just stood still. As if I could walk into my father's office, just open the door, and he'd still be there. But then I remember..."

Devon waited, watching the memories in her eyes. And then he saw her come back to the present, to realize what he had really asked.

"There's no one there. It's empty. And it should be safe. Even if anyone's watching, they'll never see us enter through the tunnel. And I closed the kitchen shutters."

She looked up to find his eyes on her face, their concern obvious. But he cleared that emotion from them even as she watched, replacing it with the detachment he had used as a shield since they'd made their agreement.

She took one last look around, then motioned him into the tunnel and locked the hidden door behind them.

He was waiting for her in the kitchens. She studied his lowered head as he leaned against the cook's table that dominated the room.

He looked up, the blue eyes gently teasing. "Have I told you that if I ever get home to England..." he began and watched her slow smile.

"That you never intend to climb onto a another horse?" she finished for him.

"No," he said and shook his head, "that I'm going to sleep for a thousand years."

"You can do that upstairs," she suggested, knowing that, although he was probably as tired as she, his intent was only to allow her to rest. And so she picked up one of the branched candlesticks and led the way to the private quarters she and her father had shared above the very public rooms of the casino.

She entered her father's bedroom, and as the candles she held flickered dimly over the shadowed corners, she realized there were no ghosts for her in this room, no painful memories, only a sense of familiarity and peace.

She turned back to find Devon leaning against the frame of the door, taking in the surprisingly luxurious appointments of the dark chamber she had brought him to.

"This was my father's room," she said in explanation. "I think you'll be comfortable. Everything you'll need should—"

"It's fine." He cut off her nervous monologue. He could see the exhaustion reflected in her wan face. "Go to bed, Julie. Things will look better in the morning."

"Is there anything I can—"

"No, Julie," he said softly. "Go to bed. We'll consider what to do in the morning. But tonight we just need to sleep. We both need—"

"To sleep for a thousand years. I know," she said, trying to smile. "You told me. I'll see you, then, in the morning."

She moved across her father's bedroom and through the doorway. He turned slightly to allow her to pass by. The desire to touch him, to feel again the solid warmth of muscle, to allow herself to rest against the comforting, familiar strength of his body was stronger than any emotion she could remember. Instead of permitting herself any of those satisfactions, she brushed quickly by and hurried to her own doorway. She heard behind her in the dark hall the closing of her father's door.

"Sleep well, Dev," she whispered and stood a moment longer, watching the closed door.

After she had dressed the next morning in the carefully selected jonquil muslin, she waited a long time, listening for sounds from her father's chamber that would indicate Devon was awake. Finally, she knocked softly and opened the door.

He was standing by the curtained window that looked down on the street. He turned at her entrance, and she could see that he had used her father's razor to remove the three days' growth of beard. His hair, lightly touched by the sun after several days in the outdoors, was neatly combed, and last night's tiredness had been erased from the tanned face.

His blue eyes studied the slender figure in the doorway. He thought how different she appeared today— no longer the dark Gypsy waif who had ridden uncomplainingly beside him. Her elegant beauty would rival any of the sophisticates who would grace the entertainments tonight in the French capital. She was so lovely in the simple dress, and he felt again the stirring of the emotions he had fought from the beginning, emotions he had thought he would never feel again, hadn't wanted to feel again. So he took a deep breath, forcing himself to look back out the window.

"I think you must be right. There's no sign that anyone has the slightest interest in this building. We should be safe for a while if we're careful to light only the interior rooms at night."

"Why didn't you wake me?" she asked, glancing around the room. There was no evidence of his night's occupation in the neatly made bed or in the items arranged in order on the dressing table.

"I thought you needed the sleep. You looked as exhausted as I felt last night."

"Thank you," she said with a laugh. "You are definitely not a rake, not with that unflattering turn of speech. And I thought that wasn't allowed."

"Not allowed?" he questioned, smiling.

"Anything personal."

He studied her face and knew that in spite of the amusement in her voice, there was also a message in her words.

"Forgive me. I know that you don't need or want a knight-errant. I'll try not to forget in the future."

His tone had been as light as hers, but she knew she had widened the gulf that lay between them. She asked, dangerously revealing that she cared, "And do you prefer your women helpless and clinging?"

"I told you. There are no women," he said, his voice closing the door to whatever lay in his past. "If you would, I'd like to look in your father's study. It's possible he may have left something I might use to help me locate the duke."

"Of course," she said in the face of his coldness, and she led the way down the stairs to the room behind the casino where she had last seen her father. She opened the door for him, but at the sight of the familiar chair and the desk covered with the dust of the last weeks, she turned away, leaving him to search alone.

After four fruitless hours, Devon admitted defeat. The papers that remained all concerned expenses and profits, debits and credits recorded precisely in the hand of a meticulous scribe. If there were any records of the less innocuous dealings Julie's father had directed for Avon from this small room, he had been unable to find them. Either these rows of figures represented a code he couldn't break, not even with the intelligence the duke had prized so highly in his espionage work in London, or anything that might have proved the old man had indeed been the Spider had been destroyed. There were no papers in the safe and no hidden drawers or doors that he could discover.

He found Julie seated at one of the gaming tables in the enormous, shadowed salon of the casino. She had dealt endless hands of patience through the long hours. Devon stood silently and watched as she was defeated again by the cards.

"Patience," she explained, smiling at him. "It's a virtue I've tried to cultivate. But I do so hate to lose."

"I would think someone with your skills could manage to win every time," he said, returning her smile.

"But to do that, I would have to cheat. And to cheat at patience would be gulling only myself."

"I didn't mean to imply—" he began, remembering her reaction to his accusation at the Gypsy's camp.

"It doesn't matter," she interrupted, her fingers laying out the next game. "Everyone assumes, I suppose, that those who make their livelihood at the tables have no inner strictures against taking whatever advantages their hard-earned skills might provide. My father's house—" Her voice broke suddenly at the memories, and she looked up. "My father didn't cheat. Nor do I. In spite of what I was forced to do for the Gypsy."

"Julie," Devon said, seeing the pain revealed in the dark eyes, "I didn't think—"

"What did you find in my father's office?" she asked, her eyes on the cards she manipulated quickly across the broad surface of the table.

"Nothing," he answered, giving in to her change of topic because, under the conditions of the agreement he'd proposed, he had no choice. He couldn't take her in his arms and kiss away the painful memories. "At least nothing that seemed to have any bearing on his work for Dominic. He seems to have destroyed all evidence of those activities before Fouché's men came. Or Fouché now has whatever papers might have provided that connection. I found indications that I wasn't the first person to evince an interest in whatever the office might have held."

"Someone else searched my father's papers?" she asked, the movement of her hands over the cards arrested. "Of course," she whispered, "I should have known that was inevitable. It seems such an invasion of who he was."

"He would have expected it. He knew the game he played was dangerous. And that those he opposed were ruthless."

"He was very ill," she said softly. "I think that at the last he held on only for whatever service he could provide for his country. A last act of expiation, perhaps. But I don't think he had any regrets when he pulled that trigger, Dev. That's the only thing that's made me able to accept his death. That and the fact that his life meant something, had been valuable to your friend's efforts."

"Expiation?" Devon questioned. "Expiation for what?"

"Someday," she said, her eyes again on the cards that rested, waiting under her fingers. "Someday I'll tell you my father's story. But not today. I think I've dealt with enough ghosts today. Would you like to play a hand against the house?" she offered. "You may choose. Whatever you like—ecarte, baccarat, basset, faro, piquet."

As she talked, the small, graceful hands picked up the lines of patience and then shuffled the cards in long, ruffling falls, almost faster than his eyes could follow. She dealt the four aces in a row across the table, and he wondered how she had arranged the deck so those cards fell at the top. Her voice broke into his fascination with her skills.

"Hearts, truly loved; diamonds, ever courted; clubs, blissfully married; and spades, forever single. Would you like for me to tell your fortune, Devon? There are so many ways for the cards to talk, to reveal the secrets they hold," she said.

"These are the ancient kings," she continued, glancing up under her lashes at him. She then began to place the next four of her fixed deck in a row below the aces of the suits she had just named. "Charlemagne," she pronounced, laying the king of hearts under its ace. "Caesar." She placed the king of diamonds. "Alexander and David," she finished and began to shuffle the remaining cards.

"And the knights," she said, leaving a space between the kings and the cards that she began to place below them. "La Hire? Hector? Lancelot?" she asked, her voice teasing as she smiled up into his eyes again.

He shook his head as he recognized her association of him with the heroes the French face cards had traditionally represented.

"Or are you Hogier?" she suggested, placing at last the jack of spades.

"Distinguished company," he said, smiling, "but too courtly for a simple soldier."

"But most of these were soldiers, too—simple or otherwise," she argued, gesturing to the kings and their matching knaves. Her hands began again to ruffle the cards in colorful streams between her fingers.

"And having seen your back," she began, and then stopped, remembering his reluctance to discuss what had happened to him on some distant battlefield.

"It's all right," he said at her pause, wondering why she would refer to something his reticence had clearly placed off-limits. But then Julie's matter-of-fact acceptance of his scars had also been surprising. "Having seen the damage to my back, you think . . . ?"

"That you belong in this distinguished company."

His laughter at the compliment he thought ridiculous was genuine. "And your fortune, my lady of the cards? Where is your portrait?" he asked, because he knew the assembly of heroines the French queens encompassed.

"I'm not here," she said, still smiling, placing the queens in the space she had left under their corresponding kings. "Perhaps the women you know in London are here, but for my representation we'd need another game. The As-Nas deck has the dancing girl,'' she said easily.

''*And* the soldier,'' he answered. Her eyes lifted to lock suddenly on his face. And he added softly, ''Perhaps we both fit better there.''

The silence that followed his suggestion was finally broken by her low laugh. ''You know the cards,'' she said, gathering up the display she had made with the face cards.

''I told you. I was a soldier. I've played cards all over the world. With a hundred different decks in a hundred encampments. And I understand a little of their mystique.''

''Then you're an unusual Englishman. I thought silver loo and whist were your limits. And faro considered very daring.''

''What a poor opinion of my countrymen you have.'' He laughed. ''Surely we're more sophisticated than that.''

''My father was English. And, I suppose, so am I. I've never thought about my nationality beyond the circumference of these rooms. What I do with the cards opens many doors. Even those curtained doorways of the Gypsy's camp.''

''For someone with your talents,'' he agreed.

''And what would those talents be worth in a London drawing room? I neither paint nor sew nor play the pianoforte. I have none of the skills of your world.''

''My world?'' he questioned, laughing. ''Do you honestly believe...'' he began and shook his head again. ''Julie, I don't belong to that world any longer. Mud and heat. Tents and campfires and half-cooked game. Dysentery and fevers. My God, surely you're not picturing me at an afternoon's musicale listening to some simpering debutante's efforts? What we did on our journey to Paris was far nearer what my life has been than that."

"And to the life of the woman you love?" she asked.

At her question his teasing smile faded.

"The woman I *loved* married someone else," he said, emphasizing the past tense of that verb, but she misinterpreted what was in the shadowed eyes, mistaking his bitterness over that betrayal for pain occasioned by loss.

"Why?" she asked, unable to conceive that any woman would be so foolish as to refuse his love, if it were offered.

"And on the day you tell me about your father, I'll tell you that story," he said, closing the door to her questions.

"Play cards with me?" she said suddenly, accepting his refusal. "Piquet," she suggested, her favorite. "You're safe there, I promise, from any tricks I know. Only mind to mind with piquet. The cards—"

"The cards don't lie. And they don't cheat those who respect them," his quiet voice interrupted. "I'll play with you, Lady Luck, but you may find my skills paltry compared to yours."

"Did you win their money, Dev, when you played before battles? Were you lucky?" she asked idly.

"'Lucky at cards, unlucky at love,'" he quoted lightly and pulled out one of the elegant chairs at the table and sat across from her.

"My unlucky knight of the spades," she suggested, laughing, and dealt by twos the twelve-card hands.

"And what do you suppose those would reveal about our respective fortunes?" he asked as she quickly placed the remaining cards facedown between them to form the stock.

She met his eyes and said, "Look and see. It's your play, Dev."

She watched as he examined his hand and discarded. He quickly took the allowed cards in the stock, studied the others, then smiled to signal his consent to her play.

"Carte blanche," she said, announcing that her hand contained no face cards. She glanced at him to smile with the question. "I think that term has another meaning in London?"

"Yes," he admitted, "but it's not a term I've ever had occasion to use, except in cards."

"No London mistress, either," she correctly interpreted his comment. "Unlucky in love, indeed," she said, making her own exchange from the stock. "And I think I'll leave you in the dark as to what remains here. One should never reveal something an opponent can later use for his triumph."

As the game continued, she found him to be a worthy opponent. He was coldly logical, his play was faultless, and he seldom took chances that went against the odds, which, she realized, he was able to calculate as quickly as she.

At the end she was the winner, but only due to a lucky *carte rouge* on the last deal.

"And today," Devon said, acknowledging his defeat, "not even lucky in cards."

Their conversation through the hands had been limited to scoring, both too intent on the play to continue the double entendres that had begun the game.

"But you're very good," she said. "I had the better cards, not the superior skill. Will you play me again sometime?"

"Any time you wish, Lady Luck. I think we'll have some hours to while away as I try to decide where we go from here. I'm no closer to finding Dominic than I was when I entered France."

"If Fouché is responsible for my father's death, and if he was working for your friend . . ."

"Then Avon's disappearance can certainly be laid at Fouché's door," he agreed, having already come to that frightening conclusion when she had first shared the story of her father's death. Neither Fouché nor Napoleon could allow Avon's intelligence network to reveal their very separate plans. One of them, probably the minister of the secret police, had begun to unravel the network. He had lured Avon to France where he had disappeared, unable to warn the allies about what was about to happen to a Europe that thought they'd seen the last of French upheaval.

"Fouché's a very evil man, Dev, if one believes half the stories that circulate about his actions. One who will stop at nothing to advance his plans. If he captured the duke—"

"I know," Devon said, "but I have to believe that Avon is still alive. And I have to find him, Julie. I owe him more than I can ever repay. And I can only pray 'that it's not too late."

"How long has he been missing?" she asked, but his eyes didn't lift from the long fingers that were gripped together on the surface of the gaming table.

"More than three months," he answered, and his lips tightened with that admission.

"Three months in Fouché's hands? My God, Dev."

"No," he said sharply. "Whatever you're about to tell me about Fouché's methods, I don't want to hear. I've wasted enough time. What I would like to hear are some suggestions as to where he might hold a prisoner of Avon's value. Do you know?"

"Almost anywhere in Paris. He has that kind of power. But I would imagine that it would be somewhere other than the official prisons. Especially—"

"Especially with Bonaparte's return. Fouché's power is certainly curtailed by the Emperor's," he said, thinking out loud.

"But Napoleon has a history of forgiving him. He's done so time and again. But it's said that Bonaparte has his own spies within Fouché's network, so that he always knows what's being plotted. They're all intriguers. It's their life's blood."

"So Napoleon would be aware of everything his ex-minister of police is doing? Is that what you're suggesting?"

"That's what the gossip suggests," she corrected.

"And is the source of that gossip reliable?" he asked.

"You'd be surprised at the powerful men who have visited these tables. And at the things they discuss quite openly before a woman who deals cards. I suspect that my father's value to the duke was originally founded on the tidbits of information he picked up in these very rooms when he ran the casino. But I don't see how knowing that Bonaparte will almost certainly be aware of your friend's whereabouts can be helpful."

"No," he admitted finally, "nor do I. But I learned from Dominic that all information is valuable. And we have little enough. I wish," he began bitterly and then stopped, trying to think of any other avenue he might explore.

"That you'd never become involved with a boy stealing apples," she suggested, imagining how frustrating the lost days he had spent on her rescues must be to him now.

But his answer surprised her.

"No," he said, smiling. "I think becoming involved with your plight was the most incredible piece of luck I've ever had. The few names I'd been given when I left England couldn't be traced. Those agents had disappeared long before I tried to contact them. You led me to the Rom, whom I would never have found on my own, and who will always be available now to help. And you know far more about Paris than I. I can only hope that you'll be willing to help me continue the search here."

She smiled at his doubts about her cooperation. "I wish I felt that I've been as valuable as you suggest. I have as much reason to want to do Fouché a disservice as you do. I'll help find your friend, if only as revenge for my father's death."

"To our continuing partnership, then," he said and held his hand across the table. She hesitated, wondering if he remembered that their agreement was only until they had reached Paris. Perhaps that's what he was implying.

When she failed to answer, caught in the confusion of emotions, he said, laughter coloring his voice, "Or like my friend the Gypsy, do you think we should seal our bond in blood?"

Her eyes lifted to his face, and she shook her head slightly. "No, Dev. Remember? I'm the dancing girl.

We seal our oaths with a kiss." And saw the laughter die in his eyes.

"I don't think that's very wise," he said softly.

She smiled at his refusal. "Only a kiss, Dev," she mocked. "Nothing else. No other commitment. Just a kiss for the dancing girl. I assure you, I know my place," she said with a carefully controlled bitterness.

"For days that place has been at my side," he said quietly, acknowledging her courage and endurance. But that was not, of course, what she wanted.

"Are you afraid?" she asked, goading him. She was tired of his nobility. She wanted the touch of his mouth. *His whore.* The drunk's words at the fair suddenly leapt into her mind. She could never be anything else to him, so why shouldn't she have the crumbs from this table.

"One kiss," she offered again, and her eyes were soft and dark with the dangerous invitation.

Although he understood that danger very well, he, too, wanted what she'd suggested. He had thought about touching her, making love to her, too many long hours after they'd stretched out, carefully separated by the fires he'd built each night. One kiss. What could it hurt? He couldn't want her any more than he already did. His control had proved strong enough in the long nights to fight that temptation. Surely it would be strong enough to cope with one kiss.

And so, against all his self-imposed limits to their relationship, he stood to again offer her his hand.

"Lady Luck," he invited softly.

She put her fingers into that strong grip, and he helped her rise. She hesitated a moment, wondering if he really meant to give her what she had asked for.

And then the long fingers that held hers tightened and, using their strength, he pulled her around the table to stand before him.

He raised her hand to his lips and kissed the fingertips. She was watching his face and saw the question appear in the slanted brow, offering her one more chance to change her mind.

"Perhaps you should..."

"No," she said softly, denying his suggestion.

"Then so be it," he agreed finally, giving in to his own desires as much as hers. He placed her fingers against his chest. She allowed her palm to flatten, and her hand moved upward to lie warmly touching his neck. Her thumb brushed along his jawline, delighting in the slightly rough, masculine texture of his chin.

He could see the pulse in her throat increase as she looked up, and at what was revealed in her eyes, his heart lurched against the wall he had tried to build around it.

His head lowered to her mouth, which moved, sweetly caressing, over his own. He could feel her soft breasts press into his chest. Her hands found his shoulders as she stood on tiptoe, and then his arms, unbidden, circled her body protectively. So small, he thought, and so alone.

His tongue moved against her lips, pushing to get inside, and they opened, inviting his invasion. Her tongue began to answer the movement of his, tenderly matching his sure mastery. And finally, fighting the tide of passion that had too quickly flooded his body, he raised his head to look into her face.

Her eyes were closed, and the tip of her tongue appeared from between her lips to touch the moisture the kiss had left on the soft, full underlip. Her eyes opened to reflect unmistakably the same emotions that had shaken his resolution.

One small hand found the back of his head to pull his mouth down again to her body, to invite its brush over the pulse whose fluttering movement he had watched earlier. Suddenly he was lifting her to bring the smooth ivory of her skin in contact with his hungry lips. They traced over the hollow of her throat, and then his tongue trailed lower, burning against the tops of her breasts and finally into the dark cleavage between them.

She was lost in the sensations. How she had wanted this.

She turned her cheek against the silk of his hair and whispered his name, but it was not in denial. And he carefully lowered her body to see what was in her face. He touched her with his thumb, moving it caressingly from the still-throbbing hollow of her throat into the valley between her breasts, which his lips had just deserted. He saw the quick inhalation of reaction.

Again a shuddering breath shook her slender frame, and she stepped back, away from his thumb's touch. He allowed his hand to drop, and then he waited.

"Julie?" he whispered, questioning, and finally she met his eyes.

"Yes, Dev," she said, agreeing to what she had denied in the barn that day, knowing that what she felt was beyond her control. And that she could destroy his.

Lost in the feelings that had been created in the shadowed room, neither heard the entrance of the man who listened to the whispered exchange. And who had watched what had gone before.

Devon's only warning was the widening of her dark eyes, and then he was pulled around by a strong hand on his shoulder and the first blow struck his unprotected chin. The second was a right that landed solidly in his stomach and sent his body crashing into the gaming table, its edge striking against the back of his head.

Julie, he thought, as he went down, and the last thing he heard before he lost consciousness was her scream.

Chapter Seven

When Devon came to, Julie was pressing a handkerchief against his bleeding mouth. For a second he couldn't remember why he was down, but then the image of a dark, scarred countenance and of a fist driving into his chin created a surge of adrenaline. He tried to rise, and with that movement was forcibly made aware of the results of the second impact.

"Julie?" he whispered, his eyes closed briefly against the pounding darkness in his skull.

"Shh," she said, "it's all right. There's nothing you need to worry about. Just lie still. I promise you everything's all right."

"Who?" he finally managed, relieved that, although her eyes held concern for him, there was no fear.

Her hesitation was a little too long, and then she said simply, "A friend. An old friend of my father's. He thought..."

And watching the rush of color stain the translucent skin, Devon said, acknowledging his guilt in the situation, "I know what he thought."

"I explained," she began, and then her voice faltered. "I told him that I had asked you to..."

He took the cloth from her hand and pressed it tightly to his lip. The sting was a welcome distraction from the crescendo of pain in his head. Despite that, Devon put his other hand against the floor and pushed himself up, leaning back gratefully against the table that had inflicted the damage.

And he saw again the sardonic smile of the man who had hit him. He was standing near enough to have heard their conversation, and his opinion of Devon's actions was clearly revealed in the glittering eye.

"We still thrash cads in France," he said softly in English. "Or horsewhip them."

"Stop it," Julie commanded angrily, turning from her attention to Devon's injuries to face him. "Haven't you done enough?"

"Apparently not," he answered mockingly. "He still appears to be alive."

"I told you—" she began furiously.

"I know what you told me. And I know what I saw. And you, *monsieur,* I wonder if you would treat a woman of your circle as you just treated Julie."

There was no easy answer for that soft accusation. Devon had acted in a way that certainly broke his personal code, if not the mores of his society. Because of Julie's occupation and her past, because she was a woman who was surely not innocent of sexual pleasures, most men of his class would view her as fair game. But he had agreed to bring her to Paris, under his protection, to help him find Dominic and to avenge her father's death. Under his protection, his conscience reminded him, and he had violated his own definition of what that implied.

"No," Devon said softly. The honesty of his regret was revealed in his blue eyes, which did not drop before the indictment in the hazel intensity of Jean's. "No," he repeated, and turned to look into Julie's white face.

"I hope you'll accept my apologies," he said to her. "Please believe that what happened between us in no way reflects a lack of respect for you or for the invaluable help you've been."

"Don't," she said bitterly. "Nothing happened between us. Do they write that speech out for you to learn? What to say on being caught kissing the upstairs maid? I don't even know what you're apologizing for. I asked for a kiss, and you gave it. You don't owe anyone an explanation of your actions. I enjoyed your kiss, my soldier knight. The dancing girl thanks you."

And she turned defiant eyes to the man leaning gracefully against the wall.

"Very pretty," he said mockingly. "I'm sure your father would have been enchanted to hear you characterize yourself as a 'dancing girl.' Or have you changed so much since his death?"

"You're right," she said, her tone as cutting as his. "Not a dancing girl. A faro dealer. My father made me that. Whatever dishonor lies in who I am, you're creating, Jean. Not Dev. In the days I've spent with him, he has treated me with—"

"In the days?" Jean interrupted, repeating her words in disbelief, and his posture was no longer relaxed. He looked again like the avenging angel he had perhaps pictured himself when he had knocked the Englishman to the floor. Very definitely a fallen angel, but a man who still had enough integrity not to make love to an innocent girl. As this man, apparently, did not.

"Are you telling me that you've spent these weeks I've scoured France for you in his company? And during those days I was... *Mon Dieu,* Juliette. *Mon Dieu,*" he repeated incredulously.

At the look on her face and at the pause that stretched as he waited for her denial, he finally turned to the man he had hit and sketched him a mocking bow.

"I owe you an apology. This is an *affaire* of long standing, I take it. Forgive my untimely interruption. I had thought that I was protecting Julie from your unwanted advances. Apparently I was only witnessing—"

"Don't say anything I'll have to force you to be sorry for," Devon warned quietly.

The low laugh from the man he had just cautioned was caustic. "Pardon me if I doubt your ability to carry out that threat. You hardly appear to be in any position to do so."

"But looks are deceiving, as I'm sure you know. There has been nothing in the nature of an affair in my relationship with Julie. We..." Devon's voice ground to a halt, because he had realized that, without the intervention of this arrogant Frenchman, that accusation would almost certainly have become a reality. The silence in the shadowed room lengthened uncomfortably.

"Yes? I assure you I'm awaiting the revelation of your amatory adventures with ill-concealed impatience." The eyebrow on the unscarred side of the Frenchman's face slanted upward with his sarcastic prompting.

"I should hate to have to kill you," Devon said softly, the tone of quiet regret devoid of any other emotion. But there was no doubt in the minds of either of his listeners that he was deadly serious.

"And I think that perhaps that threat might better come from my mouth than yours. You have spent some time with him, unchaperoned, I assume?" Jean paused to ask the girl, who was still kneeling beside the man he had knocked down.

"You may *assume* whatever you wish," she answered, emphasizing his choice of verbs. "You're going to, no matter what I say."

"Several days, unchaperoned, in the company of a young woman for whom I am responsible," the Frenchman finished, ignoring her taunt.

"For whom you're responsible?" Disbelief colored Julie's question. "By virtue of what, may I ask, do you feel yourself responsible for me? Not only do you *assume*," she repeated more sarcastically than before, "you also apparently presume, Jean. You were my father's employee. And that's all you ever were, to me or to him."

The impact of her words was clear, briefly, in the dark face. And then he controlled his pained response. The unscarred corner of his mouth moved into a bitter smile. "I think that is not the entire truth, *petite*, and you know it. I'm sorry what I've said today has hurt you enough that you would deny what your family meant to me."

He waited a moment, but she was silent, a silence prompted by her knowledge that she had given a less-than-honest evaluation of their relationship. But she didn't acknowledge his right to judge her. Or to condemn Devon.

"Your father told me to take care of you, whether you want to believe that or not. They were the last words he said to me before he asked me to send you to his office, before Fouché's agents broke in. But when I looked for you, after your father's death, you were gone. And I searched for you—believe me, I searched."

"I'm sorry," she said softly. "He told me to disappear, to hide myself as far from Paris as possible—and to trust no one."

She waited and saw the negative movement of his head. The low light cast blue-black glints into his hair as he denied the implication.

"But you must have known that he didn't mean me, Julie. Surely you knew that I would do anything to protect you."

"I didn't know what to believe. I never thought that you might be looking for me. And then I met Dev."

Her eyes returned to rest on the face of the man who had become an interested, if silent, spectator to their exchange. Her lips moved into a slight smile, unconsciously revealing what the memory of that meeting meant to her.

"Or rather he found me," she amended softly. "In the grasp of one of the agents Fouché sent to find me. And he rescued me. We decided to travel together. That's all there was."

But the Frenchman had watched her eyes as she talked. Because he had known her so long and, although she had never been allowed to suspect, because he had loved her, he had recognized what was revealed there.

His gaze searched, too, the handsome, unmarked face of the Englishman, and then he hid the bitterness of his discovery in his sardonic questions.

"And if you had spent some days in the company of a woman of your acquaintance, a woman of your class? Some days in the company of young woman of your circle in England? What would be your response to the concerns of her family, I wonder? As a result of her father's last words to me, I still consider myself responsible for the Viscount Ashford's daughter."

The blue eyes had turned to ice at the beginning of that speech, but the Frenchman had not misjudged his target. And Devon's smile became as dangerous as Jean's as he considered the challenge in the revelation of who Julie was.

"The Viscount Ashford," he repeated finally, and at the recognition of all that name stood for, a recognition clearly revealed in his tone, Julie heard again what her father had faced before he had been driven from his country. "I think I'm beginning to understand," Devon finished, the pieces to the puzzle Julie represented falling finally into place. She was, as the Frenchman had pointed out, a woman of his own class. And she was certainly not responsible for the actions of her father. Or for whatever direction her life had taken as a result of those actions.

There was no response except a mocking half bow and the slight movement of the undamaged side of the mouth that had asked those unanswerable questions.

Devon took a deep breath and turned to the woman who was still watching the Frenchman. He couldn't tell what she was thinking from the still, alabaster paleness of her profile.

He took her hand and saw her come back from whatever memories of her father's bitterness had made her, momentarily, unaware of him. Unaware of what he must now be thinking. She had never intended that

he should know who she was. There was no need for
what Jean had done. For that betrayal. Devon would
have gone as soon as he found Avon, and he would
never have had to know that her father was the center
of a scandal that had rocked London.

"Julie," Devon said softly, aware suddenly of the
tears tangled in the dark sweep of her lashes. His heart
beat once, hard, and then he caught the breath her
pain had robbed and raised the hand he held to his
lips.

She watched his movements, and he saw her throat
move as she swallowed, trying for control.

"Julie," he said again in concern, and he smiled
into the eyes that finally met his and waited like an
animal at bay for whatever he intended to say.

"Would you do me the great honor of trusting
yourself to me in marriage? I promise that I will, from
this moment on, do everything in my power to make
you happy. Will you marry me, my beautiful Lady
Luck?"

She had never dreamed that he would offer her
marriage. But, she realized suddenly, she should have
known. Everything he had done since she'd met him
had indicated that this proposal would be demanded
by his concept of honor. Not because he wanted to
marry her, of course, but because it was somehow, to
him, the right thing to do. There was probably no
other gentleman in London, she thought, who would
have offered marriage to a woman of her background, despite the nobility of her birth. Her father's
dishonor and her own past would have made that idea
an anathema to anyone else.

Only you, she thought, tracing again his features.
And I will never allow you to make that sacrifice.

Her eyes swam with unaccustomed tears, and he watched one escape its shimmering pool to trace downward over her paper-white cheek.

I never cry, she had told him, and thinking that he knew what those tears signified, Devon smiled at her again and raised her fingers to the gentle touch of his lips.

The small hand was ripped from his hold, and she was on her feet before he realized her intent. She walked to stand trembling before the Frenchman. His face was free of the mockery he had so effectively employed against the Englishman. And then she slapped him as hard as she could, the blow resounding in the echoing emptiness of the casino's vast salon like a pistol shot.

The imprint of her palm showed white against his dark skin.

"You bastard," she whispered. "You bastard," she said again more strongly, and then she ran from the room, leaving the two men, enemies from the inception of their acquaintance, alone.

Jean had not reacted in any way to her assault other than the involuntary recoil of his head in response to the force of her hand.

Devon watched as the Frenchman put his hand up to the mark she had made, and he was pleased to note the slight tremor in those long fingers. They finally touched the blood that had begun to well from the corner of his lip.

"Yours, I believe," Devon said, holding out the stained handkerchief he had used on his damaged mouth. "At the moment, you seem to have more need of it than I."

He was satisfied to see the mockery had also disappeared from the hazel eye. The Frenchman took a deep breath, and his fingers moved to touch the black patch above the scars.

He waited a long moment and finally moved to stand over the fallen man. Jean took the handkerchief, but instead of using it to blot the blood from his lips, he returned it to his pocket.

And then he put out his hand and allowed the tanned fingers of the Englishman to lock into his.

When Devon was standing, the blue eyes rested again on the brutally scarred face.

"I haven't made love to Julie. What you saw..." Devon paused, wondering why he felt compelled to explain his actions to this man when Julie had denied his claim to speak on her behalf.

The Frenchman found himself believing that quiet assurance. He recognized that he had, in his impetuous defense of Julie's honor, probably marked paid to his own hopes.

"Then why did you offer? There's no one but we three who know."

"Maybe," Devon said, "but I can't be sure of that. We traveled together. We shared our meals, our resources and—" He remembered the times he had kissed her, the night he had held her trembling body against the warmth of his.

He acknowledged to himself, at least, the real reason he'd made that offer. He loved her. He'd fallen in love with the woman who had ridden by his side these last days, in a situation, like battle, in which one's true character could not be disguised or hidden. And he knew that she was not indifferent to him. She had revealed that in her response to his every touch. But discussing his feelings was not something he intended to do with this arrogant Frenchman.

"And Arthur Ashford was a friend of my father's," he substituted instead of confessing what he'd been thinking. "She didn't use that name when she told me her story. Believe me, I had no idea who she was."

"Very revealing. Thankfully we've abandoned those class distinctions in France. Had you known she was one of your own, you would never have—"

The words were cut off at the sudden blaze of Devon's blue eyes that warned him against a further defamation of character.

"She's always used her mother's name," Jean said, realizing he'd overstepped the boundaries he had tacitly agreed to. "Her mother was French, one of the old families. Despite the name's aristocratic associations, Julie found it better for her work here."

"Perhaps because it wasn't familiar to the Englishmen who frequented these rooms."

"The event that drove her father from London is a very old scandal," the Frenchman suggested. "I'm surprised that anyone remembers. Or cares."

"A peer caught cheating the members of his own club? I should think that would be remembered even in Paris." Devon said and saw the quick amusement.

"Certainly a brief notoriety, *even* in Paris," Jean admitted. "But a twenty-five-year-old story about a minor aristocrat would hardly be *au courant* in France. You were only a child when it happened, and yet you recognized the name immediately."

"I told you. Ashford was a friend of my father's. I heard the stories about my father's friend as I grew up. But my father never discussed the incident at all."

Realizing fully, perhaps, what, in his anger, he had forced the Englishman to do, Jean spoke aloud the question Devon had already begun considering.

"And what will your father say about your marriage to the Viscount Ashford's daughter?"

The blue eyes glanced up, and Devon smiled at the Frenchman for the first time since their encounter had begun.

"I think I'll worry about that after I've secured the lady's acceptance. Do you know where I can find Julie?"

"If I did, I wouldn't tell you. But I'm beginning to believe you were telling the truth. And if so, then there's really no need for that very gallant sacrifice," Jean mocked. "I think for Julie's sake it would be better if you left her in my protection. In view of the scene I interrupted, yours seems to be suspect."

"And I really don't think that your opinion of what lies between Julie and me is going to affect what I think is necessary."

"Necessary?" Jean broke in, his tone biting. "But that, my English nobleman, is exactly what I object to. You'd marry Julie because you consider it necessary to satisfy your ideas of honor and the image you have of your own nobility. And I think that she deserves more than a husband who will wallow in his self-sacrifice and never let her forget what he gave up for her sake."

"A husband—such as you?" Devon questioned, smiling. "I think I'm beginning to understand your objections here. You want her for yourself."

"I want what's best for Julie," Jean argued. "I know Julie. I understand what her life has been, and I value her for who and what she is. I want her, but not because of some twisted idea of honor. I think Julie deserves more than that."

"In other words, you think what I'm offering isn't good enough," Devon said quietly. "That your motives are somehow more..." He paused, searching for a word that wouldn't denigrate what the scarred gambler wanted to give her, because he had recognized the sincerity of Jean's concern.

"More honest," the Frenchman finished for him.

"You'd be surprised at the honesty of my motives," Devon said. "But whatever they are, I think I have the prior claim. Until Julie refuses my offer."

"And you expect me to wait patiently in the shadows while you convince her that, in taking her to London as your wife, you'll be doing something fine and noble. I'm sorry, but I think you should understand that I intend to do everything in my power to show Julie the worst possible thing she could do is to allow you to marry her out of your noble sense of guilt."

"Then," Devon said finally, "I suppose I should begin my convincing. Are you sure you don't know where I might find her?"

"Go to hell," the Frenchman said softly. "You'll bring her nothing but the bitterness her father lived with. Leave her alone. Go back to London and a world you understand. You know nothing about hers. You'll only hurt her if you stay."

The Englishman didn't answer that accusation because he was afraid there was some logic there. But he had seen the hunger that had briefly flared in Julie's eyes when he'd asked her to marry him. And in spite of what the Frenchman thought, there had been no self-sacrifice in his proposal. On the contrary, for once in his life, Devon had done exactly what he had wanted to do, with no considerations for his family, his honor or his country.

Devon nodded slowly, not in agreement with what Jean had said, but in acknowledgment of the conditions. And then he turned and left the room.

Behind him the shadowed salon was silent. Finally the man standing there alone flicked one of the cards Julie had left on the table, and under his expert fingers it turned to lie mockingly, face up, revealing the king of hearts. And the laughter that echoed under the high ceiling and bounced back from the empty spaces was bitter.

Jean found Julie a short time later where he had known she would take refuge, in the small room she had long ago claimed as her domain in the vast maze of salons and private parlors that occupied the lower floor of the casino. She was sitting at the elegant secretary where she had once placed the orders for the choice delicacies and the fine wax candles and the expensive sea coal used to fill the huge fireplaces—all the details that were necessary to run the successful business she'd directed for the last three years.

He entered quietly and stood a moment watching her. Although she was certainly aware he was there, she made no acknowledgment of his presence. The anger she had expressed over his interference was no longer apparent in the small body. She sat, lowered head resting in both palms.

"Surely you're not grieving over rejecting that sanctimonious *aristo's* proposal. Did you really want to trail him to London, kissing his hands in gratitude every day, properly humble because he was honorable enough to marry you despite your father's fatal mistake?'' His voice was as mockingly sardonic as it had been downstairs.

"He's not an aristocrat," she answered. But she had known, despite his denial of a title, that Devon was.

"Oh, God, Julie, of course, he is. You've dealt with enough London fops to recognize one by scent alone. He fairly reeks of wealth and position."

"He's a soldier."

Jean's laugh was short and pointed. "And so is Wellington, who is also an English nobleman, as are most of his officers. Do you imagine your nobleman as a recruit? That arrogance brooks no impudence from the rank and file. He's accustomed to command, all right. Probably staff. Christened with enough names to choke his own charger and related to half the peerage. No matter what he told you, that noble air is too inbred to hide."

"It doesn't matter. Whatever he is, he's beyond my reach, and I know it."

"But what matters is that, clearly, you want him," Jean said, his amusement evident. "Buy a hair shirt. It's cheaper. And when you've had enough pain, at least you'll be able to take it off. Unlike matrimony with your nobleman who'll require a permanent penance for who you are."

"You *are* a bastard," she accused bitterly, still without raising her head.

"Of course," he agreed, laughing. "I thought I'd told you. My mother professed to have had no idea—"

"Why must you mock every human emotion, everything that's fine and decent and noble?" she asked, her eyes raised in fury to meet his, her voice echoing the contempt he had earlier instilled in the word "no-ble."

"Perhaps because I am none of those things," he said, relieved to see that flash of fire back in her dark eyes. He moved to prop himself gracefully against the edge of the desk at which she was sitting, looking down on her. "Or because I've come to believe that most of the people who profess to possess those qualities are hypocrites. As he is. Surely, Julie, you don't think there are still knights on white chargers waiting to ride to your rescue. As you told me, you're a little old for fairy tales."

"I'm a little old for everything. But that doesn't mean that I can't believe there are still good and honorable people in the world."

"And the man I just found putting his lascivious mouth on your body? Do you classify him as good? Somehow that wasn't my impression. But then I have been, perhaps, more disillusioned by my past than you. I had always thought you understood the ways of the world. That you and I were alike in that," he finished gently, inviting her to remember the rapport they had once shared.

Her eyes searched his face, and he allowed their scrutiny, although she knew his inclination would be to turn away, to hide, as always, the damaged profile from the interested or horrified stares it evoked. But Julie had seen his scars, at least the external version, for years, and so he endured her gaze.

"I know," she whispered finally and touched the small smudge of dried blood in the corner of his mouth, the only physical evidence remaining of her anger. "I know that we are. That you and I are alike. But he's not what you believe. He's like my father.

Surely, Jean, you can't deny my father's standards were unusual in our world. He—''

"He cheated his London friends at cards and then spent the rest of his life trying to make up for it. He raised his only daughter in an environment most men of his class would never have permitted their women to know about, much less participate in. And he did that because he was selfish enough to want the support of your love, your daily presence. He apparently also worked to defeat his adopted country, spied on the nation that had taken him in when his own had kicked him out, had exiled him because of that very nobility you're now so enamored of. Do you want to know why your father became the bitter old man he was? Look at your hero if you want to see the cause of your father's heartbreak.''

"Then if you believe Devon is the villain you've just painted him, why would you make the ridiculous suggestion that he marry me?'' she asked, and again he could hear the bitterness that underlay her question.

"Because... God, Julie, I don't even know any more what I felt when I walked in and found him making love to you,'' he said harshly.

"Jean,'' she protested, and he interrupted, knowing what she was about to say.

"All right,'' he acknowledged. "You tell me that nothing has happened between you, and I believe you. But I was so—I don't know. Furious. Jealous,'' he suggested finally, and her brown eyes widened at the word.

"Jealous?'' she echoed, unbelieving.

The unscarred side of his mouth moved suddenly, the ability to mock himself undiminished by the real feelings he had for her.

"Ironic, isn't it? Especially after the lecture I just read you. But I had always believed, had at least hoped, if anyone could succeed in melting the cynicism that has encased your heart in ice, that I would be that someone. I waited so long. And then I walked in here today, after weeks of searching for you, and find you in the arms of another man, apparently enjoying his lovemaking."

Her face, when he glanced down to read her reaction, was very still, but her eyes held no trace of amusement or disbelief.

"Then why..." she whispered.

"Why would I demand that he marry you? Because I thought he'd refuse, and you'd see him for what he was."

"And if he had?" she questioned, and he smiled at her before he answered.

"Then I thought you'd realize there is someone else who loves you. I know the idea of taking your place in London society at the side of a man who has a right to be there is far more romantic than the thought of living with a scarred bastard who was raised in the stews of Paris and has known nothing of that nobility you seem to admire. I know that I'm no woman's image of a white knight, especially someone as idealistic as you."

"Idealistic," she repeated, laughing. "Of all the terms anyone has ever applied to me, that—"

"—is the one the person who knows you best in all the world would choose," he said softly. "I just hope, Julie, that when you eventually decide you're going to survive this infatuation with that very noble Englishman, you'll think differently about someone who has loved you for a long time. Someone who will accept you with no caveats or restrictions on who you are or on the woman you will eventually become."

Finally she smiled at him. "And when I decide I'm over that infatuation," she invited softly, "what do you suggest?"

"I had thought," he said speculatively, a slight smile hovering over his lips, "a small and very select card room..."

"Perhaps somewhere near the Palais Royale," she pretended to muse, "very exclusive, only the most *noble* clientele. Is that what you had in mind?" she asked, smiling at him.

"Exactly. When you're ready, I'll order the wine, my darling," Jean promised softly, the only endearment he had ever used to her, "and deal the first hand."

Chapter Eight

When Jean had willingly allowed himself to be dispatched to care for the horses and to buy in the nearby Les Halles market the provisions they would need to remain safe in the midst of their enemies, Julie decided she'd hidden long enough. Devon would eventually have to be faced, and the proposal Jean had forced him to make would have to be answered.

Remembering the gambler's carefully worded avowal of his feelings, she knew that she was better prepared for that ordeal than before Jean had sought her out. Again he had provided support. Not the protective cotton wool Devon seemed to feel her situation called for, but a reassurance of his willingness to stand behind whatever decisions she made. And so, taking a deep breath, she left the sanctuary of her private office and returned to the main salon where she knew Devon would eventually find her.

She automatically began to gather the cards she'd left scattered on the surface of the table, scarcely noticing the upturned king of hearts. When she realized what she was doing, she stacked the deck and left it. She walked across the salon and into the dimness of her father's office where Devon had looked for some trace of information that would help him find his friend. The afternoon sun was filtered by the heavy draperies, and the resulting gloom softened somewhat the impact of entering the room where she had spent so many happy hours.

She thought again about the judgments Jean had made of her father's actions, ideas she had never even considered. She knew she had blindly accepted that what her father had done was right, accepted those decisions because he was her father and because she loved him. But she wondered what her life would have been had he left her with the nuns. Would it then have been possible, as clearly it now would never be, to have what she wanted? As if conjured by her thoughts of him, she heard Devon's voice from the doorway.

"I think we need to talk," he said simply, walking across the small room to stand before her. He was somehow relieved to find no trace of tears, despite the emotional scene in the salon. He thought he understood something of what, between them, he and Jean had done to her.

"I know," she said softly.

"Somehow, when I finally asked a woman to marry me, I didn't expect it would occasion flight. Is the thought of marrying me that terrifying?" he asked, smiling slightly.

She allowed her eyes to rest on his face a moment before she replied.

"I should think it would be the other way around," she said softly.

"And I had thought you'd decided that I'm really not a rake. I don't offer for women I'd be terrified to marry. You're beautiful and brave, intelligent—"

"And I deal faro and vingt-et-un in the most notorious gaming house in Paris. I wonder how your family would respond to your bringing home a wife with those credentials."

"I think I'm old enough that I don't need my family's approval of the woman I choose to marry. I asked you to marry me, Julie, and I'm still waiting for an answer," he said.

When he had met her tear-glazed eyes, he had known that his proposal had been a matter of his emotions and not his honor—emotions he had fought throughout their journey to Paris. And he was tired of denying what he wanted. During the last two years, he had certainly been shown that life was too precious to allow conventions to stand in the way of living.

Caring for Julie was, he had realized sometime in the difficulties of the last week, exactly what he wanted to spend the remainder of his life doing. Something in the Frenchman's calm assertion that he would be better able to make her happy had made Devon grimly determined to prove that allegation wrong. Given the chance, he had no doubt he could ensure her happiness. Her responsiveness to his touch had shown him that she was as emotionally involved as he.

Her hand lifted involuntarily, wondering what he was thinking, and the slender fingers touched the bruise that was already beginning to darken the side of his mouth. When she felt his smile move against her sensitive fingertips, she forced her hand to drop.

"And old enough, I think, to know what would happen if I said yes." She added reality to his list. "I've known no other life than the one I've led in these rooms, but I saw what exile from his world did to my father. I couldn't do that to you, Dev. Even if I thought this sudden desire for my hand was prompted by anything other than your misguided nobility."

"My nobility," he said mockingly and shook his head. "That wasn't nobility between us in the salon today. You know better than that, Lady Luck. And I'm not really concerned about my family's approval of whomever I marry. They would be the first to support my right to make that decision."

"Because?" she asked, trying to read what was hidden in his tone.

He shook his head again. "Marry me," he said, smiling invitingly, "and I'll reveal all my family secrets."

"And all your own?" she asked, cherishing his slow smile.

He was a man who didn't undertake promises easily or make oaths without considering the costs.

But he pledged finally, "And all my own."

It was a vow whose implications she recognized and valued.

She wanted what he offered, all that it represented, and most of all, of course, she wanted him. She fought to keep her fingers locked around the fold of yellow muslin they had found, fought to keep them from touching again the bruised mouth or the faint lines that fanned from the corners of the dark blue eyes.

"And would your sister, who calls you Dev, welcome me into your family?"

"Of course," he said easily, but somewhere in the back of his mind a faint whisper of doubt about Emily's reaction stirred.

"And your brother-in-law, the Duke of Avon? Will he take me to court on his arm?" she questioned.

"He'll adore you," he assured softly, knowing Dominic's abilities too well to doubt his recognition of her quality.

"And perhaps I can open a small card room, something very private and exclusive. For your friends and his?" she suggested, thinking of Jean's response to that same proposal. But instead of the support the Frenchman had offered, she saw the faint crease grow between his brows.

"Julie," he began doubtfully and realized from her eyes that he had walked into the trap she'd deliberately set. He cleared the question from his voice and said, laughing, "Won't that take a lot of money? Remember you're marrying a simple half-pay soldier. Not even a minor title."

"I can imagine the titles your friends would bestow on you if you were foolish enough to marry me, Dev. I wonder how many faces I'd meet across the dinner tables of London that I've faced across the gaming tables of Paris. And I wonder how many of them you'd be forced to meet on some deserted field at dawn to protect my honor," she said, and saw a pained reaction to her words move across his carefully controlled features.

"Think," she demanded forcefully, knowing her arguments were having some effect. "Think what you're suggesting and what it will mean to your life. I can't live with you in London, and with Bonaparte's return, I don't think you want to live here in Paris. Venice, perhaps, or Florence?" she suggested, imagining how he would hate the separation from his country and his family. "Think, Dev, if you want that exile. That loss of who and what you are. The loss, perhaps, of everyone and everything you love."

She waited. His lips tightened, and she saw him swallow, the movement too strong and sudden. And then the blue eyes were smiling again, their serenity unbroken.

"You haven't answered my question, Julie. Will you marry me?" he asked calmly, as if she had never spoken. She could see none of the images she had sought to create in the lucid blue.

"No, Dev," she whispered, and finally she allowed her hand to touch his cheek. "I won't marry you, but I will never forget that you asked me. I'll never, ever, my beautiful soldier knight, forget that you asked."

She watched his lips tighten and the blue eyes drop before hers. But she had always known that he wanted her. She had had no doubt from the first about the sexual attraction that had flowed between them. But he'd said nothing about love. *"The woman I loved..."* Perhaps he was still in love with that woman. She'd never know. She only knew that she couldn't marry him. Marriage to him would be exactly what Jean had said. A hair shirt of punishment. His in answering the slights made because of what she had been, and hers because of what that would eventually do to him. It would be better, then, that nothing come of what they both felt, rather than that pain.

"And I think that perhaps your gambler friend found you first," he said, and she looked up from her regret to find his eyes calmly searching her face.

"Jean?" she questioned softly, lost with the sudden shift of subject. She couldn't know of the antagonistic understanding the two men had reached regarding their very different plans for her future.

"We talked. He knew where I'd be," she explained. "Where I always go to hide, to think."

Her words revealed something of their shared history, an affirmation of their closeness that Devon would rather not have heard. He found himself wondering suddenly about their relationship. He blocked the thought of whatever might have happened between them in the past. In that way, too, lay madness. A particularly dangerous insanity for their situation.

If he accepted his love for Julie, it would have to be with a blindness for whatever romantic liaisons her past contained. Or the Frenchman would be right. If he couldn't control the images of someone else's possession of her before he had entered her life, then he had no right to seek to make her his. He would only end up punishing them both. But because his inner strength was very great, having been tempered in fires of self-examination that few men are ever forced to confront, he buried that question and smiled at her.

"Then apparently he's had an opportunity to produce some compelling arguments against your acceptance of my proposal," he said. His comment invited her confidence or her assurance that nothing important had been said between them. He could tell by the slight flush that spread upward from her throat that she wouldn't be able to offer that comfort.

"I see," he said finally as she allowed the silence to grow. "Somehow I think I prefer his assessments of my character be made in my presence. And I don't like the idea of your discussing my suit with someone who's made it clear he considers me obligated to marry you, but at the same time unworthy to touch the tips of your fingers."

"We weren't discussing *your* suit," Julie answered softly, her emphasis clear.

"And was he more successful in pleading his cause than I've been?"

"No, but Dev, you don't understand—"

Her voice cut off in unconscious appeal, and he waited a long time for her to go on. Finally his grim expression softened.

"Do you realize how much you've been asked to deal with in the last few weeks? Your father's death, your flight and its dangers, my rather clumsy attempt to offer you both the protection of my name and my physical protection from Fouché. And now, apparently a counterproposal from someone who has known you far longer than I," he said, trying for a lighter tone than the deep disappointment he felt. "But I want you to remember you don't have to make any decisions you're not prepared to make. I'm not going to push you into anything, Julie. I hope you won't allow your friend to, either."

Listening to that quiet commitment, she knew, despite the proposal she had just received from someone far more knowledgeable about who and what she was, that she had not mistaken her feelings for this man.

"Dev," she said softly, "could we go back to the way things were before, to whatever there was between us before Jean came? I want what we felt then. Not what he's blackmailed you into offering out of your sense of honor."

"You'd be surprised at my motives in offering for you, Lady Luck. I was rather caught off guard by them myself," he admitted softly. "But I think you're right. Perhaps what you need now is the assurance that you can count again on my self-control. And as soon as I've told you that exercising that control is going to be the most difficult task I've undertaken in some time, I'll begin. And I think this time..." he said, holding out his hand.

She looked down at the outstretched palm, the red line of the Gypsy's knife still clear, and laid her fingers against the scar.

He turned her hand in his and raised it to his lips for a brief kiss.

"Until I find Dominic, my Lady Luck, you're safe from *my* proposals," he promised, stressing the pronoun.

"And do you have a plan for achieving that, now?" She removed her hand to gesture at her father's office.

She was sorry she had asked when he shook his head, his lips tight with frustration.

"I didn't believe I'd simply come into France and find Avon's agents ready to help me locate him. Nor did I think I could just walk out of a hostile country with Dominic in tow, but I did hope there would be something or someone remaining that might offer a clue. It's as if the duke and his network have simply disappeared."

This time they both heard the footsteps crossing the salon. Devon turned so that his body was between Julie and whoever was approaching through the vast room beyond the office.

"It's Jean," she said, brushing by him to prevent any more of the hostility that had been so evident between them when she had fled upstairs.

Devon watched her walk quickly to meet her friend and felt a sudden jolt of anger at the thought of her rushing to greet the Frenchman. Jealousy, he admitted, mocking himself, but he didn't bother to deny the validity of his identification of the emotion that was tightening his stomach muscles.

"Dev, come and eat," she called, her voice coming from the shadowed passage that led to the kitchen.

He took a deep breath to banish the possessiveness, which he acknowledged could destroy any chance of happiness between himself and Julie. He realized he had been gripping the frame of the door so hard that its ridges were still clear on his fingers when he removed them. He looked at those marks a long time, and then, obeying Julie's suggestion, he forced himself to walk across the wide salon to join them in the shuttered kitchens.

He found Julie unpacking supplies on the huge cook's table. He didn't even glance at the man who stood leaning against the wall, also watching her.

"Jean's brought enough so we won't have to venture out again for a few days. We may not enjoy a wide variety, but at least we won't go hungry. You know I can't cook," she said, looking up at him from under those impossibly long lashes.

"I can," he said, smiling at her confession, and he knew she was remembering, as he was, the simple meals they had shared on their journey. "I don't think, however, that building a fire would be a very wise move on our part."

"I agree," said Jean. "That's why there's nothing there that requires cooking. I suggest that we eat the meat pies first and save the less perishable items for later."

"Of course," she said and held one of the still-warm pastries out to him.

When he had accepted it, she unthinkingly licked the gravy off her fingers and lifted another pie from its wrappings to hand to Devon. When she realized that she was holding this pie in the same fingers she had just delicately cleaned with her tongue, she pulled back the offering just as his hand reached for it.

"I'm sorry," she said, embarrassed by her lapse of manners in front of him, conscious that she had forgotten to maintain the social niceties with this man with whom she had lived so intimately.

The corners of his mouth moved in quick amusement, and his brow quirked in question.

"I don't think you need be so concerned about your fingers. After all..." he suggested, daring her to remember that her tongue itself had only recently caressed his mouth.

But she, at least, was very conscious of the man who had stood watching throughout the exchange.

Devon took the pastry she held out to him, and then with his other hand he quickly captured her fingers, licking the pie's juices from them, all the while holding her eyes with his.

She was fascinated by the texture of his tongue against her skin for a heartbeat, and then her fingers struggled, demanding freedom, and he released her. Her knees were weak, and there was a peculiar sensation in the pit of her stomach, but she turned and found the third of the pastries in the grease-stained paper.

She didn't look at Devon again, and finally she heard him move to prop one hip casually on the top of the table while he ate.

"Devon," she said finally to break the oppressive silence, "Jean thinks that you were right. There seems to be no one watching the casino. Apparently Fouché—"

"Devon?" Jean's voice questioned harshly, shockingly forceful in contrast to her casual comment.

Two sets of eyes, velvet brown and hard blue, locked on his face.

"Devon?" he asked again, more softly but with more meaning than the first startled response to the use of the Englishman's full name. "Is that a common name in England?"

Julie's eyes flew to the narrowed blue gaze that seemed to be searching the question for any hidden aspects.

"No," Devon admitted at last. "I was named for my mother's family estate. It's not really a proper Christian name at all, not one that I've ever—"

"Devon," the Frenchman said again, smiling. "And did you really come from the pits of hell?" he asked, the mockery full and derisive in the soft question.

"Jean," Julie whispered, shocked by what he had asked. She hadn't understood the comment she took to be an insult, but she saw Devon's face drain suddenly of color and the pupils widen, a contrast to the diminishing ring of cobalt surrounding them.

He never stopped to consider what he might be revealing. He was too relieved to consider the consequences of letting this man, whose convenient appearance had already made him suspicious, know more than he apparently already did.

"Where is he?" Devon asked dangerously, and watched the smile that lifted only the undamaged side of the Frenchman's lips. "Where the hell is the man who told you that?"

"But he didn't tell me, *mon ami*. I was simply in a position to overhear his delirious ravings. Your name and that phrase repeated over and over."

Julie wondered how someone could move as quickly as Devon did then. He was across the space that had separated him from the Frenchman and was holding Jean's wrist almost before her eyes had registered the motion.

She watched Jean's eye move from an unintimidated confrontation with the furious blue ones to rest pointedly on the fingers that held him captive. Eventually Devon released his grip, and she saw his struggle to regain the control that had, at the Frenchman's words, deserted him. He stepped back, allowing a less threatening space to open between them, and waited until the flush had died from the high cheekbones of his adversary before he spoke again.

"The man you just spoke of," he said quietly, exercising an enormous force of will to modulate his tone, "is my friend. And I owe him more than my life. I'm sorry for what I just did, but I have to know what you can tell me about him. You said he was delirious?" he asked, feigning a calmness he didn't possess and waited again.

"And what would you give for the information you seek?" the equally restrained voice asked.

"Anything," Devon answered without hesitation. "I told you. I owe him more than my life. I'll give you anything you want—anything I have."

The scarred lips lifted in the bitter, one-sided smile, and the tone of the answer made the girl listening shiver suddenly.

"Julie," he said simply, and at first she thought he was speaking to her. But then he finished with even darker malice coloring his words. "Will you give me Julie in exchange for your friend?"

"No," she whispered and was forced to clear her throat against the sudden constriction. She didn't want to hear whatever answer Devon might have made. "No," she repeated, louder than before, and they both turned to her. "He doesn't have me to give, Jean. I control my own fate. I'm not a stake to be fought over. You tell him or not, but don't bring me into whatever you're doing here. I won't be a party to this."

Jean looked at the pale face a moment. Some of the tension seemed to leave his body and he, too, stepped back, widening the distance between them.

"Your friend was Fouché's prisoner. He was being held in the Luxembourg Palace. After the raid on the casino, I was briefly incarcerated in the same cell, held for questioning because I worked for Julie's father and was therefore suspect. That's all I can tell you. Except that, if you're planning to try to liberate that man, I will warn you you'll never succeed. You'll never get him out of France, or even out of that building, alive. And I'm urging you not to try. You can't beat Fouché, not alone and not with the odds all in his favor. And not given the condition of your friend. Go home and forget him. Your friend is beyond your help. Beyond anyone's help. And you might as well accept that."

The blue eyes considered the sincerity that rang in the quiet voice. Julie was holding her breath and didn't realize it until she watched the slow smile break the rigid control Devon had forced over his features.

"In the pits of hell?" he asked quietly. "Is that where you're suggesting Dominic is? But, my friend, I've already been there," Devon said truthfully. "And returned. Thanks to Dominic. And nothing you can say will make me leave him in Fouché's hands. And whatever I choose to do with the information you provided is surely, after all, my choice." He waited for his opponent to absorb that idea, and then he finished softly, "Will you tell me about my friend?"

The Frenchman stood still, held by the surety of that calm voice, which Julie had seen affect all those with whom they had yet come in contact. And then, almost imperceptibly, he nodded.

Jean's story was told without embellishment, and most of it could have been predicted by the other two based on their experiences in avoiding Fouché's reach. He had left the casino the night Julie's father had died, his sense of danger too well-honed to think he would get away unscathed by whatever was happening. He had disappeared during the aftermath that followed the agents' break-in and the patrons' shocked response to gunfire in the middle of a peaceful night in this well-run establishment.

"My first thoughts were of getting you out, Julie, before you could be taken for questioning, but you weren't here. You'd disappeared. I watched the casino for several days, and there was still no sign of you."

"My father told me to leave Paris, but we hadn't had time to discuss where or how. He only had time to issue the warning and then to give me money. Enough for several weeks, but it eventually began to run out."

"And then you met Devon?" he probed.

"No," she answered, laughing. "Then I became a boy."

"A boy?" he questioned, considering the vision of femininity she presented in her fashionable gown.

"A very believable boy," she said lightly. "I have it on the best authority."

Her eyes rested teasingly on Devon's face, and it was obvious that she was reminding him of some shared memory. That thought was enough to cause a strong surge of jealousy in the Frenchman.

"But why?" he asked.

"It seemed safest. And I thought no one would expect it of me," she explained.

"No wonder I had no luck in finding you," he said. "I'm looking for the most beautiful woman in Paris, and she's pretending to be a boy. Pardon me, *petite*, but in spite of your friend's assessment, I personally can't imagine you in that guise."

"If you had seen the dirt under her nails and had smelled…" Devon began. It was the first time he had spoken since he had demanded the Frenchman's story, and Julie was glad the darkness of his vow was gone from his voice.

"I beg your pardon," she interrupted in response to his description. "I assure you I did not smell. I was a very clean urchin, at least below the surface dirt I carefully applied."

"Your hair smelled of flowers," he said softly, remembering. "That was the first indication I had that the child I had just stolen from his enemies was something other than he appeared."

"And the second indication?" Laughing, she invited him to confess.

"The second was perhaps a certain *je ne sais quoi*— a certain echo of womanliness," he finished, smiling.

"That's not—" she began, still smiling at his reluctance to admit what he really meant.

"We seemed to have strayed from the point," the Frenchman interrupted bitingly, aware again of the teasing intimacy of the verbal exchanges between his companions. "Or are you no longer interested in the whereabouts of your friend?"

"Did it appear to you that my interest had waned? If so, I assure you, you're mistaken," Devon said quietly, his eyes no longer on the girl's face. Instead they rested with somewhat bitter inquiry on the scarred countenance of the man who had just spoken. "I await the point in your narrative at which you arrived in Fouché's prison with much anticipation, I promise you."

Jean's mouth tightened slightly in anger, and then his control was reimposed. However, that icy discipline didn't prevent his longing to see the Englishman stretched out at his feet, the victim once more of a fist that was itching to wipe out the polite boredom, which was the only emotion the handsome features now displayed.

"I came back to the casino finally because I had nowhere else to look. I had exhausted every acquaintance of yours I knew and had asked as many questions as I dared. I was afraid that my search might direct theirs to wherever you were so successfully hiding. But then I made the mistake of entering this building, and of course they were watching. They took me to Fouché, but since I was not who they'd been waiting for, they seemed unsure what to do with me. They knew I'd worked for your father, which naturally made them suspicious of my activities. But their questioning was cursory, if rather painful. And then they threw me into a cell, a cell occupied by what appeared to be a still-breathing corpse.''

He stopped at the strength of that memory. As cynical as he imagined himself to be, he had been affected by his encounter with the man in that cell. But it would be impossible for him to admit that.

"And?" Devon prompted, wondering at the look in the hazel eye, a look he had not seen before in his rather hostile dealings with this man. But with his question, the emotion, whatever it had been, cleared, and Jean went on with his story.

"He was in high fever, suffering from what appeared to be an inflammation of the lungs. And he was delirious. I honestly doubted that he would live out the night. I found out later that Fouché, only a few hours before, had him brought from the dungeon. Apparently he'd changed his mind about letting him die. But he cut it close." His voice fell almost to a whisper as he repeated, "Damn close."

There was a long silence at the unexpectedness of the feelings revealed in that whisper, and then the Frenchman seemed to shake off the memories of that experience.

"What had they done to him?" Devon asked, knowing that if he were to be successful in freeing Avon, he had to understand what he would be dealing with. And in light of Jean's earlier warning, he had to know Avon's physical condition.

"They'd inflicted some damage, apparently, in the capture. They'd taken him in the street outside the casino. Obviously, they'd been waiting for him to contact your father. He fought them. He recalled a blow to the head and something—" he stopped and looked at Devon's carefully controlled face "—some

injury to his leg. I don't know what kind of damage
because I have no idea what it was like before, but..."
Again he paused, and the slight shudder was involuntary.

"Go on," Devon said, his voice rigidly emotionless.

"Fouché used cold water to bring him around during the interrogation, and his clothing was soaked.
Then they threw him into that hole," he said, looking
up suddenly.

"And?" Devon prompted softly.

"They fed him. At least they put food in the cell and
he crawled to it. As long as he was able to crawl. I
don't know how he'd stayed alive as long as he had.
Sheer force of will, perhaps."

"Yes," Devon said again, his voice even softer than
before.

"And the thought of someone named Devon who
had promised to come from the pits of hell," Jean
finished his story, watching the face of the man who
knew better than he the meaning of that determination. "And you are that man?"

"Yes," Devon admitted, "and knowing what
you've just told me, you still think I should leave. You
believe I should let him remain in the hands of the man
who arranged that imprisonment. Do you know who
Fouché's prisoner is?" he asked suddenly, hoping to
catch the Frenchman off guard, to surprise information from him in the midst of what appeared to be
honest emotion.

"No," he said simply, and a remembered amusement lightened his voice. "He told me it was dangerous to know him. I assumed, because they had
questioned me about espionage for the English, he was

involved in that. Especially when I learned Fouché had stationed a guard outside the cell we occupied in hopes he might overhear something that would link me to his prisoner. They knew we were both connected to the casino, and they hoped I'd reveal something that would allow them to hold me. Luckily for me, Fouché's listener was disappointed. And to give him credit, your friend warned me, as soon as he was able, about what Fouché was doing. I'm afraid it had never crossed my mind he might have had ulterior motives in placing me in that particular cell."

"And then they let you go? Are you trying to tell me they released you with no more assurance that you were not involved in the passing on of information to the English, than a lack of conversation? Frankly, I find that very hard to believe."

"And I really don't care whether you believe it or not. By that time, I think Fouché had other things besides external enemies to consider. The Emperor had returned, and Fouché might have simply lost interest in your friend. But since you are far more knowledgeable about my cellmate's importance to your government than I am, you're the better judge of that. He certainly lost interest in me. I was released after little more than two weeks' internment. I didn't question my good luck. And I don't care if you do. I was happy enough to leave his hospitality. But I don't think your friend will be as lucky."

"No," Devon said, shaking his head. "Fouché knows very well—"

The words were cut off when Devon realized he'd been thinking out loud. He didn't trust this Frenchman. He wasn't sure how much Jean knew and how much he had surmised from Avon's delirium. Either way, Devon didn't intend to add to his knowledge.

So he asked instead, "Who had access to his cell? Who entered it each day? Who has freedom of movement within the prison? Guards, officials, anyone else?" He halted the running questions as the other man simply shook his head and continued to shake it in response.

"No one. The guards slid the food each day through a slot in the door. No one entered. Not in the entire time I was there, except—"

Devon smiled in satisfaction as the significance of Jean's sudden pause was clear to all of them.

"Who?" he asked softly. And at the continued hesitation, he said again, "Who? You obviously thought of someone who was allowed to enter."

"A doctor," Jean answered, his disdain clear. "Some pompous, arrogant poltroon who tried to bleed him."

"To bleed him," Julie repeated in disbelief. "I should have thought that would be the last thing a man in his condition would need."

"Yes." Jean smiled at her. "So did I. I'm afraid I rejected his professional services," Jean admitted grimly.

"Then you probably saved Dominic's life," Devon said quietly. "And for that alone, I'm in your debt."

"What I did for your friend I would have done for anyone. I don't want your gratitude or your friendship. Save it for your hopeless mission."

"Why hopeless?" Devon answered easily, ignoring the hostility. "Now that you've just given me a way to get in. Another doctor, a repeat visit."

"And if Fouché has already sent another physician? Or if your friend has staged a remarkable recovery, although I can't tell you, given his condition when I left two days ago, how remarkable that recovery would be. Or perhaps, by now, he has instead—"

"No," the Englishman interrupted, "and you don't believe that, either. He's waiting. Just as he survived in that hell Fouché put him through, Dominic will be gathering his reserves of strength and waiting for me because he knows that I'm coming. There is not now, nor has there ever been, the least doubt in his mind as to that fact."

"You're a fool," the Frenchman said softly. "You'll never get him out. For one thing, he's in no condition to walk out, and they certainly aren't going to stand by and watch you carry someone out, no matter what role you're playing. Even the guards aren't that stupid."

"I won't have to carry Dominic out. He'll do it. Don't doubt what he's capable of. I should think that even a brief meeting with him would have convinced you of that."

"You haven't seen him. You can't imagine—"

"But I know him. He'll walk out. All we have to do is come up with the plan that will give him that opportunity."

"All right," Jean said abruptly. "Even if I grant you his physical ability to leave his cell, what makes you think you can get him past the guards? Don't you believe someone will recognize that the man who's walking past them is the prisoner they've guarded so long?"

"But you just said that no one ever entered the cell. The guards carried an unconscious, delirious body upstairs. Not a man. It's a chance we have to take. And the guards aren't hired for their intellect.''

"If he's important to Fouché, and only you know how important he might be," the Frenchman argued, "then our friend won't be careless enough to allow you to walk out with him. No matter how distracted he is with Napoleon's return."

"Jean, I want your help in getting Devon's friend out of prison," Julie said, and they both turned to her in surprise. She had been so quiet throughout the last part of the discussion that they had almost forgotten her presence. "You have more information than we about the conditions under which he's being held. Your assistance can be invaluable."

One corner of the scarred mouth lifted in the familiar mocking smile as he asked, "And why should I do that, *petite?* Because you wish it? Do you think that's enough reason to convince me to help a man I don't like?"

"No," she answered softly, rejecting his cynicism. "I expect you to help a man whom you clearly admire. A man who is still suffering in Fouché's hands. I'm going to help because Fouché was responsible for my father's death, and you're going to help because that man's life came to mean something to you. That was evident in your voice when you told that gruesome story. You left him in better condition than you found him in because you took care of him. And I know you well enough to fill in the parts of the narrative you deliberately left untold. You stopped the doctor, and then you accepted the responsibility for the life you'd saved. You're going to help Devon rescue him because you couldn't prevent yourself if you tried. We are too much alike to hide our feelings from one another."

"You think you know me so well," Jean said, his voice caressing. "I wonder what it would take to surprise you."

"Only the thought that you could let someone die out of jealousy or anger. That would truly surprise me," she said.

"I hope you're not endowing me with the noble sentiments you believe you see in your own rescuer. I'm not your knight, *petite*. And I never will be."

She studied the saturnine features, familiar and well-loved, before she answered. "But I never wanted a knight. However, I do want your help. And I think you have all the attributes necessary to play this role. It doesn't call for nobility at all. Only a certain single-minded determination and a great deal of shrewdness. Those qualities you have in abundance. And unlike us, Devon lacks certain skills. Skills like thimblerig, which make people think they see one thing when in reality..." She stopped, knowing that he understood what she was suggesting. "He needs our help. And I need yours. It really is a very simple choice."

"Then if this is what you desire, my love, I shall be delighted to help your white knight. How could you ever doubt it?"

"I never did," she said and smiled at him.

The Frenchman's voice had been light, but something had underlain the amusement, something dark and haunted. Again Devon felt the apprehension he had had from the first moment he had learned about Avon's mission. However, he was too relieved by

Jean's agreement to endanger that cooperation by any questions. He'd let Julie deal with her admirer. And he would stand by, for Avon's sake, and grit his teeth while she did.

Chapter Nine

The plan they finally devised was simple. Devon would enter the prison posing as a doctor and, using Jean's directions, go to the cell where Dominic had been held. They hoped that his assurance in finding the place would, in itself, be convincing as to his right to be there.

"The passage from this entrance leads straight to the few remaining cells. It's a busy corridor, used by people in the building who have no connection to the prison. You'll probably be challenged somewhere between your entry into the building and the cell. The more unconcerned you are about answering those questions in any detail, the better. Your attitude should be, how dare these peasants ask a man of my learning and position his business. Use Fouché's name. You have nothing to lose by showing them contempt. If they doubt you enough to check, it's already too late."

"I can't believe you think you can just walk in," Julie argued as she had for the last twenty minutes. They planned no diversion, no attempt to occupy the guards' attention. A straight bluff that, gambler though she was, she couldn't believe would succeed.

"This isn't the Conciergerie. There," Jean said, shaking his head, "there is a real prison. With a lot of experience at keeping its prisoners and foiling escapes. This would never work in that atmosphere. Luxembourg, however, was designed as a royal residence. With the requisite dungeons, to be sure, but the main building itself hasn't been used as a prison in nearly ten years. You're lucky that Fouché wants to keep his affairs secret. We may have a chance at the Luxembourg."

If Jean had been reluctant before, it seemed that once the decision to lend his aid was made, he entered into the planning with every appearance of enthusiasm.

"The key is your ability to overpower the guard who is stationed outside that cell. The door is solid, except for the high grill. If you can get him inside, where you'll be hidden from sight. And if you can manage—" Jean began, and then halted. Having made his evaluation of the Englishman's fighting skills, based on the success of his own surprise assault, he seemed doubtful that Devon would be able to carry off this vital aspect of the scheme.

He looked up from the rough plan of the prison rooms in the Palais du Luxembourg to find a pair of amused blue eyes. A quick drop of lashes hid the expression, but Devon's voice when he answered the implied doubt was calm and absolutely sure.

"He'll come into the cell, and he'll remain there when we leave. Avon dresses in the doctor's clothes and exits, following the route by which I entered. You'll be waiting outside in the hired carriage to drive him to the Gypsy's encampment. In the meantime I change into the clothing concealed in the false bottom of the satchel I'll carry, and leaving the guard unconscious in the cell, make my way out some other entrance as unobtrusively as possible. And I'll ride to meet you at the Romany camp."

"The key . . ." Jean began again.

"The key is my performance at the prison. But I'm the only one who can do this. And I will do it, despite your doubts. Your face might be recognized, and Julie, while having managed to become a believable boy, is going to fool no one masquerading as a doctor. I understand. And I'll get him out."

"Or become Fouché's prisoner yourself," Julie said softly.

"No," Devon promised, but she wasn't comforted by the smile that accompanied that quiet denial.

"This is your one chance. And his. If you fail . . ." Jean said.

The Englishman's smile widened slightly, and his eyes rested on the dark, marred face.

"If I fail, then you get what you want, don't you? Or is that what you're hoping for?" he asked quietly.

The eyes of the two men held for a long time, and it was Jean who broke the silence.

"Not that way," he said, and finally the Englishman nodded.

"Then tomorrow," he agreed quietly.

"I'll have to go out again to get the props you'll need and to arrange for the carriage," Jean said.

"And to find a suitable stick," Devon commanded.

"A stick?"

"For Avon. A walking stick. Make sure it's sturdy," Devon instructed. "And Jean," he added as an afterthought, and again the Frenchman waited. "See if you

can find one with a silver head.'' He didn't bother to
answer the quizzical look that met his, but he smiled,
and the Frenchman shook his head over whatever had
prompted that ridiculous request.

Julie followed Jean into the tunneled passage to secure it from the inside and to make the necessary arrangements as to when she should again open the
secret entrance for the gambler's return.

It seemed to the man who waited in the kitchen that
she took a long time over that task. Devon forced
himself to bury the anxiety caused by the minutes she
was spending alone with a man who had also offered
for her hand. The sooner he removed Julie from the
influence of that dark gambler, the better he'd like it.
But until they had rescued Avon, he knew he'd have to
be patient and trust her not to be swayed by the
Frenchman's arguments. But that didn't mean he had
to enjoy exercising that patience.

He glanced up to find Julie standing in the kitchen
doorway watching him.

''I still think—'' she began.

''No,'' he said too sharply, ''for the thousandth
time, no. You'll meet the carriage at the Observatory.
If, for any reason, we aren't there at the agreed upon
time, you go to the Gypsy. I don't want you anywhere
near that prison tomorrow. I mean it, Julie. And I
want your promise that you'll do exactly as you've
been told.''

''Exactly as I've been told?'' she repeated incredulously. Had he known her longer, he would have recognized the dangerous undertone. His response to her
suggestions for how she might help tomorrow had
been so different from Jean's. And she felt a surge of

anger at Devon's refusal to consider what she'd been urging since they'd begun planning.

"And have I given you the right to dictate my actions? Even had I agreed to your ridiculous offer, would that have given you the right to tell me where I'm allowed to go or what I'm allowed to do?"

"My ridiculous offer?" he asked, his voice as revealing of his dark mood, provoked by her prolonged absence, as hers had been. "And why do you find my proposal so ridiculous?" he asked, wondering how seriously she was considering the other that had been made.

"I suppose it was occasioned by your desire to take as your wife a woman of my background. You know why that proposal was ridiculous."

"Your father is dead because of his efforts on behalf of my country, and you've been left with no one to protect you. You traveled in my company for several days without proper—"

"And so you feel compelled to offer for my hand? Because my father is dead? Because we traveled together?" She laughed a little bitterly before she continued. She had known there were no other reasons for his offer, but to hear him acknowledge that so openly hurt unbearably. "Or is it because your lover married someone else? And I'm even beginning to suspect why she did that. She probably discovered how pigheaded you can be," she mocked.

"Pigheaded?" he repeated furiously. "Because I don't want to take a chance that you'll be taken by Fouché? Do you know what would happen to you in a prison? Do you have any idea of the treatment the guards submit female prisoners to?"

"Of course, I know what would happen to me. Believe me, I know." She stopped. Why reiterate that she knew far more about the underside of Paris than he did? And arguing with him, now that they had so little time, was not what she had intended. She had only wanted to help tomorrow, and she knew she could, but for his stubborn, idiotic English pride.

"Do you know that they would take turns," Devon began, remembering the atrocities on the Peninsula and with the image, sudden and sharp, of that happening to Julie, his voice lost the anger that had colored it. The diversion she had offered might make it easier to get Dominic out. But not at the expense of Julie's life, he thought. Not at the cost of even one hour in a French prison.

"I can't stand that thought, Julie," he whispered and pulled her tightly against the solid warmth of his body.

Just as I can't stand the thought of losing you tomorrow, she thought, but you don't want to allow me to help. And I can. Tomorrow she would watch him walk into Fouché's private hell, and she didn't know if he would ever walk out again, but she knew that she intended to do everything in her power to make sure he and Avon would escape. Escape to return to their London world of safety and nobility. Away from the lies and deceptions of her world that he found so repugnant.

She allowed herself to rest against the hard strength of his chest a moment, listening to the heartbeat that was dearer than her own.

She stepped back and found his eyes, still clouded with his vision of what could happen to her if he allowed her any role in tomorrow's rescue. But she had no doubts about her ability to survive, to carry out the plan she'd devised. Because she had been surviving without his protection for a long time now. She wished suddenly that she was the sheltered, protected lady he deserved. But she wasn't. And never could be.

"Please let me help," she whispered and watched the slow, negative movement of his head. And when his mouth lowered to find hers, as she had known it would, she turned her face away, avoiding his touch. She pulled her hand free and walked across the kitchen without another word.

I don't need or want a knight-errant, she thought again. And I make my own decisions. The Gypsy girl will be at the Palais du Luxembourg long before you arrive, Devon. Bluff and counterbluff, my darling. Never wager against the professionals.

They had all been subdued at supper, each lost in private thoughts about the endeavor they would undertake in a few short hours. Julie was conscious that Devon's eyes rested frequently on her face, and she knew that he regretted as much as she did the bitterness of their last exchange.

She didn't want to let him walk out of her life with that memory between them. But she had responsibilities to carry out in the morning, and if she allowed herself any intimate moment with him, she feared the loss of the control that must be used to keep her intentions secret.

He had been forced to offer her his name, a marriage that could only take place at a cost to him that, based on her father's life, she was certainly in a position to weigh. But she wondered how she had found the resolve to refuse what she wanted more than breath

or food or life. And tomorrow he would be gone—by
her choice and because she loved him.

Jean watched her as, head lowered, she picked at
her food. When she looked up, she smiled questioningly at him, but he simply allowed his considering
gaze to rest on her unhappy face. There was nothing
he could do to alter what was happening here. She was
in love with the Englishman, as incredible to them
both as that might seem. And the only hope for the
fulfillment of what Jean wanted was if Devon and his
friend were successful in leaving France tomorrow.

"I think I'll make it an early night," Devon said finally, hiding his frustration over Julie's refusal to meet
his eyes. He pushed up from a gaming table in the salon where they had spread the remaining selection of
foods Jean had brought from the market. "Unless,
Julie, you want to try to improve my accent over the
next several hours?" he asked, a slight smile on his lips
as his eyes rested on her averted profile.

"No," she said simply. "Jean can try, but I'm going up, too. It's been a long day." She didn't turn to
face him, but continued to play with the edge of her
wineglass as if it were the most fascinating object she'd
ever encountered.

"No," Jean said, his eyes still on her face. "Pari-
sians don't think anyone else speaks French anyway.
Your accent's good enough that the guards will assume you're simply another provincial. And it's too
late for any last-minute tinkering. It either works, or
we end up as fellow guests of Fouché."

"Then good night," Devon said, and he stood a
moment watching her, waiting for some indication
that she felt as regretful about their estrangement as
he. He didn't want to walk out that door tomorrow

with her anger as the only legacy of the time they had spent together. Despite his assumed air of confidence, he was well aware of the odds of his leaving the Luxembourg Palace tomorrow.

Give me something, Julie, he thought, some sign that all that remains between us isn't this brittle politeness. He waited a long time, and then became aware the Frenchman was watching him with that mocking half smile. His eyes fixed for a moment on that arrogant face, and then he nodded his good-night and left the room.

It seemed she had made her choice, he thought as he walked away, and maybe that was for the best. At least there would be someone who would look after her when he was gone. Someone who cared perhaps as much as he did.

Devon was used to imposing his will by the sheer force of his personality on those around him. Early in his career his superiors had recognized that he was a born commander, his troops ready, if he led them, to attack hell itself. For him, leadership had always been easy. But with Julie, he acknowledged, he might as well be trying to force his will on Dominic.

With a reluctant grin, he contemplated what an interesting combination of personalities that would be. If only, he thought grimly, I can bring that meeting off. And then he began the climb to her father's bedroom to face a long night spent trying to forget what would occur in the morning—and the very real possibility that after tomorrow he might never see her again.

"Dev." The voice floated to him in the middle of the horror that held him, its concern pulling him away from the chains that confined him. He couldn't move, couldn't resist their weight, which was crushing the life out of him. He couldn't breathe. The darkness sat on his chest, hot and fetid, but he was helpless to fight its hold. Helpless.

"Devon," she said, and he struggled to find her voice, to use it to fight his way out of the mists of the nightmare. He hadn't dreamed about the paralysis that had been the immediate result of his injury in so long. He had pushed it deep into his mind, had buried it, denying its power to make him again its prisoner. And now once more it was here, its horror undiminished by the months that had passed.

"Devon, please. Wake up, darling. Whatever it is," she whispered, frightened by the shivering convulsions that still shook his entire frame.

He was drenched with sweat, the sheet clinging like cold hands to his nude body. It was always that way. God, he hated it. Hated the helplessness of that endless battle.

He was aware enough to know that her warm hands were touching him. He could feel them caressing his cheek, and he needed to know if he could also...

He took the slender fingers in his own and forced them over the muscles of his bare chest. He pushed hard against their softness, grinding his hand down over the light bones of hers, forcing it lower, over the ribs and then to the flat, ridged plane of his stomach. He had to know that he could really feel her touch against his skin.

And he could—not paralyzed, not helpless. With that realization, he suddenly relaxed his hold. He released her hand and allowed his own to fall to his side.

He tried to breathe naturally, to control the harsh gasps he could feel. He knew he was frightening her.

"What is it, Dev?" she said, her hand moving of its own volition against the smooth skin that covered the strength of his body, her intent not to arouse but to comfort, to soothe away whatever terror had gripped a man she knew to be absolutely fearless.

She shook her head at the frightening remembrances of his reckless courage. Whatever had caused this man to react in the way she had just witnessed was beyond her imagination.

She eased down on the bed to sit beside him. He was still breathing as if he had run a race. Long, hard breaths that shook his body. She could feel the clamminess of the sweat-drenched sheet against the warmth of her hip. She leaned over his chest and took his right hand in her left and felt the long fingers close tightly over hers. Her right hand continued to stroke the damp satin of his skin. And finally she watched the rigid muscles begin to relax under her touch.

Unconsciously, her thumb found the small peak of his nipple. She brushed over and around it, her eyes following the circling movements of her fingertips against the darker brown that surrounded it and then over the nipple itself, which suddenly pearled hard under her touch. She looked up to find the blue intensity of his gaze, aware now, on her face. This, at least, she would have to remember. She had touched him, had felt the strong, masculine length of him under her hands.

"It's all right," he said softly. "I'm sorry I woke you. It was just a nightmare."

"I thought I had seen nightmares," she teased gently, smiling at him, "but that—"

"I'm sorry. Did I—" He stopped the question, but she knew what he wanted to know and how much he would hate to ask.

"I heard you. I thought at first you were talking to Jean, and then there was something strange about what I heard. Your voice wasn't loud, but different. I didn't know what was happening, but I knew something was wrong. Do you want to tell me about it?" she invited. Her hand moved lower, fingertips following of their own accord down the ribs that were clearly marked under the overlaying muscle. Her thumb traced along the center channel of his chest to pause when it encountered the rough hair that began above his navel and disappeared under the twisted sheet that wrapped his hips.

Her touch was soothing to him, reassuring with each inch her fingers caressed that it was over, that he could feel, could move his legs, his arms, his hands. He raised his left hand and watched as the fingers flexed easily under his brain's command. God, he thought. I wonder if anyone ever appreciates what that means unless . . .

"Dev?" she said again, arrested by the wonder in the blue eyes. At her question, his gaze left the contemplation of the movement of his own fingers closing into a fist. He touched her chin with his knuckle and then used his thumb to trace over the softness of her bottom lip.

"Do you know . . ." he began, and his fingers spread to span the side of her face, to feel the fragile cheekbone, the fine brow, the small, delicate curl of her ear, the soft black strands of her hair. She allowed her head to lean into his touch, and turned her cheek to rub slightly against the palm.

"Do you have any idea how much it means to be able to touch you, to feel your smile start under my fingertips?" he asked softly, the motion of her lips against his thumb preceding his words by only a fraction of a second.

"No," she said, loving the tenderness in his voice, "but I'm willing to have you explain."

"It's like being dead and then coming to life again. Can you imagine what you would feel?" he asked.

She shook her head, and his palm cupped her face, savoring that movement.

"Did you dream you were dead?" she asked softly, thinking that would be horror enough, perhaps, to cause what she had seen.

"No," he whispered, "but I wanted to be. And I couldn't even manage that." The grim smile that lifted his lips was not directed at her, but she shivered at whatever emotion had caused it.

"Dev," she said again, to bring him back to her, and finally his eyes focused on her face.

"You must think—" he began, and then his eyes closed tight. "God, I can't imagine what you're thinking."

She looked down at the man she loved, and finally she whispered, uncaring of the consequences, "I think I'm about to show you what I think, my heart."

His eyes opened then at what was revealed in the husky whisper. She leaned down, giving him the opportunity to avoid her kiss, as she had moved to deny his today. Instead, his mouth opened, welcoming the hesitant invasion that remembered all they had shared before. His tongue slid smoothly, hot and demanding, against the brush of hers. She was so warm, so alive. And he had been so cold.

Her hands found his, locking tightly together with them to rest against the pillow on either side of his head, small fingers intertwined with strong brown ones. He used those locked hands to pull her down to lie against him, never stopping the cherishing movements deep within her mouth.

Her breasts, covered only by the thin silk of her nightgown, pressed into the steel of his chest. And at their contact she could feel the searing breath he took and heard the low groan from somewhere deep in his throat.

Life and death. The agony of the past and the uncertainty of the future. They were all mixed up in his mind. He hadn't had time to escape the throes of the nightmare, to find the control he needed to resist what she was offering, the temptation of feelings that were so much a part of what it meant to be alive.

And so he buried his tongue in the softness of her mouth as he wanted to bury his body, hard and tight, into the dark, honeyed warmth of hers. It had been so long. Such a long, aching, lonely time, and he knew that this woman had been made to ease that loneliness, had been created for him to love and to protect. He had never been as convinced of the rightness of anything in his life as of the rightness of Julie in his arms. No matter what the past, no matter even the future.

She raised her head and smiled into the smoky, sensual midnight of his eyes. He lay still as she touched her tongue to the corner of his mouth where his slow smile always began. She had wanted to do that for so long. She couldn't remember when she had first known that she wanted to touch him there. She dropped small kisses, relishing the salt-sweet taste of his skin. Her tongue smoothed across the skin of his eyelid and then down his nose to meet his mouth, which lifted, open to welcome her.

"Julie," he breathed as his lips moved, turning slightly to fit, as if they had always known their place under her mouth. His hands freed themselves to find her body. One slid possessively into the short, dark curls that touched her neck. His fingers opened until they cupped her head, holding her against the sweetly ravaging kiss. The other spread wide against the small of her back, hard fingers pressing insistently into the depression at the base of her spine. She arched into their touch like a cat.

He tightened his hold around her body and rolled, pulling her completely onto the bed with him, so that she lay on her back, the strength of his broad chest and wide shoulders leaning over her. His eyes watched her face and then, smiling, he lowered to find her lips.

Her hands moved to fit along his shoulders and then to steal around his neck, feeling the long line of the muscle that led from under the thick hair curling over his nape. Her fingers found, and had forgotten, the ridges of the scars she had seen that morning beside the stream. And they paused, afraid to hold, to smooth, to touch there, as she had been allowed to caress the rest of his body.

She became aware that his mouth had deserted hers, and that the blue eyes were shadowed with some question, but he waited. Finally with one finger she gently followed the longest of the weals she had felt.

"I'm afraid I'll hurt you, Dev," she whispered.

"They don't hurt," he said and then hesitated. "They're not sensitive, but if you'd rather not touch me there—"

She lifted her mouth to cover his, to stop whatever he had been about to suggest, and her hands moved across his back, unhindered by fear. She felt his muscles clench beneath her fingers as she deliberately deepened the kiss, drawing from his lips the reassurance that he wanted her. In spite of whatever motives had prompted his offer, in spite of the woman in London, here and now, at least, it was she he wanted.

"I want to touch you. I want to feel my lips on your body," he said softly. "I want to see you. Julie, just let me touch you. I just . . ."

As he whispered, his fingers found the narrow ribbons that held the tube of silk. They grazed against her skin as he used his thumbs to slide them over her shoulders and off her arms. And then his hand lifted to smooth the cool touch of the material away from her body.

Her breasts were small and perfect ivory globes, the tips touched with rose. As he watched, the nipples lifted as if straining toward his lips. She saw the smile catch the corner of his mouth, and felt the breath he gathered and held.

"I knew," he said softly, awe filling the deep voice, "I knew you would be this beautiful."

Her throat closed tight and hard. Touch me, her mind begged, but she couldn't speak, lost in the wonder she saw in the hard contours of his face.

And finally his thumb moved, as light as the breath of summer breeze, against the tip of one waiting breast. It rested there a moment, caught in the spell of her.

His fingers caressed under the milk white globe, lifting slightly, while his thumb moved, teasing, over the growing hardness of the rose nipple, exactly as hers had moved before against his body. Sensations, gliding like silk pulled through a ring, rippled deep, low inside her body. Her breath was thready, and she was mesmerized by what his eyes said and by what the hard fingers were doing. The smile she loved tilted the corners of his mouth at the pleasure that began to glow in her dark eyes.

And then slowly, her anticipation so great that his slowness was almost cruel, his head lowered. His tongue, warm and wet, circled where his thumb had been and then flicked with deliberate strength over the hardened bud. Some sound, like the caught breath of a child before the first tears, moved through her throat, and in response to that appeal, his tongue laved again, rough against the smoothness, soft against the hardness.

She watched the intimate movement of his mouth against her breast without any sense of reservation or of shame. This was Dev, and it was right.

With my body, I thee worship. The words came to her from some shred of memory, unfurling like ribbon in a brain that had almost ceased to think, lost in a body that craved only feel, touch, caress—but she knew with unshakable certainty that worshiping was what he was doing. With my body...

The waves of sensation that had begun to curl somewhere deep inside moved, arching upward to flicker like summer lightning into her stomach and downward through her thighs. Her knees were boneless, floating, and only he was aware that they had opened, already welcoming what he knew she wasn't ready for.

Not yet, my sweet, not now. But no one else will ever again touch you like this, he vowed silently. No one else. You are forever mine.

And thinking that, he allowed his mouth to finally possess her, to close over the reaching peak he had created. He suckled and heard again the softly gasping wonder of her response. His teeth found and captured, gently teasing as her body arched beneath his touch. He could feel his control slipping, draining from his mind as his body filled with desire, taut and demanding. If he didn't stop now . . .

And so the movement of his hard lips stopped; his tongue caressed once, twice, and then lifted away. He took a shuddering breath, its strength vibrating through the entire length of his body. Finally the blue eyes, starred as the night sky, raised to find hers, whose black lashes sparkled again with the diamonds of her tears.

"Julie," he said, leaning to kiss the moisture away, first one eye and then the other, tenderly caressing against the movement of closing lids. He moved back, and when she opened her eyes, he was smiling at her.

"Why are you crying, my beautiful Lady Luck? I'm the one who should cry. I have never seen anything as lovely as you are. Do you have any idea what you're doing to me?" he asked softly, trying to restore the discipline her shivering reaction to his mouth had destroyed.

Slowly she shook her head. His smile widened lovingly at what was reflected in her face as he took her hand and guided her fingers to brush lightly along the hard evidence of how much he wanted her. She pulled away from his hold as if she had been burned, and then she knew that she had. Branded by the knowledge that she could do that to him. He had made no effort to keep her fingers. She was so trusting in his arms, allowing him to do anything.

And with that thought, he realized he had been doing exactly what that bastard had accused him of. She wasn't his. At least not in the eyes of the church and the state. Not yet. But under heaven, he vowed, she will be. Because she is mine. We just proved that beyond any doubt. Regretfully he lifted the slender straps over her shoulders, the tempting beauty of her body at least covered by the sheer gown.

"I thought..."

"Don't," he whispered. "Don't say it. There are limits to whatever fragments of control I'm piecing together here. And the imposition of that control is a second-by-second operation. And you, my delight, are trying to shatter whatever I have left."

"I don't want you to have any control. I want to feel your mouth against me, Dev. I've thought about having you touch me there, wanted you to, since you kissed me in the salon. Oh, God, Dev, I'm so afraid that this will be all we'll have," she said. Tomorrow had intruded, had broken against the constraints they had placed on the world that had, until now, encompassed only this room, this bed.

"If—" he began.

"No. No *if's*. I don't want to hear them. We have tonight. You know this may be all we ever have. Please, Dev. No *if's*." And she watched his eyes, and hoped.

His face was relaxed, the harsh emotion of the nightmare defeated by the effects of what they had just shared. She knew he had forgotten whatever horrors had driven him into her arms. Whatever had stolen the self-control he had promised. He lay on his side beside her, the long length of his body touching hers. She could still feel the heaviness of his erection against her thigh.

He was silent a long time, and she wondered what he was thinking. And then his hand lifted to find her trembling lips, already anticipating its movement against her body. He let his fingers follow the line of her throat, the silk of her skin contrasting to the rough, callused palm that paused briefly to hold the slim column of her neck, savoring the movement of the pulse at its base. He allowed his hand to brush down her body, and it was large enough to span the peaks of both breasts. He felt their response and saw her eyes close, the lids dropping suddenly at the flood of warmth, stealing again, coiling hungrily in her body.

Down to touch the depression of her navel, outlined against the fine material of her gown. His hand turned, the fingertips moving lower to rest at the beginning of the V made by the joining of her slender legs that were still relaxed, waiting for his body to move between them. Empty and waiting for him. And then he stopped, his palm holding the slight convexity of her belly. She opened her eyes finally, wondering why the seductive movement of hard flesh against the smooth glide of the silk had ceased.

"And what if..." he began, and the picture that had stopped his hand, the image of her slender, perfect body filled, tight and hard, with his child, caught at his throat. He wanted to make love to her more than he had ever wanted any other woman. But she was, he discovered, capable of arousing emotions he had never felt before. He had never even dreamed of creating a child, never even thought of how he would feel to hold the turning movement of his son under his palm, inside the body of the woman he loved, separated from his hand only by the warm velvet of her skin. And now the vision was so strong he could almost sense the stretching movement of tiny limbs.

"I'm not walking into Fouché's hands tomorrow with the possibility that you're carrying my son, a son I might never see."

She hadn't realized what he had been thinking. His touch had been so gentle that she had simply been lost in the caressing tenderness of whatever he was feeling, but this... Only after he spoke did she know how much she wanted the reality of the image he had just created.

"Dev," she whispered and lifted to kiss the lips that had just given birth to a dream.

He met her mouth, allowed a brief and insubstantial touch against all she had hoped for. And then he moved away from the reach of her lips and removed his hand from her body.

"After tomorrow. After I find Dominic. Then, Lady Luck, you and I have an appointment," he promised softly.

"But—"

"You're my luck. After tomorrow," he said and touched a finger against her mouth to stop the questions he could see in her eyes. "Go back to bed before I forget all my good intentions. And Julie, I don't want to see you in the morning. If—" he began, and remembered that she had rejected those possibilities. And said instead, "I want to remember only this. Here and now."

And because he had given her no choice, she nodded.

He lowered his head suddenly, and his lips closed around one small, rounded breast. His mouth pulled strongly, the silk no barrier to the movement of his tongue against her skin. She cried out softly against the sudden heat that jarred deep within her body, roiling and arching, so intense it was almost on the edge of pain. She hadn't known anything could feel like his mouth, moving warm and darkly demanding against her softness.

She wasn't aware that her fingers had found his shoulders, nails biting deeply into the scars she had touched so tentatively before. Unaware and uncaring now that she was hurting him. She wanted into his skin, to become a part of him, and she would not even have known how to find release for those feelings. She only knew she wanted, and he was leaving her unsatisfied. Unsatisfied as he was.

She heard his quiet, delighted laughter at her response, and then he had encircled her body in hard arms that held her crushed tightly enough against him to deny the possibility of any separation, protected as only Devon could.

"After tomorrow," his lips promised against the smoothness of her skin. She could feel his warm breath on her temple, and then his mouth rested over her own to whisper, "After tomorrow, I promise, my Lady Luck."

He leaned back and lifted her hand like a courtier. She stepped down from the high bed, one bare foot finding the floor, hoping her trembling knees would be strong enough to support her.

She thought nothing in her life had been harder to do than to leave the shadowed safety of this room, but because she loved him, she trusted him and, for once, obeyed. But she touched him again, slender fingers tracing lightly across the shivering skin of his chest, and then she moved away, beyond arm's length, removing herself from the temptation that was his body. She turned finally and slipped across the room, her bare feet making no sound on the thick carpets.

He lay awake a long time after she had left, her body's perfume tangled in the sheet he pulled up over the stinging marks she had made on his shoulders. The image of Julie cradling a child they had created moved into all the dark corners that his nightmare had occupied and erased the premonitions about tomorrow. He fought the force of his blackest memories with the promise of ones yet to be made, and finally, when he closed his eyes, there was nothing of that darkness that remained.

Chapter Ten

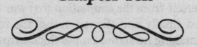

The doctor's elegant carriage stopped close to the service entrance of the palace. The morning's cold had already given way to a springlike sunshine that made the guards on duty relaxed and desirous of escape from their posts along the gray portico at the rear of the building. The entertainment that had begun in the courtyard almost a half hour earlier had pulled everyone who wasn't as confined as they to watch the Gypsy girl's hands tantalize even the wise eyes of this urban audience. From the kitchens and offices of the gracious stone edifice the watchers had wandered, drawn by the sense of excitement that had floated like a pleasant aroma through these businesslike halls.

And now, almost the only workers who were not being entertained by the laughing eyes of the magician who moved the shells over the elusive ball were those standing disconsolately isolated from the amusement, still tied to the duty of guarding the entrance to the corridor leading to the prison area.

The figure that stepped down from the coach was tall and stooped, bent perhaps with age. And then the guards noticed the heavy cane and the way the lean body rested painfully against its support a moment, gathering strength before he would be forced to begin the halting journey to their door. The black satchel marked his profession for them, confirmed by the severity of the finely cut frock coat and the elegant hat he wore.

The doctor allowed his eyes to glance toward the crowd at the far end of the square, which was formed by the shape of the building's wings. The Gypsy girl's dark curls were occasionally visible through the heads of the taller watchers who surrounded the portable table. He could hear her laughter clearly, along with the morning noises of bird song and the traffic along the street. And then, as if pulling himself back to the unpleasant demands of his duty, he limped heavily to the guards' station.

He waved a dismissing hand at their challenge, and at the assured gesture, the barrels of the rifles they held lifted away from the doorway across which they had perfunctorily dropped. The soft, muttering explanation he had begun was halted as he thrust the bag he carried in his left hand at one of the guards. He never looked at the man whose fingers closed over the handle in automatic response. Instead, with an eloquent groan the doctor used his left hand to lift the crippled right leg up over the threshold of the entry. Then gripping the stone facing with that same hand, he used that and the cane to support the leg as he pulled the left one up alongside it. That painful maneuver accomplished, his fingers fumbled in his waistcoat pocket for a large white handkerchief with which he wiped his forehead, careful not to dislodge the gray wig he wore.

"Gout," he grunted finally in explanation, calling forth a smiling condolence from the younger and a

head-shaking tsk from the other. "The disease of
kings," he offered, stuffing the handkerchief untidily
back into his vest pocket. He reached for the satchel,
which was politely replaced in his outstretched fingers.

"But not of emperors." The guard laughed as he
released the bag. Louis XVIII's suffering from that
infirmity was widely known, but as the soldier reminded them all, no longer of concern to any loyal
Frenchman. Bonaparte was not a victim.

"Thank God," the doctor said softly and, leaning
on his stick, took two steps into the shadowed hall. He
paused as if confused and asked over his shoulder.
"Fouché's pet?" he questioned and hoped.

"To the left along the corridor and then the first
right. The third cell. It's rather a distance." The young
guard's apologetic voice hesitated.

"No matter. When Fouché commands..." the
doctor said and began his limping journey.

As the visitor disappeared into the gloom of the interior corridor, the guards turned back, their attention once more directed toward the laughter of the
crowd in the courtyard.

Devon paused briefly at the turning, as if resting.
His performance down the secondary hallway was as
convincing as his earlier one. There was a quick flare
of interest in the eyes of the huge guard who stood
duty before the door of the cell he sought, but he could
almost see the mental relaxation as the mud-colored
eyes appraised the limping figure. He wondered briefly
if Jean's doubts about his ability to handle this giant
might have been justified, and then he no longer allowed himself to even consider the possibility that he

could fail. Not now, he thought. Not this close to success.

He gestured imperiously at the door when he reached it and again made a show of mopping his forehead, a show that had effectively hidden his features, as he waited while the thick fingers fumbled for the key.

When the metal latch released with a discernible clang, he waved vaguely back along the passage he had so painfully traversed.

"I'll need water, hot water from the kitchens," he ordered, and then entered the cell without waiting to see if his command had been obeyed. He was not surprised, however, to hear the retreating footsteps fade into the distance over the stones behind him. A few minutes alone with Dominic, to assess his strength and tinker with the plan according to what he judged the duke would be capable of.

His eyes gradually adjusted to the dimness to find the figure of his brother-in-law. The Duke of Avon was sitting on the low bed that appeared to be the only furnishings of the room. His shoulders, covered by a coarse cotton shirt, were propped with his usual elegant grace against the wall behind the bed. His right leg was stretched out along the mattress, but the left had swung off the bed to touch the floor. Devon was relieved to see that he was dressed, dark trousers covering the long length of leg and his feet in low boots. Except for the terrible thinness and the increased spread of silver that fanned back from his temples into the coal-blackness of his uncut hair, he appeared, reassuringly, the same.

The silver eyes rested without surprise on his face, but the firm lips were touched lightly with his smile.

"You have every right to ask," Devon said softly, and watched the familiar lift of one dark brow in questioning response.

"To ask what took me so long." He explained his attempt at humor. Almost before the words had left his mouth, the eyes of the man on the bed shifted to the right, and the cold muzzle of a rifle was thrust against the artery that pulsed under Devon's jaw. In the sudden stillness he could feel the increased tempo of his heartbeat thud against that rigid tip.

Avon's silver eyes were again on his face, and Devon managed to whisper past the sick disappointment of his failure, "How long?"

"They've been here over an hour," the duke answered softly. "Waiting."

Betrayed, Devon thought bitterly, and his hot rage made him wonder fleetingly if he could move quickly enough to wrest away the muzzle. But his hands were still encumbered by the props he carried, and the rifle of the other soldier rested with unwavering certainty on Avon, who might be unable to move quickly enough to escape a ball if he started anything. And with the report of the gun, the other guards would come. Betrayed, he thought again with hatred, as the options presented themselves in a series of lightning images, each of which was rejected by the quick fighter's brain. No chance. Not now. Not and get Dominic out, too. And so he waited, praying that there would be another opportunity.

The door opened behind him, and the guard reappeared, without, of course, the requested hot water. At a gesture from one of the soldiers standing in tableau to Devon's left, his massive figure lumbered across the cell and lifted Avon in his muscular arms. The duke quickly hid whatever emotion had stirred momentarily in the too-thin, harshly controlled face. Pain or humiliation or both, Devon wondered briefly, as Dominic was carried, as easily as if he had been a child, across the stone floor. The increased pressure of the muzzle was used to guide Devon out of the way, but the soldier's eyes never left his face, anticipating any sudden action.

The giant skillfully turned the long body in his arms to facilitate their movement through the doorway, and then he and his burden disappeared into the shadows.

The soldier's eyes directed his prisoner to follow. Devon moved also through the cell door, the satchel and stick still held loosely in either hand. His long stride, however, in no way resembled that which he had adopted in his passage down the corridor.

"Fouché's orders." The familiar mocking voice was audible now. The sunlight ahead of them filtered from the open courtyard into the gray recesses of the prison. The speaker was silhouetted against the entrance, explaining something to the guards who had been so sympathetic to the physician's disability. Devon's mind identified and accepted the reality of the voice, and with an unspeakably painful effort he fought to restrain his rage.

"And I'll sign for the release of your prisoner," the speaker continued, folding and returning to his breast pocket whatever document he had been showing. "We intend to interrogate all of them at the ministry. Your cooperation in the capture of these additional conspirators will be noted on your record of service. My congratulations on a job well done."

The trace of officious condescension in Jean's voice had been obvious to both Englishmen, but the soldiers appeared to preen under his commendation, accepting his praise as sincere and as their due.

The Frenchman moved away from the door to allow the enormous figure room to maneuver the prisoner he carried through the entryway. The duke's silver eyes rested briefly on the scarred face that quickly disappeared from their gaze as Avon was carried into the sunlight and toward the waiting carriage.

Devon, however, had the opportunity to convey all the contempt he felt for the man who had betrayed them. His cold blue eyes locked on that marred face. The hazel eye allowed the meeting, lazily and sardonically accepting his hatred. He bowed with courtly elegance to the Englishman who walked under the watching bores of the two rifles trained on his spine.

"And I think you may safely relieve our friend of his theatrical trappings," Jean instructed. Devon allowed the props to be taken from his fingers, and removing the wig, handed them that also. His hands, now, at least were free. As he moved toward the waiting carriage, Devon's mind began to hope. The Gargantua was carefully arranging Avon into the seat, and Devon could see the cost of that procedure in the perspiring features of his friend. But he knew that if they allowed him to also enter those confines, he could count on Dominic's support of whatever he could devise that might give them a chance. Their opportunities were surely better in the carriage, a conveyance that offered a means of transportation for the duke, in spite of his condition, the seriousness of which was becoming more obvious with each passing minute.

Wait, Devon urged against his anger. Wait and think. You'll only have one chance, and it must be the right one.

"Get the Gypsy." The traitorous voice spoke from somewhere behind him. "She's one of them, too. A diversion."

A soldier who had been standing by the carriage when they emerged from the building started toward the crowd, still focused on the flashing promise of the shells.

They all watched as the trooper efficiently scattered the spectators to their forgotten obligations and pulled the slim, writhing figure across the cobblestones that separated them. As she had in the village, she fought every foot of the way, but she was too small to do any real damage.

Devon flinched against the casual backhanded blow the guardsman gave her when she managed to bite fingers that had foolishly moved within reach of her teeth. The rifle's muzzle, which Devon had felt sliding down his shoulder, and by which he had been judging the distraction of the two soldiers behind him, shifted again into vigilance at his reflexive response to that slap. Not wise, he reminded himself and fought to relax the tension that corded the muscles of his shoulders.

The soldier laughingly controlled her, and the struggling duo moved closer, ever closer to where he stood waiting. And it seemed that his prayers were about to be answered as she was being dragged to become a passenger in the coach on which now rested the frail hope of escape. And then the dark voice spoke again behind him.

"No," the Frenchman ordered authoritatively. "Not in the carriage. She'll go with me. Put her on one of the horses. I have some special entertainment planned for the girl."

All he had to do, Devon thought, the plan instantly leaping into his mind at the implication of those words, was to inflict enough damage on the three people surrounding him to allow Julie to reach the driver's seat. Or if Dominic must be sacrificed, to reach one of the waiting horses and to make a bolt for freedom. The huge guard who had carried Dominic had disappeared somewhere behind his line of vision, but he couldn't be sure he had reentered the building. However, it was a chance he had to take. In the distraction he planned to cause, Julie should be able to break away from the one soldier holding her.

Think, my darling, he prayed, the muscles in his legs gathering for the movement that would provide the distraction that might allow her to take the opportunity to flee.

The odds seemed fair, as long as Julie would be safe. And if this failed, they would be, perhaps, no worse than they were now. At least he would have the opportunity to get in a blow or two on that scarred bastard.

"Too bad all these elaborate plans were destined to fail, my friend," Jean's voice taunted, closer to him than he had dared hope.

Devon knew where the enemy was, and he could still feel the tip of one of the rifles resting lightly against his shoulder. He dropped suddenly, his body turning and his quick hands reaching to grasp the muzzle. He used it like a scythe, swinging in a hard arc against the temple of the man from whose surprised hands he had wrenched it. And then back, to strike with a thud against the skull of the other soldier who had stood dumbfounded by the speed of the attack.

He turned then to the Frenchman, and allowed himself a brief moment of satisfaction at the shock that had, as yet, arrested any reaction. Two down, he thought grimly and swung the improvised club again. Jean lifted his arm to ward off the blow that struck painfully against his raised forearm instead of the side of his head.

Before Devon could recover from the momentum of that swing, the Frenchman dropped street-fighter quick and barreled his shoulder into the Englishman's stomach. The movement threw Devon back to crash heavily against the side of the coach. As always in battle, the adrenaline was pouring into his system so that he was barely aware of the pain. He managed a hard right into Jean's gut and heard the grunting response. Due to the closeness of the carriage door behind his elbow, he had not been able to get enough force into the blow to do a great deal of damage. He worried briefly that the remaining soldier hadn't joined the fight. Surely, with this going on, he wasn't still holding Julie.

"You stupid, arrogant son of a bitch," Jean said under his breath. He then began to curse softly and very fluently while he struggled to control the muscled arms that fought to free themselves enough to strike another, more successful, blow. Neither was aware that the carriage door on the far side had opened to welcome the scrambling figure of the girl, who was helped into the safety of its enclosure by the man inside.

"Get into the carriage, you idiotic bastard," Jean ordered desperately and was relieved to see, finally, the third soldier appear peripherally in his line of sight.

"Help me get him into the carriage," he grated in relief, just before Devon's knee slammed up hard into the vulnerable area between his legs. The Frenchman's body went limp with the agony of the blow, and he fell to his knees, retching, against the cobblestones. Devon turned to meet the advance of the remaining member of the opposition, who appeared to be approaching with reluctance.

The Englishman backed against the coach, waiting in the loose, relaxed crouch of a born fighter. He was surrounded by the groaning bodies of three of the soldier's comrades. The remaining man looked as if he might be considering whether he was getting paid enough to get killed.

Strong fingers reaching from the window of the coach at his back found the vital arteries on either side of Devon's neck and pressed hard, skillfully blocking the passage of blood to the brain. Devon's hands lifted to pull against their constriction, but already the air was beginning to shroud with mist and the scene before him to darken. The soldier, suddenly realizing his opportunity, darted daringly to direct a fist against the unprotected chin. Devon's head rocked back with smashing force against the frame of the carriage door, and he dropped like a stone, a victim of the combined assault.

"Dev. My God," Julie cried from inside the carriage as he fell, "you're going to kill him."

Through the efforts of the soldier and of the huge guard, who had finally responded to the commotion, his limp body was lifted easily, if not gently, into the coach. She could see the giant toss a comment over his shoulder to the guards at the door, who had started to come out into the square. At whatever he said, the two returned to their positions. It did, indeed, appear that the fight was over.

As Julie cradled Devon's head in her lap, wondering what damage had been done in the struggle, the men who had just loaded him into the coach turned to help Jean. In response to his angry rejection of their attentions and his agonized whisper, the soldier mounted the driver's box while the guard helped the two who had been injured by Devon's improvised club. But it only took a few minutes to gather their weapons and mount the waiting horses, the proceedings watched by the prison guards, except for the giant, who had disappeared into the palace.

In short order the small procession, led by Jean, whose fury was clear both from the set of his shoulders and from the livid features, was riding out of the sunlit courtyard and into the main thoroughfare that would lead to their destination.

The man seated opposite Julie in the carriage watched her slim fingers smooth Devon's disordered hair as she bent to kiss his lips, slightly parted in unconsciousness. When she raised her head, she met for the first time the impact of the Duke of Avon's silver gaze. One dark brow rose in response to what was in her face.

"Why did you do that?" she said, disbelief coloring her voice. She had just watched the Avon's sure fingers render his friend, his rescuer, his brother-in-law, unconscious. "How could you possibly..." She stopped as the amusement he had been feeling at her genuine puzzlement was allowed to move finally into

the dark, classically perfect features of the man who
watched her from across Devon's body.

"Because someone had obviously made a serious
error in judgment. And if I didn't do something rather
quickly, I was afraid our friend here was going to spoil
it all. And it was such an entertaining farce, my dear.
Your idea?" he suggested softly, smiling at her.

Her mouth was suddenly dry at the force of that
smile and at the intelligence in the unusual gray eyes
that rested on her face in absolute enjoyment and with
sincere compliment.

She nodded slowly, arrested by his reaction, but
compelled to answer by some force in the gentle question.

"But Devon wasn't allowed to know all the details?" the low voice continued softly. "And no one,
of course, thought that he would be foolish enough to
take on a garrison?"

She shook her head, ashamed now that she had
agreed with Jean's assessment of the Englishman. She,
who had seen, who had known what he was capable
of, had allowed Jean to make her doubt him.

"We never dreamed..." she began, then faltered as
the duke's beautiful mouth slanted quickly into a
smile.

"Then I assume your acquaintance with my brother-
in-law has been brief," Avon said, amusement in the
rich voice. "And he nearly carried it off. I wonder
what you would have done had he left the members of
our escort too seriously injured to carry out their pretended duties. If they had been replaced by real soldiers from the detail assigned to the palace—"

"Don't," she begged softly, shivering. "I didn't
think— No one would have believed he could—"

"I would have," the duke said with conviction, "but then obviously I know him far better than you. I would have known exactly what action Colonel Burke would have taken under those circumstances. You should have told him, Mademoiselle de Valmé. It would have been far easier on him." His eyes dropped deliberately to watch the slim fingers, which had been unconsciously caressing Devon's face. "And, I think, on you."

"How do you know who I am?" she breathed, but it took him a moment to answer.

Color stole suddenly into her throat and cheeks when she noticed, as he had, of course, intended, that he was watching her touch his brother-in-law with the familiar, rather possessive fingers of a lover. At that unexpected blush, Avon, who was very wise in the ways of women, revised his opinion of the one seated opposite him, an opinion that had been based on her profession and on her reputation.

Whatever his sources had led him to believe about Ashford's daughter was obviously not the entire story. Not considering that revealing blush, and certainly not if Devon were involved with her. The duke pulled his thoughts away from that interesting possibility to answer her question.

"Who else could you be?" he suggested softly. "Besides, I was in Paris watching your father's establishment for several days before Fouché—" He stopped suddenly, the remembrance of all that had been done to him blocking his explanation with a flood of emotions so strong he was powerless against its force. He closed his eyes, fighting the weakness that had stolen his usual iron discipline, and then locked the dark door of those memories.

Julie watched him struggle to regain control. He made himself open his eyes and continue the answer he had begun. "And I had heard a variety of descriptions of the Divine Juliette."

He had meant nothing disparaging by his use of the nickname all of Paris called her. But had he not been lost in a battle with his own demons, Avon would never have unthinkingly inflicted the pain that was reflected in the white face raised to his.

She blocked that reaction to his knowledge of her reputation to ask the obvious question.

"But even so, how could you possibly have known that they weren't Fouché's soldiers? That it was all..." She stopped and shook her head.

"Some slight difficulties with their uniforms. A grenadier's belt on an infantryman's uniform. A minor problem with regimental insignia on another. Who are they?" Avon finished his critique to ask.

"An out-of-work actor, a mountebank, gamblers Jean knew. I don't really know. They all owed Jean money. I suppose it must have been a lot of money to make them willing to take the chances they did. The uniforms came from a rag shop. We thought they would..." She paused, embarrassed by their obvious errors.

"I had a great deal of time to study them," the duke said forgivingly. "But Dev... It would have taken Devon only one glance to sum up their deception. I'm sorry that he didn't have that opportunity." His eyes moved consideringly to his brother-in-law, whose head still rested in the girl's lap.

Her eyes followed his, and their drop allowed the duke the opportunity to study her. He saw the small thumb brush over the abrasion on the chin of the man she held.

Dev looked so helpless, she thought, so defenseless. And then she smiled slightly, thinking that he had been anything but defenseless. He had almost foiled it, had almost defeated them all. He had only been stopped by the collusion of someone who knew him so well and who, for his sake, had mounted a rear assault.

"God, I hope..." she said softly, thinking out loud, and then she paused, knowing how Devon would hate any expression of concern about him.

"He'll be all right," Avon reassured, wishing he were as certain as he sounded. "He's survived far more serious injuries than that."

"I know. I've seen—" she began softly and then stopped in embarrassment. The duke's eyes lifted suddenly to her face at that unconscious disclosure of the intimacy of her relationship with Devon.

"But don't tell him I told you that," she finished, knowing it was too late to deny what she had just revealed. And then for the first time Avon was exposed to the teasing sparkle in the smiling eyes that had enslaved half the men in the French capital.

The duke glanced again at his brother-in-law, lying in the arms of a woman who clearly loved him very much. His eyes closed tightly as the memory of Emily in his arms flooded his body, hot and demanding, moving with all its remembered heat into his groin. He took a deep breath and looked up to find the girl watching him anxiously.

"Are you all right?" she asked softly, concern for him written in her features. This was Devon's friend.

"No," he whispered finally, "but I will be. If I can just get home, I will be." He leaned his head against the side of the coach, suddenly exhausted, the limits of his uncertain strength reached, as they often were now, without warning. "If . . ." he breathed.

"No *if's*," she said softly, seeing the beautiful profile revealed in sharpened purity by his ordeal. Although he didn't answer or lift the fall of thick black lashes that hid the charcoal-rimmed silver irises, she knew he had heard her. The corners of his mouth stole upward in response, and watching, she thought irrelevantly that she liked his smile also. She wondered if she might watch for it with the same anticipating pleasure with which she had always waited for Dev's.

With that thought her eyes fell again to Devon's face. No, she revised, there will never be anyone whose smile I'll long to see as I do yours. She remembered the gentle weight of his hand resting against her stomach and thought about a child of his growing there. She tried to banish that image, and then suddenly wondered why she shouldn't be allowed to think about what he had suggested.

Everyone is entitled to dreams, she told herself. Even if they are aware that they'll never come true, everyone is allowed to have them. She brushed the tips of her fingers against his forehead, the sunlight from the carriage window alternating there with the shadows cast by the tall trees that lined the road they took. And at the end of that road, she knew what she had to do. But until that time . . .

Until that time, my darling, at least I, too, am allowed to dream.

Chapter Eleven

Julie didn't open her eyes again until the motion of the coach began to slow. She didn't think she had slept, as her companions still did. Surely Jean wouldn't have called a rest this close to the city.

When the carriage had come to a full stop and was standing under the shadows of the trees, the voices that floated back to her weren't loud, nor should their indistinct cadences have been enough to cause the frisson of fear that was her immediate reaction. That was caused because she knew that whatever was happening now was not part of the carefully devised scheme she had outlined in detail to Jean.

She glanced down at Devon and was surprised to find that his eyes were open, watching her face. And he was obviously listening with the same breathless concentration that held her motionless to whatever was now happening in the road before them. They heard the clattering movement of several horses, the unmistakable jingling noises of armed men riding. Then through the windows they watched as their disreputable crew of mock soldiers was replaced by a group whose extreme efficiency of maneuvering left no doubt that here, at last, was the real thing.

The coach began to move again, and the pace was far sharper than that at which they had been traveling. It no longer mattered, it seemed, if they attracted attention. Indeed, it would be impossible not to, surrounded as they were by a detachment of hussars.

She was unprepared for the upward movement of the body that had rested so quietly in her lap. Devon had noticed Avon half-sitting, half-lying on the facing seat. The duke's eyes were closed, and he rested against the wall of the coach. It was apparent by the unchecked motion of his head in response to the pitch of the rapidly moving vehicle that he was unconscious.

Devon grasped Dominic's thin, white wrist, which lay limply in his strong fingers. She could read the worry in his face as he felt the faintness of the pulse. His eyes, filled with concern, lifted to meet hers. "Julie?" he asked, but she shook her head.

"He talked to me," she said, watching the man she loved care for his friend. She smiled in remembrance of the duke's gentle teasing. "And then he just went to sleep. At least, I thought he was asleep. What's wrong with him, Dev?"

"I don't know. Maltreatment. Starvation. The results of the fever Jean described. But surely by now..." he began and then discarded the possibility that Avon might be more ill than he had thought.

"Maybe it's just exhaustion. He was strong enough to—" she stopped suddenly, and the blue eyes swung to her face at the hesitation.

"Strong enough to what?" he questioned.

"He's the one who stopped you. He did something to your neck, and then the soldier hit you. I think the coach really did most of the damage."

She stopped, his face clearly indicating that what she was explaining made no sense.

"Avon stopped me? Is that what you're suggesting? That Dominic would try to keep me from getting us out of there?"

"No," she said, smiling, "but he would try to stop you from ruining everything. And you almost did. It was a trick, Dev. Deception. The prison officials thought they were helping foil an attempted escape. Jean had forged papers ordering them to cooperate with him, to catch you trying to free the English spy. He hired the fake soldiers, bought the forged documents, everything.

"But we thought that it would be more believable if you reacted naturally. If you thought you really had been betrayed. We couldn't be sure, of course, of your acting ability. I'm sorry, Dev, but we never dreamed that you'd react like you did. And then no one could stop you. So the duke did," she finished her explanation.

"Then if what happened at the palace was a deception, what's taking place now?" He halted, waiting for her explanation.

"I don't know," she admitted. "It's not part of anything I planned," she continued. "I don't—"

"You planned?" The disbelief was dangerously evident.

"It was my plan we used for the escape. Jean had to carry out the details. He was the only one who could go into the city to make the arrangements. But the plan was mine. I thought your scheme needed a few diversions, a little deception," she mocked, suddenly tired of his continued denial of her values, of the methods used in her world. "What we did worked. At least until you decided to slay dragons instead of giving in to overwhelming odds, as we'd anticipated any sensible person would. Jean said if you'd been a soldier, it would be obvious to you that there was no way..."

Her voice faded. Overwhelming odds or not, he had defeated them. Had it not been for Avon's intervention, Devon would have accomplished what they had never even dreamed he might attempt.

"Then you have no idea who these soldiers are or where they're taking us?" he asked.

"No," she whispered. "But I'm afraid that, in spite of it all, we haven't succeeded."

"Fouché," he said softly. "Damn him. He has probably expected an attempt to rescue Avon since he was captured. He's probably just been lying in wait for whoever was foolish enough to try it."

"We knew the odds were very long."

"Which is why I never wanted you involved," he said softly. "Why didn't you listen to me, Julie? By now, you'd be safely away in the care of the Gypsy."

"Because," she told him truthfully, "no matter what happens, I'd rather be here with you. No matter what, Dev."

Devon recognized where they had been brought as soon as the carriage and its escort wheeled into the entrance. The Emperor had made the Tuileries Palace his headquarters when he'd entered Paris. Fouché would almost certainly have rushed here to reestablish the old comradeship with Napoleon.

Soon, he supposed, they would be forced to face the man who had led them all to this moment by plotting his own climb to power months ago. A climb that had been threatened only by the existence of Avon's network. Devon suspected Fouché feared his proposed coup, which would replace the Bourbon king with a claimant controlled by Fouché himself, would be exposed to the outside world before it could be carried out. So he had set out to destroy the network, and then, having lured the duke to Paris, to destroy Avon himself.

But with the arrival of Napoleon in France, Fouché had obviously decided that Avon might be more valuable alive than dead—hostage, pawn. No one would ever know why that twisted mind had made the decision to move Avon from the dungeon. Perhaps, as Jean had suggested, the duke had been carried up to share his cell simply as a test of the gambler's involvement. But whatever its original purpose, that move had brought the duke within reach of rescue. A rescue that had now, apparently, failed.

Devon's speculation about Fouché's motives was interrupted by the halting of the carriage. He glanced again at Avon's pale face, and his lips tightened in frustration. Dominic had already suffered so much at the hands of the French.

They were very professionally guarded as they unloaded the coach, and the litter on which the soldiers carried the duke inside had disappeared before the others were herded into the courtyard.

The room to which they were finally brought was a simple office. Maps and charts and dispatches were spread in a seemingly careless array over the surface of the huge table that dominated. The rest of the furnishings were plain, almost Spartan, in comparison to those of the rooms they had passed through on their way here.

The small, dark man standing behind the table looked up briefly at their entrance. He took the time to make a carefully considered mark on the map he was studying. Then he gestured dismissal, and the young officer who had escorted them here saluted, turned on his heel and, closing the door behind him, left them alone with the Emperor of France.

Napoleon's black eyes had dropped to his map again even before the young lieutenant shut the door. He rubbed his chin a moment and moved to another position to study from a different angle the terrain and then the notations he had made. And finally he seemed to become aware of the presence of the three who waited before him.

"I am led to understand that you carried out quite an entertaining diversion at the Luxembourg Palace this morning. Let me congratulate you on the daring of your attempt. However, I'm sure you must realize that I could not allow you to spirit such a valuable political prisoner out of France."

"Then they weren't Fouché's soldiers," Devon said softly, trying to think what the Emperor's hand in the game might mean.

"The Duc d'Otrante," the Emperor corrected carefully, using Fouché's proper title, which he himself had bestowed, "*has* no soldiers. Only Bonaparte commands the soldiers of France," he said. "My minister of police seems to have forgotten that. He arranged for your capture and conveyance here. He had also hoped to meet with you personally, but I'm afraid he has been . . . detained." His slight smile suggested his amusement at the thought of Fouché's frustration over his interference. Devon remembered what Julie had told him about the relationship between the two. Napoleon used Fouché, but he didn't trust him. He even spied on his own minister of police. Apparently that was how he had known of their capture. But he couldn't imagine why Bonaparte had chosen to interfere.

"I've sent a physician to see to your friend," Napoleon said to Devon, the accent of Corsica still coloring his French. "Not my personal physician, who unfortunately is not in attendance at the present. But an army surgeon, a very good one. I understand that the duke's treatment since his capture by the minister of police has not been particularly gentle."

"Fouché wasn't your minister of police when he imprisoned the Duke of Avon," Devon commented carefully. By the slight tightening of the Emperor's lips he knew that both the points he had just made had been acknowledged.

"The Duc d'Otrante has occasionally been known to assume powers that do not rest within his domain. I am aware he was not acting in an official capacity when he imprisoned the duke. However—"

"The Duke of Avon is a fully accredited representative of the Court of St. James's. I am sure that, as such, he falls under the protection of the sovereign of France. Although, of course, it was not to this government that his diplomatic mission was undertaken. Even so, an ambassador of His Royal Highness, the Prince Regent, would certainly not be subjected to any further disrespect by the French Crown." Devon's face was perfectly calm. It was the highest level of bluff. A game of diplomacy played against a master.

"An ambassador from the Court of St. James's?" the Emperor questioned softly, his amusement deliberately revealed at this reckless maneuver.

"Indeed, Your Majesty. If, however, you would care to assure yourself of the Duke of Avon's credentials, I'm certain—"

"Of course. We are all certain." Bonaparte gestured impatiently at the formal language of the protest. "But whatever the English Crown would now claim, you and I both know why Avon came to France."

"I know if an accredited diplomat who holds one of the oldest titles in England suffers any harm while in your court what the nations assembled at Vienna will do."

Devon was aware that he was threatening the man who had controlled almost all of Europe. A man whose power over their lives was still undisputed. He could do what he liked here and worry about diplomatic repercussions later.

"Do you think they could hate or fear me any more than they already do?" the Emperor questioned softly.

For the first time Devon was allowed to feel the power that emanated from this potbellied, insignificant-looking man, dressed in the simple green uniform of his own Chasseurs of the Guard, who was leaning, both hands resting on the annotated map before him. And Devon knew that he was deliberately being made aware of the Emperor's displeasure.

"And you?" The Emperor's soft voice was not in any way threatening, but Julie shivered suddenly. "And are you, too, an accredited representative of the English Crown?"

Both Devon and the Emperor were aware that whatever protection the Court of St. James's chose to exert on behalf of the Duke of Avon, it would not extend to his brother-in-law. And so Devon told the truth, a truth that he hoped would still mean something to Bonaparte.

"No," he said, and there was a quiet arrogance in the claim with which he answered Napoleon's question. "I'm not a diplomat. I'm only a soldier."

There was a pause while that information was evaluated. Devon's carriage and something indefinable about the pride with which he had brazenly spoken appealed to the general's mind which still dominated Bonaparte's thinking.

"But my soldiers wear uniforms. And you don't appear to be wearing one. Perhaps you have fought for your country in a different way. Perhaps you, like your friend, have chosen espionage as your method of service to the English Crown," Bonaparte said gently.

"I am not, nor have I ever been, a spy. I told you. I'm a soldier. Nothing more."

Everyone was aware that one of the Emperor's favorite conceits was the idea of himself as, still, only a soldier. It was Bonaparte's often-noted affinity for his fellow soldiers, of any nationality, that Devon had been gambling on.

"You enter my empire under false pretenses, attempt to rescue the man credited with directing England's intelligence activities and then tell me that you are 'only a soldier.' And I wonder, my English friend, why you think I would accept that claim, in the middle of this entire web of deception, as true?"

The silence, disturbed only by the ticking of the gilt and marble clock on the mantel, was complete as they waited for Devon to answer the Emperor's question.

Pride, Julie thought, suddenly afraid. Your stubborn English pride is about to cost you your life. Show him, she urged mentally, *prove* to him that you are exactly what you've said. But the silence stretched dangerously.

And when he didn't speak, the quiet waiting was shattered by her voice, which rang clear and calm.

"Make him show you his back," she said to Napoleon, knowing that was proof beyond dispute of Devon's assertion, and that the Emperor would certainly be able to identify the cause of those scars.

Bonaparte's gaze had moved to the girl's face and softened unexpectedly. He had a notorious weakness for beautiful women. And in spite of the nature of her rather bizarre costume, this one was very beautiful. Judging by her speech and manner, she was not what she appeared to be, either. This was turning out to be far more entertaining than he had anticipated. He smiled at her and was treated to a practiced and very provocative dip of dark lashes and then an upsweep, which revealed smiling eyes.

"Take off your coat," he said to the tall Englishman, his eyes still resting on the girl's heart-shaped face. Far paler than he would have thought with that black hair, but remarkably beautiful.

"No," Devon's soft voice answered, and the Emperor's surprise pulled his attention from the eyes of the girl, which had suddenly widened.

"Don't be a fool." Devon heard Jean's whisper from behind him, but he was so furious he was almost trembling.

"I can always have someone remove it," Bonaparte said simply. He didn't seem to be particularly angered by the refusal. "But I don't think you would enjoy that. And to preserve your own dignity..." he suggested.

Julie held her breath until the long fingers began to remove the dark coat he had donned this morning for his role as doctor. Devon dropped the coat and reached behind with one hand and, locking his fingers into the material of the shirt, pulled it over his head in a single, furious jerk.

He heard Jean's quickly suppressed gasp behind him, and then he turned slowly, so that his back, held as straight as if he were on parade, was to the Emperor. His ice-cold blue eyes locked on Julie's, and by the bitterness that was revealed in his she knew how much he hated what she had just forced him to do.

But in watching her reaction, Devon missed the soft footsteps that crossed the carpet behind him. The gentle touch of fingers tracing the ridges of scar tissue sent a shiver across his marred back, like the flickering skin of a horse that has felt the touch of the spur.

"I think sometimes it's a very hard thing to be a soldier," one old veteran said finally to the other and, bending, the Emperor of France lifted the discarded shirt and draped it gently over the English colonel's shoulders.

He walked by Devon, who was still trembling slightly with reaction. Bonaparte's eyes deliberately did not look at the face of the Englishman, but he allowed his gaze to openly study the scarred countenance of the Frenchman.

"And I think that's something you, too, understand," he said to Jean. "I remember your face. Before those scars." He paused and met the unwavering intensity of that hazel eye. "It was in connection to a certain position at Wagram, a position that had to be held at all costs, and a young captain who promised that it would be."

There was no answer for a long time, and then Jean said softly in response to that memory, "And it was."

"Yes," the Emperor acknowledged the quiet pride of that claim. "It was. I understood that you had been wounded. I looked for you, but the surgeons hadn't expected you to live. You'd been sent from the front, and I'm afraid I assumed..." he paused in the midst of that remembrance. "But I must confess, I'm surprised to see you in this company, or have your loyalties changed so much since then?" And he lifted one hand in a brief gesture at the burns that marked Jean's face.

"I hope you know that they haven't, sire. But there are extenuating circumstances," the gambler said, smiling slightly in return.

The Emperor's dark eyes watched the twisted movement of that damaged mouth, and then he nodded. "There always are. We are seldom allowed to do the things we believe are right without extenuating circumstances. I assume you also would like for me to intervene with the minister of police on behalf of you and your companions."

"If..." Jean paused, unwilling to ask.

"If I remember what I owe you?" the Emperor finished for him.

Jean's gaze fell before that ready acknowledgment of that debt, and then he glanced up to say, "I would never ask, but..."

"Extenuating circumstances?" Napoleon suggested softly.

Jean hesitated.

"It doesn't matter," the Emperor said, watching the conflict in that dark face. His eyes traced the seared flesh and the black patch. "I don't forget deeds of valor. And whatever business Fouché has with you, I think he can be compelled to forgo its completion."

"And the woman?" Jean asked into the silence that followed the Emperor's promise of his freedom.

"And is she the circumstances that drew a loyal Frenchman into this nest of spies? Perhaps, if love is involved, your lack of judgment is explained," the Emperor suggested, smiling.

Jean allowed his eyes to turn to Julie's for the first time since he had seen, overlying the brutal damage the shrapnel had inflicted, the fresh marks of her nails on Devon's back and shoulders. He knew she had not been aware of them, or of what they had revealed to him. Her concern had been for Devon, and not for him.

But Jean had loved her for a long time, and he wouldn't abandon her now. The Emperor would let her go if he claimed her. No matter what he decided about the two Englishmen, Napoleon would give him the girl.

"Yes," he said softly. Her eyes met his, but nothing was the same.

He held out his hand, and her small fingers locked into it.

Seeing her response to the Frenchman's invitation, Devon looked away, his mouth as rigidly controlled as that straight, scarred back.

And Napoleon again considered the Frenchman before he smiled at the girl.

"Make him tell you some day how he got those scars. It's an interesting story."

"I will," she promised softly.

Suddenly the door that led to the Emperor's private quarters behind this office opened. It was the military doctor Bonaparte had sent to examine the duke, and they all turned at his entrance. Even Devon, who had not touched the shirt that had been thoughtfully placed over his shoulders.

The surgeon's eyes seemed to rest on Devon's figure a moment too long, but after all, it was certainly unusual to find a half-dressed man in the presence of the Emperor, and his gaze eventually shifted to his commander's face. Bonaparte's black brows lifted in question. Again the physician's hesitation was almost noticeable.

"Let him go," he said softly.

"I've told you who he is," Bonaparte began, and the surgeon interrupted, an obvious sign of the respect in which his opinion was held.

"He's not a threat to you. Not any longer. Let him go," he said again.

The Emperor waited, considering the options available to him and the English soldier's warning about the possibility of international repercussions. Perhaps it was the simplest way, after all.

"He's dying. I don't know that he'll survive the crossing." At the involuntary reaction of the man standing nearest him, the man whose bare chest heaved hard once, reacting as he had seen men react to a saber thrust, the surgeon paused, and his next words were clearly addressed to Devon.

"There's an abscess of the bone. It's too deep for surgery. And for the hip, of course, amputation, which is the only treatment, isn't possible. Take him home. I'll give him something so he can stand the Channel."

Devon nodded once.

Having made his decision, the Emperor walked back to the table and, finding materials, wrote a scrawling message that represented freedom for them all. He turned and gestured to Jean, who released Julie's hand and moved to accept the document.

The Emperor's lips lifted slightly, and he rested his hand a moment on the shoulder of the man whose scars would make an interesting story. One he had no doubt the girl would never be told. And smiling, he patted the hard arm and turned back to his table and the endless maps and charts. They had been dismissed, and the surgeon and Jean were certainly aware of it.

The doctor moved his head in a slight gesture toward the front entrance, and Jean knew that he would arrange for Avon to be carried there to meet them. He walked across the room and touched the English soldier's arm. Devon started slightly and, still in shock, followed him.

Julie waited until the two men had passed, and then she turned to the man who stood looking down on the Empire he must try to re-create. Re-create without his *Grande Armée*. Without many of his most experienced marshals, who had refused to break their oaths of loyalty to the Bourbon king. Without his wife and son, who would not, of course, be allowed by his Austrian father-in-law to rejoin him.

Julie knew that the people who had been judged here this afternoon had already been forgotten, but she said it anyway, whispered the words that no one else had thought to say.

"Thank you, sire," she said softly, and in the Gypsy skirt that was so short it touched well above slender ankles, she gracefully performed a deep and formal court curtsy. And held her position until the dark eyes, enjoying the picture she made, smiled their reply.

* * *

It had begun to drizzle rain, and the courtyard was dark with the heavy clouds that overhung the city. Under the direction of the military surgeon, the soldiers were carefully transferring the English duke into the waiting carriage, one clearly marked with the imperial crest, larger and more accommodating transportation for the sick man.

When the three of them reached the coach, Jean put out his hand to help Julie inside. She hesitated, looking at Devon's set face.

"No," she said softly. "I'll ride. The air will do me good. I need . . ." She couldn't think of an excuse for her sudden desire for hours spent sloughing through the muddy roads. But it really didn't matter.

"You ride inside with the duke," she said to Devon and walked toward the waiting horses, who, sensing the coming storm, milled against the experienced hold of the soldiers. One of the imperial guard eagerly helped her mount the gelding, which she had instinctively chosen, and the young guardsman blushed in response to her smiling thanks. She forced her eyes not to return to the man standing beside the Emperor's carriage.

Jean's hand grasped her bridle suddenly, and she watched the raindrops pattern against his dark skin. She couldn't meet his eyes.

"Why?" he said. "Why in God's name did you do that?"

"To save him from a firing squad," she answered. "I thought it was the only way."

"You must have known how much he'd hate being forced to show those scars," Jean said, thinking that if anyone understood what Julie's suggestion to the

Emperor had cost the Englishman, it was he. "He'll never forgive you," he warned.

Her eyes rose to meet his, and she pushed at his hand, demanding her release.

"It doesn't matter. It was just a dream. You've told me from the first how impossible . . ." she began and then shook her head.

He held the bridle until the restive protests of her mount finally broke through the confusion of his thoughts. He released his hold and watched her calmly soothe the gelding's display of temperament.

"It doesn't matter," she whispered again, the rain beading in the dark curls, and he couldn't tell whether those drops caught in her lashes were rain or tears. But her eyes were clear and wide on his face. He stepped back and mounted the horse the watching soldier held and waited for the signal that would allow them to leave Paris behind.

Devon climbed into the carriage, and hidden finally from those who had surrounded him since the surgeon's diagnosis, allowed his eyes to close against the sting of unshed tears. Only for a moment, here alone, would he allow himself to remember Avon's hand holding his through the long horror of surgery. To remember the hours he and Dominic had spent that fall and winter in London as they had sought the traitor who threatened the lives of British soldiers fighting to defeat the monster whose presence they had just left. Who was not, of course, a monster at all.

"Put your shirt on," the French surgeon commanded softly. He was leaning in to make a final check of the placement of the pillows the soldiers had piled on the seat to cushion the duke from the jolting of the carriage over the rough roads. His dark eyes moved from Avon's limp form to Devon's.

"I should hate for my best work to have been in vain," Larrey, Bonaparte's chief military surgeon, said softly. "In spite of the confidence I expressed when the Duke of Avon asked me to go to London to operate on his brother-in-law, I didn't believe the results would be this good. You owe him a great debt."

"And you and your skills. I am grateful. I would be more grateful if there were anything you could do—"

Devon stopped because he saw and didn't understand the twinkle that began to grow in the physician's eyes. And then his smile.

"I'm a hell of a surgeon, Colonel Burke, but diagnostics is not my forte. Get another opinion when you get to London. It's highly possible that I may have made a mistake. But I shall leave it to you to protect my reputation," he said softly. He withdrew his upper body from the coach and closed the door. He signaled the driver, and the carriage and its outriders clattered out of the courtyard.

"He told me what he was going to do," Avon's voice spoke from the shadows of the opposite seat. "I was afraid you'd try to kill Bonaparte and then fight your way out of the palace. Those were the longest minutes of my life." The familiar amusement colored the confession.

There was no response from the man who sat, elbows on his knees and his head bowed in his hands. No sound at all except the rain against the roof and the horses' hooves ringing on the stones outside.

The duke reached carefully and touched his knuckles lightly against one of the hands that held the lowered head of his friend.

"Dev?" he questioned softly.

And finally, after a great while, the voice of his brother-in-law, who sat shivering, still bare to the waist, spoke into the silence.

"Just give me a minute, Dominic. I'm having a little trouble adjusting to the idea that I'm not going to lose you, too," he said softly, remembering Julie's small hand, which had been placed so trustingly in the gambler's.

The silver eyes watched that bowed head a long time in the dim interior of the coach. And then they closed, content because Avon understood Devon's strength and knew that he would somehow manage to deal with whatever had happened in the Emperor's office.

Chapter Twelve

The weather called a halt to their progress long before the lieutenant, ordered to see the party safely to the coast, made the distance he had hoped to cover. But he had received explicit instructions from the surgeon as to the care he should take of the sick man inside the carriage, and the condition of the roads had certainly gone beyond those proscribed limits. The small inn had appeared almost miraculously, but the weather had also guaranteed its crowded conditions.

The soldiers were perfectly willing to bivouac in the attached stables, but a private parlor was all that the officer could convince the host to make available to the travelers in his charge. Under his direction, his men made up a pallet not too far from the parlor's welcoming hearth with sheets and blankets provided by the innkeeper. Those and the pillows from the coach ensured a suitable bed for the duke.

When the four travelers were finally alone, there was a decided lack of conversation. Julie stood with her hands outstretched before the blazing logs in the fireplace.

"Do you know where we are?" she said as her fingers began to thaw.

"Somewhere near Argenteuil, I think," Jean answered, watching the slim, straight back. She had thrown off the heavy military cloak one of the troopers had finally persuaded her to take against the cold rain, but the thin peasant blouse was slightly damp, the vertebrae of her spine outlined by the clinging material. And the vision of another back, broad and scarred and scored by the marks of her nails, intruded into the room.

"I think we need to discuss what happens when we reach the coast," Jean continued, and she turned from her contemplation of the fire.

"I don't believe that's anything we need to decide tonight," she began.

"But I do," he said, challenging, and watched the sweep of color in her cheeks.

"No, Jean," she begged softly. "Let it go. At least for tonight. Everyone's exhausted, and—"

"I don't understand the problem," Devon broke in. His voice was calm and reasonable in contrast to the Frenchman's obvious anger. "Dominic and I cross the Channel. After that, you're free to follow whatever agenda you were pursuing before. Unless you want asylum. If you think Fouché will try to take some sort of revenge, in spite of the Emperor's intervention."

"I'd be delighted to arrange protection in England," the duke offered. "Considering all that I owe you, it seems the least I can do."

"You owe me nothing, and I'm not interested in asylum," Jean denied, "but you haven't mentioned what Julie should do."

"I thought Mademoiselle de Valmé had arranged her own future," said Devon.

"And your offer?" the Frenchman asked, the mocking sarcasm back in force.

"I think any offer you coerced from Colonel Burke in Paris has certainly been negated by the events that have intervened," Julie said calmly.

Don't do this to me again, she begged silently, her eyes held on his scarred countenance by sheer force of will. Don't make him ask again what he certainly doesn't want to ask. Don't, Jean. Not if you care about me.

"On the contrary, my dear. Whatever event left the marks of your nails clearly visible on his naked back seems to me to demand some response. Unless, *monsieur,* you managed to introduce into the casino last night some other female whose lust for your body left it further scarred with that distinctive signature of shared passion."

Julie realized then that in forcing Devon to reveal to the Emperor proof of his military service, she had also led him to expose what had happened between them. But it had not, of course, gone as far as Jean was imagining. He would never believe that now. She didn't remember using her nails on Dev's back, but considering the emotional state his touch had reduced her to, she didn't doubt the truth of Jean's claim.

Unconsciously, in remembering, her eyes had sought Devon's. And found, instead of the memories of what they had shared reflected in their blue depths, only a cold formality.

"Of course. Mademoiselle de Valmé is still welcome to the protection of my name. If she desires it," he said and bowed slightly, his smile as sardonic as Jean's had ever been.

"No," she said simply. And the bitter smile widened in response.

"No," he repeated, "I didn't think so. *Mademoiselle* made her choice clear in the Emperor's office."

"That's not—"

"There's really no need to defend your decision. And I'm sure you'll be much happier in your friend's capable hands. You have so much in common," Devon said, gently mocking.

"But I'm not offering my hand," Jean denied softly. And only Julie saw and recognized his pain. "I find that I no longer want her, *monsieur*, now that you've made her your *putain.*"

At Julie's response, a gasp she couldn't control, Devon's fists closed, and he made the first step toward the Frenchman.

Avon's voice interrupted harshly. "Dev," he shouted.

His career had instilled an automatic reaction to that tone of command, and Devon fought to impose a control he was far from feeling, unaware of how revealing of the true state of his emotions that unthinking defense had been.

"I would like to offer Mademoiselle de Valmé another option," Dominic said softly.

Devon's gaze swung to Avon's calm face and rested there unbelievingly.

"*Mademoiselle,* your father worked for me for years. I would like to offer you a home, a refuge from the dangers you've recently faced because of his employment in my service and for his country. I hope you'll come to England as my ward. I promise you that my protection is given willingly and with no conditions attached. You will be free to come and go as

you wish, and you will be welcome to my hospitality
and my support as long as you like."

"As your ward?" Devon asked explosively, thinking only of Avon's reputation before he had married
Emily. "You can't be serious," he said.

"Why?" Julie asked quietly, imagining all the
wrong reasons for the disbelief in that strained voice.
"Because even the Duke of Avon wouldn't dare take
your whore into London society?"

"God, Julie," Devon said, "you know that you're
not— Don't say that," he commanded softly, his anger dissolving suddenly, destroyed by the knowledge
of what he had made her feel.

"It's what they both believe," she whispered bitterly.

"But it's not true. Why are you saying this?" he
asked.

"Because it would have been true. Last night. If you
hadn't . . ."

And the memory of what he had said, and of the
caressing touch of his hand, destroyed her bitterness,
too. She met his eyes, and there was none of the coldness that had been there earlier. They were as tender
as they had been last night.

Only last night, she thought. So much had happened. She could no longer depend on Jean's support. And she didn't understand why Devon had been
so angry. Perhaps, as the Frenchman had warned her,
he would never be able to forgive her for what she'd
forced him to do in the Emperor's office.

Only two things were the same. Fouché would still
like to find her, for revenge if for nothing else, and she
could never become Devon's wife. For it would be a
marriage forged out of his sense of noblesse oblige and

destined, in the closed world of London society, to become nothing but a cause of bitter regret.

"Marry me, Julie," he said softly, as if in mockery of that thought. "Let me take care of you." And he waited.

But it was not the reason that might have moved her to change her mind. She had never wanted his protection. Only his love. And he had never offered her that. She knew he wanted her, wanted to make love to her, but it was not the same.

When she finally spoke, it was to the man on the pallet, whose silver eyes had watched with concern for them both.

"Yes," she said to Avon. "If you meant it, then, yes, I'll go to London as your ward."

She didn't look at Devon, whose proposal she had rejected for the second time. And she didn't attempt to explain again the impossibility of accepting what he had just offered.

"That's probably a wise decision," she heard Devon say bitterly. "As the Duke of Avon's ward your future will certainly be assured. My congratulations on the shrewdness of your choice. Ever the opportunist. And who knows, perhaps in London an even better offer will come along."

And because she didn't look at him, she didn't know until she heard the door of the small, comfortable parlor close behind him that he had left the room.

She never knew where Devon spent that night. In a carefully maintained silence, she and Jean had occupied the chairs in the inn's front parlor, and Avon's weakness and exhaustion had ensured his night's sleep. But she didn't see Devon again until he met them at the carriage the following morning. He didn't look as if he had slept at all, the skin surrounding the blue eyes dark and bruised. But he had established a laughing camaraderie with the soldiers who accompanied them, and she supposed he had bedded down with them when he had left last night.

He walked up to the gelding she had ridden yesterday, quickly adjusting the stirrups to their normal position. The roan reached back to dip his nose gently into the broad shoulder, and Devon whispered into his ear with serious concentration. He patted the massive neck and then swung smoothly into the saddle. The horse turned, dancing slightly in response to the familiar weight of his rider. Devon's blue eyes met Julie's watching brown ones and lingered briefly over features that revealed that her night had also been sleepless. And then he skillfully controlled the gelding's excitement and edged the horse to a position close to the young lieutenant, who looked up with a smiling welcome.

Julie forced her eyes away and found the silver gaze of the duke on her face. He smiled at her as she entered the carriage to take her place across from him.

"I think this will be a good opportunity for us to become better acquainted, *mademoiselle*," he suggested softly.

"Of course," she said, closing the door. "But if I'm to be your ward, I think you might begin to call me Julie." She wondered again why he had made the offer she thought as ridiculous as Devon's.

A twenty-three-year-old woman, especially one who had seen as much of the world as she, didn't become anyone's ward. Her acceptance had seemed the only solution to what had been happening last night, but here in the light of day, she thought he might be as embarrassed by his proposal as she was by her agreement.

Even as ill as he obviously was, it was hard to imagine that someone whose sheer vitality was so evident in his eyes and in his intellect had so little time to live. And she would never allow him to spend one moment of whatever time remained worrying about her future. She was, as Devon had reminded her, perfectly capable of arranging that for herself.

The duke didn't speak again as the carriage began to roll out of the yard and onto the mire of the road. Their journey would be as slow today as yesterday, she supposed, staring out at the rain-washed countryside.

She looked up to find Avon watching her face with something approaching compassion, and so she decided that she might as well put an end to this farce, as well.

"I want to thank you for what you offered last night. I'm sorry that what was taking place when you made that offer was so uncomfortable for everyone. But we both know society will never accept the idea that you've suddenly decided to adopt a female faro dealer. And I've no doubt your wife would be less than delighted to welcome me into her home. I wouldn't blame her."

"I've found that the ton generally accepts anything, no matter how outrageous, as long as it's presented from a position of wealth, birth and power, and with a certain arrogant *bravacherie*. All of which I happen to possess," he said. She could hear the amusement and the gentle invitation to join him in making fun of his own class.

"I'm sure you could carry even that off, but I don't intend that you'll have the trouble."

"I assure you, my dear, that I'm quite looking forward to presenting you to London society. I think they'll be enchanted. And as for Emily—"

"No," she interrupted softly, and her eyes were very serious. No wonder Devon had been so determined to find this friend. He was making plans for her future when his own seemed so bleak.

"Am I allowed to know why?" he asked.

"Because you'll have other things you'll want to do. Before . . ."

There was a delicate pause, and when she looked up from her twisting fingers, the gray eyes were alight with laughter.

"Forgive me," he said. "You must think I'm remarkably slow. But I had forgotten."

"Forgotten?" she whispered.

"My impending fate. My untimely demise. My unfortunate—" And at her sudden obvious enlightenment, he smiled.

"You're not dying," she said frankly.

"I don't think so. And neither did Larrey."

"Then why?" she breathed and knew the only answer. "To save your life. To make the Emperor release you. But why would he do that?"

"I'm not sure my life had a great deal to do with Larrey's decision. Dr. Larrey was the surgeon who removed the most damaging piece of shrapnel from Devon's back. I think, like a painter, he couldn't stand to have his greatest masterpiece destroyed. He'd worked too hard to watch Dev shot down by a firing squad. If he could convince Bonaparte that I was no longer a threat to him . . ."

"But Dev had, I think, already convinced the Emperor to release you. He'd claimed you were an accredited diplomatic. He seemed very assured that the English Crown would corroborate that claim. He was extremely convincing."

The duke's slight smile told her, without the arrogance words would have displayed, that that part of Devon's assertion had almost certainly been true. Avon had been too valuable to the British government for them to deny him any aid.

"So Larrey's deception wasn't necessary," Avon suggested.

"No, I didn't mean that. I think it was the deciding factor." She paused, remembering the scene in Bonaparte's office.

"I *am* interested in what happened. When Larrey told me you were meeting with Napoleon rather than Fouché... I don't even understand how that was accomplished."

"Apparently the Emperor was aware, even before his escape from Elba, that Fouché had been planning a coup. In spying on his minister of police, he discovered our attempt to rescue you."

"I understand the diplomatic repercussions of holding me, but why would Bonaparte decide to release the rest of you?"

"My father and I never knew anything about Jean's background, but it seems that at some time he was a soldier. An officer. Napoleon called him captain. He managed to hold some position in Austria. And in the process... You've seen Jean's scars, which the Emperor indicated were acquired in his service."

"And because of that service Bonaparte was willing to release Jean?"

"And me. He asked if I belonged to Jean. I accepted because I thought if we were free, we had a better chance of arranging for Dev's escape. He'd already ensured your safety. But then Dev said . . ."

"What?" Avon prodded softly at her pause.

"That he wasn't a spy, but a soldier."

"Which is true," Avon agreed, watching her face, which had drained of all color as she remembered what had happened next.

"But Napoleon wanted proof."

"And?"

"And then I made Dev prove that was true," she whispered, seeing again what had been in his eyes as he had stood, stripped, before the Emperor.

"You made Dev— But how could he prove—" the duke began, and then he knew. "You made him show Bonaparte his back?" The duke's voice clearly expressed his doubts about the possibility of that having occurred. "I would be very interested, my dear, in hearing how you were able to convince Devon to do that."

"The Emperor ordered him to, but only because I suggested it. I thought they were going to execute him if he didn't. But he hated it. Jean said he'd never forgive me."

"I think never is too long a punishment for an action that was undertaken with the best intentions."

"That was when Jean saw . . . You heard what he saw. But I promise you—"

"You owe me no explanations." Avon interrupted whatever assurance she was about to give. "Indeed, I am the last person to whom you need explain any action you were forced to take after your father's death. I'm only sorry I was unable to offer you my protection then. And I know Devon very well. I know the kind of man he is. There's nothing you need to defend in your relationship to my brother-in-law. I'm well aware of Devon's code of conduct. It certainly extends to his treatment of the woman he loves," the duke said quietly.

"He told me he was in love with someone in London," she said.

"At one time. But she married someone else because of his injuries. If your refusal of Dev's offer was in any way influenced by the thought of that woman in London..."

"No." Smiling, she shook her head. "I knew she existed, and I also knew she had married someone else. I refused Devon because I know what marriage to me would mean. You know who my father was. Can you imagine me entering, on Devon's arm, any of the homes of the people who knew my father's story? I wouldn't mind so much for myself, but I would care very much for Dev. And he would hate them for the way they would react to my presence. Hate them enough to kill someone, I think," she finished softly.

"And if that barrier were removed?" Avon questioned, watching her face. "Would you accept his offer then?"

"An assumed identity?" She laughed. "Even if no one learned that I'm the Viscount Ashford's daughter, I assure you I couldn't attend a single dinner party in London where some gentleman wouldn't recognize the Divine Juliette." The epithet was lightly spoken, but the duke remembered the pain his use of it had caused. "I don't want him killed in some pointless duel to protect an honor only he believes I have."

"Then you love him?"

"Of course," she said simply, and smiled at him again. "I thought you knew."

"Forgive me. Sometimes the workings of the female mind defeat me," he said.

"I doubt it," she denied, smiling.

When his soft laughter came, she swept the thick lashes up to show him the hidden sparkle. Somehow she had been instantly at ease with this man. She already considered him a friend. And, she decided, if he were serious, she was going to enjoy being the ward of the Duke of Avon, however ridiculous anyone else thought that might be.

The inn they found that night was almost empty, the sudden clearing of the weather freeing the travelers who had been stranded there by the storm. There were rooms for them all. She knew that Devon had seen to the meal that was carried upstairs to the duke, and he didn't join them in the downstairs parlor. She and Jean ate with the young officer, grateful for the restraining presence of his company. But eventually he retreated from the warmth and the polite conversation to rejoin his men, and she and Jean were left alone. She began some excuse that would take her safely to her room without having to face what now stood between them, but he put his hand on her arm, and so she waited.

"I'd like to talk to you," he said. "I wanted to tell you that I'm sorry for what I said."

"I know," she whispered. "But what happened wasn't what you thought."

"Come with me. When we reach the coast. In spite of the fool I've made of myself, you know how I feel about you. And if you're really determined not to accept his offer, then let me take care of you. It's what your father wanted.''

Her eyes rested on the face of a man who, knowing how she felt about another, was willing to give her his love. And because of what had happened in the emperor's office, she was very conscious again of his brutal scars for the first time since she had come to be more aware of the value of the inner man.

"You were a soldier, weren't you? Like Dev. That's where you met Bonaparte. You fought for him. And that's what he meant about the scars. He told you to tell me about this," she whispered, her fingers touching the textured discoloration that marred his face. He turned away, moved slightly so that she couldn't caress his cheek.

She let her hand fall and watched him a long time. And then he smiled.

"In the course of the last ten years, almost everyone in France has fought for the Emperor. And in spite of what he told you, these don't make a very interesting story. But I'll tell you sometime," he promised, "if you'll come with me tomorrow. You know you don't want to go to London. Think, my darling, what your life will be like. You're too accustomed to the freedom you've enjoyed so long. You'll never fit in. And you don't really want to. You can't."

"I'd give my life if I could," she said truthfully, and heard the rasping breath he took when he understood what she had just said. "But I won't marry him. I won't make his life the hell my father's was."

"Then why won't you come with me? What do you hope—"

And suddenly he knew from her eyes what she intended, knew before she confirmed it, her voice stumbling a little over the words. "If I can't become his wife, and you and I both know all the reasons that's impossible, then I'll be his mistress."

"He'll never allow it," Jean whispered.

"I thought you didn't believe he was that noble. And perhaps you're right—maybe he won't want me. But I have to try. It's the only chance I have."

"And if you don't succeed?" Jean asked. He hadn't touched her, but he knew he would. Before he left. Before he let her go to the man she had chosen over him. "What will you do if you don't succeed?"

"I don't know," she said honestly, smiling over the limited choices left to her. "Become a Gypsy fortune-teller," she said, remembering the Romany camp. "Or convince the duke to back a small, very select gaming room in London. I haven't thought that far."

"Julie, my love, if you ever need help with that genteel establishment in London, you have only to send word. You know that, don't you?" Jean asked softly. "Or if you ever decide that you need me for anything else."

"And like Dev, you'll come from the pits of hell for your friend?" she said, reading clearly what was in his face and in the tenderness of his voice.

"Of course," he said, smiling.

She lifted on tiptoe and placed her lips against the cruelly marked corner of his mouth where the damaged nerves created the slanting, one-sided smile.

"I can't feel you there," he said softly, his breath stirring against the gentle touch of her mouth. And very carefully, as if she were a fragile piece of porcelain, he enfolded her in his arms. His lips found hers, and his tongue forced an invasion. And a response. For a fleeting moment, she allowed the comfort of his love to envelop her. But he wasn't Devon, and finally he knew.

He released her and forced himself to smile into her eyes.

"I hope he's not a fool," he said. "For your sake, my darling, I hope he has sense enough to know what you are. But remember . . ."

"I know," she said. "And I will, I promise. I'll never forget."

He was gone the next morning, and although Avon asked, she could say quite honestly that she didn't know when he had left or where he was going.

Chapter Thirteen

Despite Larrey's denial of the death sentence he had imposed for Bonaparte's benefit, Devon was still concerned about Avon's health. For more than one reason now, he wanted to get the duke back to London, to put an end to this seemingly endless journey and then attempt to arrange his own future.

He pawned the gold and emerald seal in Le Havre to provide funds for their passage. He arranged for the mare to be sent back to the old man and for the gelding to be loaded on the vessel he had hired for their crossing. Then he returned to the inn where Julie and the duke waited.

"Tell Moss how valuable that seal has been. And I promise to retrieve it for you, Dominic. I'm sure you could simply order our journey on the basis of aristocratic arrogance, but when I showed up on the wharf, they all demanded their money in advance," Devon said, smiling.

"I don't care about the damned seal, and I don't think I could convince anyone to do anything right now, Devon. I can't even seem to command myself most of the time," Avon said bitterly.

Devon recognized the duke's frustration with his continued illness. Avon's inability to make his body recover, to become strong enough to do more than sit up for short spells before he fell asleep like an exhausted child, was, Devon knew, driving him mad.

Dev touched his shoulder in unspoken sympathy, and somehow, at that gesture, they both were back in those small rooms in London where Devon had lived his confined existence before Larrey had freed him.

"Dominic," he advised, knowing very well what the duke was feeling, "give it time. When we get to London—"

"Sandemer," the duke said, and looked up with more of that familiar aura of command than Devon would have believed possible only minutes before. "Not London. I want you to arrange for me to be taken to Sandemer. Send for Moss and for Dr. Pritchett. But I'm not going back to London until I know..."

The blue eyes that met his were carefully controlled. Devon in no way revealed that he was well aware of the fear that had necessitated the decision.

"And Emily?" he asked, watching the duke's face.

"When I've talked to Pritchett," Avon said. "When I know what the hell's wrong with me."

"Dominic," Devon began to argue.

"No, Dev. Whatever you're going to say, whatever argument you intend to make, I've already considered. Believe me. You have no idea how much I want to see Emily, but I want some answers first. Just get me to Sandemer and then get Moss. You've wasted enough time on my affairs."

"I hope you don't mean that," Devon said, anger coloring his voice. "How can you believe that I've begrudged a moment I've spent in this search?"

"You know I didn't mean it. If you want my apology for that idiotic remark, you have it. I just—"

"You don't have to explain. Especially to me. That's a road I've been down, my friend. But if you don't send for Emily, you're going to hurt her more than you ever have before. By now, she's bound to know that something's gone wrong. And if you come back and hide at Sandemer, then she's going to think—God, I don't know what she'll think. But don't do it, Dominic. You're wrong. Stubborn, arrogant, proud—as always. And wrong."

Blue eyes locked with gray, and for the first time in their friendship, Avon's fell, hiding what he felt.

"Sandemer, Devon. I know what I'm doing," he said, the blue-blooded aristocrat accustomed to immediate obedience commanding once more.

Devon studied the averted profile a long time, but the duke refused to meet his eyes.

Finally he turned away and found Julie watching the scene. She smiled at him tentatively, but his lips tightened rather grimly. She knew she was just another problem.

Since her refusal of his offer, he had spoken to her only out of necessity, the words polite and formal. As one might treat the friend of a friend, someone whom one was not especially fond of. And she supposed that described their present relationship rather well. Finally she turned away, and she didn't know that his gaze rested on her a long time before he left the room.

When she heard the closing door, she glanced at the duke, but his eyes were closed, the smudged circles of exhaustion dark around their hidden vitality. She wondered about the woman they had been discussing, Avon's wife, who was apparently to be denied the opportunity to care for her husband in his illness. She understood her own guilt, but she wondered what the Duchess of Avon had done to deserve her punishment.

The Channel was rough, the waves chopping whitely against the sides of the small vessel. Devon worried about the wisdom of trying to make the crossing considering Avon's condition, but he knew the duke was a good sailor and more than eager to make the attempt. He couldn't imagine the effects a bout of seasickness would have on Dominic, so he simply closed his mind to that possibility.

But it was not Avon who suffered that indignity. It was the Parisian, the sophisticated cosmopolitan, who had never before been on the sea. Devon had arranged for two cabins, and having helped the willing crewmen install the duke in the narrow bed of one, he had returned to find Julie standing by the rail, fascinated by the activities of the busy docks.

They were barely out of the harbor, the gray-green water churning against the planks of the laboring vessel, when Julie turned suddenly and fled below. Not understanding at first, Devon followed and found her in her small dark cabin where the odor of fish and stale bodies overlay the scent of brine. She was sitting on the bunk, the clammy pillow held crushed against her face. He could see her shoulders beginning to heave as she fought the growing nausea.

He found the bucket, conveniently placed by the door, and knelt before her. He forced her to release the pillow, and at the desperation in her dark eyes, he smiled comfortingly at her. She lowered her head and swallowed hard, fighting her body's betrayal.

Only a few seconds later, her small fingers found the rim of the bucket he held, and then he was holding her, too, as she was thoroughly and violently sick.

When he judged the first paroxysm had eased, he sat beside her, pulling her to rest against his chest, and fumbled in the dimness for the discarded pillow. Its casing, however, proved to be too noisome for his need, and without hesitation he used the sleeve of his shirt to gently wipe her mouth.

She made a token protest with fluttering fingers, and then allowed his strength to overrule her sensibilities. She really didn't care what he did. There could be nothing more humiliating than what she had just been forced to endure.

"Go away," she said hoarsely. Her throat ached with the violence of the attack.

Her hands pushed weakly at his chest, but he didn't loosen his warm embrace. And instead of the smell of fish, which had increased her sickness, the scent of Devon rested under her nose. She breathed in the masculine aromas of his clean body, and wondered vaguely how he managed to smell so good in spite of the conditions of their journey. She was sure she didn't. And remembering the events of the last few minutes, she was again horrified that he was seeing her like this.

The toast of Paris, she remembered suddenly. What a bitter jest. The one man she had ever cared about impressing, and instead . . .

"Go away," she said desperately, and managed this time to sit up, to pull her swimming head away from the comfort of his hard chest. He let her up, but she knew he was still there. She could hear his breathing, magnified in the swirling vortex of her nausea. And then the fish. And the rocking motion of the world beneath her.

Her fingers dug suddenly into his arm and she whispered, pleading, "Dev." And miraculously the bucket was there again when the next convulsive retching made her forget everything, her humiliation lost in her gratefulness for his hands, which seemed to know exactly what she needed.

She was sick a long time. A maelstrom of confusion, of being held closely, cherished between the agonizing spasms that robbed her of thought, of dignity, of humanity, it seemed. Until finally, exhausted, she thought it might be over. Her stomach still gave an occasional heaving motion, but there was no longer any need for the bucket. There was literally nothing left.

He laid her at last against the cold sheet. She was aware that she held, with trembling fingers, the warmth of his shirt against her face. At some time during the ordeal, he had removed it to wipe her face, and she had latched onto it as to a lifeline. It was Devon. As were the hands that had held her head, as gentle as a woman's would have been. And his voice, whispering against her icy cheek. She wanted to remember what he said, because she thought it was important, but it had been lost in the devastation.

She was aware that he was kneeling beside the bed. Her eyes closed, so she wouldn't be forced to see whatever was in his face, she said, "Go away. I don't want you. Just leave me..."

"Alone?" he finished softly, and the word echoed somewhere in her consciousness, reminding her of how alone she was now.

"Yes," she said, fighting the urge to just let him take care of her. To just give in and let Dev again protect her. "Go away," she whispered instead.

But he was back almost before she had realized that he really had obeyed her. He lifted her to sit leaning against his chest, as he had cradled her between attacks. He held a brandy flask against her lips and tilted it suddenly so a few drops of the spirits it held entered her mouth. She was afraid she was going to be sick again, but the container was insistently presented.

"Drink it," he commanded softly, and she did, trusting him.

When he judged she'd had enough to relax her, but not enough, considering her empty stomach, to precipitate another bout of nausea, he found the stopper, his arms still holding her against him while his fingers secured the flask and then laid it on the floor beside the bed.

"Sit up," he said in that same soft tone of command. She leaned forward and then he was sitting with his back propped against the wall behind the bed. He pulled her against him, shifting her body so that he could stretch out his long legs beside hers. Her back was against the solid warmth of his bare chest, and his arms encircled her, his hands crossed loosely in her lap.

"Are you going to give me back my shirt?" he asked, his mouth against the top of her head, his breath stirring the fragrant curls.

"No," she said.

"Not ever?" he asked, and she could hear the smile in his voice.

"No," she denied, snuggling closer to the pleasant closeness of his body.

"Why not?"

"Because it's yours. And I like to hold it."

The brandy he had forced her to swallow was making inroads on her ability to think. But it didn't matter. This was Dev. Whatever she said was all right. Was right. Because he was warm. And he was holding her.

"I love you," she said finally.

"I know," he whispered again, and she felt his lips nudge against her temple. She closed her eyes at their touch.

"I'm going to seduce you," she said, and his steady heartbeat against her spine hesitated and then resumed.

"I'm delighted."

"Not now," she explained carefully. "In England. But now... I don't suppose you'll want me now."

"And why would you suppose that?" he questioned, and again she could hear the smile.

"Because how could you?" she said simply. It was so clear. No one could still want someone whom he had... She lost the thought. And it hadn't been very clear anyway. "You know," she said instead.

"No, I don't know. And I don't care. I think I've made you drunk, my darling."

"I like that," she whispered.

"Being drunk?"

"No, the darling part. I wanted to have your babies," she said rather incoherently, and the tears started unbidden, but she blinked them back. There had been that lurching break again in the strong rhythm behind her.

"Little Gypsy girls with dancing eyes," he suggested softly.

"Or soldiers. No, not soldiers. Soldiers get hurt. I don't want our sons—" Her voice broke, and his arms tightened. "But mistresses don't have sons," she finished. "At least in Paris."

"I wasn't planning on having a mistress," he explained.

"But she's married. You can't have a wife who's already married to someone else," she reasoned. "You told me."

"I told you a great deal of nonsense, all of which you seem to have remembered. And I have my doubts that you'll remember this. But I'm going to try anyway. You're going to marry me. You might as well get used to the idea. You may think that you'll convince me otherwise, but you won't. You won't be my mistress. And you won't fall in love with anyone else. You belong to me, and you know it, and I know it. And you're just going to hurt yourself fighting against that truth. And you're going to have my sons one day. And my daughters," he said softly. His palms had found again the curve of her stomach, and he tightened his fingers to let her feel his possession there. "Don't break your heart, my darling, fighting the inevitable. It won't do any good."

"No," she argued softly, and shook her head. She could feel the roughness of his unshaven chin catch a strand of her hair. "You need a shave," she said, sounding very much like a wife.

"Yes, dear," he whispered, and she wondered vaguely why he laughed. But the feel of that gentle

movement against her body was so pleasant that she
closed her eyes, and he held her while she slept.

Devon and his shirt were gone when she woke. The
motion of the ship had stopped, and she knew they
were in England. Her father's home. And now hers.
At least for the time being.

She straightened her clothing as well as she could,
and wrinkled her nose at the unpleasant odors that
surrounded her. She wanted fresh air and the salt
breeze against her face. And out of this awful hole.
She walked to the door and noticed the bucket he had
brought her, washed out with salt water and standing
innocently in its usual place. She wished she could remember all he'd said, but she remembered enough,
and her eyes were suddenly haunted. She gathered her
courage in both hands and climbed the narrow steps
to the deck.

She wondered if they had left her. There was nothing and no one in her bustling surroundings that
looked familiar.

"My lady," a voice at her elbow said hesitantly, and
the sailor had to repeat his assertion before she realized he was talking to her.

"His grace asked if you'll wait on board until the
arrangements for transportation have been made. The
colonel's already gone ashore."

"Of course," she said softly, wondering how he
could possibly call someone as bedraggled as she was
"my lady." How ridiculous. And she had long since
ceased to think of Avon as "his grace." But, of course,
he was.

Once Devon's initial resistance to the duke's plan
had been voiced and rejected, he had privately de-

cided that Sandemer's location on the coast might be easier, given the duke's condition. The French captain, however, had adamantly refused to accommodate his unscheduled and unsought passengers by landing them in those unfamiliar waters, so the colonel had been forced to make arrangements for their transportation to Avon's home overland.

When Devon returned, he found Julie sitting on a pile of hempen rope watching the harbor. The look he gave her was slightly challenging, but there was a new element in the blue depths that she hadn't had time to identify before he turned to continue below decks to discuss their imminent departure with Avon.

In the carriage she and the duke slept most of the way, and it was dusk before they turned from the well-maintained road up the winding mile that led to Avon's estate. And she was unprepared for the vast expanse of the structure that suddenly rose before them out of the mists that had begun to gather with the twilight.

Her eyes moved from the imposing sight to find Avon watching her.

"I used to get lost," he said, smiling.

"I can see why," she said, laughing. "You didn't tell me..." She stopped because he hadn't told her anything except that she would have the protection of his name. She couldn't imagine why she hadn't realized his name would entail all the privileges his title automatically carried.

"I know it's an architectural horror," he said. His head was resting back against the corner of the coach, and she knew he couldn't see the castle. Only in his mind's eye. "But it's..."

"Home," she suggested, and he smiled.

'Thank God,'' he said softly, and the smile faded. "Devon's right, you know."

"Don't you start, too."

"Why not?" she said. "I'm your ward, remember. I'm supposed to be concerned about your welfare. And I'm a woman. I know how your wife will feel."

"I know how she'll feel, too," he said softly. "That's the bloody hell of it."

And wisely she left him alone.

Julie had certainly not grown up in any sort of impoverished situation, but she had not previously encountered anything on the scale of the wealth and the elegance of Avon's estate. Her fingers trailed over the ivory silk hangings of the bed in the enormous chamber she had been carried to. The dignified footman who had escorted her had in no way expressed surprise over the condition of her apparel or her disheveled hair, but she found herself fighting to keep her lips from moving into a smile as she imagined the story he would tell below stairs when she had been safely disposed of.

She noticed her broken nails and decidedly grubby knuckles and quickly removed her fingers from the priceless material before she could damage it. She looked at the inviting tub and the steaming, fragrant water that had appeared, almost like magic, under the direction of Avon's efficient majordomo. She touched the soft lawn of the nightgown that had been laid over the lavender-scented sheets.

Impostor, she thought, but she undressed quickly and lowered her body into the warmth of the water. After she had washed her short curls, she leaned her head against the back of the tub and wondered if

Devon were soaking in the soothing warmth of a similar bath. She almost dozed, surrounded by the realization of what it meant to be the ward of His Grace, the Duke of Avon. And then she smiled.

I'm still the dancing girl. No matter what my surroundings, that hasn't changed. And I know it.

She waited until the noises of the house had ceased. And then she forced herself to wait another long hour, carefully measured by the hands of the mantel clock.

The smell of beeswax and lemon oil permeated the upstairs hallway, and her bare feet made no sound on the gleaming oak.

Standing before the heavy door, she wondered briefly if she should knock. But in the silence she decided against that urge, and so she turned the handle and allowed her eyes to adjust to the dimness.

Devon was standing by the window, his body marked by the shadows of the mullions. He didn't turn, and she thought he hadn't heard the opening of the door. The scars on his back were dark fissures against the liquid glow of the moonlight that washed his skin. She stood, drinking in the tall perfection of his body, the broad bare shoulders, the muscled length of thigh under the skintight material of his pantaloons.

"I've been waiting a long time," he said softly. "I was beginning to think you'd changed your mind."

"No," she said, and at the uncertainty of that single syllable, he turned and smiled at her.

"You seem a remarkably reluctant seducer," he said finally into the long silence.

"I had thought you might help," she suggested, smiling.

"No," he denied, and he didn't return her smile. "I want to be courted. I'm tired of being rejected, Julie."

"I've never rejected you," she said.

"Forgive me, but when you accepted Avon's proposal, it felt very much like rejection to me."

"I refused to marry you. That's very different—"

"No, it's not. If you've rejected my name, you've rejected me."

"That's not why. And that's not fair. You know I can't marry you. I've told you what would happen."

"Do you think I care what anyone else thinks? Do you honestly believe that what anyone would say about you would make any difference to the way I feel?"

"Eventually," she said, very sure. Remembering her father's exile.

"God," he said softly. "You have to know—"

"Make love to me," she interrupted. And saw the words stop him.

"Why?" he asked.

"Why?" she repeated, incredulous. "Because I want you to. Because I thought that you— You do still want me, don't you, Devon? What happened on the boat hasn't changed that, has it?"

"Julie," he said, laughing. "Yes, I still want you. Do you remember what I showed you in your father's bedroom?" he asked softly. And saw by her face that she did.

"Would you like me to show you again how much I want you?" he asked, his voice seducing her. This was not what she'd imagined, but it was better. He wasn't resisting as she'd been afraid he might.

She nodded slowly, unable to move. So he walked across the expanse that separated them and closed the door behind her, and then the chamber was lighted only by the moonlight.

His eyes were very dark, and she could barely read his features. He bent to touch his lips gently to her throat, ivory in the silver glow that poured into the room from the tall windows behind him.

Her head fell back, too heavy suddenly for the slender column against which his breath glided, caressing. He hadn't touched her except with his lips. And with the shivering weakness moving into her knees, she put her hands on the strength of his shoulders.

"You should probably pretend to resist. Simply for convention's sake," he said, whispering the words into the soft fragrant skin between her ear and the silk of her curls.

"No," she breathed.

"No," he agreed, his fingers tangling in the ribbon that secured the low neck of the lace bodice.

His thumb traced into the unfastened V. And he waited. She opened her eyes and looked into the cobalt depths of his.

"Marry me," he suggested quietly, his thumb moving side to side, skimming just under the swell of each breast.

"No," she said, and swallowing, watched his mouth lift at the contrast between those words and her tone. "I love to see you smile," she whispered.

"You will," he promised. "And I don't think we need this." The gown was lowered over the cream of her shoulders, pushed by hands that were dark and demanding against the smooth slide of the fine cotton that slithered softly to fall on the carpet. And then he smiled.

He held out his hand as if he were escorting her onto the floor of some ballroom, and she rested hers in his and stepped out of the small pool of material.

But he didn't lead her to the high bed she had been aware of since she had entered the room.

He looked at her a moment, his eyes caressing the entire trembling length of her slim figure.

"Not at all boyish," he teased softly.

At the tension suddenly released, she laughed.

"You can't be afraid of me, Julie?" he asked softly, having felt her shivering anticipation. And he was reassured when she shook her head.

"You know I'll never hurt you," he whispered.

"I know. I'm not afraid."

He bent again and allowed his lips to touch beside the pink-tipped bud of her breast. He moved his tongue slightly against the silken skin, and her breath caught and held until his mouth finally closed over the hard nipple and pulled, teasing gently.

"Dev," she said, her breath released in a whispered plea that consisted only of his name.

He concentrated first on the prolonged adoration of only one perfect globe, and then with the trembling direction of her fingers, moved to the other. And then both. Endlessly teasing, deserting and returning until the quivering waves of sensation that grew upward from between her legs threatened her balance. Her fingers dug into his shoulders as she felt him go down on one knee, still caressing with his mouth nipples that were now swollen and aching and wet with what he was doing. And then to the other knee. Until his hair was caressing the valley between her breasts, his strong fingers kneading the outside of their aching swell as his tongue trailed lower.

It found at last her navel, and buried there, his teeth biting gently around the edges, while his thumbs rubbed over and around the throbbing peaks his mouth had created and then deserted.

Her body was one long flame, wanting something she couldn't find. Wanting what his mouth was doing everywhere. And not really knowing where. Wanting something. Everything.

And at the first knowing flick of his tongue over exactly what she had wanted him to touch, she arched against him, her body exploding inside. She would have fallen had his hands not held her hips, cupping and supporting, as she was lost to anything but the sensation of his mouth moving with sure command against the most sensitive part of her body.

He held her imprisoned by the pressure of his hard fingers as the shivering torrents shattered and then, under his mouth's assault, built again. And again. He wouldn't let her go, demanding her response. And she was powerless to do anything but convulse against the force of her love for him. She hadn't known. Hadn't imagined. And finally he wrapped his arms around her waist and held her as she leaned, exhausted and sated, against him. She cradled his head to her, the silk of his hair moving against her skin as her panting eased. And when her knees finally gave way, her shivering body slid down beside him. And they knelt together in the moonlight.

"If this isn't temptation," he said softly, "then God forgive me, I don't know what would be."

She couldn't speak, couldn't think, but her fingers moved across the harsh landscape of his back and delighted in the roughness of the marred skin. Devon. Always Devon.

"Marry me," he said after a long time. After her body had stopped trembling, its cold warmed against the heat of his skin.

And he waited.

"No," she said, and put her lips against his eyes. "I'm still the dancing girl. The faro dealer. And the only hand I've ever held is carte blanche."

"I'll never ask you again," he said softly. "If you don't know... After that, if you don't know you're mine..."

"I know," she said. "But I won't marry you. I'll be your mistress, Dev, your lover. I'll live with you openly or in some discreet address on a quiet London street. I'll be whatever you want me to be. But not that. I can't be your wife."

He held her. And she hoped. At last he rose and helped her to her feet. Her knees were still weak and she felt fragile, brittle. As if she might fracture if she moved beyond the strength of his arms.

"If I accept what you're offering," he said softly, "then you'd eventually believe that I have also accepted your evaluation of your place in my life. And you mean too much for me to do that. It's all or nothing, Julie. And I'm not going to make love to you. Not beyond what happened tonight. And I didn't know..." He stopped, the memory of her response still shaking the foundations of what he thought he knew about making love. "But some day you're going to decide that I'm right, that none of what you fear really matters, and you'll want to be my wife. And I'll be waiting. I'm not leaving that choice up to you so that you'll have to give in or give up or admit your feelings. But because it has to be what you know is right. Your decision. Do you understand?''

"No," she whispered. "I want you. How can you just deny what's between us?"

She waited, and in the moonlight, she saw him shake his head.

"I can't believe I'm saying this," he said softly. "It sounds like ... I don't know what it sounds like. The sheerest stupidity. Or the blindest arrogance."

She waited, and finally he whispered what he had been thinking.

"I love you too much to make you anything less," he said softly.

He didn't touch her, and he didn't wait for her response to something he had thought she must have known as long as he had. Instead, he turned away from the strongest temptation he had known in his life and left her alone in the seductive spill of moonlight. Inside her head she heard the echo of the words he had spoken. Hearing them again and again as her eyes filled with tears that this time spilled unchecked.

Chapter Fourteen

Julie didn't think she had been awake the next morning when the soft knock sounded, but so nearly so that she wasn't surprised by the entrance of the smiling chambermaid. She had been dreaming, she thought, or remembering the trembling response of her body to Devon's touch last night. He had known how to touch her in ways she had not been aware were possible between a man and a woman. And he had read her response and fed on it, stoked the fires he'd created as if he shared her mind.

But the cheerful entry of the servant put an end to that pleasant reverie. She could smell the rich aroma of the chocolate the maid carried in the blue-and-gold porcelain pot. She thought, after the hardships of the last months, that it was very welcome to be waited on.

"Good morning, my lady," the maid said briskly, carefully depositing the heavy tray with its Sevres chocolate set on the table beside Julie's bed. She moved to the windows and pulled back the draperies to let in the morning sun.

"I'm to be your ladyship's maid, as soon as you're ready to get up and dress. And the colonel gave me a letter. Said you was to have it as soon as you was awake," she carefully repeated her instructions, searching the voluminous pockets of the heavily starched apron she wore over her neat serge until she found the missive, a single sheet folded and sealed with a wafer and the seal Devon had borrowed from Avon's desk.

"Thank you," Julie whispered, her pulse racing suddenly at the thought of what he might have written. But she waited until the maid had left the chamber to break the wax.

> My Darling,
> I'm returning to London to provide Whitehall with information concerning the Emperor's current situation and conditions in France. After that, I hope to join Wellington, who, Avon's servants inform me, left for Brussels on the fourth. You should have plenty of time to decide what you want before I see you again.
>
> Devon

"To join Wellington," she read aloud. "My God, Dev, what have you done?"

Unmindful of her state of undress, she threw off the covers and, taking the letter, fled to the only person who might have some hope of stopping him.

Avon's majordomo was serving the duke his morning coffee and could not prevent a small betrayal of his surprise at her entrance, clad as she was in only her night rail. The servant's mouth gaped slightly, but he was too well-trained to allow the reaction to be anything other than brief and quickly hidden. Especially before the duke.

At the quick gesture of dismissal from Avon, who rested against the banked pillows of the bed in which he and his father and his father's father had been born, the butler departed without the least appearance of haste or embarrassment. As soon as they were alone, Julie handed Devon's letter to the duke.

"They won't let him, of course," Julie argued, as she watched him read it. "Surely he can't just rejoin his regiment."

The gray eyes lifted to rest consideringly on her face. "But he can," he corrected her softly. "You and I have cause to know that he most certainly can and will do whatever he sets out to. Believe me, Julie, Wellington will welcome Devon with open arms, one of his beloved staff with considerable combat experience. Most of the Peninsular veterans are in America now. And in his gratitude, Wellington won't look too closely at whatever strings Dev has to pull in Whitehall to be put back on active duty."

"But he's doing this..." She stopped because she couldn't discuss what had occurred between them last night. She was no longer sure of the validity of her reasons in refusing Devon. But even if he were convinced he could overlook her background, would London let him? God, she thought suddenly, what does it matter? Dev's gone, back to the hell that war is. He had warned her last night that the next move must be hers, and then he had left her no way of making it.

"I'm sorry," she said finally. "I don't know why I thought you could stop him. I know Devon well enough by now to know that if he's made up his mind, then nothing will prevent him."

"In spite of my inability to help, I'm glad you came to me," Avon said. Having nothing else to offer her, he held out his hand.

She walked to the bed and took his long fingers, which gripped her own, reminding her bitterly of Dev. She sat down suddenly on the edge, her fear for him making her knees as weak as they had been last night. She had already seen the horrors of what Devon was about to face forever imprinted on his back.

Avon, remembering all she had endured, pulled her against his chest and allowed his arms to enfold and comfort her. He was offering her the only consolation he was capable of. Devon was gone, and if he were determined on this course, then nothing either of them could say would convince him that his rightful place was not in Brussels with the forces that were massing for an attack against Bonaparte.

Lost in the unpleasant realization of how little they could do, neither heard the opening of the door or saw the sudden check of the figure who had rushed up the stairs past the majordomo, whose efforts to intervene in that swift ascent had been made far too late.

"My God."

Julie freed herself from Avon's hold and sat up to face the door. The duke's only reaction to that shocked voice was a quick dilation of black pupils in the silver eyes.

Julie waited for him to speak, to order out of his room whoever this was who had dared to interrupt his privacy without even knocking. But as the duke's eyes calmly met the intruder's blazing green ones, the tension grew until finally she spoke.

"I'm afraid there's been some mistake," Julie said politely to the slim figure who stood rigidly in the

doorway. Mud-splashed breeches and riding boots
seemed almost a desecration of the elegance of the
chamber. And on second glance, curiously out of
place with the jade velvet cloak thrown back over one
shoulder and the hat, which was suddenly ripped off
to reveal a spill of long, red-gold curls.

"And you, madame, have made it," the Duchess of
Avon said scathingly, advancing toward the bed.

Julie stood quickly to face the fury of that accusation, perhaps even to protect the duke from the obvious hostility, but she couldn't help but admire the
coldly brilliant beauty rage gave the woman who
stalked across the chamber.

"And in *my* nightgown," Emily said bitterly,
reaching out to flick the priceless lace at Julie's throat.
"Really, Avon, you might have had more taste than to
dress her in my rail."

"But it's so becoming," the duke said softly. "Or
don't you think so, Emily? I had always considered
that that particular shade of ivory set off your com-
plexion to perfection, but now, seeing it on Julie, I
wonder..." He let his voice trail off suggestively.

"Julie?" his duchess repeated icily. "You should at
least have found someone with a real name. Is this the
very best that Paris had to offer?" Furious emerald
eyes traveled contemptuously down and then back up
the small figure standing before her.

"I beg your pardon," Julie said dangerously, her
own temper beginning to flare in response to the
mocking insults of the tall, slim redhead standing before her.

"Julie," Avon said from the bed behind her, his
voice as relaxed as if making introductions at a gar-
den party, "I would like to present my wife, the

Duchess of Avon. Emily, my dear, this is Juliette de Valmé."

"Get out of my husband's bedroom," the duchess said with great dignity.

"Your wife," Julie whispered, realizing what Emily thought, and that Avon, for some reason, was encouraging that belief.

"Oh, God," Emily jeered. "Don't tell me. He forgot to mention he's married." She laughed, but they both had heard the small, revealing break in her voice.

"This has gone far enough," Julie said furiously, turning to the duke. "What are you doing? Why are you doing this? Whatever she's done, surely she doesn't deserve to be treated like this."

"Whatever *I've* done?" Emily repeated. "What the hell do you mean, whatever 'she's' done?" she demanded hotly.

"I'm sorry," Julie said. "I don't know what you've done. I don't know what you *could* have done that would make him decide not to come home. I told him he was wrong to treat you this way, but it's not—"

"You told him? Good God, Avon," Emily said. "Must I be forced to ask this chit in *my* nightgown to offer an explanation for *my* husband's betrayal? Why are you doing this?"

Julie, recognizing how muddled her helpful intervention had become, once more faced the duke. "Tell her," she demanded. "Tell her who I am, Dominic."

"You tell her," he said, his face absolutely expressionless, but his eyes were fastened still with that strange intensity on his wife's features.

"Yes," Emily said, smiling rather bitterly. "You tell me. I can't tell you how impatient I am to hear this explanation."

"I'm the duke's—" Julie stopped, realizing suddenly that if she had thought Avon's proposal was ridiculous, how his wife would feel, especially since she had just been discovered in his bed.

"The duke's what?" Emily questioned sarcastically at her hesitation. And in unconscious imitation of her husband, one perfectly shaped brow rose in inquiry.

"Ward," Julie finished truthfully, unable to come up with a more acceptable lie.

"His ward," the duchess repeated softly, and then more loudly, incredulously, "his ward?"

"Yes," Julie whispered.

"Dominic?" Emily questioned suddenly.

"My ward," the duke agreed calmly.

"My God," she said again. "I could think of a better story than that, even caught *en deshabille*. Really, Avon."

"That, my dear, is one story you had better never have cause to create," her husband threatened softly.

At his tone, something in the emerald eyes flared and then eased, so that they rested, with considering intelligence, on his face. And softened unexpectedly.

"Dominic," she began, seeming to notice for the first time his thinness and the increased spread of silver in his midnight hair.

"If the duke's story is perfectly unbelievable, then it's probably the truth," Avon's valet said from behind Emily. He had heard most of the conversation, although he had proceeded more sedately up the stairs, given the difference in the ages of the duchess and himself.

And when he had arrived, Moss had taken time to study his master, always his first consideration. The signs of Avon's illness, signs that Emily was just becoming aware of, had already been carefully noted.

"After all," he continued to reason calmly, "Dominic could certainly have thought of a better explanation than that. You know he could, Your Grace."

"How old are you?" Emily asked suddenly, her eyes returning to the delicate features of the woman who stood between her husband and herself.

"Why?" Julie countered softly. "How old are you?"

Emily smiled, but there was no humor in the movement of her lips. "*My* husband, *my* house and *my* nightgown. So I think I'll ask the questions."

"Old enough not to leap to conclusions," Julie answered challengingly.

The green eyes studied her face a long time, and Julie calmly allowed their scrutiny. After all, she had nothing to hide. There was nothing between herself and the duke beyond friendship.

"Who are you?" the duchess asked again, and there was only politeness in the careful voice.

"Juliette de Valmé," Julie answered.

"And why are you in my husband's bedroom?"

"Because Devon's going to Brussels, and I hoped Avon would stop him."

"Devon? To Brussels?" The duchess's voice had lost the polite control again.

"To join Wellington," Julie explained, recognizing in that loss of control a possible ally.

"My God," Emily said, no longer listening. "How can he? After all he's been through. All that we've been through together. How could you, Dev?"

"Because he's a soldier. It's who Devon is. You know that, Emily," her husband said quietly. "It's all he's ever wanted to be. And what's shaping up in Europe is—''

''I know what's shaping up. Another bloody damned battle where men get blown up like cinders in a chimney. I damn well know what's going to happen. Don't patronize me, Dominic. I've been there. And so has Devon. Don't you understand? First you're gone. And I thought— And now Dev. Or don't you care? Either of you? Don't you care what you do to the ones you leave behind?''

''Of course they care,'' Moss said quietly, putting a comforting arm around her shoulders. ''You're over-wrought, Your Grace.''

Avon's valet pulled his mistress protectively against his chest and held her there tightly.

''And as for you, boy, I don't know what game you're playing here, but you ought to be ashamed. She's ridden all night to come to you. And how do you greet her? With tricks and riddles. What the hell's wrong with you?''

''I don't know,'' the duke said softly, meeting the furious eyes of his valet, which narrowed suddenly at the sincerity in that unexpected response. But in obedience to Moss's demand, Avon's gaze returned to the blanched face of his wife.

''I'm sorry,'' Avon said.

''Why would you do this? Why would you pretend that she's . . .'' Emily asked.

''Because I'm a fool,'' he said, hearing the hurt that echoed in her broken question.

''You've never been a fool,'' she whispered.

''Only about you. I've done some remarkably foolish things because of my feelings for you.''

"And was that what this little scene was all about? How you feel about me?" Emily asked.

"Believe it or not."

"I'd much prefer to believe it. But why?"

His eyes fell, and he forced his fingers to stop playing with the edge of the sheet.

"Because I needed to see exactly that response," he acknowledged finally.

"And what other response could you possibly expect? God, Dominic, you're frightening me. Please, my darling." The duchess stopped again, waiting for an explanation that would make sense of this entire episode.

At what was in that whisper, the duke met her eyes. And then the same hand that had been extended in friendship to Julie was offered to the duchess. But the simple gesture was eloquent this time with some other emotion. When his wife's slender fingers were placed on his outstretched palm, Avon conveyed them to his lips with something that, to Julie, looked very much like worship.

And then the duke lifted his silver gaze to find his ward's dark eyes glazed with tears that she was forced to blink to control.

"Julie, forgive us. The worst kind of family contretemps. I can offer you no excuse. Only my apologies. And those of my wife, which, I assure you, you'll have when I've made mine to her. Moss, if you'd take Mademoiselle de Valmé back to her chamber and make sure that she has everything she needs. And Emily, I'd like to talk to you. A few overdue explanations. If you'll be kind enough to hear them."

"Of course," his duchess said, still studying her husband's face. "Moss, please provide whatever my husband's ward requires from my wardrobe.'' There was no suggestion of mockery in the quiet appellation.

"I'd be delighted, Your Grace," Moss said. It wasn't clear which of their Graces he was addressing, and it didn't matter. He stretched an inviting hand in the direction of the chamber door, and Julie, after a quick glance at Avon, smiled at the valet and allowed herself to be led from the room. After what she had seen in the duke's eyes as they rested on his wife's face, she knew they were definitely *de trop*.

When the maid had finished altering one of Emily's morning dresses, Julie put it on and waited for someone to tell her what to do. She knew that they had probably forgotten all about her, but she wished she could do something to make up for that scene in the duke's bedroom. Although, of course, it had been his fault. And deliberately done, she'd decided, but she couldn't begin to imagine why.

Finally she wandered out into the silence of the wide upstairs hall and was surprised to find the duchess sitting at the top of the grand staircase. The door to her husband's room was closed behind her, and she was alone, her head resting against the tall post of the banister. From where she stood, Julie could see that Emily was still dressed in the stained breeches and the shirt she had worn before.

Julie hesitated a moment, looking down at the surprising Duchess of Avon. She couldn't see Emily's face, but she watched her surreptitiously wipe at her eyes, and she knew by those furtive efforts to hide the fact that she'd been crying that the duchess was aware of her presence.

"Pritchett wouldn't let me stay while he examined Dominic. I don't know why. I already know every inch of his body. I would know, better than that damned doctor, what's wrong."

"Maybe that's why he put you out. Professional jealousy," Julie suggested and was pleased to hear the slightly watery laugh in response.

"I'm sorry about this morning," Emily said. "If Avon wants a hundred wards, he can have them. As long as he's all right."

Julie eased down to sit on the step beside her.

"That's really all I am. I know how it must sound, but when he offered and when I accepted— The situation was— Neither of us saw any solution to what was happening. And I'm still grateful that he offered. But I'm no threat to your relationship," Julie explained and saw the amusement in the tear-washed emerald eyes that were raised in response.

"I know that. If I hadn't let my temper get the better of me, I would have known it when I walked into the room. But he's never before given me cause to be jealous. He always let me know that I was—" The duchess stopped and shook her head. "I don't know why I'm telling you all this. You can't possibly be interested. It's just that I can't stand this damn waiting. It's taking Pritchett too long. I'm going to kill him. And Dominic, too. Damn them all," she said again, feelingly.

Julie was surprised when the slender white fingers found her hand and held it tightly.

"Have you ever been in love?" Emily asked after several more endless minutes had passed, the door behind them firmly shut.

"Yes," Julie admitted, and she was unaware of the pain revealed in that word.

"Not with Dominic?" the duchess asked softly.

"No," Julie said and smiled. "I'm sure you can't understand that, but no, not the duke."

Emily's answering smile was, for the first time, given with its usual warmth.

"I'm sorry," she said softly. "What happened?"

"Happened?" Julie repeated.

"To the man you love? What went wrong?"

"Well, nothing, I suppose. But considering he's on his way to Brussels . . ." she said and waited.

"Dev?" Emily breathed. "You're in love with Dev?"

"I know nothing can come of it. I told him. But I can't help how I feel. I promise you I understand how impossible it is."

"I think—" Emily began, and then shook her head. "You're going to have to explain all that. If you love Devon, then why can nothing come of it? You make it sound as if—you're not married?"

"No, of course not. What do you think I am?" Julie asked.

"Avon's ward," Emily replied. "That's all I know about you. And that you're in love with my brother. Who's lost his mind and is going to rejoin the army. As soon as I've finished killing Dominic for going to France, I'm going to do the same to Devon."

"I'll help," Julie promised grimly.

"And does Dev love you?" the duchess asked.

"Yes," Julie said, and her eyes were very sure when she met those of Devon's sister.

"Then why would you say that nothing will come of it?"

"Because no matter how much I want to, I know I can't marry Dev. And he won't let me be his mistress," Julie added, almost an afterthought.

"Then I take it that you've offered," Emily asked, fascinated by the idea that her brother might inspire that kind of sacrifice. "To become his mistress."

"Yes," Julie answered, without any explanation to soften the effect.

"So that's when Avon made you his ward?"

Julie hesitated and then finally admitted, "It was a little more complicated than that. We thought Fouché might still be looking for me in France, especially after what we'd managed to accomplish in rescuing the duke. And Jean, who was going to take care of me, thought I'd— He believed Devon and I..." Julie's voice faltered over confessing what Jean had believed. "So I accepted Avon's offer because I had nowhere else to go," she finished truthfully.

"And Devon?" Emily asked.

"He wanted to marry me. And I told him I couldn't, and then he left for Brussels. So if anything happens to him there, I suppose it will be my fault," Julie said, putting into words what she had felt since she'd opened his letter.

"Can you tell me why you can't marry my brother?" Emily wasn't making much sense of this disjointed narrative, but she had always been able to focus on the essential.

"Because I'm the daughter of the Viscount Ashford. If you don't know the story, I'm sure there will be any number of people in London eager to tell you. And because I've spent the last five years of my life as a dealer in one of the largest and most notorious casinos in Paris," Julie said calmly. "Either situation seems insurmountable to me, but together..." She gave a small and very Gallic shrug. "And so I told Devon no. He seems to think that all those things don't matter and that eventually I'll realize that and change my mind."

"And you, on the other hand, are very sure they matter a great deal?" Emily said softly, and she couldn't hide the pity in her eyes.

"Aren't you? You know London. I saw what the viciousness of the ton did to my father. And Dev will be forced to overhear the same whispered remarks, endure the same cuts and snubs, the open insults. It broke my father. He never recovered from losing the world to which he had once belonged. To which he still desperately wanted to belong. And I couldn't bear to watch that happen to Devon because of me."

"But Dev... Don't you know how little Devon cares about those things? I don't know your father's situation. But I do know Dev, and I don't think all your reasons put together amount to a row of pins as far as he's concerned."

"Not for himself, perhaps. But do you think Devon would tolerate any insult to his wife? Or his children? I've seen his reaction," Julie said softly, remembering his fury with the drunk's taunt at the fair and with Jean's accusation. "And I *wasn't* his wife. I wasn't really anything to him then. How many duels do you think he'd survive? And he'd fight them. You know he would. And eventually he'd either kill someone or be killed."

"And so you'll refuse to marry him because you're afraid he isn't strong enough to deal with your past."

"It's not a matter of strength," Julie began to deny, but Emily's assertion that that was the essence of what lay between them was something she'd never considered before.

"What you're really afraid of is that Devon's love isn't strong enough to deal with all that without turning into something else, the same bitterness that ruined your father's life. But Devon isn't your father. And I think you must trust that he *can* handle every objection you just expressed. If that's all that stands between you, surely..."

"I wish I could believe you. You don't know how much."

"Then believe me. Because I know him very well. And when Devon asks you again—"

"But he won't. He told me that. I have to ask. I have to know that it's right. And now, even if I were convinced that that's the right course for us both..."

"Dev's gone."

"And it's too late."

"Why don't you let me see to it your place in the ton is so assured that when Devon returns, all your doubts will have been laid to rest? And you'll be free to make the offer, and Dev will accept. That won't be an exactly novel approach in this family," Emily said. Julie saw the softly remembering smile, but couldn't know the significance of that memory.

"You really think so?" Julie asked, wondering.

"No, I really know. We'll let Avon..." The pause recalled the situation that had brought them together at the top of the elegant staircase. Hearing the sudden doubt in the low voice, Julie put her arm quickly around the Duchess of Avon and held her as tightly as Moss had before.

* * *

Pritchett's face was unreadable when he finally opened the door. Emily stood to meet him, still holding onto Julie's hand. Julie could see the sheer terror in the emerald eyes of Dev's sister, and she supposed the doctor could, too, for the first words he said were intended to be reassuring.

"I can find nothing too seriously wrong with your husband, Your Grace. Beyond a troubling weakness of the lungs and a loss of strength caused by prolonged malnourishment and mistreatment. Considering the conditions of his imprisonment and the virulence of the pneumonia that resulted from it, I think he's very lucky. But I've prescribed bed rest. A month, at least. With nothing more strenuous to occupy his time than an occasional game of chess. I don't want his man of business or his estate manager to have access to the duke at all. I mean complete rest. I'll check on him periodically and have the local man look in between my visits. And I think if that regimen is adhered to carefully, he may, in time, recover fully. The lungs don't seem to be irreparably damaged as yet, but I'm sure you know how tricky such things can be. Even the slightest chill," he suggested ominously and then shrugged.

Realizing from her face that he had made his point, he kindly and rather unthinkingly patted Emily's shoulder. It was a familiarity he normally would never have allowed himself, but somehow this mud-stained duchess seemed far less intimidating than she should, considering the ancient title she bore. The women watched as he made his way down the steps and allowed the majordomo to help him into his coat.

"Do you know how to play chess?" Emily asked.

"No. Do you?" Julie answered.

"Not yet, but I intend to learn," the Duchess of Avon said, and turning, went into her husband's room, closing the door firmly behind her.

Chapter Fifteen

London—July 1815

The temperature of the crowded ballroom was enough to make several young debutantes swoon, and the officers who had unwisely worn their woolen uniforms were already regretting that decision. But somehow it had seemed appropriate that the military should turn out for these celebrations in full regalia, even if it were nearly August. Had it not been for the Duke of Wellington's stunning and decisive victory over the French five weeks before, none of these lavish entertainments would now be taking place. London, at this particular time of the year, should have been empty of members of the ton. But not this year. Not in the summer of 1815.

This was a time to glory in being English. In spite of the cost of that victory, named Waterloo, after Wellington's custom, for the village where he had established his headquarters. Even the name inspired a thrill, except in the hearts of those whose loved ones had appeared on the extensive casualty lists. But tonight society was attempting to forget the darker side of battle in honoring those who had assured the final defeat of the Emperor. Tonight was for celebration, and the swirl of uniforms and fashionable ball gowns that decorated the floor seemed to argue their success in forgetfulness.

The tall man who stood watching those waltzing couples had arrived more than was fashionably late. He had, however, been greeted with pleasure by his host and hostess, despite the fact that he was also un-invited. And he alone, it seemed, had chosen not to appear in uniform tonight, although he was certainly entitled. He was dressed instead in the somber black of formal evening attire, unrelieved except for an onyx stickpin and the fall of his snow-white cravat.

His blue eyes had searched the floor only a moment before finding the small, whirling figure held too closely in the arms of a handsome young hussar. The cap of gleaming ebony curls was longer than when he had last seen her, almost four months ago. But even the cropped hair was becoming the rage. Because, despite the whispers that still followed her passage through a ballroom, whatever the beautiful ward of the Duke of Avon had chosen to do or to wear since her arrival in London in the middle of May had ultimately set the mode.

Anything Juliette de Valmé did was charming in the eyes of her many suitors. It was rumored by those who knew about such things that Avon had already re-fused a half-dozen offers on her behalf from the few men who were courageous enough and deemed them-selves eligible enough to brave the duke's cold reception.

Devon found he had been unconsciously supporting his left elbow with his right hand, and he knew his decision to discard his sling had not been a prudent one. But he'd be damned if he'd show up at a victory celebration like Banquo's ghost. There were enough painful reminders in the room of the realities of war. He didn't intend to be another.

"Devon?" A voice interrupted his reverie, and he turned to find an old Peninsular comrade considering him with questioning eyes. "I'd thought you were still, that is, I'd heard you hadn't yet come back to town."

"This afternoon," Devon said easily. "I'm afraid I wasn't invited. I've made my apologies."

"Which were unnecessary, I'm sure, considering your current reputation and the occasion."

"Our hostess very graciously forgave me," Devon said, ignoring the knowing smile that answered that unnecessary comment.

"I should imagine she would. Have you seen Emily? She's here. And even Avon. Guarding his treasures."

"His treasures?" Devon questioned.

"His duchess and his ward. The Divine Juliette. I suppose, being part of his family, you'll be in a position to cut us all out. Somewhat of an inside track."

"I'm afraid—" Devon began.

"Of course, you may be too late. You'll have to line up behind half the bachelors in the city. But I'd forgotten. You'd already joined Wellington before Juliette rescued Avon. Surely Emily wrote you?" his informant asked, seeing the confusion in the colonel's features.

"The post was uncertain. I don't seem to have heard about the rescue. Perhaps you'd be so kind," Devon suggested, the faintest smile beginning to hover about lips that had lately had little to smile about.

"Damned most romantic thing I've ever heard. I understand you knew about the duke's role in the war, that you even worked for him while you were... incapacitated."

At Devon's nod, his informant continued eagerly, "Well, it seems Juliette was Avon's agent in Paris. Or rather, originally, her father was. The Viscount Ashford. The government needed someone in position in France to spy on Napoleon. Avon approached Ashford, despite the circumstances under which he'd left England, and he agreed. And then later, when he became ill, his daughter took his place. She provided Avon with invaluable information that she acquired while running her father's casino in Paris. The duke went into France to get her out when Bonaparte finally discovered what was going on, but she ended up rescuing him.

"I don't have all the details. It's been very hushed, as you can imagine. Only the barest bones of the story. They say Avon was furious that his role in the war has finally become public knowledge. But too many people knew about Mademoiselle de Valmé's bravery to keep it quiet. Although, to be honest, I doubt half of the men that are buzzing around her give a fig about her patriotism. I would imagine most of them are attracted by her far more obvious attributes. You really hadn't heard the story?" the man asked suddenly, recognizing Devon's fascination with his tale.

"No," the colonel assured him softly, "I hadn't heard it. But perhaps I can convince Emily to present me. Familial consideration, if nothing else."

"Well, good luck. But you won't manage a dance. They're always spoken for in advance. Even Emily won't be able to help you there. It's good to see you back," he said, punctuating his words with a friendly tap on Devon's left shoulder.

As he had already turned away, he missed the quick grimace that light touch had caused. Devon unobtrusively eased his palm again under the elbow of the aching left arm and wondered where Emily could be. It was amazing how quickly he'd found Julie, considering the throng. The dark blue eyes watched her laughing figure a few minutes longer, unaware that his sister, who had found him despite the crush, was quite accurately reading his thoughts from the grimness of the smile that played over his lips.

"What's wrong with your arm?" she asked, and he only then became aware of her presence at his side.

"Nothing," he said, quickly removing the supporting fingers.

"Liar," she returned with assurance, but without rancor, and they smiled at one another.

"Are you really all right?" she asked, when he finally met her eyes. The deep blue of his was too bright, a brightness whose cause she recognized, and the flush across his cheekbones was not caused by the sun. Sisterlike, she put the back of her hand against his temple and could feel the heat of his fever.

"Don't," he said softly, and with his right hand he caught and lowered her fingers. He smiled at her again to take the sting out of his denial. "Just leave it alone, Emily. I'm staying only a moment, I promise."

"Dev..."

"Where's Dominic?" he asked, forcing a change of subject.

"In the card room. Have you seen Julie?"

"Only from a distance," he answered, waiting for whatever sisterly advice he knew she would want to give.

However, she surprised him. The green eyes rested on his face with concern, but she didn't say whatever she was thinking.

"Is Dominic recovered?" he asked and knew by her smile, knew before she told him, that her husband was again Avon.

"He's fine. He's wonderful."

"Thanks to Julie," Devon said, his tired blue eyes filled suddenly with humor.

"You've heard the story, I take it. One of Dominic's better efforts. I'm sorry your share in the rescue was lost somewhere in translation from the French. We decided that it might open questions as to the time you and Julie had spent together, and so, my dear, you were never in France. In case anyone asks."

"Of course," her brother said gallantly. "I'm delighted not to have been there."

"I'm glad you're home. Despite hearing about your exploits from half the army, I really wanted to see for myself that you'd survived. Did you have to go about proving whatever it was you were trying to prove with such recklessness?"

"Yes," he said, not bothering to explain the emotion that had driven him at Waterloo, an emotion he'd not acknowledged, even to himself, for a long time. He had gone to Brussels to prove that he was the same man he had always been, that the unthinking courage that had served him in countless battles in Iberia had not deserted him because of what had happened to him there.

"And did you accomplish whatever you set out to do? Or will you go haring off to the next war we become embroiled in?"

"If," he started softly, his eyes returning briefly to rest on one of the dancers.

She waited, watching his face until he again became aware of her presence.

"If," he began again, "I have my way, I'm going to be raising babies."

"I beg your pardon?" Emily said in surprise.

"Babies," her brother repeated. "You know. You have one. Little Gypsy girls and..." He stopped at the look on her face.

"Babies," she echoed faintly. In spite of the fact that her own son had always adored his uncle, Emily had apparently never thought of Devon with children.

"But first," he said, "I have to acquire a wife." He had come tonight because he had to see Julie. But he had also come hoping that she'd finally realized nothing stood in the way of their marriage except her own fears. He had never cared about the opinion of the ton, but according to his recent informant, even that hurdle had been overcome. Perhaps tonight.

"Any advice, my only and well-beloved sister?"

"No. No advice, but I'll wish you luck. I like my husband's ward very much. And she plays a very skillful game of chess."

"Chess?" Devon asked in surprise.

"Never mind. I'll explain later. The music's ending. You might just catch Julie between partners. If you hurry."

"No, I don't think so," he said and smiled at her raised brows. "I think I'll join Avon in the card room. I have something of his I need to return," he continued, remembering the duke's emerald seal, which he carried once more in his pocket. And, of course, the next move must be, perhaps now more than ever, Julie's.

The Duchess of Avon watched her brother stroll through the crowded ballroom toward the small antechamber where the gentlemen who chose not to dance were occupied with their card games. He never glanced at the floor where her husband's ward was surrounded by the usual bevy of handsome men.

It was Emily who was waiting for Julie the next time the music ended. She used her prerogative as her chaperone to charmingly dash the hopes of the young man who owned the next dance and sent him callously on his way. When she turned back, Julie was smiling at her rather questioningly.

"I thought you deserved fair warning," Emily said.

"He trods toes," Julie suggested. "I know. But poor dancing isn't a reason to..."

"Devon's here," Emily said simply, and was well rewarded by what was suddenly revealed in the dark eyes.

"Avon said it might be weeks before he concluded his duties with the army of occupation. I don't know why everyone else seemed to have had leave to return, and Dev had to stay."

"There apparently was a reason for that delay. I'm afraid my husband has been as deceptive about Dev's duties as about your background."

Julie wondered why Emily was being so cryptic if Devon had been working again for Avon. Since the fabricated story about her past that Avon had "revealed" to carefully selected sources—sources the duke was sure wouldn't be able to keep such a delicious and slightly scandalous secret—everyone was aware that espionage was Avon's vocation. But that, of course, was not the pertinent part of Emily's information.

"Where is he?"

"He went looking for Dominic."

"But not for me?" Julie asked softly.

"Well, to be fair, you were rather surrounded. And I think, from what you've told me, Dev's still waiting for your decision. Avon's in the card room. Shall I dance with your next beau?"

There was a long pause, and then Julie smiled serenely. "I don't think so. Thank you, Emily, but I'll attend to my own obligations."

She turned to find her next partner standing patiently at hand, and with a smiling apology, she allowed him to sweep her into the waltz that had already begun.

And so it wasn't until later, during a respite from dancing demanded by the heat, when her partner had been dispatched for refreshment, that Julie looked up to find Devon's blue eyes resting calmly on her face. He was thinner and deeply tanned from the summer's maneuvers, the fine lines around his eyes a pale contrast to the darkness of his skin. His hair was streaked with gold burned by the sun, and she thought he had never been more handsome.

"Julie," he greeted her softly.

"I've never seen you in uniform," she said, glancing at his quietly elegant evening dress, starkly understated in the sea of military paraphernalia. The smile she loved began to lift the corners of his mouth.

"I had thought," he said, looking around him, "that I'd try to fit in. I didn't realize that parade-ground wear had become de rigueur for an evening in London. My apologies."

Then the silence between them stretched uncomfortably. There were no social niceties to be exchanged. And they couldn't talk about anything else here.

"Would you dance with me, Dev?" she invited. It was an acceptable way to have his arms around her. She thought from his smile that he knew exactly what she was thinking.

"I was told that the beautiful and popular Mademoiselle de Valmé never had an open spot on her card."

"I don't," she answered, her dark eyes flashing with mischief. "But I'll lie to my partner if you'll dance with me."

His eyes left hers to watch a waltzing couple sweep gracefully by. And then returned to smile at her regretfully.

"Forgive me, Julie, but I've been traveling most of the day, and..." He took a breath, but he didn't finish the explanation.

"Of course," she said, embarrassed by his refusal. They seemed almost strangers. "Then...perhaps another time."

"I'd give an arm to be able to dance with you tonight," he said, and the old, familiar teasing note was back in his voice. "Would you like the heart of a one-armed suitor to go with all these others you've managed to collect while I've been gone?"

"No," she answered, smiling at his flattery, "I don't think I would like that at all. But I would like your promise that we'll dance together. If not tonight, then eventually," she begged, hoping for something.

Dev seemed so contained, and into her joy at seeing him again, a faint prickle of unease moved. Devon had always been so sure of the depth and permanence of his love. Surely in the long months they'd been separated he hadn't decided that he no longer wanted her. Her hand involuntarily found his, seeking reassurance that he still felt the same.

"We have an audience," he reminded her softly, but he lifted her fingers to brush his lips across them, and he found that it was suddenly hard to breathe. "And I think we've given them more than enough to talk about for the evening."

"You're not leaving?" she asked, correctly interpreting that last remark, in spite of what the touch of his lips on the back of her hand had done to her emotions.

"Yes, my darling, I'm going home," he said and then added, "I'm at my father's, Julie, if you decide—"

"Devon?" a beautifully modulated voice inquired softly, breaking into whatever he had been about to tell her.

Julie forced her mind from its fascination with what was in Dev's eyes. Something was definitely wrong. But before she could formulate any coherent explanation beyond that first terrifying thought, she became aware that Devon's attention had shifted, rather gratefully she suspected, to the tall, slender blonde at his side.

Elizabeth, now the Countess of March, extended a shapely white hand, and her lips smiled in what Julie, at least, recognized clearly as an invitation.

Dev's gaze fell to the small fingers of the woman he had guarded so tenderly through France as they rested, still safely held in his. Julie gently began to extract her hand from his hold and felt an unfamiliar tremble in his strong fingers as he reluctantly released her. Again the flicker of unease stirred in her consciousness.

"I wanted to introduce you to my husband," Elizabeth said. "Since you are my oldest friend in the entire world, I would very much like the two of you to be friends. It would mean so much to me if, Dev, in spite of everything..." Her voice trailed regretfully.

"I'd be very honored to meet March, Elizabeth," he said to the lovely woman at his side. He kissed the hand she offered and then released it. But her fingers tucked familiarly into the crook of his right arm.

"I hope you'll excuse Colonel Burke, Miss Valmer," Elizabeth said charmingly, making Devon's excuses for him. "We haven't seen one another in several months, and my husband is so seldom in London I'm afraid I won't have this opportunity again for some time." Her eyes smiled into Devon's, clearly conveying information she wanted him to have. "March much prefers the country, although I'm generally bored to tears there. But he's most generous in sharing me with my family. I often come up to town without him."

"De Valmé," Julie corrected softly, watching the interplay.

"Of course. Mademoiselle de Valmé. I remember. Forgive me, but I have a dreadful memory for names. Devon had to prompt me throughout my season, or I should never have managed at all. When someone approached, he was always there to whisper the proper title in my ear." Her smile to him was deliberately intimate, and then, to avoid rudeness, was redirected at the last possible second to include Julie. "And French names," she said, shaking her head helplessly over their seeming impossibility. The softly clustered curls bobbed gently, releasing a breath of lavender. "While you're in London, perhaps you might consider using your— Oh, forgive me, my dear. I'd forgotten that your father's name might not be something that you wish to remind people of."

"Why not?" Julie said, smiling easily. This was certainly not the first derogatory reference to her father she'd endured in London. It was, however, the least veiled. And clearly for Devon's benefit. "I loved my father very much. I'm not ashamed to be his daughter."

She met Dev's blue eyes, which were resting consideringly on her face. He had said nothing in her defense. But, of course, nothing was really needed. She had already dealt with the worst London could offer and had found that even the most pointed remarks had gradually lost their power to wound.

She had thought that when Devon returned it would all fall into place. Emily had been so sure that he would be able to deal with the ton's lingering doubts about her suitability to be included in their small, tightly knit circle—doubts only the feminine guardians of that sacred *beau monde* seemed still to harbor.

But nothing was going as she'd planned. Devon was so different, so reserved. And all the old fears began to resurface. Was he acting so strangely because he was ashamed of her? Or wondering what the countess thought about her background? Apparently Emily had been wrong, she decided bitterly, and all her confidence about the future began to ebb in a wave of panic. Devon's distaste for her notoriety was exactly what she had feared.

"If you'll excuse me," she forced herself to say, "I need to find my next partner. I'm being extremely rude. Devon, I'm glad you're back. I'm sure I'll see you again soon at Avon House."

He looked down briefly at Elizabeth's hand resting possessively on his arm, and then back up at Julie.

"Until then, my Lady Luck," he said softly, and smiled at her. It was the old smile. There were no shadows there. And her lips moved unconsciously to answer it. Their eyes met again, and then he was gone, guided across the floor, still looking into the smiling face of the beautiful Countess of March, who was probably reminding him of all they had once shared. "My oldest friend," she had said.

Julie stood a moment, allowing her eyes to follow him until the somber black of his evening attire was swallowed up in the swirling sea of crimson and green and blue uniforms. She turned and blindly threaded her way through the dancers. At some point in that near-headlong flight, she felt Emily's fingers catch her arm, but she didn't pause until she had reached the safety of an alcove, sheltered from the ballroom by its ornamental greenery.

"Who is she?" Julie asked bitterly, knowing Emily well enough to know she would have been very aware of the interrupted reunion.

"The Countess of March," Emily answered, the tone of her answer as caustic as the question. "Didn't Dev introduce you?"

"Dev said barely three words to me," Julie said. And then, "She's very beautiful."

"Yes."

"And she seems very popular. I've noticed her before, but I never knew that she and Dev..."

"Why wouldn't she be popular?" Emily said, but the small laugh that accompanied the question was mocking. "She has everything the ton admires—birth and breeding, wealth and power. She's beautiful. She married well and produced the required heir within the year. The Countess of March has done everything that London considers necessary for perfection."

"You don't like her," Julie said softly, comforted by the obvious loathing that had been in Emily's voice as she had spoken those compliments.

"Like her?" Emily repeated in surprise. "My dear, I once came nearer to murdering that woman than I have ever come to killing anyone. I despise her. She's the woman—" Seeing the sudden pain in Julie's eyes and realizing what she must think, Devon's sister decided on sharing the truth about the Countess of March, a truth she had told no one but her brother.

"When Dev was wounded, he made me write to her, to destroy whatever commitment had been between them. But then we brought him home from Spain and we were so afraid he was going to die. So I went to her. I broke my word to him, but— I know it's difficult to believe, seeing him today..." Emily's voice faded with the remembrance of those dark days.

"Emily?" Julie probed softly.

"I begged her to go to him, to tell him that it didn't matter. That she loved him still, despite what the doctors said."

"And she refused," Julie guessed.

"In order to marry March." Emily shook her head slightly in disbelief. "And then, when Dev—after the surgery, when he found out, he thought her family had forced her to marry the earl. I told him the truth. I wanted him to know exactly what she is. So why my idiotic brother would allow himself to be kidnapped by her tonight, I shall never know."

"Dev seemed so— I don't know what he was. He went with her, but I thought... His hand trembled when he released mine. He was so strange."

"I don't know what's going on. But I know someone who will. After all, Avon has very good sources of information. And as for Elizabeth, I doubt my brother will be taken in again. She has everything she wants except, apparently, Dev. But that's one game at which she won't succeed. My brother is not that big a fool.''

Emily pressed a swift kiss on her cheek and went to find her husband who, she seemed to feel, would have all the answers.

It was very early the next morning, after a night spent endlessly reliving the few minutes she had been allowed with Devon on the crowded ballroom floor, that Julie had dressed and sought out Emily, hoping for the promised explanation for Dev's behavior. But the duchess was not in her room, and Julie never considered seeking her in Avon's. Her questions would simply have to wait until her host and hostess rose and joined her downstairs.

Unless Emily was out on one of her early-morning gallops, she thought suddenly, and in that case, she might already have returned and be downstairs, breakfasting alone, as was her custom on those occasions.

Julie hurried down the long staircase, one hand holding up her gown so that the slender ankles of the Gypsy girl were again exposed. She halted at the raised voices in the dining room. Avon and Emily, obviously engaged in some argument. That alone was enough to cause her hesitation. She had never before heard them even disagree.

She had turned and begun to steal back to the upper levels of the vast Mayfair mansion when something Avon said caught her attention. And after that, she could no more have stopped listening to what was, undoubtedly, a very private conversation, despite the raised voices, than she could have ceased to breathe.

"Because Devon didn't intend for Julie to know. And I gave him my word, Emily."

"But why? That's ridiculous, Dominic, and you know it. Dev's my brother, and I love him, but this makes no sense."

Avon's answer was too low for Julie to hear, but Emily's denial rang clear.

"Oh, God, Dominic. Poor Dev. It's so unfair."

The rest was muffled, inaudible, and in spite of the chaos of her shocked mind, Julie was certain that the duke had taken his distraught wife into his comforting arms.

Avon's explanation was softly spoken, so that Julie, trying desperately to hear, caught only broken sentences. But those were enough to force the suddenly trembling knees to bend, and eventually she sat alone on the massive staircase and learned the truth that Devon had hidden from her last night.

"...too widely spread...amputation...very dangerous in his condition...near the shoulder," and then clearly, "this afternoon, but Pritchett thinks he may have waited too long..."

Julie swallowed the fear that had grown as her mind began to make sense of those scattered phrases. And she remembered Devon's question. *Would you like the heart of a one-armed suitor to go with all the others?* And her laughing denial.

She took a deep breath and rose, forcing her numbed body to begin again to react, as she had forced her mind. She calmly retraced her steps to the landing and then down the winding servants' stairs and out into the humid heat of the London morning.

* * *

The ride in the hackney coach seemed endless, Avon's words echoing painfully over and over. *Amputation... near the shoulder... waited too long* repeated in her head until she thought she would scream. Not Dev, Emily had protested. Not Dev, her own heart agreed.

But Julie knew exactly what his reaction would be, the smiling pretense that it didn't matter. That it was nothing, as the devastation she had seen before on his back was nothing. Shrapnel, he'd said. Nothing.

She knew how he'd hate this. The forced dependence. The brutally obvious imperfection of his body. But she'd make it up to him, she'd show him that it didn't matter. That she loved him in spite of...

And if he would hate the other, how he would despise that. I've refused you when you were whole and strong, and now that you no longer will be, I'm rushing to tell you that I want you. At least that's what you'll think. Because last night, last night when I had the chance to ask you, before I knew... Before I knew, she repeated, struck by that thought, because she had suddenly realized that no one could know that she knew. Not Avon nor Emily nor Devon.

Dev would marry her if she went to him now, full of loving concern for what was about to happen to him. The doubts about his love, which had been created by his behavior last night, were banished by the revelation of what he had been hiding from her. He hadn't wanted her to know. That's why he had come last night. He hadn't told her then because he had given her one last chance to come to him simply because she

knew it was right. Her decision, he'd said, one that he
hadn't wanted forever tainted by her pity.

She remembered again the teasing, off-hand question, *Would you like the heart of a one-armed suitor?*
And her denial. If only she'd asked him last night. But
now he would always doubt her reasons. Somewhere
would always be the thought that it was pity or guilt
for sending him into that battle that had brought her,
full of regret, to ask him to marry her this particular
morning.

He didn't need to be weakened today by her tears,
her concern. He didn't want her pity. He didn't need
it. Not Dev. He needed all the strength he possessed to
endure, with his smiling confidence intact, the blow
that would fall today.

And from somewhere, like a miracle, Avon's words
to Emily came into her head. *I needed to see exactly
that reaction.* And Emily's reaction, which Avon had
cherished in circumstances similar to Dev's, was jealousy. Bloodthirsty fury. And an open declaration that
no one else would have the man she loved.

The carriage jolted to a stop, and the jumbled confusion of her mind cleared. Deception, she thought.
No one can possibly be aware that I know. One more
deception, my darling. And this one not for the hand,
but for the game. A simple bluff to win the game that
will last the rest of our lives. And I *am* the professional.

She scrubbed at her cheeks to remove any lingering
trace of the tears that had been her first reaction. She
bit her lips to give them color and pinched the pale
skin over her cheekbones. She ran shaking fingers

through her tumbled curls, thankful for the summer's humidity, which ensured their spring.

She glanced down at the pale pink morning gown she had so carelessly chosen. She hadn't known she would be dressing for the most difficult role she'd ever undertake. Far harder than the urchin or the Gypsy girl. Far more important. She gave a mental shrug and tugged the short sleeves farther off her shoulders so that the neckline scooped as low as the peasant blouse she had worn so long ago. The material skimmed the top of ivory breasts that heaved once with the deep, fortifying breath she took. And then she grasped the driver's hand and stepped out before General Burke's home.

Chapter Sixteen

She knocked imperiously on the front door, then pressed trembling hands against the skirt of her simple dress. She dried the telltale moisture from her palms and wished she had gloves. He would never believe she had left the house without bonnet or gloves and wearing what was obviously—

The aging butler opened the door in response to her knock, and suddenly the calmness she had sought settled over her. Like the almost supernal calm of that endless moment before the ball in the roulette wheel stops, or the dice fall, when the betting is heavy enough to ruin the house. Then, as now, there was no need for fear. Whatever the outcome, it had already been decided by the fickle gods of chance. My Lady Luck, he'd called her last night, and unconsciously, she raised her chin and allowed the full force of her smile to dazzle the old man.

"I'd like to see Colonel Burke, please. And would you pay my driver. I seem to have come away without my reticule."

She didn't wait for his response, but swept by him and into the hall. In spite of her air of confidence, she closed her eyes in relief at the conversation behind her, evidence that she had been obeyed.

"I'm sorry, my lady," the butler said as he reentered the house through the front door he hadn't bothered to close behind him, "but the colonel isn't receiving guests this morning."

He glanced rather pointedly at the hall clock, and she was surprised to find that it was only half past nine. Since most of the ton went to bed at four and seldom rose before the early afternoon, she realized how bizarre he must think this call. A woman scorned, she reminded herself grimly of the role she was playing, will do any number of bizarre things.

"He'll see me," she said aloud. "Tell him..." She paused and then knew her inclination was right. "Tell him Lady Ashford would like to talk to him."

"But, my lady—" he began to protest.

"And I'll wait." She raised questioning brows and allowed her eyes to consider the doorways that stretched on either side of the central hall.

"I'll ask," the butler said grudgingly, but he tottered ahead of her and waved her rather ungraciously into the main salon. When she was safely ensconced there, he disappeared, and somewhere from across the hall she heard a door close.

She shut her eyes, trying to think what she was going to say to make him believe her. She remembered Emily's furious eyes that morning at Sandemer, but she was afraid that when she saw Dev, she'd betray herself. Afraid that her eyes would stray, searching for evidence of the injury. Banishing that thought because she could feel the sting of tears, she pictured instead the Countess of March's graceful white hand against the black of Dev's sleeve.

Not the right arm, she thought suddenly. He had used his right arm to hold her hand. To raise it to his lips. She shut her eyes, trying to visualize the few minutes she had spent with him last night. The left, she knew without a shadow of a doubt. He hadn't moved his left arm at all. It had hung awkwardly at his side the entire time. And that's why he hadn't danced with her, she realized. Because he couldn't. Or she would have known immediately.

"The colonel will see you, my lady. But he's dressing. He asks if you'll wait. And I'm to offer you tea."

Tea, she thought vaguely. Why would I want tea? Because the English drink tea for breakfast. And because I've come calling at the crack of dawn. I wonder what he'd do if I asked for brandy, she thought irrationally, but she controlled that impulse and simply shook her head. After all, Devon might be suspicious if she reeked of brandy. Or, she thought daringly, it might be a nice touch. But before she could make that decision, the old man had disappeared again.

She wandered aimlessly to the windows overlooking the street. Her coach had disappeared, and there was no traffic so early in this quiet residential neighborhood. The trees were green, and their leaves drooped heavy in the summer heat, but their vividness faded as other scenes filled her mind. The caravan where she'd shaved him. The kiss beside the stream. The shadowed barn with its reaching fingers of light. Her father's room above the casino. And Sandemer.

Lost in those images, she was unaware of the entrance of the man she was waiting for. He stood watching a moment as her fingers traced the edge of the window. He wondered who had told her. Emily, he supposed. Avon had known, of course. And whatever Dominic knew was eventually shared with Emily. It didn't really matter.

Only one more thing to be faced, to be endured. And there would be compensations. But first the concern, the dark, tear-glazed eyes trying to avoid looking at his arm. And then eventually he'd be allowed to hold her. And he knew, despite his reluctance to face her pity, that holding her this morning would make the afternoon bearable. And perhaps she would be there when it was over. Compensations. But first . . .

Somehow she became aware that he was there. She knew suddenly that he was watching her. She bit her lips as she had in the coach, and forced herself to visualize again March's beautiful wife laughing up into Devon's face. And his answering smile.

She turned to face him, to begin the deception she'd planned.

"A late night, Colonel Burke?" she asked softly. "And whatever did you do with the lady's husband?"

She walked away from the window, the simple gown swaying gracefully as she crossed the floor that stretched between them. Away from morning sun that had created a corona behind the ebony curls, so that finally he could see her face clearly. And in the dark eyes were none of the emotions he had dreaded. They were the flashing eyes of the Gypsy girl—and they held no tears. And no pity.

"The lady's husband?" he repeated questioningly. He was leaning against the frame of the doorway, his pose perfectly relaxed. His right shoulder was propped on the wooden molding, and his left arm was bent at the elbow, the slightly curled fingers resting near his waist. He had hooked his left thumb in the last buttonhole of his blue silk waistcoat to support the injured arm, but the back of his hand hid that. His long legs in tight doeskins and gleaming Hessians were crossed at the ankles, and although he wore no coat over the snow-white shirt and waistcoat, he looked as elegant as any London gentleman she had yet encountered. And as much at his ease. Her lips almost lifted at his deception. Bluff and counterbluff, my darling, she thought, as she had once before.

"The Countess of March," she said haughtily, forcing her mind back to the game.

"Elizabeth?" he asked, and she was pleased to hear his disbelief that she could imagine there might be anything between them.

"And was she as entertaining as before?" she asked boldly. His head tilted slightly, questioning something in her tone or in her wording. Something that must have rung false. Careful, she cautioned herself. Don't overplay.

"She must be very talented indeed. Somehow she doesn't look that...passionate," she finished carefully. "But we both know looks are deceiving."

"Julie, that's not—"

"You walk back into London after all these months," she interrupted furiously, "after the time we spent together, after that night at Sandemer..." She allowed a small, throbbing catch in her voice before she continued her angry tirade. "And all she has to do is to crook her finger, and there you are again, her devoted slave. Emily was sadly mistaken in her judgment of her brother."

"Emily?" he questioned in surprise.

"She said you weren't that big a fool. Apparently," she added sarcastically, "she gave you more credit than you deserve."

He shook his head, and his eyes dropped, hiding his sudden amusement. Elizabeth, he thought in amazement. God, she's jealous of Elizabeth. If she could only know how little he cared. He straightened, intending to put an end to Julie's misconception about what had happened last night after he had forced himself to walk away from her. But the pain occasioned by even that slight movement of his arm reminded him of what he had steeled himself to face when Ashton had announced her. And instead . . .

"She can't have you, Dev," Julie whispered, and the blue eyes of the man she loved raised again. They looked so tired, she thought, so ill. *Maybe already too late.* Avon's words echoed, but she blocked them. "She had her chance, and now you're mine. And you always will be."

"Julie," he said again, and at what was in her face, he knew his long wait was over.

But before her control broke, she had succeeded in what she had set out to do. When her lips trembled and her eyes filled, he never thought it was out of pity. He accepted at face value what she was offering. He believed that she had come today only because she thought he still cared for Elizabeth.

"She may be more experienced at... She may know more ways to please you than I do," Julie said, stumbling a little over the admission. And her lips trembled again. "But I'll learn, Dev. You can teach me. Like you did at Sandemer. And you'll never regret it. I swear to you, my darling, I'll make you happy. She can never give you little Gypsy girls, and any sons she bears you will all carry his name. You *said* you didn't want a mistress," she argued, knowing she was losing control.

"Don't cry, my darling," he said, helpless in the face of the tears that were streaming.

"Oh, God," she said, wiping at her cheeks with the back of her hand. "I never cry. I darken my lashes, and if I cry, they run," she explained disjointedly. "I never cry," she protested again, and raised her eyes to meet his.

And found he was smiling at her. He had straightened away from the support of the doorway and stood watching her.

"Oh, Dev, don't still be in love with her. I couldn't bear it if I thought you cared about someone else. I've been so stupid. But I've always loved you. You knew that. Please, don't want her instead of me. Not when I love you so very much."

"Enough, Julie?" he asked softly.

And knowing what he wanted, what he had demanded from the first, she took a deep breath, feigning a moment's hesitation. And the blue eyes again waited.

"Devon Burke, will you please, please marry me? I don't give a damn what anyone says—about my father, about Paris, about anything. Finally, I know that

you don't, either. I just want to be your wife. And I
hope I'm not too late. You do still want me, Dev?''

He opened his right arm invitingly, and somehow
she was across the room, being crushed fiercely against
the strength of his body. Where she had always belonged. She never thought about the left arm that had
not moved to welcome her. It meant nothing. Less
than nothing that it rested, caught between their bodies.

And finally he released her enough to look into her
eyes, searching them briefly and finding only love.

"Yes," he said unnecessarily, crushing her against
him again. "And Julie," he added, whispering the
words into the gleaming softness of her fragrant curls,
"I have no idea where the Countess of March spent
the night. But it wasn't with me, my darling. I was very
busy dreaming." He paused, and she pulled away to
look into his eyes.

"Dreaming?" she questioned, knowing what he
would say.

"Gypsy girls," he whispered, and lowered his
mouth to hers. There was nothing gentle about the invasion of his tongue. He was hungry for her, had been
hungry through too many long, lonely nights. But her
need was as great as his, and she answered as he had
hoped she would. Her arms circled his neck, and he
lifted her with the sure strength of his right arm. Her
mouth clung, warm and demanding.

The fingers of his left hand moved between their
straining bodies. He touched the nipple of her breast
through the soft cotton of her dress and felt the gasping response of her mouth against his. He caught the
hardened bud between his fingers and caressed its tip

with his thumb. But even that small movement sent tremors of agony up his damaged arm.

He needed to tell her. He knew that it wouldn't matter, but she deserved to know. She belonged to him now, but it would be some time before he could make her completely his. And he needed to explain that to her.

He bent to let her toes touch the floor and loosened the grip of his right arm. He heard her murmured protest, and welcomed the clinging refusal of her mouth to release him.

"No," she protested, her fingers locked in the sunstreaked chestnut of his hair, pulling his head down to follow the unwilling descent of her body.

"Julie," he said against her lips. His right hand caught the fingers of her left, which circled his neck, and he removed them, holding them tightly in his own. "Julie," he said again, laughing, as she pressed her small body more firmly against the hard erection that was so reassuring of his feelings for her.

"Listen to me," he said, his amused response to her demonstration of how much she'd missed him clear in his voice.

"No," she said again, struggling to gain the release of that tightly held hand.

"Julie," he repeated, and then finally, knowing what would demand her instant attention, he whispered against her forehead, "You're hurting my arm, darling. Please, let go."

She stepped back as if he'd slapped her, released him so suddenly she might have fallen if he had not still held her trembling fingers. He supported her a moment, hating the terror in her eyes.

"It's all right. Just a small souvenir from Boney, but it's still a little uncomfortable."

She swallowed suddenly, and finally allowed her eyes to trace down the length of the left arm, from the broad shoulder to the slightly swollen fingers, once more curled rather unnaturally against his body.

His smile was as quick and readily given as it had always been when she finally raised her eyes to his face.

"No tears," he whispered, releasing her fingers to catch her chin between his thumb and forefinger. "Remember what they do to your lashes. Promise me, Lady Luck, no tears." He released her chin, and smiling, wiped at a small, dark smudge beneath her eye. His fingers trembled suddenly when they touched the velvet of her skin.

"No tears," she promised, willing herself to calmness to hear him say finally what she already knew, what she had known before she had come. She would never confess that her performance had hidden that knowledge. Only a small deception between them. And the only one, she vowed silently, that I shall ever be guilty of, my love.

He remembered, through the daze of pain and weakness and laudanum, that Pritchett had explained it to him. They had found what was contaminating the wound. And had removed it. A thread, he thought the doctor had said. A gold thread from his uniform, driven deep into the gash by the downward force of the saber. And suddenly he was back in the choking smoke of Waterloo, watching the saber's slow, dreamlike descent, watching the blade strike over

and over into his arm. That must be what was hurting
so badly. That must be . . . He awoke again to be violently ill. The laudanum always made him sick. He
hated it—what it did to his brain, to his control. He
thought he had cried out when they'd helped him to
lean over the basin. God, it hurt so bad. But that was
good. The arm was there, and the pain was reassurance. They hadn't taken it, and maybe now they
wouldn't have to. He thought that's what Pritchett had
said.

"Yes," Julie's voice came softly into his confusion. "It's still there," she whispered. He opened his
eyes and found hers, smiling at him.

"Gypsy eyes." Somehow he managed to form the
words as he thought them, and saw her smile.

"Go to sleep," she whispered, and he felt her lips on
his forehead. He closed his eyes in response to that
command, but he needed to know, and so he forced
his lids up again. They felt as if they weighed a thousand pounds.

But it wasn't Julie who was holding the water to his
parched lips. He sipped gratefully, and then his father eased his shoulders back against the pillow.

"Julie?" he asked.

"Avon came for her. She has to sleep. It's almost
midnight. You'll be better in the morning and she'll be
back. You can tell her everything then."

"I'm going to marry her," Devon said to his father
and was surprised at the smile that remark occasioned.

"I know. You've told me. At least a dozen times.
I'm glad. And I know all about the babies. Go back to
sleep, Dev. You can tell me again in the morning."

"Then you don't mind?"

"Mind? I may be an old man, but I'm not an old fool. And I don't think it would matter to either of you if I did. But no, Dev, I don't mind."

He lost the struggle to keep his eyes open. It was after midnight, his father had said, and Julie would be back in the morning. And they hadn't taken his arm. He thought that's what Pritchett had said. Maybe he should ask his father, to be sure.

"No, my darling," Julie said, and he could feel her touch his fingers. They were cold, and hers were warm against their numbness. "Stop worrying. I'm here, and I'm holding your hand."

"And you're going to marry me?" he asked again. He watched her lips slant suddenly, and then she laughed.

"Yes, Dev, for at least the hundredth time, I am going to marry you. Now squeeze my fingers," she ordered gently, and was relieved to feel the slight movement of those swollen fingers against hers. Pritchett had been afraid the surgery had been so extensive it might have limited whatever use he would have of the arm. She felt the tears start at his successful obedience to her request.

"Why are you crying?" Devon asked.

"I don't know," she said. "Maybe because I'm happy," she whispered, smiling at him through her tears.

"You never cry," he said, closing his eyes, satisfied by the smile that she was really all right.

"Maybe," she began, and then realized how true it was, "maybe I've just never been happy before."

She knew he hadn't heard her because she had felt his hand relax into unconsciousness before she had told him that. But it didn't matter. She'd tell him again later. They would have a lot of time later to talk. She smoothed the curls off his forehead and touched the stubbled cheek. You need a shave, my darling, she thought idly.

He mumbled something in his sleep, and she glanced up to make sure his eyes were still closed. And they were, the lids resting without moving, hiding the cobalt eyes. Because what she thought he had said, what he could not possibly have whispered in response to that thought, had been a very softly spoken, "Yes, dear."

Julie could never remember much of her wedding. Only the warmth and strength of Devon's hand holding hers and the look in his eyes when he repeated the ancient vows, his voice as firm and commanding as it had been the day she had met him in the French village. She hated the whispered responses that were all her treacherous throat was capable of producing, but no one seemed to think it was unusual for a bride to be emotional. And perhaps they were especially forgiving of a bride who was so beautiful.

Later, at the reception at Avon House, Devon had finally danced with her. She alone had been aware of the slight awkwardness of his left arm. To the watching guests they had moved together in perfect unison, surrounded by an almost visible aura of happiness.

She glanced up finally to find Devon's eyes on hers.

"My father says you have the Ashford eyes," he whispered, thinking how grateful he was for the general's unfaltering steadiness today, for his support through the difficult weeks of his convalescence. He had allowed them privacy, precious moments that had sustained them during the enforced wait.

"Most people think they're from my mother because she was French, but for those who knew my father..." Her voice faded, and despite the watching throng, she laid her cheek against Devon's chest and relaxed into the pleasure of floating across the polished ballroom floor, securely held in his arms.

But his words reminded her of all the kindnesses the general had shown her since she had come that morning to ask Devon to marry her. He had treated her as he treated Emily, like a much-loved daughter.

And it had been the general who had finally told her the story that explained so much about her father's bitterness, a bitterness that had been for reasons very different from those she had always imagined.

Devon's father had secured her promise to accompany him to the last ball of the extended victory celebration, feeling, like his son, that she'd spent too many long hours in the sickroom. No one in his family had attempted to deny her right to care for Devon, despite what the ton might think. Only Devon's insistence on his full recovery before the wedding had prevented their immediate marriage.

And so she had stood beside the general in that sweltering August ballroom and watched again as the Countess of March floated gracefully across the floor in the arms of almost every man but her husband.

"She's very beautiful," the general said, clearly reading her thoughts.

"Yes," she agreed, smiling at him.

"You're not imagining that Devon still feels anything for her, are you?"

"No, I think Dev was quite clear on that point."

"She committed the unforgivable sin, you know."

"The unforgivable sin?" Julie questioned, wondering why they were even bothering to discuss someone who mattered so little to their lives.

"Cowardice," the general said, his eyes returning to watch that graceful figure. "The one thing Devon could never forgive."

"But I was a coward, too. And he forgave me," she said.

"But you were afraid of quite different things."

"I was afraid that Dev would eventually feel the same bitterness my father felt at losing his place in this world." She glanced around the magnificent room, wondering how she could have been so foolish. Dev didn't want this at all. He had told her how little he cared, but she hadn't believed him because her father had, apparently, cared so much.

"It was March, you know."

"March?" she said, wondering what the general meant.

"That night in White's. It was the earl. Didn't he ever tell you?"

"The night my father cheated? He cheated March?" she asked, thinking how ironic that would be.

"Your father never cheated anyone. I can't believe Arthur never told you. But, of course, knowing him as I did, I should have realized that he wouldn't. That was part of who and what he was. He made his deci-

sion that night and he never reneged. He gave everything up rather than betray the woman he loved."

"The woman he loved? I don't understand. What
woman? What are you talking about?"

"The Earl of March's sister. Your father was in love
with her. And he knew what would happen to her
family when it was discovered that March had been
cheating. So instead of allowing that to happen, instead of permitting her life to be destroyed, he took the
blame. He 'confessed' that the marked deck was his.
No one but he and March could be sure which cards
had been used. And the earl was very willing to let
Arthur assume his guilt. Another damned coward.
They deserve each other," the general said bitterly.

"And his sister? She never knew what my father
had done for her?"

"She knew. I told her. I thought she'd go with him.
We all knew that leaving England was the only possible course open to Arthur. And I thought, if she
knew—"

"But she didn't," Julie said softly. "In spite of what
he'd done for her brother, she didn't. And so he went
alone. No wonder he was so bitter."

"But he never told you."

"No. England was very dear to him. He talked
about all this. It all meant so much to him." She shook
her head, wondering what there could have been about
this hollow show that he'd never forgotten. "But we
never talked about that night. I never knew more than
the stories I heard from the Englishmen who, despite
believing the old scandal, were quite willing to play at
his tables in Paris."

"I'll tell them, Julie, if you want me to. Only my promise to your father has prevented my speaking out before. But Arthur's dead, and you belong to my family now. I can clear your father's name. And yours."

"At the cost of March's," Julie said, wondering how the countess would deal with that blight on all that she'd accomplished. On everything that the ton considered important. She was perfect, Emily had said. And now Julie knew it was all built on a lie and a sacrifice.

"No," she answered the general's offer, not even tempted. "It's what my father wanted. But I'm glad you told me. I'm glad he didn't break his code, after all."

It was somehow comforting to know that her father's life had not been a lie. Jean had been wrong, she thought. Wrong about my father and wrong about Dev. And I hope you find someone someday, my friend, who will restore your faith that there are people who are truly noble.

She'd looked up to find the general's blue eyes on her face, and they reminded her of Dev's.

"Dance with me, please," she asked him, and smiling, he led her onto the floor. And his arms had been an acceptable substitute then for Dev's, which finally held her today as tenderly as she had always known they would.

Epilogue

And on their wedding night, deserted at last by both their family and the discreet servants, they were finally alone. The decor of the chamber to which Devon guided her was decidedly feminine, its hangings and draperies done in soft rose, the matching tones of the carpets deep and rich against the dark wood of its furnishings.

"And this is yours. My father had it redecorated. His wedding gift for you, Julie."

"It's beautiful," she said softly.

"But I'd like to invite you to share my room tonight, my Lady Luck."

"You haven't called me that in a long time," she whispered, remembering the night of the ball when she had been so afraid what they would share tonight might never happen.

"But you are. You always will be."

"Give me a few minutes then, and I'll join you," she promised softly.

"Only a few. And if you're longer than that, I feel I should warn you, I've had a great deal of experience storming citadels."

Devon caught her hands, holding both tightly for a long minute while he studied her eyes. Finally he turned her hands over and, almost reverently, kissed the palms. And then releasing her, he entered his adjoining room, closing the connecting door behind him.

He had nearly decided to launch the assault he'd threatened when the door opened again.

"That's almost as beautiful as the moonlight on your bare skin," he said, as she stood poised hesitantly on the threshold, dressed in the ivory silk nightgown Emily had had made for her, the exact shade of the one she had been loaned at Sandemer.

"Avon has impeccable taste," Emily had assured her with a laugh, "and if he says this is your color, then trust me, my dear, it is."

"Avon picked it out," Julie said and smiled at Devon's expression. "Well, not really," she amended. "Only the color."

"But how could he know," Devon said, crossing the room to stand before her. "He's never seen the moon's glow caressing this," he continued, his lips touching her shoulder, bared by the daring design of the gown.

"But you have," she said, and smiled at him again.

"All too briefly."

"And then you left."

"Do you think I could have spent another night under the same roof with you after what had happened between us and not make you mine?"

"I am yours. I was then," she argued.

"Not as completely as you're going to be."

"I couldn't be any more yours, Dev, if we'd been married a hundred years."

Devon took her fingers and kissed them, but when his eyes returned to her face, they were no longer teasing. He pulled her against him and simply held her close, his chin against the top of her head. And smiling slightly to herself, she slipped her hands into the opening of his dark dressing gown to touch the smooth warmth of his chest. She could feel the increased pounding of his heart as her fingers explored the skin exposed by the V of the lapels. She pushed open the robe as far as the material would allow and then began to struggle with the knot of the belt.

"Knotted, Dev?" she mocked, still smiling, and finally the cloth gave under her determined fingers. She released the belt, and as the garment parted, she put her arms around him inside the robe and leaned against his exposed body.

"You feel so good," she whispered. Her dark curls brushed his chest as she turned her face to rub her cheek into the fragrance of his skin. And then his hands caressed her back to pull her up into the hard arousal she had already been aware of.

"Yes," he said in agreement.

She slid her palms up to his shoulders, watching his eyes. They were the same smoky navy as they had been at Sandemer, slightly narrowed as they waited for whatever she intended. She pushed the robe off his shoulders, and it dropped to lie at their feet, only the silk of her gown separating them.

She gently touched the angry red scar that extended almost completely around his upper arm. She hadn't dreamed that it would be as extensive or as ugly. No wonder the doctors had despaired of saving his arm.

"Surely you're not going to quibble about one more mark on my less-than-perfect body, are you? Coals to Newcastle, my darling. Or something to that effect," he said, smiling. "And no, it doesn't hurt."

Julie said softly, "Liar."

As if to prove his contention, he suddenly scooped her up in his arms and carried her to the huge bed. She again enjoyed the sensation of being in Devon's charge, and of being therefore totally and completely safe.

He laid her on the bed and leaned over her, his left knee bent to rest beside her and the other foot still on the floor. He seemed completely unconscious of his nudity, but her blushing fascination must have been obvious, because he said softly, "As always with the French, my darling, you seem to be overdressed for the occasion."

"Or perhaps, always English, you think dress doesn't matter," she suggested, willing her eyes to his face.

"Well, it certainly doesn't matter here," he said, solving the mysteries of ribbons and design with an expertise that fascinated her. His hands managed to brush all the most sensitive spots with teasing accuracy as he expertly divested her of Emily's gift.

"You did that..." she began, and paused because the rough pad of his thumb was moving over her collarbone with tender wonder.

"What?" he asked, but clearly his mind was on something besides her words.

"Emily said you had always been popular with the ladies, but that show of knowledge of intimate apparel was rather—"

"Emily said? My God, Julie, what else did you and my sister discuss about my disreputable past?"

She was sorry she had brought it up, because the movement of his hands against her body had stilled.

"Only that when you fell in love, you... Something she said made me think that you hadn't... That it had been a long time since..." She stopped, sorry she had begun that particular line of thought.

"It has been. Far longer than you can imagine. There was Elizabeth. And then I was wounded. And then there was you. And then I was wounded again. That's rather frightening, don't you think?"

"That you seem to have a propensity for attracting violence?" she asked, smiling at his relaxed tone.

"No, I meant the possibility that I might have forgotten whatever... expertise in lovemaking I'd acquired in my misspent youth," he suggested.

"No," she said, remembering Sandemer and the responses he had called forth so easily.

"No," he agreed, his mouth lowering to find the peak of her breast. She had not been prepared for the sensation, and her body arched uncontrollably. His hand found her hip, and he soothed the force that had moved within her.

"I want to please you, Dev, but you'll have to teach me, as you did at Sandemer. Just be patient. I want to learn everything."

She realized suddenly in the middle of that breathless invitation that he was simply watching her, his eyes shadowed in the subdued lighting of the chamber.

"You said that before. About Elizabeth. That she might have more experience in pleasing me."

"Did you make love to her, Dev?"

And he smiled at the scarcity of any really intimate moments in the long history of his relationship with the Countess of March.

"I don't think Elizabeth was interested in the physical aspects of love. I don't remember her ever even touching me in any way that might—" He stopped suddenly, aware of what he was discussing with his wife on their wedding night.

And felt her small fingers steal to touch his chest, to skim downward across the ridged muscles of his stomach, and lower. She tentatively explored with a lightness that revealed far more than she could know, especially to a man with as extensive a misspent youth as Devon had enjoyed.

But for some reason, he didn't allow her to continue that hesitant exploration. He caught her fingers and raised them as he had done so often to the gentle caress of his lips.

"I think—" he began.

"No," she whispered, freeing her fingers to touch the fan of small lines at the corner of his eye. "Not tonight. Don't think. Only feelings, sensations. But no thoughts," she urged.

He allowed the movement of her hand against his face, but his eyes were considering, remembering, and suddenly she was afraid.

"Dev, what's wrong?"

"I don't..." He swallowed, and the dark blue eyes again considered the worried concern in hers.

"I think you're going to have to explain what you meant, Julie. I'm beginning to believe... My God, my darling, I'm beginning to think I've been a very great fool."

"I don't understand," she whispered. "Explain what, Dev?"

"What you meant about Elizabeth having more experience than you. And that I'll have to teach you how to please me. Believe me, Julie, nothing could change the way I feel about you, but I'm beginning to think that perhaps I've been mistaken. Would you please tell me, Lady Luck, *why* I'll have to teach you to make love to me?" His soft question stopped and, waiting, he lowered his head and touched his mouth again, as reverently as he had kissed her palms, to the pulse that fluttered erratically at the base of her throat.

Her hand found the soft silk of the hair that curled at the nape of his neck. His head was still lowered over her body, and her eyes were wide and dark as she thought about what his words implied. And then she realized what he thought, what he had thought through the long weeks he had sought to make her his wife, and finally she knew how much he loved her.

"Oh, Dev," she whispered. "I didn't know you thought there had been someone else. Someone before you. Only one man has ever touched me. Only one man ever put his mouth against my body. In Paris and at Sandemer. Only you, Dev, and I thought you knew. I thought you must have known or you would never have asked me to be your wife."

"Forgive me, Julie. I thought that was part of why you refused. Because you were unsure—"

"That you could love me enough to overlook that? There's never been anyone else, Dev. My father may have allowed me to run his casino because his illness necessitated that, but I was as protected from his customers' advances as if I'd been the cherished English girl he would have liked me to be. Protected by him, and then later, of course, by Jean."

And in the darkness, with the sudden upward slant of his lips, hidden by their glide over the velvet softness of her skin, he released, at last, his jealousy of the scarred Frenchman, an emotion he had not even been aware intellectually that he still held.

"Then," he told her softly, the moist warmth of his breath tantalizing between her breasts, "I will be very careful with you, my heart, because you gave me something very precious a long time ago. Then you gave me your trust, that I was the man you'd chosen. And tonight—" he paused, thinking about what he wanted this night to be for her "—I may hurt you, my darling, despite the care I intend to take. I don't think I will, given your responsiveness and my intent. But I want you to want me."

"I want you, Dev. You have to know that."

"I know. But not like you will. Not when I'm finished," he vowed softly, and when his lips again found her breast she knew that she truly didn't understand all he could make her feel. But he was right. Before the night was over, she would know just how right he had been.

With the tenderness of his fingers and with his worshiping lips, he took her again to the place he had shown her before at Sandemer. But this time he allowed her no release. Again and then again he drew her slowly to the edge of the precipice that she now longed to soar over. And slowly, with tantalizing cruelty, he retreated. His hands moved to gentle or to soothe, to touch her cheek, her shoulders. And his lips deserted the flame he had ignited to brush against the corner of her mouth or over the tears he drank from her lashes or to touch the perspiration that gathered under her breasts. But never to release her.

And then he began again. Almost taunting her with his power over her body, which was now totally in his control. She had lost the will to do more than move in response to what he was making her feel. Her hands had found his shoulders and gripped too hard, making their own appeal, which he also ignored. Her fingers fell between them to catch his hard nipples, which moved involuntarily with the roll of the underlying muscles caused by the hard, gasping breath that suddenly shook his body. He said her name then, whispered it into her mouth.

But when she touched him, his fingers paused in what they had been doing, and so she arched against them in her need, demanding, wanting.

"Dev," she begged. Her mind was incapable of any coherent thought. He began to touch her again, and she knew that what she sought was very near, and she wanted it so. And wanted him.

"What, my heart?" he said softly, his lips finding hers.

"Don't stop again," she breathed.

"Stop what?" he whispered.

"Loving me," she said, having no other reference. Her body had begun to shiver, to tremble, and it was very hard to think of the words he wanted.

"You have to tell me," he commanded, but there was only love in the soft demand.

"I don't know how," she whispered.

"Yes," he said. "You know what you want."

"You," she said. "Only you. Forever."

"How?" he asked. But as he spoke, the implacable demand his touch had made had cruelly stopped again. And he waited.

"With me?" she asked, hoping that it was what he wanted. Her body moved again, involuntarily lifting to seek his fingers. "Within me?"

"Yes," he agreed and touched her. But the focus of his caress had shifted. His fingers slid suddenly into the pulsing need he had created, into the warmth and dark sea of her desire. Her breath stopped, held by the wonder of that movement. And then his thumb touched, caressed again, demanding, and the chasm was there. But before she could plunge, both his hands had shifted under her hips, and as the air gathered around her soaring body, he entered her, hard and strong, thrusting into her even as she fell. And again. Slow and sure, and she convulsed into his strength. Held secure by Dev's arms so that she could fly without fear.

And when it was over, her body no longer racked by the force of its surrender, she opened her eyes to find his blue ones watching her face and what had been reflected there. She knew he had watched throughout her response to his gift, to this miracle that he could create within her body. And he smiled. And then he began to move again, to push deeper within her. She could feel him exploring the walls that no longer had any barrier to what he sought.

She became aware that her hands were on his hard buttocks, her nails pulling him even closer into her. There was something else he was trying to teach her, something beyond what he had already given her, but she didn't understand how there could be more than the swirling disappearance of the universe that happened when he touched her. But something was happening. Building. Changing. Melting. And she knew she wanted this, too.

And finally he said, "Open your eyes, my darling."

And so she watched, as long as she was able, as what she had given him in return began to happen. He held her eyes until he felt her join him there, and the waves of sensation that swept through her sent him over the edge of her imagined chasm also. And so they fell together.

She didn't know how long they lay entwined, his weight deliciously warm and heavy against her slenderness, almost as heavy as the languor inside her body. She felt the hard thud of his heart against hers, and she smiled because she had been aware of the gradual slowing of that measured rhythm.

And finally he shifted to lie beside her, and although she protested the desertion, she was comforted by his hand that moved over her, spanning the moisture that dewed her breasts and stomach. And finding the different wetness below. His fingers stroked, almost in memory, with no intent to arouse, but she convulsed, an aftershock to the eruption that had drained them both. And she felt the small spurt of his laughter her involuntary reaction caused.

"You are," he said softly, his lips in the fragrance of her disordered curls, "probably going to be the death of me, poor wounded veteran that I am."

She smiled at that, having no doubts about his strength. And then she said, the thought having come to her sometime before, but she had not had the strength then to utter it, "I'm very glad that you were wounded before, my love."

His lips hesitated briefly, and then knowing that whatever she was about to say was not something to be feared, he asked, "And why would you be glad of that?"

"Because that must be when you learned patience. All that wonderful patience," she said in remembrance, and turned her small body so that it pressed against the entire long length of his. "But, Dev," she continued softly, "I've never learned patience, so I'm afraid that, like a child, I want my pleasures immediately. Do you suppose . . ." she asked.

His fingers found hers and conveyed them gently to the answer to her question.

"In some things patience is considered a virtue, but in others, I believe you're right. If pleasures are immediately at hand, why shouldn't they be enjoyed?"

"But pleasures are always more meaningful when they're shared," she suggested, and his body moved to fit into hers like two halves of a broken coin rejoined.

"Like this?" he asked softly a few minutes later.

"Exactly like this," she whispered, her fingers moving over the scars on his back that were as familiar to her now as the blue eyes and as the smile she had loved from the first.

* * * * *

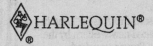

Harlequin® Historical

WOMEN OF THE WEST

Exciting stories of the old West and the women whose dreams
and passions shaped a new land!

Join Harlequin Historicals every month as we bring you
these unforgettable tales.

May 1995 #270—**JUSTIN'S BRIDE**
Susan Macias w/a Susan Mallery

June 1995 #273—**SADDLE THE WIND**
Pat Tracy

July 1995 #277—**ADDIE'S LAMENT**
DeLoras Scott

August 1995 #279—**TRUSTING SARAH**
Cassandra Austin

September 1995 #286—**CECILIA AND THE STRANGER**
Liz Ireland

October 1995 #288—**SAINT OR SINNER**
Cheryl St.John

November 1995 #294—**LYDIA**
Elizabeth Lane

Don't miss any of our **Women of the West!**

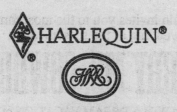

HARLEQUIN®

PRESENTS
RELUCTANT BRIDEGROOMS

Two beautiful brides, two unforgettable romances...
two men running for their lives....

My Lady Love, by Paula Marshall, introduces
Charles, Viscount Halstead, who lost his memory
and found himself employed as a stableboy by the
untouchable Nell Tallboys, Countess Malplaquet.
But Nell didn't consider Charles untouchable—
not at all!

Darling Amazon, by Sylvia Andrew, is the story of
a spurious engagement between Julia Marchant
and Hugo, marquess of Rostherne—an engagement
that gets out of hand and just may lead Hugo to
the altar after all!

Enjoy two madcap Regency weddings this May,
wherever Harlequin books are sold.

Harlequin invites you to the most romantic
wedding of the season...with

MARRY ME, COWBOY!

And you could WIN A DREAM VACATION of a lifetime!

from HARLEQUIN BOOKS and SANDALS—
THE CARIBBEAN'S #1 **ULTRA INCLUSIVE**™ LUXURY RESORTS
FOR COUPLES ONLY.

Harlequin Books and Sandals Resorts are offering you a
vacation of a lifetime—a vacation of your choice at any of
the Sandals Caribbean resorts—FREE!

LOOK FOR FURTHER DETAILS in the Harlequin Books
title MARRY ME, COWBOY!, an exciting collection
of four brand-new short stories by popular romance
authors, including *New York Times* bestselling author
JANET DAILEY!

AVAILABLE IN APRIL WHEREVER
HARLEQUIN BOOKS ARE SOLD.

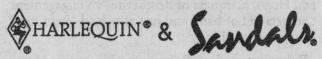

HARLEQUIN® & *Sandals*®

**Fifty red-blooded, white-hot, true-blue hunks
from every State in the Union!**

Look for MEN MADE IN AMERICA! Written by some
of our most popular authors, these stories feature some
of the strongest, sexiest men, each from a different state
in the union!

Two titles available every month at your favorite
retail outlet.

In April, look for:

FOR THE LOVE OF MIKE
by Candace Schuler (Texas)
THE DEVLIN DARE
by Cathy Thacker (Virginia)

In May, look for:

A TIME AND A SEASON
by Curtiss Ann Matlock (Oklahoma)
SPECIAL TOUCHES
by Sharon Brondos (Wyoming)

You won't be able to resist MEN MADE IN AMERICA!

HARLEQUIN®

Don't miss these Harlequin favorites by some of our most
distinguished authors!
And now, you can receive a discount by ordering two or more titles!